THE MATTHIAS SCROLL

A LOST TESTAMENT UNEARTHS THE SECRETS OF HISTORY'S MOST NOTORIOUS INJUSTICE

Abram Epstein

THE MATTHIAS SCROLL
A LOST TESTAMENT UNEARTHS THE SECRETS OF HISTORY'S MOST NOTORIOUS INJUSTICE

Certain characters in this work are historical figures, and certain events portrayed did take place. However, this is a work of fiction. All of the other characters, names, and events as well as all places, incidents, organizations, and dialogue in this novel are either the products of the author's imagination or are used fictitiously.

iUniverse books may be ordered through booksellers or by contacting:

iUniverse LLC
1663 Liberty Drive
Bloomington, IN 47403
www.iuniverse.com
1-800-Authors (1-800-288-4677)

ISBN: 978-1-4917-3348-6 (sc)
ISBN: 978-1-4917-3349-3 (hc)
ISBN: 978-1-4917-3350-9 (e)

Library of Congress Control Number: 2014909861

Printed in the United States of America.

iUniverse rev. date: 08/26/2014

THE MATTHIAS SCROLL

Acknowledgments

To my parents, Lillian and Joseph Epstein, both of whom set an example of intellectual prowess matched by pioneering social and medical accomplishments. If I have measured up to their expectations, I will have exceeded my own.

And to those formidable teachers who opened my eyes to the vistas of first-century religious history. Their names are withheld to protect the innocent, lest they find themselves embroiled in controversy not of their choosing.

With gratitude to my brother, Simon, a prominent psychiatrist who never once told me how delusional this project made me seem. Solving the riddles surrounding Jesus' life and death could not have sounded like a sane pursuit. But every page and every insight always had the benefit of his encouragement. Thank God believing in the impossible runs in my family.

Finally, to Denisse Medina, for believing in me and making sure I did too.

Introduction

For nearly three centuries, the New Testament has been a source of scholastic and religious controversy.

Unlike rabbis past and present, who continue to argue about interpretations of the Hebrew Bible but are not in conflict about God per se, Christian theologians and scholars have an ongoing debate about the character and role of Jesus. Facing puzzling passages in the Gospels and ancillary books of the New Testament, various voices are raised to pronounce evolving edicts about his activities, both transcendent and mundane.

Naturally, in the wake of his cruel death, his circle of devotees faced the question of why it had happened to the one God had sent to save mankind. As they mourned and sought an explanation for their devastating loss, a realization dawned on them: faith in the identity of Jesus, and faith that his death and resurrection were God's plan, changed the individual from unsaved to saved. This was to be the faith that *in itself* had saving power.

In the 1700s, with the Age of Enlightenment, a revolutionary era of New Testament analysis began. "Reason" was placed on a pedestal as a profound sign of man's special relationship to God. Therefore, those Christian theologians who undertook analyzing the Gospel texts for similarities and contradictions in language, style, and content were empowered to pursue their reasoning as an inspiration from the heavenly Jesus—not as a challenge or heresy.

When, before too long, several among them, using sophisticated linguistic methods, discerned differences between Jesus' actual activities and Gospel enhancements, they were faced with a monumental mystery: why hadn't Jesus ever said he was the messiah?

Put more starkly, why hadn't he ever promulgated Christian theology by confiding, at least to his disciples, that he would be arrested, executed, and disappear from his tomb, returning to his heavenly realm to rule and communicate with the faithful?

Almost unwittingly, the eighteenth-century scholarly pursuit of an explanation of Jesus' reticence had raised the most unsettling question lurking beneath the surface of their inquiries:

Did Jesus think he was the messiah?

In our own time, scholars have continued to wrestle with the Gospel texts, hoping to extricate the "historical" Jesus from the context of the church image and kerygma (message). The results have been mostly unsuccessful. Snippets of insight have been stitched together to accomplish a patchwork portrait that is always impressionistic and usually colored by the bias of its author.

Because a truly historical Jesus has failed to emerge, modern scholars have recently fallen back on poorly supported personal guesswork. One has added up Jesus' various lessons to say he was a typical Greek philosopher/teacher, spouting aphorisms. Another has said he was a magician. Others have joined in a conference to vote which things are authentic—that is, really happened—and which were added after his death. Marginal dramatizations have masqueraded as historical works, legitimizing stereotypes of Jews as Christ-killers, or professing insight into Jesus' rebellious character—all of which contain no measure of truth.

The analytical method of documenting Jesus' life as portrayed in *The Matthias Scroll* differs from others. Employing an unprecedented technique, the *Scroll* relies on finding the pearls of history in each Gospel episode, and stringing them together to reveal a startling, coherent story never before suspected, a drama of life and death offered in this novel for the first time. The doubts which have, for so long, been spawned by seemingly insoluble questions, are resolved in *The Matthias Scroll.*

Concerning Matthias' Historical Role

Matthias' choice as a replacement of Judas Iscariot is documented in the New Testament (Acts 1:21-26).

The relevant passage describing the moment reads:

> [Simon said,] "We must choose someone who has been with us the whole time that the lord Jesus was traveling around with us, someone who was with us from the time when John was baptizing until the day when he was taken up from us—and he can act as witness to his resurrection . . ." then they [voted] . . . and Matthias was listed as one of the twelve disciples (also called "apostles" after Jesus' death).

Matthias' role in creating the "new testament" is explicit. Simon says as much, with the words, "He can act as witness . . ."

Based on further documentation, one may infer he was expected to record the disciples' recollections of Jesus' teaching and life. As the group's scribe, he would take down their "witnessed" testament. (Fictionalized in this novel, Matthias eventually sets about writing his own private scroll, determined to faithfully preserve Jesus' memory, recording the events as they actually happened.)

More Footprints Leading to Matthias' Historical Identity

In John 13:23, at the "Last Supper," Simon asks "the disciple Jesus loved" to inquire of Jesus who he meant would betray him.

Sitting at his side during the dinner, this mystery disciple's relationship with Jesus is such that he is presumed by Simon to know more about Jesus' preoccupation with the betrayal and impending arrest than any of the others.

After Jesus' arrest, when he is taken to the fateful hearing before Caiaphas, Simon is excluded, but "the disciple" is permitted to enter. Only when "the disciple" intercedes with a formal request, based on knowing Caiaphas personally (John 18:15-16), is Simon permitted to even enter the gated exterior courtyard. The relevant passage indicates the individual's administrative stature, plainly a man with authority, such as that of Matthias, purportedly a Sanhedrin scribe.

> Simon-Peter and another disciple followed Jesus to Caiaphas' house (the hearing chamber). Since the disciple was known to the high priest (he) went with Jesus inside, but Simon was standing outside the door (courtyard gate). So the disciple, being known to the high priest, went out, spoke to the woman watching the gate, and brought Simon in (to the courtyard).

There, a fire had been lit and Simon was able to stay warm, along with the "servants and guards."

Several significant conclusions concerning the identity of "the disciple" emerge in this Gospel setting. First, he remained at Jesus' side, just as he had several hours earlier at the Last Supper. Therefore, we may infer it was the same person. Furthermore, having the stature of a scribe, he enabled Simon to enter the gated courtyard of the high priest. Of undeniable importance, the so-called disciple has enough political weight to be included at the hearing to witness the proceedings.

No other member of Jesus' circle is present as the interrogation begins—and plainly, only that individual could later provide any information about what occurred.

Recognizing his scribal status, one may logically infer that whatever record the Gospels make pertaining to Jesus' appearance before Caiaphas is drawn from the account subsequently offered by "the disciple"—arguably Matthias—and revised in Simon's version.

Not only was Matthias the single member of Jesus' entourage to witness the hearing before Caiaphas, but he, alone among the group, saw the grotesque mockery and derision at Pontius Pilate's Praetorium and Gabbatha scene of judgment.

Therefore, his detailed account would again constitute the only record of the event. (Although later Christianized and enhanced, it has been fully returned to the original in *The Matthias Scroll*.)

Two more chronicled appearances place him at the scene of the crucifixion and at the "empty tomb," with both accounts concealing the actual history beneath a heavy theological gloss.

As the only witness among Jesus' companions at the Caiaphas hearing, the judgment by Pilate, and the crucifixion, one may conclude that Matthias, having the skills of a scribe, could render a historical account of what actually occurred.

Why was his name expunged from the Gospels?

The evidence indicates he refused to exalt a glorified, supra-human Jesus.

As common sense suggests, whatever occurred to terminate Matthias' function as the group's scribe must have been tantamount to an emotional rupture. Almost certainly, the rift would have been accompanied by anger and, quite probably, mutual recrimination.

In the Gospels, it is worth noting that the Greek for "the disciple" is *maheeteen*. The derived nominal form, *mathetes,* indicates lack of belief in a teacher. In Acts 19:1, the term is applied to those who were ignorant of the holy spirit. Based on the Aramaic and Greek usage, one may conjecture that the Last Supper reference to "the disciple" may have originally relied on a finely drawn, disparaging vernacular.

Concerning the Portrayal of Joseph

Perhaps one of the more controversial aspects of this work is the fictionalized introduction and development of the character of Joseph, Jesus' "father" (to give him that paternal title, an issue illuminated in this novel). Admittedly, there is no statement in the New Testament that he was alive during and after Jesus' last year. While the scenes involving him, broadly considered, are fictionalized constructs, they depend on evidence.

First, In *The Matthias Scroll*, Joseph is identified as a retired member of the Sanhedrin, the Hebrew legislative body governing civil and religious law. Generally, its members were well-to-do, accomplished men who represented a broad array of constituents.

Reference to Joseph as a member of the Sanhedrin occurs in very early Christian literature (*Protoevangelium of James*), and this matches his circumstances. A betrothal to his deceased wife's niece, Mary, when she was only sixteen years old, strongly suggests there was a financial component making it a desirable arrangement. His having two homes, one in Nazareth and the other in the area of Bethlehem, further supplies a portrait of a successful man.

Second, my linguistic analysis of the name "Joseph of Arimathea" and the role he plays in the Gospels (Matthew 27:57-59; Mark 15:42-46; Luke 23:50-56; John 19:38) is significant. Portrayed as a secret disciple of Jesus, he makes his only appearance following the crucifixion and helps transport Jesus' body to a "new" tomb. According to the Gospel account, this was the only tomb to which the body was ever taken, and a full exposition of the events awaits the reader.

Regarding Joseph of Arimathea's identity as Jesus' father, the likelihood is indicated by Roman legal custom that the body could only be released for burial to a family member who had received permission to take it. Furthermore, the name, "Arimathea" is itself evidence he was associated with a family cemetery. Until this study, various translations, all tentative and incorrect, have been suggested by scholars. Some have seen the name as a cognate for "ram," meaning "heights," and so have inferred he was from the ancient city of Ramallah or from the village just north of Jerusalem, "Ramah," made famous by the words of Jeremiah referring to Jews being gathered there on the way to Babylonian exile.

My translation, the first such, asserts it was an Aramaized mispronunciation of the Hebrew *Ir Ha-mayteem*—literally, City of the Dead. The Greek equivalent—*necropolis*—makes my linguistic assessment compelling. Naturally, Jesus' father, Joseph—at least acting in that paternal role—did not live in a cemetery. Therefore, to say the man at the crucifixion was "Joseph from the City of the Dead" does not mean he was from the cemetery, but that acquaintances knew his residence to be in the neighborhood they passed on the way to visiting their family tombs.

If so, "Arimathea" (used in three Gospels as a reference to Joseph's neighborhood) would have been attached as a pseudo-surname.

While it remains educated conjecture that Joseph of Arimathea was Jesus' father and took Jesus to "Arimathea/Ir ha-mayteem," the necropolis near his home for burial in the "garden tomb" (John 19:41), the fact he is marginalized as a devotee—mentioned once—and only once—in each of the four canonized Gospels accords well with the supposition.

The Holy Spirit

As the reader may be aware, the term is today a cornerstone of Christian dogma, theologically embraced as one of the three manifestations of God: "the Father, the Son, and the Holy Spirit."

Almost certainly, if one were to ask a knowledgeable Jewish individual, including scholars and rabbis, about the "holy spirit," most would say it is part of the Christian "Trinity."

In fact, its origins are Hebrew, and its spiritual role in the Torah is one of pervasive theological importance. In a word, had the Hebrew religion not engendered belief in the "holy spirit," nobody would have known what Jesus was talking about when he referred to it. In the earliest periods portrayed in Genesis, it is referred to as "the spirit/the spirit of Adonai." Later, about 1250 BCE, Moses laments: "If only all God's People were prophets, and the Lord put His spirit upon them" (Numbers 11:29).

The exact use of the Hebrew term ("ruach ha-kodesh"=holy spirit) first becomes explicit about a millennium before Jesus, in the period of the Hebrew monarchy (Saul, David, and Solomon), a discussion of which is beyond the parameters of these brief remarks.

It does repeatedly recur in sacred Hebrew texts, playing an important role in God's communication with the prophets (for example, Ezekiel and Joel) and in the Dead Sea writings ("Thanksgiving Hymns" and other sections).

Our primary question is therefore strikingly simple: what exactly was the role of the "holy spirit" as Jesus understood it, and what were its characteristics in the Gospels?

At the moment of his conception, the holy spirit appears in a procreative function. The announcement by an angel (known in Christian vernacular as "the Annunciation") of Mary's impending pregnancy is portrayed as an act of the holy spirit, since she "has no husband" (Luke 1:34-35). And, according to the passage, "the child will be called the son of God." (Matthew 1:18 is a parallel passage.)

Also in the Gospels, it is associated with the baptism. When Jesus is immersed by John, he emerges from under the water, and the holy spirit "descended upon him" (Luke 3:22). Matthew 3:16 and Mark 1:10 say only that "the spirit of God" or "the spirit" descended on him. All three quote a voice from heaven declaring, "[This is/thou art] my beloved son."

Therefore, we may deduce the holy spirit in the Gospels could turn an individual into a "son" of God. Though no Hebrew scripture ever attributed actual conception to the holy spirit, precedent was well-established that individuals touched by its presence, could be "sons of God." Jesus himself quotes Psalm 82:6 (in John 10:34) to make the same point.

Imbued with a belief in these "powers" of the holy spirit, assuredly drawn from earlier Hebrew scripture, Jesus would have encouraged his disciples to feel like legitimate members of the Jewish community, inheritors (sons) of the Covenant. His Torah-teaching, imbuing them with the holy spirit, reflected the established perception and practice of venerated rabbis of his era. Such teaching was an act tantamount to vitiating all doubt about their family tree, so that their newfound knowledge of Torah might make them "sons of God" (the title they would earn by study with him). Therefore, Jesus believed the holy spirit flowed from Torah and could end his disciples' social and religious exile for their possibly doubtful lineages, reinstating them as fully covenanted members of the Hebrew People.

***

On a somewhat personal note, I hope the reader is not averse to my historical reconstruction. It is intended to illuminate Jesus' teaching as a profound expression of early first-century Judaism, contrasting it with the messianic glorification that followed his death. In the spirit of that endeavor, no imaginary fabrications of his words or activities occur in Matthias' own scroll. Everything he says and does in the scroll itself is attested, or supported by inference, in the Gospels. However, varied translations, recontextualized, paint an altogether different and far more historical picture than has been heretofore rendered. Further, the postmortem sequence immediately following his crucifixion is adduced from the Gospel texts themselves and rises to the level of logical certainty.

While ancillary characters and embroidered scenes lend color and background to the exposition, they complement the story—and are not fanciful inventions.

CHAPTER ONE

*A*fter nearly two hours, the peaceful jostling of James' horse-drawn cart should have calmed his disquieting premonition. But it did not. If his warning carried no more weight with Matthias than it did with the disciples under Simon's sway, the future of the Jerusalem Center would be bleak.

Of the several who liked him, even they mostly sought some semblance to Jesus in what he said and did. Always they introduced him as "the brother of the Lord," rendering any other identity incidental. Their hope, it seemed, was to return to the days when his brother was with them, as if his own voice or manner might evoke a measure of that past, enabling them to again bask in his light. Naturally, they believed Simon when he claimed Jesus was speaking to him from heaven.

Matthias was different. If anybody was disturbed by the idea that God had planned the death of his brother, it should have been him.

James had been to his home in Ephraim only once. Nearly a year had passed since then, but the gate to his small enclave and the houses to either side of the road were familiar. His brother had come here and sometimes stayed for several weeks or even longer. No doubt these were yards and gardens he knew. As he guided the horse, making a turn toward Matthias' street, James felt oddly responsible for noticing the details of the surroundings, standing in for his brother who could not.

Not too far from the end of the pebbled road, he pulled back on the reins and called out, "Matthias?"

"So you remembered," came a reply from behind the cart. "I was just getting some water."

"It's the fourth of Sivan, isn't it?"

"Go inside. I have a few things to take."

Moments later, when Matthias followed James in, carrying the flask, he asked how James was doing as "praesidere" of the Center.

"Fine. I am doing fine," James answered.

"Then take off your sandals."

Surprised he had forgotten so simple a courtesy, James quickly removed and placed his sandals alongside those of Matthias, just outside the door.

"It doesn't take a priest to see you're not so fine. Here, hold this."

Obediently, James held open the large sack for provisions as Matthias put in packages of cheese and almonds.

"These should do us some good. And you smell the bread?"

James stood watching as Matthias took several hot, nearly flat pittot loaves from the clay oven under the side window. "Smells delicious. Things are changing, Matthias."

"As things usually do."

With his neck prickling slightly from sweat, a familiar reaction to his own embarrassment, James searched for words he had been rehearsing on the road from Nazareth. He intended to tell Matthias about Simon and in his mind, this scribe who had befriended Jesus would immediately concur. *"You're right. Something has to be done about Simon,"* James imagined Matthias agreeing.

"Some are saying Jesus' death was ordained by God," James finally managed.

"But you must have influence, no?" Matthias asked, shutting the door as they departed the house. "They should show you respect."

Climbing aboard the cart without immediately answering, James turned to give Matthias a hand. "You will see that Simon is more the one who presides than I," he said.

"It's hard to believe it's already two years," Matthias reflected. "And Mary? How is she?"

"She may come with Jude to Jerusalem for the holiday. Perhaps you will see her."

Positioning himself next to James, as the cart lurched forward, Matthias inhaled deeply. "I always miss the aroma of freshly harvested barley. When the wheat comes up, it's all but gone."

Exiting Ephraim's town gate, James guided the horse past patches of grass so it wouldn't stop to eat. Nearly a mile farther on, as they reached the main road, he gave a short wave to the legionnaire standing guard as the cart passed an outpost. "We're on our way to Jerusalem," he called out.

"And it's like nothing has changed," Matthias mused. "The Romans are everywhere."

"Meanwhile, Simon tells everybody God caused Jesus to die for some special purpose," James persisted. "It wouldn't surprise me if . . ." He stopped midsentence, seeing Matthias' attention was drawn to the corner of a nearby field, where an elderly woman shook a sheaf of standing barley to fill her belted sack. "These fields must have a lot of memories for you," James said.

"Your brother and the disciples ate barley left in the corner of one much like this. Some young Pietists said they were stealing grain . . . but I'm sure you know a man who is hungry may eat what isn't harvested from the corner of a field."

3

"Simon will tell you he was above Torah laws," James answered, waiting for Matthias to show at least a measure of concern, but his gaze was still on the woman.

As the horse stepped on branches of a fallen juniper, stumbling slightly and nearly jerking the reins from his hand, James could not hide his aggravation. "You will see for yourself, Matthias," he muttered under his breath, annoyed that what he had been saying made no impression, and for the next hour they traveled with few words.

Finally, the Valley of Cheesemakers was just ahead. Jerusalem's goats had been milked in the early morning and full clay cauldrons on glowing naptha embers simmered, sending sweet-smelling steam into the air. "Can you imagine?" James asked, slowing the cart so he might finish saying what had been on his mind. "If Simon tells them he died for some divine reason, next they will be celebrating my brother's execution as a cause for joy. And you are part of his plan."

"Oh? Is there something I should know?"

"You'll see," James replied, satisfied to have cracked Matthias' veneer of seeming indifference. "He wants you to be their scribe, the twelfth disciple taking Iscariot's place."

"Me? Are you sure?" Matthias responded, squinting into the sun.

Not choosing to elaborate, James blared, "Sa!" commanding the horse to climb the hill to the Center.

The two-story stone building was larger inside than it appeared from the street, its upper triclinium windows wide enough for the disciples to contemplate Jesus' teaching in the comfort of Jerusalem's late afternoon breezes—and view the terraced hills adorned by olive and fig trees, their leaves shimmering.

Unobserved, watching from that vantage point, Simon waited for James to tether the horse to a post, considering only briefly the remote possibility that Matthias might decline their impending offer.

Below, Matthias' advice that James not worry was barely audible over Simon's boisterous welcome, "Baruch haba-eem!"

"Shalom to you," Matthias responded cheerfully, as he permitted James to help him down from the cart's iron step.

Hearing their voices, Simon's brother Andrew appeared. "Shalom, Matthias. But you look fine. We were wondering what became of you."

"Now you can relax," Matthias said, handing Andrew his sandals. "But it is pleasant in here."

The first-story space was divided into a small triclinium, alongside a cooking chamber with a closet for pots and amphorae. Sleeping rooms, small but each adequate for several pallets, were behind doors off to the sides.

"It's good to see you too, James. It is always good to see our master's brother. I know everybody will be pleased you're here."

"John should be back," Simon said. "He went to buy fruit. Andrew, go to the cistern and bring some water. But let's sit together. You've had a long trip."

James found a familiar place on the straw floor covering, leaning his elbow on a large pillow.

"But tell us, Simon, where are the others?" Matthias inquired, lowering himself next to James.

"We'll see them soon," he answered, and then, with a slight smile, added, "Peter. No matter. If you call me Simon, I'll know you mean me."

"A man has the right to call himself whatever he wishes," James scoffed.

"Of course that's true," Simon replied. "But James, I'm still stunned that Jesus chose me to be our spiritual leader and gave me the name."

"As you should be," Andrew's voice rang out, entering with a red clay pitcher of water. "Maybe he should have called you something more fitting."

Kneeling down, Andrew took a cloth, soaked it in water from the pitcher, and began wiping Matthias' feet.

"Peter, do you remember what you said when Jesus did this to you?" he asked, wringing out the cloth. "That you wished he would wash all your body from head to toe so you might be completely cleansed by him. And he told you he was sure you didn't need a bath."

"These are different times," Simon observed, ignoring the joke, just as the older Zebedee, holding a sack of dates and his brother by the sleeve, entered. "Look who I found," he chortled.

"Just in time to serve our guests," Simon suggested.

"Shalom, James!" John said. "But you are hardly a guest!"

"And Matthias," his brother added, eagerly bringing a plate for the dates. "It is wonderful you have time to stop by."

Turning his back to James, Simon changed the subject. "I think you will be interested to hear we have something special planned for tomorrow."

"Shavuot is the festival when they read the Ten Commandments. But you must know that," John the Zebedee said to Matthias. "He told us they were to be sacred forever."

"Of course he knows!" his brother scolded. "Why do you think he's in Jerusalem? Go ahead, Peter, tell them what you're planning."

"Or would you prefer to be surprised?" Simon asked.

"He must tell us," John joked. "Look at him, just bubbling over."

Acquiescing, Simon announced, "Our prayers tomorrow will not be in Hebrew! So we don't need to know any of the old words. We have a different, superior language."

Sneering at whatever Simon planned, James could not help noticing Matthias was listening intently.

Freeing a date from the cluster, taking a bite, and chewing slowly, he continued, "The new time is beginning. It's true. You think Jesus likes to hear the old words? Words that make us feel like insects because we can't even pronounce them? There was a time long ago . . ."

As Andrew and the Zebedees listened in rapt awe, or so it seemed to James, Simon raised a hand toward the ceiling.

"You all know the story about a tower people were building to reach the heavens," he intoned dramatically. "Punished for trying to become gods, their intention was torn asunder, their words scrambled, so they had to stop laying bricks."

"And they began speaking different languages," Andrew interrupted.

"Like Hebrew," Simon said, his voice suddenly dropping, a habit borrowed from Jesus. "A language of separation and punishment . . . for trying to reach the heavens and become gods."

Pausing to give his small audience a chance to fully fathom the profound insight he was about to offer and then suddenly looking upward and raising his voice, he declared, "And we will see that for us—we who were his disciples—and for those who know he is still alive, all sin is forgiven, and we may pray in that first language, telling him we depend on his heavenly guidance!"

"And you have chosen Shavuot, the Feast of Weeks, for this?" Matthias asked.

"Tomorrow! Then we will receive his teaching from heaven and again speak one language. So Matthias, what do you say?"

"I think we may speak in different tongues, but when we pray to God, we are all speaking one language."

"Of course you are right. But you believe what I am saying, don't you? A new time is at hand!"

"I am not the one to ask, Simon. A scribe's work is only to record what others say. But will I be pleased to see a change for the better? Most certainly." As Matthias stood up with effort, he said, "These old legs don't like to stay in one place too long. James, I need your assistance in the market."

Promising to return before sunset, Matthias leaned on James' arm, and they were soon pressing their way through the clusters of shop patrons along the narrow streets.

Made slightly hoarse from inhaling the pungent cumin spread in vendors' trays, James cleared his throat, "You were there two years ago, in Caesaria Philipi," he proffered, as if arguing a point that had not yet been resolved.

"Yes, I was. And?"

"He's lying. Jesus never chose Simon. You must know that."

"I don't like to say such things about others."

"Did you hear my brother say his name should be Peter?"

"People hear what they want to hear."

"And what about you, Matthias?"

"Your brother was fond of Simon. And you should understand something. These disciples were regarded as outcasts. Only your brother saw they were worth his effort."

"Half of them don't know how to pray. The Zebedees and Thomas still babble, not even knowing when to stand or sit! Illiterates! Isn't that why he gave them a simple prayer to practice in private? He hoped they wouldn't show their ignorance in public. Now Simon spits on our ancestors. His Galilean dialect scrapes in my ears."

"What greater revenge on his killers could we hope for than a Center to study his teachings?" Matthias replied. "Anyway, I hope when I die, people will exaggerate about me—the good things, that is. Maybe they will even recall something I said that they go on to think about."

"So what about being their twelfth when they ask you?"

"I have other obligations," Matthias said. "And it makes no sense. I was not Jesus' disciple; I was his friend."

"Simon is ecstatic at the idea he will have his own episcopus," James whispered, attaching importance to Matthias' official capacity as a Sanhedrin scribe. "If your tract records his interpretations, coded messages to him from on high, Simon imagines it will eventually be added to the Torah."

"And the others? Is that what they think?"

"Several of them are upset with Simon. Bartholomew, the one whose left eye sometimes goes off on its own; Simon C'nani, James bar Alpheus—"

"The one with stubby teeth."

"Yes. Several may be wavering in their loyalty to him. Back at the Center, you will meet a friend of mine who has won a reputation as a recent apostle. A wealthy Levite named Joseph, who also calls himself Barnabas. I can rely on him."

As if this were his first time in Jerusalem, Matthias made no reply but was intently observing the surroundings, especially the women who stopped at a stall featuring colorful Greek pleated skirts and blouses.

"Almost always in pairs, so their husbands won't harbor suspicion about their companionship," he remarked, showing no apparent interest in what James had been saying.

Conspiring to make James feel altogether unimportant, or so it seemed, a familiar clopping sound of a burdened donkey, carrying sacks of debris from a fallen pediment, suddenly became a din.

Forced to the side of the cobbled street, Matthias had stepped into the open gutter trough, which was full of dirty water coursing its way down to the city limits. As he leaned away from the donkey, James could see from his place of refuge under the shaded awning of the produce stall that Matthias' feet were wet.

"Shall I find you a rag to wipe them off?" he asked politely, concealing a mild measure of satisfaction at the sight of his discomfort.

"I don't know him," Matthias said, surprising James with his response to his earlier mention of Barnabas. "Oh well, they needed a good washing anyway."

"My instruction to Barnabas is to keep an eye on Saul of Tarsus," James persisted.

"The one who works for the authorities?"

"He claims to have seen Jesus or heard his voice while going to Damascus," James confided quietly, as if exposing an absurd matter best kept secret. "According to Simon, he is to spread word that my brother isn't dead. Simon promises he will be forgiven and saved."

Stopping at a stall with grains and spices, Matthias handed the vendor a Roman denarius and took several bronze leptons in change, along with a sack of finely ground barley. "You're on your way to your aunt Elizabeth's," he said, handing it to James, "so tell her it's from me. And convey my wish for a good festival and peace."

"Of course," James replied, "but what will you tell them?"

Turning away, Matthias raised his hand over his head in a farewell gesture, as if catching a mosquito. With the perfunctory wave, he turned his back to James, indicating their conversation would be continued later, and stepped into the bright sunlight. Alone in the shade of the awning over the produce stand, James felt Matthias had little respect for him. "I never claimed to be like Jesus," he protested under his breath.

CHAPTER TWO

*T*he group, numbering eleven, were gathered in the second-story meeting room.

"Are we ready?" Simon asked.

"Shouldn't we wait for James?" Bartholomew replied, his right eye wandering more than usual, as it did when he was agitated.

"I think we should wait," Thaddeus agreed.

"Brother," Simon answered, "James has gone to visit his aunt. He will get here when he gets here."

"Let's wait a while longer," Matthew suggested.

"We know what he thinks," Simon asserted, his voice lowered. "And Matthias may return any moment. Though he was not Jesus' chosen, as we are, he was his true friend. So speak on this matter and be heard."

"Here's what I think," Andrew said. "As a scribe, Matthias has authority in the Sanhedrin. He has friends to help us if our work is criticized by the priests or Pharisees."

"He's right," Thomas agreed. "We know what they're capable of."

"A lot of good Matthias was," John the Zebedee, muttered.

"No one can stand against God's will," Simon stated flatly. "Do you think Matthias could change the outcome? If Jesus had wanted it to stop, then it would have! One day we'll know why it had to happen, but here's my opinion. I think it's good to have a scribe as part of our group—but for other reasons. It's time to make Jesus' teachings into a scroll. Aren't we the priests of his life and words?"

"And you will tell Matthias what to write?" Philip asked doubtfully.

"Not just me. We can sit together and tell him what we remember. If we recall things somewhat differently or perhaps can fill in what another has forgotten, he can keep track—"

James bar Alpheus interrupted, "You expect Matthias to spend his time doing it?"

"If he agrees and shows enthusiasm for the idea, we will know he is a good choice as our twelfth," Simon said.

"But what will you tell him is its purpose?" Matthew prodded.

"That new believers will meet Jesus when they hear our testament to his life and words, as if he were still among us on this earth. Brother," Simon added, "we are only passing along the message of the living Jesus. We know he is alive."

Simon's consternation was reaching its limit. For them not to grasp the significance of what it would mean to have an "episcopus" of standing become one of them! And for Matthew to show doubt, not even a fisherman from their same Galilean background. A tax collector . . . .

"But Simon," Matthew persisted, "should we call attention to ourselves? Why would Matthias make himself an object of derision to his colleagues in the Sanhedrin?"

"To keep our boat from running aground," Simon replied, his words isolating Matthew from the others who well knew the danger of shallows when rocks might crack their hull. "But I am glad you are asking—taking this step seriously."

"Matthias is one who watched as he died on the cross," Bartholomew contradicted. "You think he will be willing to accept what you say, Simon? That Jesus is alive and speaking to us from heaven?" His intentional emphasis of "Simon" hung in the air.

"Listen, Bartholomew," he replied coldly, annoyed to be called by his former name, "those who hear the message of Jesus from heaven know he is alive. And I will tell you something else. Think about this: the ones who hear Jesus are themselves alive. Just as he chose us to understand him on earth, speaking with the holy spirit, he continues to do so."

"Well, if that's the case," Bartholomew ventured sarcastically, "we should certainly tell James."

"You may laugh," Simon replied, trying to discern which of Bartholomew's eyes was looking at him. "But where is your faith? As for James, sadly, his mind is clouded by anger. My fear is that he will never accept what I am saying. But wouldn't it be wonderful if he did, so that he might rejoice with us? Anyway, we will see about Matthias soon. Meanwhile, I have evidence. There is somebody for you all to meet, a witness."

Simon exited briefly and returned with two men, one heavyset and the other quite thin, with hair made unkempt by his sudden, quick glances, as his gaze turned here and there like a nervous bird on a branch. Almost immediately, several in the group recognized the thin individual as Saul of Tarsus, a Jew who prospered as an agent for the Roman authorities, and they abruptly rose to leave.

"Who have you brought us?" Bartholomew hissed harshly at Simon as he brushed past him. While the heavyset man who accompanied him stepped back toward the wall, inhaling deeply to permit passage of those now pushing toward the door, Saul responded, imploring them to stay. "Don't go," he pleaded. "I've come as a friend. I am now one of you."

"One of us?" Simon C'nani challenged. "Are you making a joke? You think reporting us to the police whenever you can is suddenly erased? This must be your newest trick—trap us into saying things that are against Tiberius or Pilate and call in the authorities!"

Refusing to show any timidity, Simon C'nani was now so close to him that their chins were almost touching as he added, "Saul of Tarsus. That's who you are. We are not so foolish. Simon, take him away!"

"You must be the one they call C'nani, the one zealous against the empire," Saul responded, wiping his cheek off where some spittle had found its mark. "But your nature and readiness to fight is wasted on me. I am no defender of Rome, not anymore. I will leave, if you wish me to, but I haven't come here to collect taxes or threaten you."

Disputing each other, the few still seated, including Andrew and Thomas, as well as the Zebedees, were whispering, "Saul . . . Saul is his name. He has called for our arrest. Hunting us down as troublemakers. How can we know he is done working for Pilate or Caiaphas?"

Overhearing their remarks, Saul responded, "That is how you may think of me. And it's true. I am he. But I am not here to arrest you. Peter will tell you I usually seek out your apostles and put an end to their activity; that is, until recently, if you will give me a chance to tell about it."

Seeing James bar Alpheus and Thaddeus had decided to stay, Simon C'nani and Bartholomew reluctantly followed, scowling with displeasure as they shuffled back to their seats.

"Because I am from Tarsus and a Hebrew, a man who is also a Roman citizen by birth, I was contacted by synagogues in Damascus, complaining of intruders. Several apostles had entered the Jewish services and created a disturbance by telling about Jesus. I had papers for their arrest, which were in my satchel—papers authorized by Jerusalem."

"Tell them, Saul," Simon urged.

"I am here because I have seen Jesus, and he spoke to me. While I was walking on the road, approaching the city, a blinding light surrounded me, and Jesus asked why I was persecuting him. I didn't even know who was talking to me, but he told me who he was. So I, the very one who had come to arrest the apostles, joined them, preaching in the synagogues. You should have seen the congregants— they wondered what to do when I said Jesus was the chosen one of God. Wasn't I supposed to arrest people who said the very things I was saying?"

"Are we expected to believe this man?" Thomas asked.

Simon turned to the heavyset fellow standing at Saul's side. "Some of you have met Barnabas. You may know we are able to pay many of our expenses thanks to him. Please, Barnabas."

Accepting the apparent invitation to address them, Barnabas stepped forward. "My Hebrew name is Joseph," he began. "Though I was born in Cyprus, I am a Levite and very proud of it. These days, I am often called Justus, a surname more suitable in Roman circles. But Barnabas is what I call myself. It means 'encouragement.' And it reminds me to encourage you to share Jesus' teachings."

"And you believe Saul? You think Jesus talked to him?" James bar Alpheus called out, his mouth open to reveal odd, stubby teeth that had the aspect of a wild boar.

"Jesus will speak to each of us if we listen," Barnabas said. "You who have heard him know his words are alive in you. And why should Saul be an exception?"

Directing his words to Saul, Thaddeus demanded, "Then what do you want from us? You rejoiced over our suffering and want us to forgive you? Go ask God."

"I will earn it," Saul replied, "if you let me."

"What can we give you?" Simon C'nani said, scowling. "You speak directly to Jesus—isn't that what you're claiming? Let him forgive you."

"Barnabas, tell them what we discussed," Simon prompted.

"If you all agree it is desirable to bring Jesus' teachings to regions in the north, such as Damascus, let Saul be appointed an apostle. They know him there—not only the Hebrews but the pagans. Who would be a better choice to explain how Jesus' teachings are the key to the heavenly kingdom and eternal life? Or should we keep our master a secret, as if we are superior to pagans?"

After waiting for the stir among the disciples to subside, Saul said, "May I say a few more words, Peter? It is true the pagans have different rituals and worship different gods. Yet I have talked to several of their priests about Jesus, and they are interested to hear more. Soon, I expect even to be invited to one of their ceremonies as a gesture of good will."

"Surely you don't imagine you will convert the pagans to believing in our way," Thomas derided.

"If I can change, I imagine they can too," Saul answered.

"I agree," Simon said. "And I suggest we put it to a vote."

"What will James say about this?" Bartholomew demanded.

"Of course we will tell him about the vote and anticipate his assent," Simon said. "I am hoping he will rejoice when he hears Saul's testimony that Jesus has appeared to him. I tell you Jesus is choosing us even now. Meanwhile, Saul and Barnabas, please step outside so our votes are known only to us."

Moments later, as names were called, most raised their hands in affirmation, but Simon took special notice of the few who did not.

"Saul, your apostleship is official," Simon said warmly as he and Barnabas again entered the room. "I will oversee your work and join my brothers in solving any problems you may have. Your mission is to the pagans of the northern Roman provinces, but your responsibility for correct practices and teaching depends on our authority."

"An authority I welcome," Saul replied.

Just then the entrance door below slammed shut. "Barnabas," Simon instructed, "if that's Matthias, please tell him to come up."

A moment later, Barnabas' heavy steps were heard shuffling up the stairs, and he escorted Matthias into the meeting chamber.

"Welcome!" Simon crooned. "I hope you have fared well these past hours."

"Am I interrupting?"

"Not at all. In fact, I was hoping you would be in time to meet Saul." Breaking the silence as Matthias took his measure, Simon said, "You appear to be at a loss for words. No doubt you are thinking either we've all gone mad, or we're under arrest. Am I right?"

"Yes," Matthias acknowledged, feigning surprise at what James had told him to anticipate.

"Nobody's under arrest," Saul said.

"And that's only half the miracle!" Andrew called out. "Tell him!"

"I'm here," Saul said, "because Jesus spoke to me."

Matthias raised his eyebrows, but said nothing.

"No reaction?" Simon prodded.

"I am surprised. Actually, I'm astonished," Matthias managed.

"No doubt!" Simon said. "And James should be here to meet Saul. Don't you agree?"

"I'm sure he will be here soon," Matthias said. "And naturally, he will want to know all about it."

"Perhaps one day, Saul, you and Matthias shall sit together so every word of this great miracle is recorded. Did you know Matthias is a scribe?"

"Indeed, we are acquainted. And I have heard much of your wisdom. The Sanhedrin's deliberations owe many of their records to your point."

"I've done my best to be accurate," Matthias answered agreeably. "But have you come from Tarsus, Saul? That's your home residence, I believe."

"Yes."

"And tell us," Matthias inquired, as if catching up with an old acquaintance, "what news is there of Aretas?"

"Many say he is preparing to attack the northern tetrarchy," Saul answered, adding, "Tiberius is busy with the Parthians, and the ground is sun-hardened for Aretas' troops, should he do battle."

"Thank you for that important information," Simon said. "The coastal highway is certainly safest for those who must travel north. None of us should find ourselves in the middle of a battle. Meanwhile, Saul, I know you must attend to your own festival arrangements."

Almost ignoring his words of appreciation, Saul continued chatting with Matthias. Smiling awkwardly as if he was part of their social circle, Simon had an uneasy sense of exclusion.

"But I want to thank you for having helped us," Simon interrupted. "Now, we have news from you that our master is ruling from heaven . . ." Receiving only a perfunctory nod from Saul, as if his remark was unheard, Simon was unable to say more as, just then, he was shouldered aside by Matthew who was trying to come closer. When Matthew also paid Simon no special respect, not even excusing himself for brushing against him, he was uneasy, especially noticing how he took Barnabas' arm in a comradely manner. The bond between them was disquieting. Simon was well aware Matthew had money and still owned that house in the Galilee where Jesus had been feted as a guest. Matthias had been with them. Now, from what

Simon could see, Barnabas too was part of their cadre. But of course, Matthew knew Barnabas. Still, the way he took his arm. And James was friendly with Barnabas, soliciting his contributions. Perhaps too friendly. What if they chose to weaken Simon's role as leader?

Finally, not to be ignored, Simon addressed the others still seated. "So, brothers," he called out, "if in the weeks and months to come you, like Saul, have evidence of meeting Jesus, please bear witness. We must put to rest the notion that our master died."

"If he goes too far the Romans will step in, Parthians or no Parthians," Matthew observed, taking little interest in Simon's pronouncement. "Otherwise, my guess is that Rome doesn't mind Antipas getting a bloody nose. If you ask me, the emperor doesn't trust him, and this would be a reminder of how dependent he is on Rome."

"There are rumors Aretas' camel brigades are moving forward to positions near Macherus," Barnabas agreed, directing his remark to Matthew.

"Again, Saul, I want to thank you for having helped us," Simon repeated. "Even those among us who loved Jesus have had their faith tested by his crucifixion. Our hearts are still in pain over his leaving us. We must put to rest the notion that he died."

As Saul took Barnabas' arm and they departed, Matthias asked Simon whether he too should leave.

"Not yet," Simon replied. "First we want to speak to you about your own future with us."

"If there's something I can do to help . . ."

"You were with him as his friend. We would be honored if you would record his teachings and our accounts of his works. Matthias, we have decided you are the one to fill the vacant seat left by Judas."

"Truly, I don't know what to say," Matthias responded.

"It will be a great day if you say yes," Simon encouraged. "Who is better than you to help us codify and glorify what he did? We know he anointed us with the holy spirit so that we might become his earthly representatives. Your skills are what we need. Should we not have a scroll of his life to give life? In this, our new beginning, there will be the word, exactly as we transmit it from him to you."

"Your high opinion of me is humbling. And I have my own recollections."

"If you are one of us, you are one of us," Simon told him. "The inspiration you feel to glorify our master in heaven will celebrate our faith."

"I can think of no greater revenge on his murderers than to make him famous as a great rabbi," Matthias replied. "If you want me to, I will act as the twelfth, a scribe to record the history of his life."

"Good!" said Simon. "Matthias, you do realize he was much more than a rabbi. To most of us here, he is the one whom God sent to commence the Kingdom."

"So much the better," Matthias answered. "Nothing will make the ones who did it angrier. They could only execute him once. Let them strike their fists against thin air!"

"But what do you believe, Matthias?"

Sensing from the tone of Simon's query that his future role hung in the balance, Matthias' words were measured.

"I have not yet been blessed to hear his voice speaking to me from heaven. Nothing would be more of a miracle to me than to have that blessing. I will hope for it."

"Still, you were at the foot of the cross when he was dying." It was Thaddeus who spoke.

"Yes. I was with him until the end."

"And if he said anything to you that may have been secret—about his true identity as God's chosen one—we should hear about it," Thaddeus added.

"Perhaps one day, I will share more about our time together."

"You are right!" Simon exclaimed. "We must be patient. Like you, Matthias, there are still a few among us who are waiting to hear him again! Welcome, then, as our twelfth!"

"For which honor I extend my thanks and appreciation to all who accept my presence in your esteemed circle."

"Then remain with us for the coming few days, and let us begin. I have a scroll for the purpose, and we have ample space to spend your nights."

"My scribe's points are in my bag," Matthias said. "After sundown tomorrow will be fine. But I will be lodging in the room reserved for me in the Sanhedrin's quarters."

"Whatever you choose. We shall look forward to our time together, brother," Simon replied. "And now it is time to see if the women need our help. Do you smell that wonderful aroma? Mary makes the best pigeon. She says all the women of Magdala have secret recipes."

As the disciples made their way down the stairs, Matthias felt a hand on his arm, holding him back. It was Simon. "I need to speak with you," he said. "Just a word."

Nobody seemed to notice that the two remained behind.

"Matthias, I must seem very sure of myself. I want you to see past that facade. Actually, I'm probably as confused as any among us. I don't know why God wanted Jesus to suffer as he did. I pretend it is not a question to me. Every day I ask him to give an answer from his heavenly place."

"I share your sadness. I have no answer."

"But we must. It will be a question that destroys our faith if it echoes in our hearts."

"It has only been two years. A change will come," Matthias said.

"Two years that feel much longer. Yet it all seems to have just happened. So now I must ask something. In Caesaria Philipi, when we started out for Jerusalem, and he and I were walking together, you were just a stone's throw from us, and the group heard nothing. Matthias, did you hear what he said to me? That my name was changed to Peter?"

"I know he was speaking with you. That's all."

"I thought you might have heard."

From below, a voice called, asking that they come join the feast.

"But you should understand this," Simon continued. "Some, like James, think we have made up things about Jesus. I realize James is your friend. He is my friend too. And he presides over the administration of our affairs. He brought us Barnabas. But that was a year ago, and his efforts to raise money have been nil since then."

"I am fond of James."

"As I am! But to him, Jesus was nothing more than a rabbi, a teacher of Torah. I ask you, did he come among us only to teach Torah? Forgive me for sounding so filled with reproach. But where is James? With Elizabeth, is he not?"

"Yes."

"Still grieving with her over John—John, whose role in life should have been as a messenger of the good news that Jesus was—is— among us. With all his bathing of those pilgrims crossing the river to the Temple, did he ever speak about Jesus? No. Still, some spread the rumor that he purified our master! I suspect James started that rumor."

"I am sure James never did that."

Unexpectedly, Simon suddenly squeezed Matthias' arm tightly, as if something in the room made him fearful.

Loosing his grip and walking toward the far wall, he pushed aside the large, knitted floor cushions. As he made his way past two benches, shoving them with his leg so they were flush to the wall, Simon was all the while looking about, searching for something.

"You are fortunate to have found so lovely a location," Matthias said, uncomfortable that he was excluded from whatever had Simon so preoccupied. "The remnant of that old wall mosaic is charming."

Ignoring him, Simon's gaze froze momentarily on the large amphora of salt, their most precious commodity, in plain sight, kept dry by the sun pouring in through the courtyard window. Just next to it should have been the straw broom, used to sweep up and preserve any that might spill. "But here it is!" Simon exclaimed, obviously relieved as he returned the broom to its upright position, leaning its long handle against the wall. "Forgive me for behaving like this, my friend. It's a dream I keep having that somebody comes and steals something from this room. To have the same dream . . . it feels . . . never mind. But yes, a wealthy Roman sold this building to a Jewish family. Their heirs let it run down, and we were able to buy it."

"Ajax," Matthias observed, surveying the large, fragmentary mosaic adorning the eastern wall. He hoped their discourse had moved past worries spawned by dreams or recrimination toward James.

"We redid the walls with plaster but decided to leave the mosaic—or what's left of it," Simon said, having regained his composure.

"The great warrior. Even one sad-looking eye is enough to tell it's him."

"That's as good a guess as any," Simon said. "But the feet of a woman and a fishtail near the bottom—we can make those out."

"Yes," Matthias said. "He is often pictured in the company of a pretty nereid. Those certainly are her feet. You can see what's left of his rosy cheeks—too pink. Always a shortcoming of Roman tessareae . . ."

"Hardly enough of his face to be sure who it is," Simon said dismissively. "But Philip will tell you what we know about it. He was raised by a Greek aunt."

About to allude to Ajax' tragic flaw—that he had become infatuated with an idea of himself, finally falling on his sword when it proved a fantasy—Matthias held his peace. Oddly, it seemed Simon might take it personally, as if he were talking about him.

Again at the stairway door, about to descend to the lower triclinium and rejoin the group, Simon surprised Matthias, returning to the topic of Jesus' baptism.

"Obviously, to prevent us from thinking his brother was more than an ordinary rabbi, he will say anything. You see what we are up against?" he asked.

"But Simon," Matthias said resolutely, "I am the one who told James. I told him that John immersed Jesus."

"You? Why would you make up such a story? I can't believe it was you—his friend!"

"If Jesus had not told me, I would never have known."

"What? It's impossible. It can't be!"

"John asked Jesus the same question. He felt it was an unseemly act on his part to immerse and purify Jesus. But Jesus insisted."

"I don't know what to say. If you are intending to include this as one of your recollections, I will have to see how you word it. It must express John's humility before Jesus. For now, let the matter be between us. Will you do that?"

"I have no need to talk about it."

"That's good. But to think Jesus needed his cleansing bath when John was not fit to tie his sandal!"

Chapter Three

*E*lizabeth stood in her doorway, watching as James retrieved the sack of barley from the cart. "A festival gift from Matthias," he replied to her inquiring look. "From me, all you get is a hug and a kiss."

"How is Matthias?" she asked as they went inside.

"He's fine. They're all pleased he'll be visiting with them at the Center."

"Always so thoughtful." She pointed to an area of the room where she kept foodstuffs, saying, "Put it there, and please tell him it was appreciated. Now that the formalities are over, let's hear what's going on and how you are faring."

"You probably know more than I do."

Elizabeth shook her head. "Time passes slowly for me. I hear unimportant things. It's one of the benefits of being the widow of a priest. All the women whose husbands have died come to prop me up. Their gossip about nothing doesn't stop."

"You don't look like you need propping up," James observed.

"I don't. But before the others arrive, perhaps you will fill me in on what news is worth hearing."

"Who's coming?"

"I expect your brother Jude will stop by on the way to your father's."

"And Mary? Just a few days ago in Nazareth she told me she was thinking about it."

"Let's hope. But if she comes, I want you to take her with you to the Center. You know how close she and Matthias are. It will be good for her."

Elizabeth held a small plate and served James pistachios from a nearby table. "Persian," she announced. "These only are found in the market once or twice a year."

"Mary spending the night at the Center? I'm not sure it's such a good idea," he answered hesitantly but was spared the need to prevaricate, as voices were heard just outside.

"Shalom! Anybody home?"

"Mary, how have you been?" Elizabeth asked, holding the door open as her niece entered, with Jude just a step behind.

"Don't look too close," Mary replied, hugging her aunt and swaying back and forth. "A year can be unkind."

"I always loved waking up in Ayn Kerem," Jude said, accepting a handful of nuts as he reclined on one of the cushioned mats. "It's so beautiful here—the hills and the scent of jasmine. I remember racing around the yard with John."

"You always have a place to stay," Elizabeth said.

"Thank you, Aunt," Jude replied, "but Abba will worry if I'm not there before sundown. You coming with me, James?"

"Not tonight," he replied, taking his cue from his aunt's quick glance. "What about you, Mary? You can stay at the Center."

"I don't think they would be happy to see me, James."

"They would welcome you. What more special guest could they hope for than Jesus' mother!"

"Are you serious?" she asked, smiling broadly. "I make Simon nervous. That's what you once told me."

"I want to hear the commandments," Jude interjected, typically impervious to the conversation around him. Greeted only by silence, he added, "I'm going. You know, to hear the commandments. And you, Aunt?"

"I don't think so," Elizabeth said.

Because his plans were typically unimportant to them, a disadvantage he had always suffered, Jude seized on the latest rumor to win their interest. "I guess you've heard about Antipas and Herodias quarreling over her brother's situation."

"The murderer and his whore . . ." Elizabeth replied, as if she didn't need to know more.

Undeterred, Jude elaborated. "They say Antipas suspects that his wife's brother, Agrippa, has eyes on his tetrarchy. Because he's in debt, Herodias apparently insisted he live with them in the palace. She thinks her brother is totally innocent of any such ambition."

"I hope the two men kill each other!" Elizabeth rasped. "So . . . Mary, you were saying?"

"Then you also heard Antipas and Herodias went to a state dinner in Tyre, and her miscreant brother accompanied them?" Jude persisted.

"This is interesting," Mary acknowledged. "I'm surprised you've been keeping this gossip to yourself."

Pleased to have finally captured their curiosity, Jude slowly ate from a nearby platter of mint leaves and goat cheese while casually relating the details. "At the dinner, Antipas' suspicions were proved right. Agrippa, somewhat drunk, went on about what a great king of Galilee he would make. And that the Romans should choose him over Antipas."

"Hard to believe he'd dare such an insult!" Mary responded, a smile playing on her lips.

"Wait—the best is coming," Jude chortled. "When his anger reached the boiling point, Antipas interrupted his brother-in-law to say he was a slovenly wretch who owed money to local nobility and that they were constantly searching him out for arrest. According to Antipas, he was only able to avoid jail by hiding under his sister's skirts. But James, did you know all this?"

"Only that Antipas called him a fool and scoffed that before he became king, he would have to earn enough money to put food on his own table."

"I have it directly from Joanna, whose husband still works in the palace," Jude stated, giving his news an official air.

"So, Aunt Elizabeth, how's that for gossip!" Mary declared. "Jude, you always know what's going on."

"People say all kinds of things. What difference should it make to me?" Elizabeth replied, not intending the mild slight to her nephew. "I'm sorry Jude. I can't gossip about the man who killed my son. John was the only one brave enough to tell the truth about Herodias. What a slut, not even divorcing Philip before she jumped into bed with his own half brother! No wonder his Nabatean wife fled."

"Even if two years have passed since Antipas jailed John for his speeches," James assured Elizabeth, "her Nabatean father has not forgotten his daughter's humiliation. Aretas' camel brigades are just now moving to positions near Macherus. He has been biding his time. They may well get support from the citizens of the Galilee and Samaria . . . certainly sympathy from the inhabitants of Philip's tetrarchy. I am sure many among them knew John and heard him."

"Aretas, 'the Camel' as they call him, is a famous warrior," Jude attested knowingly.

"If I believed he had a chance of conquering that bastard and his wife I would ride one of his camels alongside him," Elizabeth responded. "Rome will never let it happen. They appointed Antipas, and he serves at their pleasure."

"Tiberius may have his reasons for permitting an attack," James proffered. "Antipas has apparently been too friendly with the Parthians. And he has a large stockpile of armaments."

"None of it matters anymore. What memory does anybody have of John?" Elizabeth asked woodenly, her private distress surfacing.

As James managed to pry open the obstinate shell of an especially large nut, he remembered how the market buzzed with gossip. John's insulting harangues were recited with glee, chastising the tetrarch for his perverse wedlock. No doubt his barbed jibes had incited popular support for an attack by Aretas, elevating the oratorical provocation to the level of sedition.

For several moments, James only vaguely heard Elizabeth's words in the background. He recalled how John was arrested, but what had Jesus done to arouse opposition to any political ruler? Carved into the wood above the cross was the charge—King of the Jews—but had Jesus ever made such a claim? Had he ever called for an attack on anybody?

"Do you remember," Elizabeth was asking, "the way our own officials mocked John for imitating the prophet Elijah and derided him as a madman?"

Nodding to disguise his lapse of attention, James assured her earnestly, "We will not forget him."

"His faith in God was an example to us all," Mary added. "He used to call out, 'Pave the way. Make a clear path. Adonai will be in your midst!'"

"And look what some even now are saying about him, or so I have heard," Elizabeth related. "That he was punished for 'ploughing in slime,' that you can't clean a person's soul with a bath. Those supposed holy men living in their caves near the Salt Sea—gehinnom is too good for them! Others pray for God's return to the midst of our people in some distant future. My son was simply counting the days . . ."

Not wanting her aunt to feel so alone, Mary recalled her own loss. "I was still carrying Jesus, living here, when he was born."

As tears welled up in Elizabeth's eyes, James turned to Mary and said, "One person I know would be especially pleased to see you at the Center. Matthias."

"He is there?" Mary asked.

"Spend the night, and your paths will cross," James said.

"It would be good to see him. But is there really sufficient space?"

"I can sleep in the sitting room," James assured her. "You will have your own bed."

"I don't know," Mary said. "Elizabeth?"

"Go!" Elizabeth prompted, wiping her cheek with the back of her hand. "It will be good for you. And we can continue our visit in the coming days."

"If you are sure . . . all right. I will go."

The sunlight on the wall opposite the front window told them the time of the third watch was passing. James gave Mary a hand, helping her up from the low couch. "We must leave if we are to get there before they serve the meal," he said.

"James, when did you last see Abba?" Jude asked, standing to leave.

"About seven weeks ago, during Passover. In case he doesn't come to hear the commandments, tell him I will be over to see how he's getting along."

"And that I wish him a good festival," Mary said quietly.

Elizabeth saw them out and nodded to James, pleased that he had persuaded Mary, despite her misgivings.

CHAPTER FOUR

*U*pon their arrival, Mary was welcomed with spicy bread cakes and warm wine and with an affectionate embrace by Matthias, who raised himself to press the side of his face against hers.

Outside, as James hitched the horse to a post and secured the last turn of hemp cord, a figure emerged from a secluded spot.

It was Barnabas. "James, I must speak with you alone."

"Yes, Barnabas, of course. Where is Saul?"

"Prattling on to his old associates, I expect. It's really gone to his head. He thinks he's been selected to open pagan hearts, like Jesus is one of their gods. Whatever he decides, he will say is true because he's your brother's personal prophet!"

"The pagans won't be interested," James said, "but keep an eye on him."

"What if Saul makes up his own teaching and says it's from Jesus?"

"I don't know, Barnabas. But you best go, so we are not seen talking privately."

A moment later, James was inside and greeted the disciples. He noticed that Mary had been provided a seat near Matthias.

"Simon has something to report. Tell James about my new job," Matthias prompted.

"I'll do even better. Let me show all of you," Simon responded with a smile. From behind the couch near a table, he retrieved a large scroll and unrolled it for display. "So what do you think?" Amid murmurs of approval, Simon persisted, "Eh, Matthias?"

"Excellent," Matthias said.

"But there is nothing written on it," James said.

"Ah, but there will be!" Simon exulted. "We will share Jesus' life and works with the world. Matthias has agreed to be our scribe, and as our twelfth, he may certainly add to our treasure of memories."

"Matthias, is this true?" James asked with enthusiasm.

"I will do my best, James," Matthias promised. "I hope you are pleased."

"Of course, my friend. May you be strong and wise in your pursuit of my brother's teaching. So you are to take Judas Iscariot's place?"

"We have voted on the matter," Simon replied, "and trust Jesus' spirit found its way into our hearts."

"I hope you agree I'm worthy," Matthias said hesitantly, addressing James.

James nodded. "I do."

"But what about you, Mary?" Andrew interrupted. "Shouldn't you be the first to tell us about Jesus? Peter, she knew him long before we did!"

Others concurred, calling out, "Mary, tell us something you remember!"

She responded, subduing any sign of emotion. "He was a beautiful child. He spent time making things out of wood. His father showed him how. And we went to the synagogue in Nazareth when he was growing up. Joseph's sons and two daughters helped me take care of him. James, you were closest to his age, and he and you, I think, had a special bond. His father was in Bethlehem a lot of the time. That's where he was born, as you know."

"Matthias, will you put this down?" Simon asked.

"On the morrow," Matthias said. "After sundown."

"Of course!" Simon replied. "No work on the holiday. But tell us, Mary," Simon continued, "you must have felt you were carrying an unusual child."

"These things are hard for me to talk about. I was sixteen. I hate to tell you how many years ago that was, Simon."

"But did you have any idea he was the chosen one of God? Angels must have protected you everywhere you went!"

"I don't know. If you believe there were angels . . . well, I love you all for loving him. If you take comfort from the idea he was chosen by God, you have my blessing. Simon, there's nothing you could have done. You shouldn't blame yourself."

"For what?" Simon snapped. "I'm sorry, but what could any of us have done? I only thought you might have known God chose him."

"As usual, Simon, you talk about secrets," James said protectively. "Can you tell us if you ever heard Jesus say he was the chosen one of God? You want his mother to tell you something he never said about himself."

"I only want Mary to know he is alive in heaven. You do know that, don't you, Mary?" Simon asked.

Mary felt threatened, like a child about to be spanked for misbehaving. She heard herself apologizing as if somebody else was speaking.

"No need to be sorry," Simon said, but rather than face her, he addressed the others as if she wasn't actually there. "There's nothing any of us could have done. Of course we couldn't. God has done it. How else would he have died? You think those filthy murderers could have ended his earthly life unless God wanted it? Mary, Jesus has been talking to some of us. You may find it hard to believe, but he has!"

33

"It's all right, James," Mary said softly. "I believe he's in heaven too. So let's not quarrel."

"She is right," Philip offered, attempting to end their arguing. "One thing we know: he wanted people to be forgiving toward each other."

"If we hope to spread his teaching," James added, "shall we be guilty of ignoring his message?"

"You see why he is our praesidere?" Simon said. "James, you remind us of his love. We are fortunate that you serve him in our presence. Thank you. Only one thing I will add. None of us talks about the miracle after his crucifixion. Mary, I say this because it is hard evidence. I say this as a wondrous consolation. What more telling sign of his ascent to heaven might we have than his empty tomb?"

Before she could reply, the sound of Mary Magdalene forcing the courtyard entrance door ajar with her foot captured their attention. Handing a steaming platter to John the Zebedee, who immediately rose to assist her, she joyfully declared, "The tomb was empty! I was there, and the only sign he had been in the tomb was a bloody shroud. Neatly folded, too. He is watching us from heaven. That's what I know."

Following Andrew's example, each of the disciples raised his glass and declared, "Lehayim—to life!" Then John the Zebedee took the tray and carried it across the room to a table with sufficient space.

"One thing is sure," James bar Alpheus joked. "This is a heavenly aroma!"

But Simon grew quiet as the two Marys discussed the recipe of beets and onions blended with carrots, which accompanied the spicy roast goat.

***

Their opportunity to chat privately did not present itself until Matthias returned the next morning and invited Mary to carry her breakfast tray outside, where they sat in the small courtyard on a bench by themselves.

Under a myrtle, with its branches forming a net of shadows, Mary closed her eyes, breathing in the scented leaves, always so aromatic in the early spring. "Last night, after you'd left to sleep in the Sanhedrin's quarters," Mary said, "Simon kept boasting that you would be recording their recollections of my son's life and teachings."

"Yes, Mary. I have agreed to do that."

"Matthias . . ." She did not elaborate but paused to see whether he showed any awareness of what she intended to say.

"Tell me what has you worried."

Nodding her appreciation, she continued, "Simon is unwilling to just let him rest in peace. Isn't that what Jesus deserves? Isn't dying once enough? Saying he's still alive . . . for what? So Simon can make his memory a ghostly semblance of who he was?"

"Not if their account depends on me, Mary. I only want to see his compassion carried on. If we could all stop acting superior . . ."

"Good luck, then," she replied, her somber tone betraying doubt. "But keep this in mind, dear Matthias. A man who can create a god is a man to be wary of."

Chapter Five

$\mathcal{B}$ecause their Galilean dialect was noticeable to others, the group edged their way up the Temple mount in silence, hoping to avoid scrutiny as uneducated locals from the north.

Turning toward the southern stairs, Mary wished James and Matthias shalom and gave a slight wave to Simon and the disciples as she found Jude by the gate of the Women's Court. Then she disappeared into the crowd of pilgrims. After the morning service concluded with the Ten Commandments, she would return to Nazareth with Jude.

Leading the way to a side courtyard that fronted the Portico of Solomon, Simon instructed the disciples to concentrate their thoughts on Jesus.

They didn't need to understand the Hebrew prayers. Unlike the priests' recitation, their own voices would make natural sounds, a language to be heard on high, with meaning all might understand. The ones who had turned him over to be crucified—theirs was the babble, soon to be forgotten in a bygone era.

"So, brothers," Simon intoned, "let us be the ones to speak to Jesus in the first of all languages, from that ancient time when God exiled the arrogant and forced them to speak in many tongues, such as the one we hear through these gates."

James and Matthias stood a ways off, observing.

Simon looked to the sky and started yelling. His broken, staccato cries were fully joined by Andrew and Thomas, while John the

Zebedee, whose voice was given to cracking, had begun screeching, causing his brother James to look at him in mild embarrassment. In their own manner, Matthew and Thaddeus made throaty and deep hissing sounds, while Simon C'nani and James bar Alpheus warbled. Philip, as best Matthias could surmise, was quiet.

"This storm of noises might well have been heard at the dawn of creation," Matthias joked to James, but his attention was drawn elsewhere.

"I don't know if their voices are reaching heaven," James said, "but they have carried to the sacrificial courtyards. Here come Levite guards."

"Are you drunk?" the senior guard demanded as he reached Simon.

"We are not drunk!" Simon replied. "How can you think we are drunk when it is just several hours since sunrise?"

"They have been drinking too much new wine," one of the passersby called out. "Get them out of here!"

"Our authority is from Jesus of Nazareth," Simon declared.

"You mean the one who was crucified when he called himself King of the Jews?" the senior guard asked.

"Two years dead, and he's still making trouble," another joked.

"Well, our authority is from Caiaphas, the high priest," the first said, suddenly appearing solemn, "and you know what he can do."

"Jesus, our master, was put into your hands by the deliberate intention of God," Simon answered. "You killed him, but God has raised him to life. We are anointed by his spirit from heaven."

Hearing Simon's accusation that they bore guilt in the execution and his claim that Jesus was ruling from heaven, the one in charge no longer thought the group simply drunk. He required the apparent leaders, Simon and his brother Andrew, be taken before their captain.

They arrived at the guardhouse, followed closely by Matthias and James, where the captain listened to the complaint.

"They are obviously am ha-aretz," one guard said. "Ignorant troublemakers. They have no fringes. And when they speak to each other, you can hardly understand them."

"They are causing a disturbance," another stated.

"Put them in the common jail for a night," the captain instructed, impatient to restore order.

As the two were about to be taken away, Matthias spoke up. "I am a scribe and member of the Sanhedrin," he said. "I think it best we have the opinion of a respected Pharisee in this matter. After all, don't we long for God to anoint us with His spirit, as the prophet Joel said would happen? Are my friends here so different?"

The captain, not wishing to dispute a man with authority, indicated the guards should delay a moment longer. "Whom do you suggest?" he asked. "Everybody has taken their places in the Women's Court to hear the commandments."

"Gamliel," Matthias said.

"Gamliel? You think he would take interest in such a minor matter?"

"He will be standing by himself near the front," Matthias said.

"We know who he is," the captain answered, and then turning to his assistant, he commanded, "Go and do what he said. See if he will come, though I doubt the rabbi will take time to give an opinion."

Moments later, as all stood waiting, the Levite guard returned, followed by the tall, thin, bearded sage, accompanied by James, who had stepped outside.

"I have invited this young man to join me," Gamliel said, grasping James by the arm. "An old man needs something strong to hold on to."

38

"Rabbi," the captain said, "these two are leaders of a group who believe Jesus of Nazareth, the one ordered crucified by Pilate—you remember, two years ago—is in heaven, acting as God's chosen king."

Gamliel turned to James and said, "He was your brother. Isn't it true you are James?"

"Yes."

"I always speak with my father," Gamliel said. "He is in heaven too." Then he added with a slight smile, "Perhaps he and your brother know each other."

"I'm sure they do," said James.

Gamliel's countenance became serious as he addressed the captain of the guard. "Don't you ever talk to those you loved in life but have gone to heaven? Will you or I spend a night in jail for having honored the memory of our father and mother, while you hear that very commandment read this holy day of Shavuot? And should the devoted followers of a teacher now gone be prevented from heartfelt yearning that he still hears their voices?"

When the captain didn't answer, Matthias, who had been silent, thanked the rabbi and wished him chag m'vorach—a festival of blessings.

"Many blessings to you as well, Matthias," Gamliel replied. "It is always good to see you."

As the disgruntled captain turned his back to them, Simon and Andrew realized they were free to go. Upon returning to the others, both bragged that no sons of men could have confined them against Jesus' will. "Our jailers looked around and were amazed they had no power to keep us," Simon told them.

CHAPTER SIX

*M*atthias sat at the writing table in the upper sitting room, listening to the plan to create the account of Jesus' life.

Having unstitched several parchment segments for the ease of transcription and arrangement, Simon now slid one directly in front of Matthias. "Whatever you put down will be the truth, my own words—and Jesus' words to me from heaven," Simon said. "Other disciples may include their versions—should any of us vary in our recollections—with the general approval of our group. Matthias, I think we should begin with the immersion of Jesus by John. We may have something that precedes that glorious moment, but we need only stitch my account farther along as the need arises."

"Yes. That's fine. But I thought—"

"That I would never admit that such a thing happened? Jesus made it a secret sign. You will hear. So let us begin." As Matthias dipped his point in the bottle of dark vegetable dye, Simon began slowly. "In those days, there was John the Baptizer, preaching that the Kingdom of Heaven was about to happen."

As Matthias skillfully completed the fine, small letters, he asked, "Do you want to say when it was, so people will know?"

"Of course," Simon said. "That's a good idea. This was in the fifteenth year of the reign of Tiberius Caesar. Pontius Pilate was governor of Judea and King Herod's son, Herod Antipas, was tetrarch of the

Galilee and eastern provinces, with his brother Philip as tetrarch of the adjacent regions."

"I will leave space to add some detail later," Matthias said. "And will you mention Caiaphas?"

"Yes, we must. 'It was in the high priesthood of Caiaphas'—you should put it down that way," Simon instructed. "You know how John would call out, 'Prepare the way of the Lord. Make His paths straight'? Well, here is how Jesus has told me to say it:

"Jesus came preaching the words: 'Behold, I send my messenger who shall prepare the way.' And all the people wondered whether John was the chosen one of God, but he answered them all, 'I cleanse you with water, but he who is mightier than I is coming, and I am not worthy to untie his sandal strap.'"

Having just spoken the last of these words, Simon paused as the door opened, and James asked whether he was intruding. "I only want to remind Matthias that if we would go and not be traveling in the dark, we should leave soon."

"Come in James," Simon said. "You may find the rest of my account about John interesting. It will only take a moment."

James sat on a nearby bench and listened as Simon continued.

"Say this: 'Then Jesus came from the Galilee to the Jordan River and indicated he wished to be immersed by him. John tried to stop him, saying, I'm the one who should be immersed by you, and you are asking me to do this? But Jesus answered, let it be so for now.'"

When Matthias finished the last letter, he held his point over the parchment, wondering whether there wasn't more. "Didn't Jesus reveal his reason for being immersed?" he inquired.

"No. Not yet. He wants us to grasp the secret meaning of his act," Simon said.

"But one day I am sure he will reveal it to you," James chided, "and that will be another secret that only you hear, Simon—the keeper of secrets."

"I regret your ill temper toward me, James. I can't help it if I believe more in your brother than you do."

"That's not what worries me," James replied. "It's that the one you believe in is not my brother. You're changing him to glorify yourself."

"Our master, your brother, told us the Kingdom would begin in our lifetimes. Those were words we all heard. When it does, he'll reward us who believe in him."

"You're right about one thing," James said. "My brother hoped to see the Kingdom, just like the rest of us."

"James, if you have faith in him as I do, he will reveal himself."

"And when do you suppose he will reveal the reason God had him tortured and murdered?" James derided.

"When he chooses to," Simon insisted.

James was again on his feet, watching as Matthias tied the scroll and several extra segments with a hemp cord.

"How long before you continue our work?" Simon asked.

"On the sixth day of the week, in the morning," Matthias answered. "I will be coming for Shabbat."

"Good! I was thinking about Jesus and the Shabbat. Some of the others will certainly recall how he talked about those laws."

If James sensed that Simon's comment invited further dispute, he resisted any temptation to pursue it, saying that he and Matthias were going to Bethlehem to look in on his father.

***

Joseph was not expecting visitors, as Matthias observed. His house had not been cleaned, and there were dried, muddy patches on the floor, probably from his sandals. The oven looked like it was full of ashes from early spring, and Joseph's tunic had a yellow food stain at the fold near his chest.

"James, tell me," Joseph said, "are things good for you?"

"They are all right, Abba," James answered.

"Then why don't you come more often? I always worry about you."

"I will."

"Yes, of course. And you, Matthias, what is new with you?"

Matthias glanced at James, meaning he would not tell Joseph about his becoming the twelfth.

"Less is new, the older you get," Matthias answered. "It is a blessing to be healthy. The service at the Temple was festive."

"Yes, yes. Happy holiday," Joseph said.

"Many ask about you," James said. "Isn't that true, Matthias?"

"Only the old-timers, my son," Joseph replied. "This generation doesn't even know what happened a few decades ago. And they wouldn't care if they did."

"I think we deserve more respect than that," James protested, offering his father a hand as he shook a cloth settee cover, freeing its surface of fine desert sand deposited by the prior winter's windstorms.

Once properly spread out, James and Matthias were seated, and Joseph asked, "Am I wrong?" Without waiting for a reply, he brought over a plate of pale purple figs, saying, "The season's first."

"We appreciate the Temple. And I remember many things you taught me," James insisted, taking a bite as his father lowered himself slowly on a nearby chair.

"Such as?"

"I recall a story about King Herod. He had faded red hair. And toward the end of his life, he dyed it with henna."

43

"You remember I told you that?"

"We'd see him standing on his balcony," Matthias said. "His belly was distended from dropsy."

"I remember him on the balcony," Joseph mused. "Did I tell you about that, James? I certainly remember his big stomach. And he often went to the hot sulphur springs. His face was like old parchment, creased with lines."

"We'd hear people say he was being punished," Matthias added.

"For executing Miriam, his Maccabean wife," James said.

"But who told you that?" Joseph asked, obviously surprised.

"You did. And he suspected she was planning to poison him," James added.

"Miriam was a genuine Hashmonean," Matthias chimed in. "That's why he married her. With her as queen, he thought he'd be accepted as the true king of Judea."

Suddenly laughing and startling them both, Joseph was animated by a vivid recollection.

"Matthias, do you remember what they said? That after killing her, he would go about raving that he didn't know how he would go on without her."

Matthias nodded, sharing his amusement. "Yes, I do. Every afternoon, he would stare at the tower he had named for Miriam. He stood on his balcony, estimating the time of day by the length of the tower's shadow. Yes, his hair was bright red—like a flame that flickers just before it goes out."

"One time I hope you will show me around the courtyards again, as you did when I was a boy," James said. "It would be wonderful to see the Temple through your eyes, Abba."

"James, your father supervised the masonry."

"I remember about the priests," James said. "They were the only ones permitted to quarry the stone for the sanctuary."

"And they never used iron tools!" Joseph declared. "We showed them how to hammer pegs of wood with mallets and then pour water on the pegs. They would expand . . ." Joseph said, his voice trailing off as he changed the subject. "We'll see. But James, how are the murderers? Have you seen them?"

Obviously perplexed by the question, James hesitated.

"He means the disciples," Matthias said.

"I don't understand, Abba."

"Is it possible you don't know what happened?" Joseph asked. "They did it. Who is their leader—that Simon? Don't you realize what he did? Ignorant, uneducated fools. I don't know why he was drawn to them."

Of all the topics James least expected his father to broach, the Center was foremost. Since the crucifixion his father had not once referred to Jesus. Whether it was because he exercised no authority to rescue him or that he felt no burden of responsibility, James could not say. Only one thing seemed certain, telling from the profound void in their past conversations: Joseph was uninterested in what had happened to his brother.

"He was their teacher," Matthias said.

"You can't teach their kind. They are born like that. Who asked them to make him king? They aren't even part of the Kingdom, and they're picking our king!" Joseph's bitter laugh eclipsed his words, and he became silent.

"Abba, some of them may be fools, but why do you call them murderers? They were devoted to him."

"As their private emissary from God. Exalting him so they'd feel important."

45

"Maybe that's how they felt. But the Romans were the ones who called him King of the Jews and that was their reason for crucifying him. I never heard any of the group say he was sent by God. At least not while he was alive."

In speaking about Jesus, James felt he was on uncertain ground and might slip fully into a grim exchange about Joseph's indifference. His father's hollow expression of concern, whatever its motive, was meaningless.

"I knew his heart," Joseph went on. "He couldn't stand people who thought they were like gods, like those Pietists in the Galilee. The last thing he would have done was act like God had sent him."

"It seems unfair to blame the ones he loved," James managed, curtailing the thought swirling within.

"They all ran away. Did any of them testify for him? Which one risked his life to speak up when Caiaphas heard those accusations?"

"None did," James admitted, "but you were a member of the Sanhedrin. Maybe you could have done something to save him!" James had uttered words that he hadn't meant to say, and Joseph reacted angrily.

"You think you know so much," he retorted. "You always think you know everything. One day you'll find out things you have no idea about."

"I'm sorry. I shouldn't have said it."

"Yesterday, James and I visited Elizabeth," Matthias said, in an effort to end their bickering. "She sends her greetings."

"Yes, that's good," Joseph replied.

His father, James realized, had become disconnected from the moment, not even hearing what Matthias said. Having ascribed his disheveled appearance and the untidy place to his seclusion, a result of growing old and being alone, James now wondered whether his father was tormented by unshared private thoughts.

"What was it you said?" Joseph finally asked Matthias.

"We visited Elizabeth."

"How is she?" Joseph inquired. "You tell her she is always welcome. Well, thank you both for stopping by."

With these words, the visit, though brief, was over, and James gave his father a perfunctory hug, promising to come again before autumn. Then, just as he exited, James thought he heard Joseph whisper something to Matthias. It sounded like, "He must not know. Not yet," although the words were too muffled for him to be certain.

"What did he say to you as we left?" James asked.

Matthias shook his head. "Nothing. But I think it's best we follow Simon's advice and take the coastal highway. I have heard that Samaria has become more violent than ever, and who knows when Aretas, the Camel, will choose to attack Antipas."

James still wondered what secret Matthias and his father might have shared, but he let it pass. For now, the air was sweet with jasmine, and early summer breezes were warm. The foreshortened shadows of cypress trees along the road told it was already an hour past the third watch.

CHAPTER SEVEN

*T*he market was busy, as always on the fifth day of the week, and Ephraim's synagogue was just ahead. Quickening his step, Matthias was relieved to pass its gate without having to greet the rabbi, who often stood there to wish worshippers a good afternoon.

Halfway down the street, pushing past small groups of people milling about, he found himself inside the tanner's shop, inhaling deeply, enjoying the redolent smell of leather and parchment.

"Good afternoon," Matthias said as Hoshea, the tanner, entered from the rear workroom.

"It's ready," Hoshea replied, taking a large scroll from a nearby shelf. After unrolling a section, Matthias took several moments to study the fine, smooth surface. "Better than any you'll buy in Jerusalem," Hoshea boasted.

"That's why I come to you," Matthias said.

"May it be a Torah all will admire."

"Five denarri," Matthias said, taking the silver coins from his purse.

"As we agreed."

Matthias placed the heavy scroll under his arm, where it pressed against his skin, and several times he switched it to the other side as he walked hurriedly in the direction of his house. Because it seemed like everybody was watching him, he kept his gaze down, hoping to reach his door unnoticed.

"You were in Jerusalem for the festival?" a high-pitched voice rasped, startling him.

"Shalom. Yes. It was beautiful."

The widow who lived in the neighboring house always knew his goings and comings.

"Of course," she said. "Why shouldn't it be? Our own service isn't worth the time."

"I'm sure it's fine," Matthias answered.

"Not like the Temple," she said, taking notice of the heavy package.

"I had to make sure it's still standing. Now you can tell everybody you've heard that Jerusalem is still there."

After securing his door to prevent any unexpected visitors from intruding on his privacy, Matthias placed the scroll on the table under the window and opened it gently. He slowly stirred powdered dye in a juglet of water and pondered what he was about to do. Whatever differences he had with Simon, this was to be the true account. For decades, his skill as a scribe met the modest goal of accuracy. Now, he would attempt to enliven a parchment with the spirit of a young man imbued by God more than any other rabbi he had known. Only this he promised himself: if, when it was done, he had not brought Jesus' memory to life, he would consign it to his oven. What they had done to him on the cross, twisting him into a grotesque image, Matthias would not do to him again in a scroll. Therefore, until it was complete, he would keep its existence a secret. After pausing to collect his thoughts, he began.

This is the scroll of Matthias, which tells the story of Jesus of Nazareth.

In the same manner they denounced him, you who read this may well accuse me of wanting to shape your world—of even believing I can. You will accuse me of thinking myself God's equal. And your inclination will be to silence me, just as Jesus' enemies did to him. So I will start by saying what I am thinking. Simply, I am the only one who will tell you about his life. Many of you will go no farther. Having heard me say this, I am certain you will exclaim, "Here's another one!" Still, if you want to know what happened, then listen to me. I was his friend, and I conversed with him about the events that follow, or I knew of them as a witness.

As he paused to permit the words to dry, Matthias was surprised to imagine Jesus sitting on the sheepskin flokati rug, just as he had two years earlier. "You seem pleased by what I am about to do," he reflected silently. "I couldn't save you, my young friend, but perhaps these words may save your memory."

Again, he wrote.

Ten years after the death of King Herod of Israel, whose appellation Herod the Great was given by his court historian, it happened that Mary, daughter of Yoakim and Anna, a priestly family from Tzipori, was betrothed to Joseph. Joseph, whose deceased wife had been Mary's aunt, the sister of her mother, was a member of the Sanhedrin and a successful builder. He was a modest man who called himself a carpenter, and he loved Mary. She was in the same generation as his sons, being nearly three decades younger than he, having celebrated her sixteenth year, when she became pregnant. Afraid because she had not conceived by Joseph's seed, she sought refuge with her aunt Elizabeth in Ayn Kerem. Elizabeth was herself with child, being six months pregnant. Her son would be known as John the Baptizer.

This was in the reign of Augustus, just eight years before Tiberius became emperor. Archeleus was ethnarch over Judea, including Jerusalem, named as the Judean leader in his father's will. The Romans were reluctant to make Archeleus king and exercised the authority to tax the people, finally replacing him with their own governors and ordering a census be taken. In a determined effort to prevent scandal, Joseph had played the husband, providing his Nazareth home as a setting for Mary during the last part of her pregnancy, and he brought her to his house in Bethlehem to be officially counted in the census.

Jesus was born in a manger, in a protected area outside the house, and eight days later was taken to the Temple for the brit milah, his circumcision.

Here, Matthias stopped momentarily, hesitant to put in more about Joseph's situation. Though Joseph had raised Jesus and during Jesus' childhood years had acted like his father, Joseph's true feelings would best be told by him directly, perhaps at a later time. Postponing such detail, Matthias wrote:

Jesus' childhood was spent in Nazareth, and Joseph, who resided in Bethlehem, came frequently to be with his family.

Living in Nazareth as a boy, mostly with his mother and Joseph's youngest son, James, as well as Joseph's two daughters, Jesus often went to the lakeside synagogues and stayed, I believe, with one of the older brothers who had a home near Kfar Nahum.

At the age of twelve, Mary and Joseph traveled with Jesus to the Temple, and Jesus demonstrated to the rabbis, in traditional fashion, his ability to read and understand the texts. In the years that followed, he saw little of Joseph but spent much time with James, his favorite brother, and continued to mature in wisdom.

At about the age of twenty-five, Jesus gathered a group of local young fisherman to study with him. One was named Simon, and there was his brother Andrew, as well as two who worked with them, named James and John, the Zebedee brothers.

This was the fifteenth year of the reign of Tiberius Caesar. Pontius Pilate was procurator of Jerusalem and the surrounding territory, and Herod Antipas governed as tetrarch of the Galilee, the Decapolis, and Perea, with his brother Philip as tetrarch of the other regions north and east. Caiaphas was high priest at this time.

After attending the synagogue on Shabbat, Jesus went with the Zebedees to Simon's house in Beit Zaida, where he and his brother Andrew greeted them. Simon's mother-in-law, in bed with a recurring fever, found the strength, upon his touch, to sit upright, and with his help, she stood from the bed. Immediately feeling better, she then waited on them, serving food.

In the evening, as sundown ended the Shabbat, people of the area came to the door seeking cures for various diseases. It may have been one of the Zebedees who had boasted about Jesus' curing Simon's mother-in-law.

When the number hoping to be healed amounted to a crowd, Jesus decided to leave and did so long before dawn.

While visiting the different lakeside villages, he taught his four disciples in outdoor places, and onlookers increasingly asked him to cure their afflictions, as is the usual practice of our rabbis. Though he was doing what the others did, blessing those who were miserably diseased and offering a compassionate touch, people who had heard about Simon's mother-in-law told others he was able to heal those with lifelong infirmities. When he overheard several whisper that he was the holy one sent by God, he beseeched them not to say such things about him, but they continued to do so.

About that time, as the number of his circle came to include others, he invited eight more, in addition to Simon, Andrew, and the Zebedees, to join his group; by name, Philip; Bartholomew;

Matthew (who had been a tax collector); Thomas; another who called himself James bar Alpheus, adopting the middle nomen "bar" to proudly certify his lineage as a son of his deceased father, Alpheus; another Simon (whom Jesus called C'nani or the Zealot, owing to his hatred of Roman occupation); as well as Thaddeus, and Judas—Judas Iscariot, the one who betrayed Jesus. These were his inner circle of twelve disciples.

Resting his hand, Matthias remembered how Jesus lamented their embarrassing ignorance at the synagogues of Kfar Nahum, Chorazin, and Beit Zaida. "They don't know any prayers," Matthias could hear him saying, as he continued the transcription.

The twelve sought to be treated as equals in the Jewish community, but there were obstacles. They stood as others stood and moved their lips in prayer as the congregation repeated the words of the rabbi: "Sh'ma Yisrael"—there is only one God. Then they tried feebly to recite, "V'ahavta et Adonai Elohecha B'chal l'vavcha . . ."—you shall love God with all your heart. Most were unable to disguise their ignorance inasmuch as their words weren't words at all but babble poorly resembling the Hebrew they heard others chant. Even the few words they knew came out of their mouths in the poor dialect so common to Galilean locals.

Again wetting the point, he touched it to the page and wrote:

It was after leaving the synagogue on a Shabbat that Jesus told them not to babble like non-Jews. "I will teach you a prayer, but for now, you should say your prayers in private," he instructed.

Matthias knew there was more to it. Jesus' purpose was not only to avoid embarrassment but suspicion. If his group prayed in unrecognizable words, people would gossip. Some would say they worshipped a different god—maybe even Beelzebul himself.

I must put it down as clearly as I can, Matthias mused:

Jesus was aware of the old superstition. Many believed that local northerners had been defiled by an idolatrous family history, intermarrying with a transplanted population of pagans after the fall of the northern kingdom—pseudo-Hebrews who worshipped Beelzebul, a satanic false god, with magical incantations. Popular belief had it that before the Kingdom of God commenced, an army of evil would follow a false teacher, twisting Torah to achieve Beelzebul's purpose. As Jesus was increasingly subjected to scrutiny, especially for imparting Torah interpretations to a circle of unobservant students, some people already suspected him of an evil purpose. Then, a few weeks later, again on Shabbat, an incident in the small Chorazin synagogue caused a stir.

A woman in the congregation, bent over from years of infirmity, approached him. The rabbi conducting the service called out to her to stop, saying that all those seeking healing should come on a different day of the week, as healing was considered work and therefore a transgression of the sacred day. And Jesus replied to the rabbi, "Aren't you hypocrites, untying your animals in the manger, your ox or donkey, on Shabbat to give it water but would deny this woman, one of our own people, healing from her torment?"

When they could find no answer, he touched her, and many said she straightened up and was better.

And not many weeks after that episode, on still another Shabbat, one of the congregation who happened to be Matthew's neighbor, invited him and Jesus to share a meal following the service. As they went toward the house, a man afflicted by dropsy, with belly distended and arms twice the size they should be, ran in front of Jesus, pleading to be healed. Other congregants well versed in Torah were on the same path and watched to see what

Jesus would do. Not healing the man immediately, he asked the gathering much the same question he had on the prior occasion. "Is it contrary to Torah to heal a person on the Shabbat or not?"

If they admitted the Torah had no such prohibition, while plainly commanding aid to a suffering animal, how would they interpret its law to be less merciful to humans?

As the sick man stood waiting, silence was their answer. Nowhere in the Torah did it say healing on Shabbat was prohibited. And Jesus laid his hands on the man, and moments later, the fellow went his way, helped in spirit if not in body.

After again dipping his point in the dye, Matthias stopped and leaned heavily on the writing table. His next words would tell of a significant development. It was a matter to record with great care. Searching for a point to broaden the heading of crucial events, he found one he would use for just that purpose and wrote:

The first treacherous slander: Jesus forgave sin

Of course, they did not say everything they were thinking. What if that poor man's dropsy was punishment from God? Some were questioning Jesus' healing as if he were claiming to forgive sin. Yeshu and I talked about it. They thought the bent-over woman was being punished. By healing her, he was acting like God, forgiving her sin. And the same with that man suffering from dropsy.

Pressing the point to the parchment and quickening his pace to prevent thoughts from escaping, he wrote:

But people whispered that Jesus should not have healed any disease that might be punishment by God because that was for God alone to do. And in Jesus' words, as best I recall them, he said to me, "They could see I was not playing God. At the dining table in the man's home, where I and Matthew were guests, I chose a seat far from the host, not acting important or distinguished, so that he asked me to sit closer. During the meal, he finally raised the question on his mind about my disciples. Why were nearly all of them am ha-aretz—ignorant locals? What did I want with students who—of course excepting Matthew, since he was at the table—mostly didn't know anything about Torah and less about their family tree? I told them I wanted to teach those who needed it. Should I help those who don't need help? What sense is there in that?"

"But what about a tax collector for the Romans?" another guest asked, apparently irritated by Matthew's presence. "Will their kind ever deserve to inherit God's Kingdom, having robbed Judea's coffers for the emperor?"

From what I gather, having made my own personal observations concerning his occasional fits of anger, Matthew might well have turned cherry red at this remark and berated his critic with ample invectives, had Jesus not interceded.

Answering with a parable, which came to him as a natural gift of expression, Jesus said, "A tax collector stood in the Temple courtyard, not daring to raise his eyes to heaven, and beat his breast, crying out, 'Al chait shechatanu. God be merciful to me, for I have sinned.' Nearby, a highly regarded citizen and interpreter of the Torah reminded God that for his part, he had not taken money that was not his, nor had he committed adultery, and he had given tithes to the Temple. Then he thanked God that he was not a sinner like the tax collector he saw praying several feet away."

Having described their manner of confession, Jesus then asked the gathering which was better as preparation for the Kingdom: to be a tax collector who repented and asked God's forgiveness, promising not to collect taxes anymore, or to be one who followed the Torah but who, in his heart, hated the tax collector, even though the tax collector repented? When all at the table were silent, Jesus said, "The one who could not forgive his fellow man was asking God for the same mercy he had refused others." Explaining further, he added, "The tax collector who asked God to forgive his sins, vowing not to oppress others again, I tell you went home at peace with God; the other did not."

Matthias rose for a few minutes of respite, going outside to bring water from the cistern near his door. The brightness of the day and the heat jarred his senses.

"They wondered about his forgiving people when that was the very thing God commanded," he muttered to himself. "Aren't we taught to forgive each other?"

The widow who always paid too much attention to him heard his lament and inquired whether he was talking to her.

"And that they forgive each other!" he half shouted, probably adding to her likely impression he was suffering the addled incoherency of old age.

If there were certain sins that were for God alone to forgive, Matthias deliberated, Jesus left those to God. When the Kingdom began, all who suffered diseases of punishment would be healed by God. The lame, the crippled since birth, the withered and the paralyzed, the possessed and the blind, the lepers. And if the Kingdom was to witness their healing, was it wrong for him to give them hope?

"But he wasn't cautious," Matthias pondered, returning to his bench to resume writing.

Again using the broad point, he headed the next entry:

The leper

As word spread, people with the maladies of punishment sought relief through his rumored powers from God.

Now Jesus was in one of the towns when a man covered with leprosy approached. His disease was one of possible punishment, and Jesus did not immediately offer his touch. The man got down on his knees and begged for his healing, saying, "You can heal me if you choose." Before Jesus replied, the man was next to him and grasped his fringes. Touching his bowed head, more with compassion than an intention to heal, Jesus said, "May you be clean. Now go to the priests and make an offering to be healed, according to the Torah. And don't tell people I cured you." But word spread, because the man himself told people about the event as if God had forgiven him through Jesus. No less than others, whose gossip crossed the borders of local villages, his own disciples were boasting that he had cured the leper, though he did not know they were saying this for quite some time.

Pausing for a moment, Matthias vividly recalled that was the first time Jesus stayed under his roof. Living up to the name given them by the Jerusalem Pharisees for always flaunting their sanctimonious lives, the Pietist hypocrites ridiculed Jesus for showing that poor leper pity, saying it proved he claimed God's power to forgive sin.

So Jesus withdrew, as crowds now sought help from the one they heard had cured the leper. And he came to my house alone. At that time, he told me that people believed he claimed authority to forgive sin, but he was still unaware his disciples were fanning the flames of that rumor.

Jesus rejoined them several weeks later. The summer sun beat down on the harvested fields, drying the grain so it was parched enough to crumble by rubbing between their hands. On one Shabbat, as his disciples picked unharvested grain to eat in that manner, several Pietists monitored their activity, asking why his students were doing something forbidden on Shabbat. The criticism for picking grain on the Shabbat, Jesus knew, was a test to see whether he considered himself superior to God's law.

When he answered them that the Shabbat was made for people, meaning hungry individuals were permitted to pick and eat unharvested grain, they twisted his words. According to the Pietists, he meant he could do whatever he chose on Shabbat, even that it was made for him.

His own students did not know any better. When they overheard the Pietists grumbling about his claim to be master over the Shabbat, as Jesus observed, they proudly agreed.

More than ever determined that they should revere Torah law and not him—as if he had authority to violate it—he told them, "If you know the Torah and know how to keep it, you are blessed. If you do not know, and you break the Law, you are a transgressor. If you do not keep the Shabbat as the Torah requires, you will not enter the Kingdom." But they did not take his words to heart.

Meanwhile, the Pietists said he was teaching them to defy Torah, pretending its laws were subordinate to him. Rumors spread that he could be the prophesied false teacher, and his words were repeatedly turned on their head.

Slowly stirring the ink, Matthias recalled the particular way Simon related to Jesus, especially how he frequently whispered when they spoke—not that any adversaries were within earshot, nor were the other disciples especially interested in overhearing what was being said. It had become a habit of Simon's, during that last year of Jesus' life, so common that it didn't attract their attention. Still, Matthias was struck by it as a mannerism of self-importance, as if their conversations were just between the two of them. Had Matthias ventured a guess, such posturing likely originated with the boat. Accrued to Simon, as its owner and the one who told them when to lower and hoist the nets, was an aura of authority. But as fate would have it, his leadership was difficult to transfer from the Sea of Galilee's daily haul to lessons about Torah. His leadership role was more established by virtue of nets than perspicacity into Torah nuance. No, Matthias pondered, finding a school of healthy fish, generally toward the eastern side of the lake, sheltered from winds that stirred up silt, Simon's superiority in locating unmuddied waters did not augment his disciple's stature or prevent his being baffled by Jesus' teaching. And when he failed to grasp the deeper stratum of his teacher's commentary, Matthias surmised, he certainly did not want the others to hear. To wit, whispering to Jesus had become his way, at least in part, of shrouding his own shortcomings in matters of Torah where intellect was requisite.

If memory further served, Jesus provided Simon whatever extra guidance he could. Still, he did it in a typical manner, not returning whisper for whisper but even with mild impatience explaining lessons in words spoken loudly enough for all to hear.

Choosing a different point to broaden the heading of crucial events, one somewhat longer and less of a strain on his fingers, Matthias tapped its tip so a large drop would fall into its receptacle. He wrote:

The hand-washing episode: insult and contempt

It was just past dusk, in the courtyard of a neighbor's house near the lake, when things took a turn.

That evening, as he and his disciples passed through a courtyard to a house for dinner, a group of Pietists saw several

*go in without stopping at the water spigot to wash their hands.
Seizing the opportunity to expose Jesus' rejection of Torah, they
asked him, "Why do your disciples not live in keeping with the
tradition of our people? We see they do not wash their hands when
they eat."*

*And Jesus answered them, asking his own question: "Where in
the Torah does it say a person must eat with clean hands, except
within the Temple courtyards? Does it not say a person need not be
clean to eat when he is away from the Temple? It is not what goes
into a man unclean that defiles him before God but what comes out
of his mouth. And what comes out of your mouths," he told them,
"defiles you far more than the food you eat, and it is dirtier than
what passes into the sewer."*

*Even as they began grumbling among themselves, Jesus said,
"You wash your pots and pans and vessels of bronze, making
your houses out to be as sacred as the Temple. But when your
needy parents come to you for money, you say no, breaking the
commandment to honor your father and mother with the excuse
that the money must go toward the required tithe to the Temple.
In this way, you reject the Torah's commandment to take care of
your parents. Do not our sages teach that you must not break one
commandment in order to keep another? Yet you make void the
word of God that you hand on, as if your twisted habits are our
tradition."*

*When Simon later whispered to him, asking about the exchange
and the things he had said, Jesus was frustrated by his shallow
thoughts and replied loudly, "Are you still without understanding,
Simon? Do you not see that what comes from the heart may cause
one to break the Torah's commandments against murder, adultery,
stealing, bearing false witness, and slander and that these are*

what defile a man? Eating with unwashed hands, except in the Temple precincts, does not defile a man, exactly as it is written in the Torah."

With the sunlight now over the other side of Matthias' house, it was too dark for him to write. At sunup he would record one of the more memorable episodes during a visit to the Galilee—Jesus' meal with Pharisees.

CHAPTER EIGHT

$\mathcal{T}$hinking back, Matthias had reason to remember that day nearly two years earlier.

From Nazareth and Tzippori, as well as smaller villages of the Galilee, rumor spread to the lakeside marketplaces, where word of scandal was plied along with grain, fruit, fish, and cheese by vendors soliciting appreciation and patronage from votaries of gossip. As the commodities were placed in burlap carrying sacks, the phrase, "So you must have heard . . ." almost became a chorus, audible above the din at every stall, enticing the women to shop for news as much as for their household victuals.

It was on the fifth of the week in late Nisan, when they all heard that Herodias would not marry the tetrarch until the counting of the Omer was finished.

In Jerusalem, such a report would certainly evoke shrill peals of laughter. Not having been divorced by her husband, Philip—none other than the tetrarch's living half brother—she intended to abide by Jewish law in setting the date of her adulterous—even incestuous— wedlock to Antipas, as if doing so would sanctify their conjugal apostasy.

"Did you hear the marriage will wait for the proper time, when the barley harvest is done?" an aproned merchant inquired as he tied a large sack top. Matthias recalled what happened next as if just yesterday . . .

With the bright sunlight prying open his still-sleepy eyes, he refreshed himself with cool water and took a piece of warm bread with grape jam, finally ready to tell of that remarkable afternoon in Matthew's house.

Jostling his memory, he recalled the fellow who had startled him at the grain merchant's stall, approaching unseen and squeezing his shoulder.

"Eh, it is you!" the man declared buoyantly, loosing his friendly grip.

"I hardly recognize you," Matthias recalled saying.

"Under my beard, the rest is as pale as ever, but we heard you were in the area."

With this image playing before his eyes, Matthias made his way to the writing table. Wetting first his broad, then his fine point, he began slowly.

Sharing a meal with prominent Pharisees

Inhabiting the land peacefully alongside the Romans has, since Archeleus' ouster as ethnarch nearly three decades ago, become a policy of Pharisees, and though Matthew had, back then, collected their taxes, there were those who forgave him that past, including several members of the Sanhedrin's judiciary, visiting his Galilean home on a certain day in late Nisan.

One guest, an elder Sanhedrin colleague, hearing I was at the market, suggested that Matthew permit him to find me among the stalls and invite me to join them. Here, I should explain that my interlude at the lakeshore afforded me valued time with Jesus, who had just arrived from the fifth day's Torah reading in Kfar Nahum and whom I had only just espied.

Amenable to sharing the occasion of a good meal at the house of his most recent disciple, we three set off together, climbing a short but steep hill, where it perched near the top.

Cordial greetings once exchanged, all of us found space on the dining couches, with Matthew pleased that his teacher was among us. After Jesus declined a center seat, Matthew indicated the most senior guest should have it. Opposite me and a colleague were two other of my Sanhedrin associates, now to either side of Jesus toward the far end.

As we ate our meal, exchanging banter about the delicious salad made of fresh greens from the yard and the colorful sight of spring flowers around, I observed the guests' unhesitant glances and obvious curiosity about the young teacher inundated by so many rumors.

Still, they did not immediately address him, except with the acknowledgment of vague smiles and nods punctuating their pleasantries. Finally, one of the visitors became somber, turning the topic to the Pietists.

"They are not like us," he said. "They show off their piety. Their phylacteries are large and their fringes long, so that all will recognize them. And they call themselves Pietists, claiming they are a kind of Pharisee from the days of Judah Maccabee. Beware the ones who use our name and ape our ways so they can have authority. They claim to have the keys to God's Kingdom, so they may exclude anyone whom they judge unworthy."

Another agreed. "Too bad for you Galileans that they've moved here." Then looking at Jesus, who was too young to recall, he added, "It was their bunch who pulled down Herod's Roman eagle from the Temple gate. And when he rounded up the ringleaders, many fled to this region."

The one just to Jesus' side then scoffed, "We know all about them, these would-be Pharisees. On fast days, they scratch their faces against the stones of synagogue walls so everybody will notice the scabs and think, there goes one who has confessed his sins to God."

Across from Matthew, a man with lips hidden by the curls of his beard recalled a joke about them: "It is told that a Pietist who sees a drowning woman will look the other way, in fear his member will become distended with excitement at the sight of her predicament."

As the laughter abated, Matthew said, "They do always seem to walk around with their eyes cast downward, as if they're worried an ordinary sight may defile their souls."

"We hear about them following their wives in the marketplace to witness any moment she may spend alone with a vendor or any other man," another especially short guest said. His voice was much larger than his body, and he was quite captivating a sight as he reclined, with mostly his head and neck showing above the table's edge. "Then, when they catch her having an innocent conversation about the latest gossip and rumors, they use it as an excuse to divorce her. This they do so they may send her away without a prutah while they take a different wife, a woman they have secretly been lusting after."

"Degrading the woman they supposedly love," echoed the one with lips hidden by his beard. "Of course, if she confesses, she is immediately divorced without any security. But has anybody here ever heard of a wife getting sick after drinking the cursed water?"

All of us knew about the supposed test by God, performed by a priest when the only evidence of wrongdoing was a husband's suspicious mind.

I was the one to answer, unable to control my anger. "It never happens. No woman ever gets sick. They make up stories that they get dropsy or their skin turns yellow. But the truth is they use the ordeal to turn her into a sotah—a straying woman. Nobody will talk to her after that. Of course, even though she doesn't get sick, everybody gossips about her. She can't go out of her house, certainly not to the market. It's impossible for her to stay in her neighborhood. So she usually agrees to leave her husband with only a small amount of the money promised in the marriage contract, and he gives her the divorce paper so he can marry another. They are a plague worse than locusts! God should have left them in Egypt!"

The one sitting across from me, a dignified-looking man wearing a brown toga, said, "So, Matthias, you have seen them," which was so obvious from my seething tone that they all laughed, including Jesus, though he still held his peace. And here, just a word about his comportment. Observing politely, he had chosen not to join the conversation. Always attentive to others, he may have noticed their frequent glances invited his opinion, but he was being true to his nature, shunning a posture of self-importance.

Still, the less he said in this esteemed company, the more an aura of wisdom attached itself to his reticence. Even as I concluded my tirade, I knew they were more interested in hearing what he was thinking.

Holding the wine pitcher aloft, so all might refill their cups, I hesitated to describe how they half-dragged the accused wife up the Temple stairs to face the priest, defiling our holiest precinct with their false pretense to a just complaint.

How well I knew those sickening prayers, asking God to cause her belly to swell and explode in a grotesque caricature of pregnancy if she were guilty of harlotry . . . letting her hair down and pulling her top to her shoulders, so that her bosom was almost exposed . . . like a zonah, a whore, while young priests looked on, hoping to catch sight of her breasts as they handed her a basket of grain we feed the donkeys, as if it was her offering to God.

"Yes, I have seen them more than once," I replied, declining to provide further testimony about that sad procession, not wishing to mar the pleasure of our afternoon repast with memories of such cruelty.

Odd how we recall details. The most senior among us that day, the one who found me at the market, pushed back his beard, which he had been holding to keep from dipping in the bowl of thick barley soup, and spoke directly to Jesus.

"I'm sure you have thought about this," he said. "Perhaps you would share an opinion."

All of us were now listening intently to what my young friend would reply, as until this moment he had not spoken.

"They clean every pot and pan," Jesus said, "but they ignore the inside. All that matters to them is the appearance of righteousness. They tithe mint and rue and other herbs but overlook justice. In this way, they show they have no love for God. And now they have become an adulterous generation."

Without taking even a moment to reflect on his next remarks, Jesus asserted, "I say that every married man who looks at a woman with lust for her has already committed adultery with her in his heart. And such a man may not divorce his wife unless she has truly been unfaithful. If your eye causes you to stray, it is better to tear it out and throw it away than to travel the path to gehinnom."

Several moments of palpable silence followed, as the rabbinic legal formulation made its impression. Jesus had won their respect, invoking the rule of the geder, protecting the Torah's commandment with a fence. If a man saw even his temptation as sin, he would not violate the commandment prohibiting adultery.

Nodding his accord, the senior jurist turned to me. "Matthias," he proffered quietly, "what could be more sacred than the vow a husband makes to provide for his wife and children? But they have desecrated it in their own lives and now are threatening us all. We are alarmed by the coming wedding. Philip may not be in good health, but he is not dead, and according to Torah, he is still Herodias' husband. Worse, Antipas is his own sibling—his brother—if by a different mother."

Observing my brow furrowed by doubt, he spoke in a cadence typical of a jurist rendering a verdict. "For supporting Herodias' divorce by the Roman court, we must make the Pietists pay a price, depriving them recourse to terminate their own matrimony by falsely accusing their wives."

Whereupon, in an oratorical flourish, the short colleague proclaimed, "Can we endure such a travesty? To them, the commandments forbidding adultery and incest have been set aside by none other than those great appreciators of our scripture—the Romans! Yes, instructed by our Sanhedrin to oppose this cursed marriage, the Pietist rabbis answer, 'The Roman authorities have granted Herodias a divorce from Philip.' And even more blasphemous, they are spreading word that the royal wedding is a coming sign from God—that the Kingdom of the Almighty is at hand. Because she is a Maccabee, they will have a true Jewish queen. That's what they are saying. But Matthias, though we have not met before, except in chambers with a formal greeting,

I appreciate your wisdom about our laws. So I ask, have we ever acknowledged that Romans can abrogate the binding vows of our matrimony?"

Suddenly beset by a cramp in his thumb and with wrist and fingers weary from the arduous task of rendering each character and glyph, Matthias rested for several moments, recalling his astonishment and confusion. How was such a thing possible as altogether preventing Pietists from divorcing their wives? Just a few more words and the entry would be complete.

Then the one in the brown toga said, "So let us create a court of three to speak with the accused woman alone, before she makes her decision to drink the cursed water. We can tell her exactly what we think. She is being pushed to accept a poor settlement and divorce, not because she did anything wrong, but because her husband is done with her."

"Yes," the one at his side proposed, "we can warn the husband that if she does not become ill, the sign from God none has ever seen, he will have to raise their children in a normal fashion and that he will no longer have any grounds for divorce. If she is found innocent by God—as they always are—he must remain married to her forever."

Again adumbrating, the Sanhedrin judge just to my side said, "Those who have coddled Antipas' favor by celebrating the adulterous union will no longer make divorce a routine habit of their lives as they eye the next object of their lust. For justifying Herodias' mockery of divorce, turning to the Roman court, they will suffer lifelong the bed of a woman they may even detest. Whatever else the Romans do, they have no interest in becoming an arbiter of Jewish marital problems. We will have authority as a direct consequence of this law we are crafting."

*"And will Herodias care? Or her tetrarch husband, Antipas?"
I ventured.*

*"It will be a message to the Pietists," the member in the
brown toga iterated in his steady manner. "Let them be guided by
authority of Jupiter and their other gods if they still wish to enjoy
adulterous fornication."*

*In a show of unanimity, several thumped the table, demonstrating
complete agreement, and one turned to me and requested that,
when I was next in Jerusalem, I put down on parchment the
language of the proposed new law, which they would bring before
the Sanhedrin as a formal resolution to vote its adoption.*

*"You know, Matthias," the senior member said sternly, wiping
a stray kernel of barley off his beard, "each of the Pietist elders is
thanked with an appointment to Antipas' council. Their edicts, as
officials of the tetrarchy, will have authority over every aspect of
Galilean religious life. These so-called 'Herodians'—the official
name Pietist elders have taken for themselves—anticipate that their
queen Herodias will grace all the land with her royal presence,
ultimately ceded to her by the very same Romans now occupying
Judea! Perhaps it will give them pause, as they consecrate that
abominable love nest, to realize as a result they will experience
the bliss of marriage to the same woman forever."*

*Agreeing to promulgate the new law establishing their special
court, I should note that only recently has it been adopted, and the
outcome is still awaited.*

*The gathering enjoyed the small roast hens garnished with
large boiled eggs and saluted Matthew's fine hospitality. All of us
were feasting on the sumptuous delicacies as a guest at Jesus' side
entered upon a new subject.*

"Many of us knew your cousin's father," he remarked softly, as if to reassure him they had his interest at heart. "Zechariah was a devout priest. His widow lives in Ayn Kerem, I believe."

"Elizabeth, who is Jesus' mother's aunt," I said, certain Jesus was uncomfortable talking about the family.

"We know," the man with invisible lips said, "your cousin John is unlikely to take our counsel. And we have no criticism of his style of dress, or what he does to welcome pilgrims, cleansing them in the river before they enter the Temple domain."

"Not at all," the one to Jesus' other side exhorted. "Don't we immerse ourselves in the flowing mikveh before setting foot in the sacred precincts? And who at this table does not hope, just like him, for another David to rout the Romans? Our festivals are filled with prayer that God will be in our midst once again . . . and . . ." Having lost the intended thought to an apparent reverie concerning God's Kingdom, his embarrassment was spared by the one next to Matthew.

"Let him dress like a prophet, and even more, let us pray he is one, but it does not take an Elijah to recognize he is in danger," he warned.

Then, remembering what he had intended to say, the first one blurted out, "Yes! Why does he put himself in danger? We all resent Herodias. But it's another thing to make speeches calling her an adulteress. Your cousin is stirring people up."

"Tell him to be careful of Antipas," advised another, who had been mostly quiet until then. "His betrothed comes from a family of murderers. You think she's so different? If Antipas believes John is encouraging the Camel—King Aretas—to avenge his daughter, he will have his excuse for arresting him—a charge of sedition. Surely you have heard the tetrarch's Arab wife has fled the palace

as if they were never married." Taking Jesus' quick nod more as a measure of naive self-confidence than acknowledgement of his advice, he added, "This is about you too. We know you compared the Pietists' teaching to feces."

Shooting a quick glance in the direction of Matthew—the only one among us who had actually been with Jesus during the hand washing confrontation—he did not reply.

Jesus listened to what they said, almost as a spectator. He may have been as startled as I when one then turned in his direction and began addressing him in a patronizing manner about his activity, with no apparent connection to our previous discourse.

"Some say you are not even welcome in your family's home. Is it true they have cast you out?"

It was a question that would make anybody angry. But Jesus hardly took a moment to consider his retort, calmly saying, "If a man wants to study with me he has to hate his father and mother, his wife, and his offspring." They were shocked. Then they realized it was ridiculous and a joke and started laughing.

"If Jonah hadn't been thrown overboard, who would have ever heard of him?" the short guest gurgled through a sip of wine, rebuking the other's mild affront.

"Then you do understand," the man in the brown toga said. "Both of you should leave the insults to us. We have our ways. They will abide by our rulings because they have no choice."

Following his admonition that Jesus desist from public derision, there were only polite and restrained musings about more innocent topics, and as the room cooled in the afternoon shade, with the sun passing to the western slope of the hill, we expressed our appreciation for the food and amenities, taking leave of Matthew and going our separate ways.

Matthias had become hungry, recalling that day's bounteous meal, and made his way toward the stove. After retrieving a spoonful of salt from the adjacent storage amphora, he sprinkled it on a cluster of small aubergine cabbages, earlier arrayed on a nearby terracotta platter. Before positioning them over the smoldering cedar twigs within, he returned the scroll to its place on the shelf, careful not to soil the parchment with food oils. A short nap later, sated by his repast, Matthias turned his attention to the impending trip to Jerusalem, where matters were already proceeding apace, guided by Simon's agenda.

CHAPTER NINE

Still half asleep, Simon propped himself up on one elbow. He had not fully emerged from a dream of a thief trying to hammer down the front gate, and awoke, determined from then on to always wear the large iron key, even suspending it on his nightshirt's cloth belt. It would remind him to lock the entrance after dark.

In the manner of dreams, when the repeated rapping noise became what it was—visitors knocking—he draped himself in a linen sheet and threaded his way carefully between the prone forms of the sleeping disciples to the door.

"Too early?" Saul asked, as daylight poured in.

"Not at all! Welcome!" Simon managed, while several disciples sat up, straining to see who the visitors were. "Please come in, brothers," he added, addressing Saul's companions, Barnabas and John Mark who had accompanied him from the north.

The breakfast of wheat cakes, with eggs of turtledoves fried in oil, had been followed by his brusque announcement that it was time for those still dozing to get up, eat quickly, and find their way to the upper triclinium. The few disciples who awoke earlier were now serving the visitors plates of dates and raisins, while Simon used his foot to gently nudge those still sprawled out. Ascending to the second story, Saul entered with his companions, and the three sat at a table near the front.

James was to arrive momentarily, but Matthias, they understood, would be absent for the coming week.

As he prepared his thoughts for what could shortly erupt in an angry dispute, Simon contemplated the problem he faced. He had been aware for some time that various disciples were not looking him in the eye when he spoke to them about Jesus' resurrection. Whether it was because they doubted such a miracle had happened, or their apparent ill-ease was a natural reaction to contemplating so holy an event, he was uncertain. Even Andrew, his own brother, fully devoted as he had been to their lord, was one plainly uncomfortable when the subject arose. Most probable, he imagined, was their disquieting doubt that Jesus was more than an ordinary son of man, like them. To have been with them as their friend and teacher, an individual whose appearance was that of any other son of man, eating and sleeping the same as they, arguing with Pietists, at times resenting his family, praying to God . . . little wonder they now struggled to accept his true identity as God's own son.

To bolster their belief in his heavenly rule, Simon knew he would have to show how Jesus' guidance was reaching them in a voice familiar from their days spent in his company. Otherwise, they well might not only avert their gaze when Simon delivered his messages but altogether turn from Jesus as the one sent to save the world.

Surveying their faces, he saw they were waiting for him to speak.

"We have a problem," Simon began. "It is a matter I feel requires our discussion. You know I recently visited Saul in Cilicia to see how things were going."

As all eyes turned toward Saul, Simon's nod in his direction expressed the group's welcome.

"Forgive me. I should call you Paul," he added politely. "Your newly chosen name is one that befits you, meaning as it does, 'the humble one.' I will say at the outset that we should all be pleased you are here with us today. Indeed, many members of the synagogue congregations in that area now have heard of Jesus."

"Thank you all for your friendly welcome," Paul answered. With each new day, he hoped they might realize his past as Saul had receded into the realm of memories, gone from view like an overgrown path.

"Shortly, we will listen as you fill us in on some of the details concerning their response to your apostleship. And Paul, we all appreciate your labor on behalf of the lord, which subject must lead to the next. As your guest, most of us are aware, I was invited to a dinner the pagan elders hosted in my honor."

Distracted by the sound of wheels creaking, Simon cast a glance out the window and observed James' cart making its ascent up the hill. If possible, before he arrived to interfere, Simon hoped to show them the immutable relevance of Jesus' teaching and assure them that on earth and in heaven, he was the same, the very one they had known.

"In attendance at that festive pagan dinner," Simon continued, speaking more rapidly, "were just a few Jews—you, me, Barnabas, and John Mark. The others were priests and elders representing their religious community. Before us on the table was a lavish feast, foods and delicacies of their world but that were foreign to me. Naturally, I inquired what they were, and you advised me rather casually that the meal included fried pig meat and a variety of shellfish that are specialties of the region.

"I admit I was surprised by my own reaction. How dare they put these things before me as if they were food! Should they expect me to eat things the Torah calls vile and dirty? And I told you I was upset by it. Does that surprise you, Andrew or Thomas? Some of you look surprised. I guess I am not known for speaking my mind, eh?"

His joke at his own expense caused a ripple of laughter.

"The lamb too," he said. "Yes, there was seasoned lamb, and it had not been properly slaughtered. I could see its platter was juicy with its own blood."

Reassured that all were now riveted to his story, and James would no longer interfere, Simon slowed his speech to dramatize the message. "Since when did Jesus teach us it was all right to eat the blood of an animal? But do not think, brothers, that I gave in to my temper. What worse insult would there have been to the pagans if I acted as if their food was sinful? Well, what do you think I did?"

His question was addressed to the group, and he waited as they pondered a reply.

"You pretended to feel ill, am I right?" asked one of the Zebedees.

"Not at all," Simon answered.

"You ate the food," James bar Alpheus guessed.

"Well, you aren't wrong, and you aren't right," Simon said. "But here's the answer. Thankfully, there was a wonderful array of vegetables to choose from, and I simply said that I enjoyed a diet that hadn't come from animals. Later, as you may imagine, I told Saul— excuse me, Paul—what a presumptuous thing he had done. It was, I said, absolutely necessary for the pagans to follow Jewish custom and law as taught by Jesus if they wanted to count themselves among us. But Paul? I think you can speak for yourself."

Just then, Simon C'nani interrupted, "Excuse me. Isn't this issue a matter of sufficient importance that we have James with us? If we are about to consider how best to introduce Jesus' teachings to non-Hebrews, it seems his presence is highly worthwhile."

"You can tell him all about it," Simon said brusquely.

Exactly at that moment, James entered the room. "I am sorry to be late. Peace to you all." Having heard Simon's remark, he added, "I appreciate your concern. But I am here so we can go forward."

"Shalom, James," Simon said impatiently as he took a seat. "We are about to consider some important new ideas."

"I should have conferred with Simon before honoring him with a dinner he could not even eat," Paul said, pausing as several laughed. "But it was prepared by our pagan hosts, and I did not feel comfortable telling them what to serve. Still, a question must be faced and answered. What shall we ask of the pagans in order for them to be members of our following? Are they to obey all Torah laws?"

Turning to Andrew, who was seated nearest and then addressing others in turn, Paul enunciated his point with a question. "Are we to become the overseers of ritual observance, scrutinizing the pagans in the same way you have been scrutinized by the Pietist hypocrites? If so, brothers, you won't need one hand to count the number who accept Jesus. But there's more to this. If I am being sent by our master in heaven to spread his word to them, shall I do it in a way that dooms the venture—or in a way that makes it possible?"

"Excuse me," James interrupted, "are you suggesting they be permitted to follow their own practices? We have heard how they strangle their food animals, causing them agony as they die. Who knows what else they do?"

"Jesus held the laws of Torah sacred," James bar Alpheus declared. "Are you saying we should tell the pagans his teaching doesn't matter?"

Simon C'nani agreed. "Jesus said Torah is eternal. How shall we justify nullifying its laws?"

Andrew differed sharply. "Its laws were made for us," he insisted. "For Jews, not for gentiles. They should not be expected to keep these laws. Did Jesus ever say everybody must follow the laws of Torah?"

Paul then responded, "Haverim, my friends, there does not need to be so much argument. Of course we who are Jews and follow the Torah will do so. Our master has shown us that Torah laws from Moses are open to interpretation. For example, did the lord not heal on the Shabbat? And when he was accused of violating that sacred day of rest, did he not say he was master over its ordinances? Brothers, do you not see his voice is the new Torah?"

"You didn't even know him," James criticized. "And now you represent yourself as an authority on his teaching."

"I have done nothing more than what I have been asked," Paul responded.

Simon sensed that most disciples agreed he was overstepping his prerogative, and he asserted that their reservations echoed his own. "Yes. Your apostleship is enriched by your sense of wonder at what we actually witnessed," he remonstrated. "But are we mistaken that you seem to exercise independent authority? Interpreting Torah as Jesus did is what makes it eternal for us, not interpreting it as Paul does."

When several gave vocal affirmation of his pronouncement, Simon raised his hand to mute their protest, a gesture of civility.

"I know the difference," Paul said quietly. "I will abide by your decision to impose laws on the pagans. Whatever enhances their appreciation of Jesus' heavenly rule, I will do, so they too may enter the Kingdom."

"For one thing, they should not slaughter their animals by strangling them," Bartholomew said. "And if there's blood of the animal on the plate, I say we don't eat it, and neither should they.

Blood contains the power of life, given to living things by our heavenly Father. Jesus never ate meat with blood in it. Can anyone here say different?"

"He never ate any of the foods that are called unclean by our Torah. Not a crab's eye or a clam's tongue," Matthew agreed. "They would have loved to accuse him of eating pork. But he never did. So they accused him of eating with me—once a tax-collecting sinner!"

"But Simon," James scoffed, "I'm sure you will explain just how the heavenly Jesus is guiding Paul to make exceptions."

When Simon turned to face James, his reply froze in his throat. It was the first time he'd seen him as a determined adversary. Only then did he grasp why Jesus had met Paul on the road to Damascus. When not only the Jews of Antioch converted but the pagans too, numbering so many, James' fortress against their lord, Jesus, would be washed away in the sea of holy immersions bound to follow. Paul was speaking for Jesus. He could see that now.

"They love pork," Paul attested, thinking they were waiting for his rejoinder. "If it's a choice between Jesus and pork, my work there is lost. And shellfish. They won't understand why God doesn't want them to have the good meals they always enjoy. And will you have me tell them not to eat meat stewed in yogurt from the weaning cow that is its mother?"

Thomas then offered what he considered Jesus' teaching. "Didn't Jesus say what goes into a man's stomach cannot defile him?"

James replied, "My brother never ate any prohibited foods."

Simon bristled at James' pretense of knowing more than he about Jesus' observance. "Our prophet Jeremiah said there will come a day of God when the Torah is no longer the only way. The Covenant will be written in the heart. Your brother is now speaking to the chosen few from heaven, revealing his word. We will carry his message to the pagans."

"Are we supposed to believe in you or Jesus?" James derided. "Or is God waiting for you to tell Him what to do next?"

"Simon, let us consider this matter among ourselves," Bartholomew said, his right eye drifting in Barnabas' direction—he noticed that Barnabas had been gazing at his own feet most of the time.

"As agreed," Simon replied, acknowledging that whenever a disciple called for a private discussion, such procedure was their protocol.

"Paul, Barnabas, John Mark," Simon said, "please make yourselves comfortable on the lower level so we may air our opinions privately." But he did not ask James to go below for fear of alienating those who would object. His excluding Jesus' own brother would wait for a more propitious occasion.

After the room had been vacated by the guests, Simon turned to Bartholomew. "Tell us what it is that requires this delay," he said.

"We should hear from our president on this issue," Bartholomew replied.

"James? Have you something to say?" Simon asked.

"You heard him yourselves," James replied. "Paul believes whatever he tells the pagans is a new Torah. What if the things he says are in his mind but have nothing to do with my brother? He will say Jesus is guiding him. Eating the meat of a strangled animal with its blood on the plate—was that from my brother?"

"Jesus said what goes into a man does not defile him," Thomas repeated. "I heard him with my own ears."

"If properly slaughtered and drained of blood," James said, as if the need to explain was monotonous and unnecessary. "You may eat that meat without first washing your hands. But my brother did not eat the forbidden animals."

"And he washed his own hands," Simon C'nani bellowed. "Just like me and some others. You must recall they did not ask him about his own hands."

"Brothers," Matthew said, "may I offer this proposal? It is Paul we wonder about. Therefore, Simon, go again to Cilicia and Damascus. Meet there with the Jews who are receptive to Jesus. Their decisions will be important. Let us not say pagans are the same as Jews. We are the ones to herald the Kingdom, not they."

Perturbed they might vacate Paul's authority and elevate James' stature beyond any chance of eventual exclusion, Simon was determined to prevent their trust in his own leadership from faltering.

"Permit me to make this motion," Simon said, addressing the group. "You are concerned that Paul is not one of us, and you are right. He is not. But I believe Jesus spoke to him, and so he, too, is chosen. Still, he must respect our authority. Therefore, let us require that he take the Nazarean oath to devote himself to the will of God. Further, if others happen to be taking the same oath before the priests, he must pay their Temple fee as well as his own for that ceremony." Murmurs of approval indicated Simon's plan was accepted. "Further, as you suggest, Matthew, before too long I shall again pay him a visit to monitor his success."

"This time, make it more than a trip to enjoy the tall cedar trees," James said. "You should insist the pagans conform to basic Torah laws or keep to their own ways altogether."

"What about adultery and the other commandments? What about circumcision?" one of the Zebedees asked doubtfully.

"Here's what I think," Philip said, winning their courteous attention because he was respected for balancing their differences. "If something they do goes against our Torah and is part of their worship of their gods, they have to stop. Adultery goes against our Torah, and Jesus called it a sin. Surely they know it is wrong to murder or steal. And Jesus' words will become their guide concerning greed and theft and false accusation. We have his teaching that they should not take oaths using the name of God. Circumcision? They can always choose to be circumcised. Therefore, if they aren't circumcised, they don't have to be. It is not against Torah to delay circumcision of an adult. And I can't think of a quicker way to cut off their interest in Jesus."

The amusement at his joke was Simon's cue to invite Paul and his companions to return.

"Here is what we have decided," Simon said, waiting as they took seats. "The pagan devotees of our lord should no longer worship their own gods or practice rites required by their religion. They must condemn adultery. They cannot eat the meat of an animal that has been cruelly slaughtered. And they must drain its blood."

"And what about the other Torah commandments?" Paul queried, sounding doubtful.

"Of course they are not Jews," James interjected. "Still, they must learn what Jesus taught."

"But you need not explain that it comes from Torah," Simon countered. "We aren't making them Jews."

"Nor should you claim authority from heaven, as if Jesus is talking to you," James asserted, noting that half the disciples concurred with nods of approval. "Your teaching about Jesus is restricted to what we permit."

Dismissing the importance of James' emendation, Simon changed the subject. "Matthias, our scribe, whom you have met, will continue taking down our recollections in the coming days. There is a meeting of the Sanhedrin this week, and I expect him. But let us turn to your own apostleship, Paul. We have decided you must undertake a Nazarean oath, and I hope that is agreeable."

"As you wish," Paul replied. "If that is your idea, I am sure the lord agrees."

***

Days later, James was informed that Simon and several other disciples witnessed Paul's oath taken before the priests, in which he swore he would observe a month of abstention from drinking any wine and would demonstrate complete devotion to God by denying himself all acts of self-concern, not even grooming or cutting his hair. Aloud, perhaps for the benefit of those observing his compliance, he prayed God would guide his activities in leading others and keep him from violating the laws of Torah. If, in his own heart, he still intended to accommodate non-Hebrew ways among the pagans, nothing of that opinion was uttered the day he made the vow.

CHAPTER TEN

*A*s Matthias washed a tunic and folded it over a hemp line just outside his door, the woman from the nearby house called to him, "So . . . did you hear? It's terrible news."

"Yes?" he replied. "Have you heard something important?"

Taking Matthias' response for an invitation, she followed him inside. "But of course you must know more about it than I do," she managed breathlessly as she commenced an account of what people were saying. "The Arab has attacked the north, going through Philip's tetrarchy. They say that as soon as word spread that Philip had died, he decided to invade."

Matthias had reports about Philip, Antipas' half-brother, falling ill, but not his death.

"They say it's because the Romans were going to make Antipas king of the north, and his region borders Nabatea," she declared, faithfully delivering the day's gossip, all the while looking around the interior to see how he lived.

"Well, thank you," he told her, his tone indicating her welcome had run a brief course. Not wishing to seem impolite or abrupt, he added, "Without you, what would I know?"

She smiled at his neighborly manner and turned to go. "You should avoid traveling. That's what they say."

"I will," he promised, shutting the door behind her.

Matthias sat with a moistened point in one hand while holding down a corner of a parchment leaf with the other. After a moment of reflection, he began writing a letter.

Shalom, Joseph,

I hope all is well with you. So if my neighbor is right, as I've just heard, Philip is dead, and Aretas has attacked Antipas, taking his forces through Philip's tetrarchy. Roman permission to counterattack, I'm guessing, may await a lull in fighting between the empire and Parthia. The Romans will think this over very carefully, because they do not want Aretas opening his Nabatean borders in support of Parthian brigades. Besides, Aretas will likely blunt his incursion, knowing Antipas has armaments sufficient for seventy-thousand men. My guess is the Camel is letting Rome know that making Antipas king will be a cause of serious warfare.

Personally, whatever disappointments befall Antipas and Herodias are as pleasant to you and me as a dessert of sweet wine.

One more thought requires a few words. I am concerned about your possible annoyance when I tell you I have joined Jesus' group of students as their scribe. Please don't scowl at my decision. Is there a better way of knowing what they are doing to his memory? Maybe I'm trying to save him as if that were still possible. I will let you know how it's going when our paths cross again.

May everything be good,
Matthias

He enclosed the furled parchment in a suitable jar and tied its lid shut with a hemp strand. Embedding its knotted ends in a glob of damp clay, Matthias sealed it with agate, leaving an impression of his name. Though an official messenger carrying letters between members of the Sanhedrin was expected the following week, one arrived the next day. Members were summoned to the assembly to discuss the attack on the north. The courier inserted the clay jar with his message to Joseph into a wide-mouthed sack, along with his overnight provisions, as well as his scribe's ink and points. Having provided Matthias a pillow for the seat, he clicked his tongue at the horse, and they set out for Jerusalem.

CHAPTER ELEVEN

*W*hile visiting the towns and villages of the pagans, Paul became better acquainted with their beliefs. Meanwhile, Aretas' attack had not caused him or his companions concern, owing to their distance from the battle.

Not too many weeks after he had taken up residence in Tyre, Paul received the anticipated invitation. In the company of Barnabas and John Mark, now elevated as assistant apostles, he traveled under a hot sun, finally reaching the cool entrance of a huge cave. There, they followed a guide assigned to greet them and had gone several steps inside when the elder of the community, who had hosted the dinner in Simon's honor, appeared.

"It is good to see you again," he said. "You may take a torch, and I will show you our sacred site. To the side, as you see, are several of the caverns we use."

The daylight, so bright a few steps back, faded as enveloping darkness obscured their way forward.

Following closely behind the elder, they peered into small, natural enclaves, their damp, undecorated walls lit by occasional oil lamps in iron sconces. Formations of stone jutting out were used as seats for a small number of worshippers in private contemplation, and farther on, from a recessed room lost from sight, came the barely audible sound of chanting.

"Do I hear the priests carrying on their rituals?" Paul asked politely, as the elder indicated they had gone far enough. "I can't make out what they are saying."

"Perhaps another time we may approach the sanctuary," he replied. "You would not know their language anyway." But before he elaborated further, a startling, loud cry of something that sounded like a screaming animal echoed off the walls.

Ignoring the interruption as if it had never happened, the elder continued, "Their words have secret meanings given only to us initiates by the true god. They ascend past the falsehoods of the ruler god—no matter how his heavenly watchmen, the archontes, may try to interfere."

"How does one become an initiate?" Paul inquired, trying to appear undaunted by the bizarre noise, which though abated, had caused both John Mark and Barnabas to look about in mild alarm.

"It takes years of study. The evil ruler god has created this world and filled us with sin to control us through our obedience to his rule. But if we devote ourselves to the true god, he frees the light within us, and we live again as we did before becoming slaves."

If Paul had been inclined to repeat his request that they go closer, he was distracted by an unpleasant odor, at first tolerable but growing stronger with every passing moment. Catching a glance from Barnabas, who had raised his sleeve to his nose, Paul wondered at the elder's demeanor, impervious as he seemed, to the noxious scent.

"But why do you use a cave as your temple?" Barnabas inquired moments later, relieved they were turning back.

"Let us go out, and I will tell you," the elder said and then whispered, "You hear how our voices carry in here. I do not want to disturb them."

After depositing their still-flickering torches near the entrance and adjusting to the daylight, they came to a stone bench and sat down.

"You see," the elder said, "the cave is the cave of death." As he paused to take a drink from a leather flask at his hip, he chuckled and continued, addressing John Mark, who seemed uncomfortable. "Well, don't worry. You didn't die, did you?"

"I feel fine," John Mark said.

"Good. And you do seem quite alive, I'm pleased to say. Yes, it is the cave of death. Those who enter it with the proper wisdom are not entering a cave; they are taking their soul through the cleansing process of death itself. When we die in the cave, the eternal light within us, the essence of the true god, becomes the principal of our being."

"It is similar to the Greek understanding," Paul said. "*Soma sema.*"

"No, not at all," the elder replied. "The body is not a prison of the inner good soul, according to our way. We do not believe that we are good inside. Our souls are sinful, and there must be the death, even of the soul, before its light can be free. The idea that the soul is good is an illusion created by the ruler god to force our obedience to his laws. He tells us, 'Obey my laws and your soul will be pure.' This is the soul he has created. Like our stomachs, it has an appetite, only not for food but for his laws."

"I don't understand what you mean by laws," Barnabas said.

"Laws are laws," the elder responded rhetorically. "Often they have to do with money. If you have money, then you spend money, or loan it, or borrow it, or owe it. Always you are bound by rules, and contracts, and agreements. You must bow down before them and obey or enforce them. Do you think the true god would live that life?

You have the divine spark within you, but it must rejoin the ultimate light, the light of the Splendid One. So we teach the initiate to start by divesting himself of his wealth. If you have little money and few valuable possessions, you are free of those laws at least. For us, it's a starting place."

"We believe the same thing," John Mark said, "though we don't worship your god. Our teacher taught us to be wary of wealth."

"Paul, here, has told me about your teacher. You believe he is a savior from your God, sent to save us all. Isn't that right?"

"Yes."

"But he died. And from what you said, it was a hideous death. How shall he be your savior if he could not save himself?"

"We don't know," Barnabas answered. "But we know he is in heaven."

"Actually, he is not dead," John Mark said. "We believe he is watching over us as he did when he was alive. We know God would never have let him die."

"And Paul, you received his words on the way to Damascus," the elder stated. "You told me that."

"It is true."

"If he was the one, there would be a great mazda—an illumination of truth. Do you understand? A great light."

"It was blinding," Paul said.

"Yes," the elder replied. "It would have been a blinding light. But it is good you do not yet grasp why he died. When the fall season turns to winter, at the time of the solstice, you may join me in the chamber of the priests and see what they do. I may shed some light on why his life ended as it did."

"Thank you for inviting us," Paul replied, "but this should be the beginning of our friendship. In time, Peter, whom you met at the dinner you hosted, will return to see how we are faring. I look forward to all of us again sharing a meal."

"Food is the one weakness to which I never say no. Barnabas, you and I seem to have that in common," he added, putting his hand on Barnabas' shoulder. "For now, peace to you all."

As they bid the elder farewell, Barnabas snapped the reins, and the three returned to the city.

CHAPTER TWELVE

Several days had passed since Aretas' foray into the north, during which time Matthias had been in Jerusalem, faithfully recording the oratory of the Sanhedrin, which beseeched Rome to protect the region against attacks.

With the tetrarch dead, the invasion route used by Aretas, apparently encouraged by Philip's own guard who didn't want Antipas to be their king, was now under the direct authority of Vitellius, the Roman legate. Vitellius did not know whether the deceased tetrarch's region would be annexed to his Syrian province or given to Antipas, but he was too far from the Nabatean camel brigades to muster arms, at least initially. From what couriers were saying, Aretas had burned several municipal buildings in Antipas' villages and still had not fully retreated.

When the Sanhedrin's session concluded, Matthias rejoined the other disciples at the Center. That morning, after a light meal of fruit and cheese, James spoke to Simon about Paul, inquiring when he would journey to Tyre to keep an eye on him.

"When Barnabas gets here, he'll tell me what's going on," Simon replied, directing his comment to Matthias as if James was not even in the room. "But Matthias, let's go upstairs and continue our work. James, I assume you will join us."

Seated in the upper triclinium, Simon waited for Matthias' signal that he should begin dictating.

"Ready, if you are," Matthias finally prompted,

"Let us start with his authority as master of the Shabbat, healing in the synagogues even during the Torah service," Simon stated. "Several such miracles occurred. There was a woman with a withered hand . . . and one with her body shrunken and deformed from countless years of infirmity . . . as well as a man with dropsy, but Matthias, write it like this . . ."

As Matthias began to meticulously inscribe every word, he was struck by the strange intensity of Simon's voice. "Jesus," he proclaimed, "healed that woman bent over with lifelong misery, her bones long weakened by a malady of erosion. And she was blessed by him for her faith!" Turning to directly address James, who showed no sign of shared inspiration, he added defiantly, "That and the others like it were on Shabbat! On the day when all such activity is strictly forbidden ordinary men."

Covering more than two segments of parchment, which gave personal testimony to Jesus' healings, Simon finally reached the episode of the disciples picking unharvested grain. Allowing Matthias to rest his hand, he interrupted his account to further chastise James. "You refuse to accept the truth that he was not an ordinary son of man as we are. Why else would he reveal his authority to work on Shabbat?"

"Healing is not prohibited by Torah," James answered. "It was a good thing to do on any given day."

"But the rabbis do not do it!" Simon insisted. "Why won't you accept the evidence, James? Or is it that he was not revealing himself to you?"

Moving his fingers along a fresh wooden point, as if strumming an invisible lyre, Matthias advised that he was ready to continue.

"We are at the moment when you were eating parched barley from an unharvested field."

"I remember that!" Matthew announced, unexpectedly entering from the outside stairs.

"Welcome, brother," Simon muttered softly, again beginning his dictation. "And the Pharisees said, 'Why are you doing something that is forbidden on the Shabbat?'"

"Simon," Matthew interrupted, "excuse me, but they were Pietists, not true Pharisees."

"What difference does it make?" Simon asked.

"The true Pharisees never accused Jesus of anything, did they?"

"He was crucified in Jerusalem. Did they do anything about it? Anyway, they were mere instruments of God's plan," Simon insisted. Then, regaining his composure, he lowered his voice. "So say, 'Some Pharisees accused him of violating the Shabbat.' I hope that satisfies you, Matthew. What Jesus then said, I tell you, is evidence of his identity—to those who are worthy. Put it this way. 'Jesus replied that the sacred day of rest was made for him and that he was its master. Have you not learned, he asked, what King David did when he and his followers were hungry? How he entered the Temple and took the loaves of offering and ate them and gave them to his followers, loaves which only the priests are permitted to eat?'" Turning to James, Simon paused and asked, "Well, James? If Jesus said he was authorized by God to do what King David did, wasn't he revealing he was sent by God?"

James replied, "You say my brother was talking about his right to take bread because David did it—and so could he. Those loaves you say David ate were not in any Temple. They were in the home of the priest Ahimelech, in Nob, when David was fleeing Saul. Ahimelech only gave food to David to fortify his men as he escaped Saul's

q

pursuit. But tell us, Matthias, did Jesus disclose anything about that episode as if he was like King David?"

"I'm not certain that Jesus told me about it quite that way," Matthias replied. "And even on Shabbat, the Torah permits anybody who is hungry to pick unharvested grain from the corner of a field." Seeing Simon become flustered, he abruptly held his peace.

"Nobody but me had to hear the exact words," Simon said. "I heard them. If other disciples have a different version, Matthias, you should record it next to mine. But I tell you Jesus has revealed himself to some and not to others, which brings my account to the healing of the man with leprosy."

"I believe that happened before picking grain on Shabbat," Matthias said.

"Did it?" Simon asked hesitantly. "It could have. Are you certain?"

"That was the first time he stayed in my house."

"Then you would remember. Well, good. Not that it changes anything very much. But if we have it in its proper order, that is good. Yes, what an event that was—the leper! Matthias, are you ready? Here it is, then.

"A leper came up to him and pleaded that he heal his affliction, and Jesus touched him, and he was made clean. Then Jesus told him not to tell anybody but to go and appear before the priest to prove he was cured and to make an offering to God, as Moses commanded. But the leper went away and talked to everybody about it, spreading word of what happened so that crowds gathered wherever Jesus went, and he was forced to withdraw."

"To my house," Matthias said. "But please don't mention that. I do not want to be a visitors' attraction."

"No need to. So say he withdrew into the countryside," Simon agreed.

"Simon, shouldn't we hear from Matthias about the leper?" James suggested.

"About what? If you have something on your mind, as you usually do, please say it so we can move on."

"Matthias?" James prompted.

"He told me the man knelt at his feet and called him 'lord.' And that he was a pitiful sight, covered with leprosy. From what your brother said, the man was grabbing at his tzizit-fringes."

"And wasn't he immediately cured?" Simon demanded.

"He didn't tell me that," Matthias replied. "I recall he was concerned that the man would tell people about the healing."

"You see, James? Exactly as I say. Your brother was keeping his identity a secret!"

"Whether he was cured or not," James responded, "was not what my brother worried about. Touching a leper as a healing was the same as claiming he could forgive sin, because Torah says leprosy may be God's punishment."

"You are right!" Simon declared. "That's the point, James. Your brother had God's power to forgive sin!"

"Matthias, did my brother ever tell you he could forgive sin?"

"Your brother forgave everybody he ever met for just about everything they ever did to him. Well, except for the Pietists who act like judges."

"He said God would forgive me," Matthew observed, as if speaking deeply private thoughts. "I believe that's what changed my life."

"Of course!" James exclaimed. "The Torah promises God will have mercy on the penitent. But the truth is he wanted to keep the encounter with the leper secret because people would say he claimed to forgive sin! Isn't that true, Matthias?"

"He never said to me that he could forgive sin."

"Nor would he have," Simon replied to Matthias. "It's obvious his identity was a secret. The Kingdom had not yet begun. Now that it is here, the truth must come to light! Please let us continue with the events at Kfar Nahum. Those of us who were there will never forget that day. Write it, Matthias."

Matthias dipped his point into the dye, and Simon paused only a moment before dictating, permitting Andrew, who had just entered, to quietly find a seat.

"And the disciples went into the village of Kfar Nahum, to the synagogue for the Shabbat prayers, and there was a man who screamed at Jesus, 'What have you to do with us, Jesus of Nazareth? You have come to destroy us! I know who you are! You are the holy one of God!' But Jesus rebuked him saying, 'Be silent and come out of him!' And the man began crying and fell down in convulsions, which passed as the demon left him, and after a short while, he was calm again."

Addressing James, Simon said, "You see? He had a demon, and the demon knew he was the one sent by God. This evidence of his divine holiness is as real as any we might wish for."

"And you will depend on demons to tell you? I think I know more about my brother than some demon," James said.

"I too hope that is true," Simon said. "But Matthew, you were there. Say what you remember."

"Mostly, I remember what happened afterward. There was a commotion as the man lay on the floor. People were upset. They seemed afraid of Jesus. And we left soon afterward."

"Of course they were afraid! Put it down, Matthias. 'The people were amazed and said to one another, with authority and power he destroys the demons. And his fame spread throughout the region.'"

Having held his peace, Matthew said, "But Simon, I don't remember his saying he knew Jesus was the holy one sent by God."

"Of course he did! And you certainly recall how he chased out the demon from that man."

"I remember his telling the demon to come out of him, and the man, who had been screaming that Jesus had come to destroy them, fell on the floor. That much, I will never forget."

"Matthew, is it not the demon that caused the man's madness, which Jesus cured by ridding him of it?" Simon demanded. "No wonder the demon said Jesus was the holy one of God and had come to destroy them. Look at what happened. The demon fled in terror because he recognized Jesus. There is your evidence."

***

When Simon did not join the others on the lower floor to relax for an interval of quiet reflection, as was his custom, his brother Andrew decided to see what he was doing. To Andrew's dismay, Simon simply stood motionless, staring out the window at the distant hills.

"Are you feeling well?" Andrew asked.

"Shouldn't I be?" Simon replied, sounding annoyed. Any extra measure of concern by his younger brother always met with indignation.

"I thought James may have upset you."

"I prefer not to talk about him," Simon said flatly.

"Then I shouldn't tell you what I think," Andrew said.

"You can tell me, if there's something I should know."

"It's his voice."

"His voice?" Simon asked. "Not his ideas, but his voice? Andrew, are you making a joke?"

"Hasn't it changed? Like it's coming from his bowels."

"If you want to insult James, go ahead. But don't be stupid about it. Please, whenever you say something for the others to hear, they realize it comes from me."

"I have my own mind, Simon."

"Of course you do. That's why you trust me. Your mind tells you to."

"And my mind is telling me James sounds different for a reason."

"He's becoming more of a problem every day," Simon noted, "but I have no idea what you're talking about."

"When you spoke about the Kfar Nahum demon and how he knew Jesus had come to destroy him, didn't you see how James reacted?"

"Of course I did. You heard what I told him."

"That's just it. Why do you think James defended the demon? At first, I couldn't figure that out. But then, when his voice started changing . . . making deep, scraping words . . ."

"What do I care?" Simon demanded. "Thaddeus can make him soup if he's getting sick. Whatever James needs, he does."

"He's not sick," Andrew insisted.

"Then what?"

"He's possessed. It was the same voice in Kfar Nahum when the man screamed at Jesus. That's why he's trying to stop you."

"You think James has a demon?"

"What better way to take revenge on Jesus than to stop you from spreading the news about his being in heaven."

"And the same demon? What nonsense!"

"They're all like that."

"It's impossible!"

"Any more impossible than killing the lord? I'm telling you. It's the same voice."

"Andrew," Simon responded sympathetically, "James has no demon. And don't start saying something the others will find absurd. You think it's James they'll call crazy?"

Andrew shrugged and started to leave the room, as if it was not something he'd further pursue, but turned to add a final thought. "Everything he says is about obeying Torah law. Didn't Jesus die so we would be free from it? But James wants us under its control, still ruled by the ones who killed our lord."

"That way of thinking makes every observant Jew an ally of Satan," Simon stated.

"That's who they are. And James is no different. He is killing Jesus—again."

"He was his kin," Simon rebutted.

"That was a different James. I'm telling you, look at his eyes. Something has to be done about him."

Leaving Simon to ponder what he had told him, Andrew returned to the group sprawled about, relaxing on the lower floor.

***

James marshaled his thoughts as he guided the horse down the steep incline in the shadow of the Mount of Olives. "But isn't it obvious Simon is having his way?" he finally asked Matthias.

"I might have put things differently," Matthias said.

"I know you weren't in the Kfar Nahum synagogue that Shabbat, but did Jesus tell you the demon recognized him as the holy one sent by God?"

"Your brother told me he did the exorcism, and the man had been screaming at him, and then when he fell on the floor, there was tohu va-vohu—complete pandemonium. But look ahead at these hills, James. We have so much to be thankful for."

"Yes, you're right, Matthias. But perhaps that man will tell me. I'll pay a visit to the Kfar Nahum synagogue to see whether he is there."

"What will you gain from that?" Matthias inquired, his tone feigning indifference that caught James by surprise.

"He may not remember what the demon said, but others will. If Simon will lie to prove my brother was the messiah, I'll do whatever I can to stop him."

Matthias felt James staring at him, waiting for a reply, but kept his gaze on the road ahead, lest his expression betray troubled feelings.

"Of course Jesus only talks to Simon and a few others," James persisted. "So if we want our souls to have eternal life, we better listen to what Simon tells us."

In an increasingly familiar demur, Matthias answered, "They are like children bragging that their father is best, but they are simply exaggerations. Isn't that what we Jews always do? To Simon, either there is a divine reason for Jesus' demise, or he is without a Creator, utterly unimportant and mortal."

"And therefore you will forswear all hesitation to amplify whatever he dictates, making him master of the Shabbat, even creating a false god who just happened to bleed to death on a cross?"

Against the backdrop of James' words, which blended with sounds of the wheels of a passing cart of warbling chickens, Matthias tried to reassure him. "I will not tread on his memory," he promised.

"Then you will refuse to record he was God's son?"

When Matthias made no reply, they rode on for several miles until James broke the silence.

"I'm afraid if you stop keeping the record, he will be forgotten."

"I will do my best to prevent that from happening," Matthias answered.

As the cart turned to Matthias' house in Ephraim, James' feelings rose to the surface. "Matthias, do you and I believe in such a cruel God that he ordained my brother's murder?"

"No. But isn't Simon trying to keep Jesus alive in heaven?" Matthias rebutted, in an unusual outburst. "He hopes to turn the hammered nails and plunged spears into an illusion—to deny the murderers their victim!"

But even as he spoke from the heart, Matthias wondered whether Jews this day would believe in God if Abraham, long ago, had plunged the sacrificial knife into his son. It occurred to him that had that been the outcome on Mount Moriah, God Himself might not have survived in the hearts of the Hebrew people.

***

After dropping off Matthias, James followed the road past Samaria and headed eastward, descending the hill just south of Tiberius. As he again turned northward, he could see in the distance what appeared to be a large plume of smoke well beyond the far side of the lake. Near the shore, shopkeepers were out on the street staring in the direction of the smoky cloud, talking among themselves in small clusters.

"What is that fire?" James called to a few of the bystanders.

"Not a fire," came the reply. "The dust of camel hooves."

"Aretas? Are his soldiers advancing?"

"We think they have turned back. The cloud has shifted to the east, toward Nabatea. If he comes this way, he won't only meet Antipas, but he'll also be fighting Rome."

"Thanks," James said as he snapped the reins and continued along the lakeshore toward Kfar Nahum.

The town entrance, a large gateway in a wall of yellow stones, held together by their own weight, seemed almost alive with the small, curious lizards that made it their home.

Although the air was clear, a southerly breeze carried the stench of dead and dying sea life from the exposed mud where the Sea of Galilee had receded due to the shortfall of winter rain.

The synagogue was just ahead, and James guided his horse into the shade of a willow tree outside its courtyard.

A custodian sitting near the door watched him as he approached.

"Shalom," James said.

"Can I help you?" the custodian asked.

"Are you in the congregation?" James inquired.

"I am Samaritan. We have our own."

"But you know those who pray here, I'm sure."

"I've had this job for two decades, and before that, my father did."

"I was hoping to meet the rabbi. Or the president."

"Come back on Shabbat. Everybody is staying home while the fighting goes on."

"I live in Nazareth," James said.

The custodian nodded, indicating he understood James did not travel on Shabbat.

"Well, he is getting on in years. And it's not like there's much to do here unless it's Shabbat or we have a wedding. Oh, I almost forgot funerals. You could hang around until somebody dies." James' laughter softened the man's attitude. "Maybe I can tell you what you want to know—if you'll believe a Samaritan."

"You help Jews by watching over a synagogue, so there's hope for all of us. A long time ago, about three years, there was a man who came here to pray. He had a demon. That same day a young rabbi was visiting with his students, and the man lunged toward him, saying, 'I know who you are, the holy one sent by God. You have come to destroy us!' I have a question about what happened that day."

For only an instant—but in a way that was unmistakable—the custodian's gaze fixed on James as if he were a poisonous snake. "I don't know anything about it," he said. Pointing to the courtyard cistern, he added, "Help yourself to a drink of water before you go. It's a hot day."

"I'm sorry. I thought you might know. But it happened inside." James hoped he had touched a nerve.

"You think I don't go in? I was there. It's just something better left alone. That was a bad day here—for all of us."

"He was a healer with powers from God. That's what I heard."

"Oh, so that's it. You have a family member who has a demon. Well, your healer is dead. And he wasn't a healer, that much I can tell you."

"But I heard he could work miracles on people."

"Miracles? The Romans put an end to his miracles. On a cross. If he could work miracles, that would never have been his end. Never mind. You've heard enough."

"Just one thing more. Did the man with the demon say to him, 'I know who you are, the holy one of God. You have come to destroy us'?"

"That's not what I heard Ephraim ben Naphtali say. He said, 'I know who you are. You intend to destroy us.'"

"Nothing about the holy one of God?"

"I told you."

"Thank you, my friend."

"There are healers near Nazareth, aren't there?" the custodian asked sympathetically.

"The young rabbis and sometimes their fathers will do it."

"So go to one of them."

"I have no need. But I will keep it in mind."

"It's nothing to be ashamed of. Many fine people such as yourself have demons."

James started the horse toward Nazareth but changed his plans. He needed to tell Matthias what he had learned.

***

The scroll was on the table, turned to the next fresh segment. Dipping his point, Matthias could not help the odd sensation that he was doing more than recording the past. He was returning to it.

It was late summer, more than two months after I had finished crafting the law for a court to hear the cases of accused women, when Jesus decided to leave my house and teach the disciples about the coming Rosh ha-shannah new year. I thought of the pleasant days of my youth spent along the lakeshore during Elul and suggested I would join him, which I did.

Soon after we reached the beach, we situated ourselves beyond a stand of nearby willows, and the setting sun warmed our backs while several of the disciples busily folded their nets.

That new year would commence the seventh of the tithing cycle— the year God had commanded the land itself be allowed to rest.

No seeds were planted, and there was no new crop. After the first of Tishrei, only wheat and spelt, as well as millet from prior plantings, could be harvested and sold, but mostly, people would draw upon their stored grain. The Hebrew nation was to be free of all earthly concerns.

All of us prayed and believed Judea would soon be redeemed by God, and the world would witness her ancient glory as His Kingdom, free of Roman rulers. Though the seventh year was always considered a wonderful time, it was one beset with concerns.

Drawn into a memory that played before his eyes, Matthias' point slowed to a halt. Jesus had talked about debt. Torah commanded that in the seventh year, money was no longer owed to the one who had loaned it. But what seemed so simple and beautiful an expression of compassion, as the complete forgiveness of debt, had resulted in the reluctance of people to give their needy friends and relatives loans to meet their most basic needs, especially as the seventh year approached, when they knew they wouldn't be repaid. Again, Matthias recalled the words as if he were just hearing them:

Jesus told a parable. "To be worthy of God's Kingdom, the Malchiyut, one should think of a king who wished to settle accounts with his courtiers. One servant, a courtier who appeared before the king owing him ten thousand talents, had nothing left, and the king ordered he pay, or his family should be indentured in order to make up the debt. With his family soon to be sent away, the man fell on his knees, begging, 'Master, have patience with me, and I will repay you.' The king took pity on him and forgave the debt. But when that same fellow came upon another servant of the king, one who owed him one hundred denarri, he seized him by the throat and said, 'Pay what you owe.' When the man pleaded for patience, promising to pay him, the other refused to wait and had him put in prison until he would settle the debt. Then the nearby courtiers, who were distressed by what had taken place, reported it to the king. Summoning the man, the king said, 'You wicked man. I forgave your debt because you pleaded with me. And should you not have had mercy on your fellow man, as I had mercy on you?' And the king delivered him to the jailers until he should pay all his debt. So God will do to everyone of you if you do not forgive each other from the heart."

As I recall, not long after he finished the parable, I was the first to notice shadowy figures of several men hanging back among the trees. Before they had a chance to withdraw, Jesus turned toward them and said loudly, "Shalom Aleichem—peace to you."

"Pietists!" James, the older Zebedee, hissed.

Jesus said to him, "You must not hate your Hebrew countryman. Reprove him, but do not become guilty before God by seeking vengeance for his wrongdoing toward you. You must not bear a grudge. Love your neighbor as yourself."

"They don't mean what they say," Thomas complained. "I don't believe any of them who wish me a good year. They are like the wicked servant in your parable. They ask God to forgive them, and then in their hearts they blame us for everything."

"If you bear a grudge, then they have a debt to you," Jesus answered. "Whatever you bind on earth shall be bound in heaven, and whatever you loose on earth shall be loosed in heaven. If you forgive them, the King will see you are good, and you too will be forgiven."

"How shall we free them of their debt to us when they turn around as soon as the ten days of atonement are past, and they are the same?" John the Zebedee protested, his high-pitched complaint sounding like a loud bird.

"If one of them wrongs you seven times a day, and seven times comes back to you and says 'I am sorry,' you must forgive him."

After saying this, Jesus went for a swim. As he was quite far out, the Pietists still lurking among the trees took the opportunity to step forward.

"We thought we heard your teacher say you don't have to pay anybody what you owe them. Is that what he said?"

"He'll return in a few minutes. Why don't you ask him?" I suggested.

"We have nothing against him. And nothing to hide. But maybe he does."

"You are the ones hidden in the shade of those trees. Tell us who is hiding if it isn't you!" Andrew demanded.

"We don't want to disturb you. So we'll go. We know about him. You should be careful of what he says."

"Thank you for your advice," I said, unable to restrain my anger. "No wonder you ran away from Jerusalem. The true Pharisees saw what fools you are and chased you out."

"No one chased us."

"Then why have you decided to bother us? Go study Torah. Maybe then you'll understand half what this young rabbi does."

"It's our job. If anybody says they don't owe taxes we report it to the tetrarch. Or if they say they don't need to obey the law. Maybe he thinks he's higher than the law. That's what we have heard."

Almost unnoticed, Jesus emerged and approached.

One of the disciples, perhaps Thaddeus, handed him a towel as he reached the group.

"And you are?" Jesus asked, addressing the most senior of them.

"It doesn't matter. We were just leaving."

"They say you are teaching us not to pay taxes," Matthew said. It was an amusing comment because he had been a tax collector.

Unaware of the joke, one said, "It is a crime not to pay taxes to Rome."

"So this is your new job? Collecting taxes?" I think it was Simon who asked.

"We are members of the Tiberius council."

"Herodians?"

"The name doesn't offend us."

"A reward for celebrating Antipas' marriage to the—" A sharp look from Jesus stopped Simon C'nani from finishing his sentence as he intended. Instead, he said, *"To the Maccabean queen Herodias."*

"In time, we will all call her our queen," another of the Pietists said proudly.

"We know the law," Philip said, *"so you can go."*

"One question, if you don't mind," another of the Pietists said to Jesus. *"Some say you teach that man's law doesn't matter, that the law they learn from you is all that matters. So, is it lawful to pay taxes to Caesar or not—and should we pay taxes?"*

"Show me a coin such as you may have in your purse," Jesus replied.

Reaching into his purse, the senior Pietist took out a denarius with the head of the emperor on it and handed it to Jesus.

"Well!" Jesus said. "Look whose face this is! Caesar's. I guess then it must be his! So let's return it to him!"

Simon C'nani's laughter erupted, causing the disciples to squeal giddily, and then Jesus became serious. "As for the things that belong to God, such as your souls, give them to God, not to some earthly ruler!"

When the Pietists left, a pall hung over the group. The confrontation, they sensed, was not over. "If I owed that Pietist or any other Roman stooge a prutah," Simon C'nani declared, "he'd wait an eternity for it."

After the Pietist Herodians were gone, John the Zebedee, his voice cracking as it did when he was upset, asked, "With the seventh year upon us, what about our money? If people don't pay us what they owe us, we will have nothing."

As they sat together, warmed by the late morning sun, Jesus said to them, *"Do not lay up for yourselves treasures on earth where moth and worm consume them, and where thieves break in and steal, but lay up for yourselves treasures in heaven where no worm or moth or thief can take them, for if you make your treasure in heaven, then your heart will be there too."*

"Where will we get food? How will we even buy bread?" Thomas asked.

Jesus answered, *"I tell you, do not be anxious about your life, what you shall eat, or what you shall drink, nor about what clothes you will have to wear. Is not life more than food and the body more than clothing? Look at the birds of the air. They neither sow nor reap nor gather into barns, and yet your heavenly Father feeds them. Are you not of more value than they?*

"And why are you anxious about what you will have to wear? Consider the lilies of the field, how they grow. They neither toil, nor spin, yet I tell you Solomon in all his glory was not arrayed like one of these. But if God so clothes the grass of the field, which today is alive and tomorrow is thrown into the oven, will He not clothe you, you men of little faith? Therefore do not be worried, always asking, 'What shall we eat?' or 'What shall we drink?' or 'What shall we wear?' For the gentiles worry about all these things. And your heavenly Father knows that you need them all.

"Seek His Kingdom and righteousness and all these shall be yours as well. Don't worry about tomorrow. Tomorrow will take care of itself. And which of you by being anxious can add one cubit to his life span?"

As if the words were meant especially for him, inasmuch as he was always talking about material possessions, James the Zebedee made light of the idea, saying, *"Well, as long as I don't have to repay anybody, it sounds fine. Maybe if somebody owed me money, it would be harder to tell him never mind. But I don't have that problem."*

"You should give me the money you owe me," his brother John mumbled.

When they all laughed, though John hardly meant to be humorous, Jesus spoke earnestly. It was one thing to free others from paying what they owed, but it was different to declare yourself free of such obligations. To many, because the seventh year in the tithing cycle canceled all debts, the summer months were a last chance to collect promised monies.

Afraid his disciples would use Torah law to default on their commitments, Jesus told them, "Even if you are offering a sacrifice at the Temple and remember that you owe money to your fellow Hebrew, leave your offering there in front of the altar and go first and repay your brother, and then return and make your offering. Make friends with your debtor and settle with him. Otherwise, he may hand you over to the judge, and the judge to the jailer, and you may be put in prison. And if somebody doesn't repay you, have it out with him alone, between the two of you. If he listens to you, you have won back your friend. But if he does not, still do not say he is a criminal, or you shall wind up before a court tribunal to decide the matter. Instead, bring two witnesses with you to talk to him. If he refuses to accept their testimony against him, exclude him from your company, like a tax collector or non-Jew."

Matthias could only marvel at the intricacy of his thought. Excluding the wrongdoer was better than having him found guilty, because it left him free to repent before God, though it did not require saying he was innocent.

That next morning after a refreshing walk along Kinneret's shore, the disciples boarded their fishing boat, which smelled of the catch and were wet from the hauled nets. I helped to push them out to deeper water and wished them a good day, and then I gathered my own belongings for the trip home. Along the road, especially before the new year, passersby invited others to share a ride, and it was not long before I was on my way.

Had I known what lay in store for Jesus, I would have stayed with him. The group, as I had been given to understand, was to visit the Kfar Nahum synagogue that Shabbat, a plan that evinced no special concern. Returning home, I prepared for my Rosh ha-shannah new year stay in Jerusalem.

"I have earned a nap," Matthias said, returning the scroll to its inconspicuous place between others on the shelf. Fatigued, he stretched out on his pallet, about to doze off, when James knocked on his door and then, having no answer, pushed it open.

"Matthias? Matthias . . ." he prompted. "Open your eyes. There's something I must tell you!"

"James, is that you? I thought I was dreaming."

"Please wake up. I'm sorry to barge in like this."

"Sit down . . . relax. I'll put some water on my face. Tell me what has happened. You seem breathless."

"I am coming from Kfar Nahum," James said. "The custodian, a Samaritan, was a witness that day."

"What day? I don't understand."

"Two years ago at this season, when Jesus exorcised a demon from one of their congregation."

"Yes, you told me you would go there to inquire."

"Matthias, what I suspected is true. The demon never said Jesus was the holy one sent by God."

"James, let's have some warm wine. I'll put it over the embers."

Seeing James was agitated, Matthias took time to formulate his words. "So you will go back to the Center and tell Simon what you have learned—that the demon in the man at Kfar Nahum never said Jesus was the messiah."

"Isn't that what I should do?" James asked.

"No. I don't think so."

"You'll have to do better than that, Matthias. It will take a good reason to change my mind."

The darkness of afternoon shadows stretched across the room, and Matthias' hands trembled slightly as he poured the wine into a glass.

"Are you feeling well?" James asked.

"Yes. Still half asleep, that's all."

"Well then?" James persisted.

"Shall you and I make your brother an ordinary man? Is that what you wish?"

The question struck an odd chord, and James tried to answer.

"Of course he wasn't. God endowed him to do these healings," James said.

"But that is all they are asking!" Matthias exclaimed. "That people know how special he was. So Simon expresses his love in his own manner."

"Calling my brother the holy one sent by God—are those just words? What entitles them to say something he never said about himself? They can call it his big secret, revealed only to them, but we know better. There was no secret!"

"But his faith in God flowed like a brook to comfort and refresh all who bathed in it. Everyone of us who heard him, as well as the sick and lost whom he touched with words or hands, received healing love. Certainly, we knew it came through him from our Creator. Am I wrong?"

"No."

"Then shall you or I snuff out the life that gave us so much and turn it into ordinary dust?"

It was the same question Matthias asked every time he put his point to his personal scroll—whether he wasn't doing the opposite of what he intended, ensuring Jesus would be forgotten, as the merely mortal usually were.

"Why, Matthias?" James asked. "Why must they say he was the messiah? Isn't it enough that we spread his interpretations of Torah? This shouldn't be the choice!"

"They are still trying to save your brother, James. They are keeping him alive. If he is dead, then they must wonder whether there is a God. If he is dead, to them God is a murderer. By saving your brother, giving him an eternal place as their heavenly teacher, they are saving God, the God your brother taught them to love."

James started laughing, an odd, broken laugh. "Simon saving God. If God must depend on Simon to save him, I'm sorry for us all."

"That may be true."

"What about us, Matthias?"

"What about us? I don't understand your question."

"How shall we save God?"

"If you want to know why God let it happen, I have no answer. I can tell you this: your brother's memory will be resurrected, not as Simon would have him be but as he was."

"You believe that?"

"I do."

After James swallowed the last sip, Matthias retrieved the glass from his hand. "But will you come by on the way to Jerusalem?" he asked.

"To take you," James answered. "I'll pass by in two weeks."

"And now? Would you like to spend the night here?"

"I'm headed back to Nazareth, in time for Mary and my sisters' cooking." James stopped as he was leaving and retraced several steps, hugging Matthias tightly.

"I will not let them create a false god from the bones of your brother," Matthias said. But watching James clamber up the side of the cart, he wondered whether his embrace wasn't clinging to a past they both had known, one that was changing to a different time without them.

"Then you believe his bones are in the earth, Matthias."

"I believe his spirit lives on," Matthias replied, and James said no more but clicked his tongue at the horse, waving as he departed.

Chapter Thirteen

*I*ncreasingly, Matthias admitted to himself that he could face a surging tide of Simon's flawed recollections. Sitting with the point gently tapping the edge of the table, he pondered the confrontation that seemed more inevitable each day. *I too am afraid the truth will be lost to Simon's,* he thought, as if assuring James they shared that concern. *But I will tell how human was this god they worship. Otherwise, they may completely take him away from us and claim him as their own.*

Like a soldier striding into unfriendly territory, his hand aimed the point, shaping the truth, as Jesus, unbeknownst to James, had related it to him.

Jesus' reputation was making it difficult to go anywhere without small crowds following him, among them people who hoped to be healed and others to hear what he was saying. Opinion was divided as to whether he was the chosen one sent by God, or was himself possessed by a demon and so showed madness, or even was, as others whispered, the satanic false teacher expected to corrupt the innocent before Judgment Day.

Perturbed when he learned that his own disciples boasted he was master of the Shabbat and that it was made for him, he was troubled even more when they claimed he had cured a leper and so forgiven sin ordained by God.

Availing himself of a broad point for the next heading, Matthias would record what actually had transpired at Kfar Nahum. Although James' exchange with the Samaritan had exposed Simon's exaggeration, there was a far greater consequence than the false reverence he detested.

The Kfar Nahum episode

It was just as these mounting rumors had people whispering he was evil that the incident at Kfar Nahum occurred. Screaming "I know who you are!" a congregant who thought Jesus was in league with Satan lunged toward him declaring, "You intend to destroy us!" It was natural that in the goodness of his heart, Jesus believed a demon was speaking. Who else would say such a thing? What good man would believe Jesus wanted to destroy him or anybody? It had to be a demon! But, as Jesus understood soon after his ill-conceived exorcism, the enraged man pronounced what many suspected. No, his screeching accusation was not the voice of a demon but of one terrified—mistaking Jesus for the false teacher, come to destroy the faithful Jews as an emissary of the satanic god, Beelzebul. Almost immediately, people began saying Jesus had struck down a righteous man, causing his collapse to the floor and paroxysm of madness as a ruse to conceal his evil identity.

His disciples were with him as he returned from the Kfar Nahum travesty to his home in Nazareth. Overhearing them talk about his power over the man in Kfar Nahum as if he were the messiah, Jesus admonished them not to. Several, however, were exhilarated at the sight of his reducing the screaming congregant to a writhing pulp at their feet. Simon was one whom Jesus later heard explaining to the others how he needed to keep his identity secret until the time was right. Acting the role of chosen interlocutor, often pretending to fathom Jesus' teaching, Simon had appointed himself leader of the select cadre about to enter God's Kingdom. Among the disciples several who were also confused by his Torah lessons, boasted they too understood, afraid they could be unworthy of the imminent Day of God.

"Their messiah has a secret message meant only for the worthy," Jesus told me. And I recall vividly how we tried to make light of their coronating him savior of the world.

Meanwhile, events were moving in an unexpected direction.

When he and the disciples reached his hometown, they could see people were keeping their distance.

Almost immediately, he was aware word of Kfar Nahum had even reached Nazareth. At home, he was received coolly by his own family, and realized they too were distressed by news of the bizarre episode.

In the market of Nazareth, like most residents preparing for Rosh ha-shannah, he and his disciples bought delicious small apples and dry figs. As they did, he heard people talking.

"He is the one possessed by a demon," a gossip told her companion. But when he turned to see who said it, she instantly averted her eyes, probably terrified that his demon might enter her.

If they did not think he was the emissary of Beelzebul, as that was the view of a modest number, they were certain he was possessed. To have attempted an exorcism on a religious man of good standing in the Kfar Nahum congregation, he had to have been mad! Only one with a demon would do that, they told one another.

Still, there were some who believed he had miraculous powers.

As Jesus and the group made their way toward a wooded hill, a man who heard he was a healer asked him for help. A companion quickly grabbed the wretch by his tunic sleeve to save him from the mistake, warning him to get back so he might be spared Jesus' touch, even as others were drawn to the commotion on the quiet street.

Showing he understood their whispered accusations, Jesus said to them, "Undoubtedly you will quote me this proverb: 'Physician heal thyself!' And you will tell me, 'If you are so good at exorcisms, like the one we heard about in Kfar Nahum, do one on yourself!'"

A Pietist, with his large tefillin box flapping on his forehead, shouted from the outer edge of the circle formed around him, "You are the one who needs an exorcism!"

Finally having retreated to the privacy of the secluded hill, Jesus listened as Simon and several disciples berated "those Jews." It was as if they were talking about foreigners.

"If you only show love for those who love you, how are you different from non-Jews? Don't even non-Jews do that?" Jesus asked, directing the question to Andrew, who was sneering in contempt.

"They don't think of us as Jews anyway, so why should we act different?" Andrew asked.

"We will be going to the synagogue tomorrow," Jesus said. "People will greet you with wishes for a good year ahead. All of you should return the greeting."

"I will give you and our group my greeting—not them," Thomas grumbled.

Jesus realized he had made it hard for them. Wasn't he asking they forgive the very Pietists he had denounced as adulterers and hypocrites? Repeatedly he had shown disdain for their distortion of Torah law, and now they were to be accorded fond regard, even though they considered his circle impure, doubtful Hebrews, probably born from a defiled family lineage.

Their disgust, he later told me, was etched in his disciples' faces, and he wondered whether he had an impossible lesson to teach. Resolving to try, he adjured them, even more strongly than by the lake, "You have heard it said, 'love your neighbor and hate your enemy,' but I tell you, love your enemies and pray for those who persecute you. Do this so you may be sons of your Father who is in heaven. And when you stand praying in the synagogue, forgive those you resent. Then your Father in heaven may forgive your sins. Be perfect as your Father in heaven is perfect. And remember that He causes His sun to rise on the evil and the good, and sends rain on the righteous and the unrighteous."

If God did not withhold His love and blessings even from those who sinned, neither should they.

Not that they knew it, but he was more uneasy about their attending the Rosh ha-shannah new year service than they were. His family was already scoffing at his supposed role as their rabbi. If he embarrassed them further, he could be shunned by his own mother and siblings. So for the sake of his family's honor, as well as his own, it was important his circle be informed about synagogue custom and shed the stigma of ignorance that cast doubt on their backgrounds.

Aware they might imitate the Pietists, seeking to appear familiar with the synagogue service and be less conspicuous as ignorant fishermen, he told them not to, saying, "Don't be like those who stand all the time so they will be seen as holier than others. Be careful about practicing your piety in front of others. If you don't know the prayers, do not babble like non-Jews.

Say words that come from your heart, like these: Aveenu she-basha-mayeem—our Father who is in heaven—asher shemcha mikudeshet—whose name is holy—yavo aleinu malcutecha—may Your Kingdom come—al pi ritzoncha, according to Your will—bashamayeem u-va-aretz—in heaven and on earth."

And because it was the seventh year, he added, "Give us each day our daily bread and forgive us our debts for we ourselves forgive everyone who is indebted to us. And lead us away from yetzer ha-ra—the evil inclination."

Then Jesus declared loudly for them all to hear, "Judge not, that you be not judged. For with the judgment you pronounce, you will be judged." Quoting a Hebrew proverb, he added, "The measure of forgiveness you give is the measure you will get."

It was the first of Tishrei, and Jesus went with his disciples to the small Nazareth synagogue, accompanied too by several young men who had been tagging along. Mary and his brothers would come later, but his sisters had gone on ahead of him. Along the street, others were also making their way to the service and greeted members of his group with a wish for a good year, which they returned with wooden politeness.

When they arrived, nobody seemed to take special notice. Quietly, Jesus said to his disciples that they should find seats near the rear of the small synagogue, making room for those who came regularly and on the new year had places in the front.

As they settled in, a Levite leaned over a scroll and sang a psalm. "Blessed are those who reside in Your house, blessed are those who praise You. Blessed are those who are bent low, for You will lift them up. Blessed are those who say Your Kingdom is forever, for Your hand satisfies their every need."

As the Levite continued, Jesus was aware that his disciples were detached from the moment.

The first along the row was Simon, who looked at the standing Pietists with contempt. When his eyes fell on the next one, John the Zebedee, he was startled by a haughty grimace. Next to him was Thomas, who had complained that if they observed the seventh year, none of them would have enough to eat. He could well have been thinking of his next meal. Simon's brother Andrew was listening but, as usual, seemed impatient—a trait he exhibited even when Jesus took time to show compassion toward the sick. And still farther along he could make out the fixed spectator's gaze of James bar Alpheus, as well as Thaddeus, who always strained to grasp the lessons, with his mouth open in a wide yawn as if to catch flies. All seemed separate from the spirit of the occasion, though the others were too far along the row for him to observe.

With the promise of the prayer—"Happy are we who dwell in the house of the Lord, happy are we whose God is Adonai"—sweeping across the sanctuary, Jesus pronounced the words, encouraging them to join in as best they could. "Adonai will provide food in due season. Adonai lifts up the fallen and protects all who love Him." But the prayer was unknown to them and never left their lips.

Following shacharit, the morning service, the disciples relaxed on a nearby knoll, and Jesus listened to their banter while they ate a light meal. Talk was about the market in Tiberius, fish nets, money for caulking, and which of them was fastest at sewing tears. Judas Iscariot, the one I recently replaced as the twelfth member of the group, seemed to listen attentively, as the Zebedees took turns showing off their knowledge of the lake. Since Judas was the youngest, this seemed natural, and as I understand, just then nothing showed of his true nature. Jesus was disappointed because they didn't even once turn to him with questions about the holy day and Torah, and so he recited verses from the psalms.

"Blessed are the peacemakers, they shall be called sons of God," he said prayerfully, "and those who are humble, they shall enter the Kingdom."

Then seeing Bartholomew was spreading oil on his bread, Jesus continued, "and God gives those who hunger and thirst for what is right, food in due season." But when his words only made them sleepy, he made no further effort.

Returning to the synagogue after a nap, with the mincha service soon to begin, they noticed a cluster of Pietists outside the gate, waiting for something.

"When the shofar is sounded, they will put money into the bowl for the poor," Jesus explained. "That way they will let everybody see how righteous they are. When you give charity, let no shofar be sounded first, as do the Pietists in the synagogue or outside on the street, so they may be praised by people." And pointing to the collection bowl, he added, "By putting charity in this public collection, your left hand will not know what your right hand is doing."

When they seemed puzzled by his comment, Jesus quoted the sages, saying, "The recipient should not know from whom he receives, and you should not know to whom you have given. This is the highest form of giving. Do not cause a needy individual to be in your debt."

Just then, a small woman, elderly and alone, made her way forward. From her mouth, where she kept several prutot in the pocket of her cheek, like a squirrel saving its nut, she took out the coins and placed them in the bowl.

"She has put in more than the others," Jesus told his disciples. "For they all are putting in money they have in excess. But she has put in money she needs to live on."

When Thaddeus seemed embarrassed because he had no money, Jesus said, "The good man out of the treasure of his heart produces good."

Inside they found their places but remained standing as the shofar was sounded, its notes alternately broken and then longer in duration, the ancient call to assembly.

Beckoned by the plaintive blast, the congregation imagined themselves again standing at the foot of Mount Horeb, awaiting God, trusting His presence would be manifest in their midst, as in the days of Moses.

When the shofar fell silent, a rabbi stepped forward and opened a small scroll from which he read Moses' instruction to the people. "You shall love Adonai your God with all your heart, with all your soul and with all your strength . . . and you shall teach these words and speak about them and fasten them as a sign on your arm and between your eyes, and put them on the doorposts of your houses."

Silently, the worshippers each offered their prayers, and then the leader of the synagogue asked who in the assembly would read from the scrolls of Isaiah and Jeremiah, words of the prophets selected for the holiday.

Jesus stepped forward.

Leaning over the scroll on the table before him, he began with the words spoken by God to Isaiah.

"Listen to me, you who seek the Lord. Look to the rock you were hewn from, to the quarry you were dug from. Look back to Abraham your father and to Sarah who brought you forth."

After completing this passage, he unrolled an adjacent scroll to the prophet Jeremiah, telling of Ephraim, the symbolic name for the northerners taken into exile by Syria centuries earlier.

"I will bring them in from the northland," Jesus recited God's promise, "gather them from the ends of the earth—the blind and the lame among them. And with compassion I will lead them to streams of water, by a level road where they will not stumble. For I am a father to Israel. Ephraim, My northern son, is My firstborn."

Just about then, there were whispers between several people. One exchange he thought he could make out was, "Does he not speak like he has the authority of God? He's not a scribe, is he? Does he speak for God? Is that what he thinks?"

But he continued without faltering.

"Hear the word of the Lord, Oh nations, and tell it in the isles afar. Say, 'He who has scattered the northerners will gather them. I can hear Ephraim lamenting: You have chastised me and I am chastised.'

"And God answered, 'Truly Ephraim is a dear son to Me. I will receive him back in love.'

"'A time is coming,' Adonai says, 'when I will make a new Covenant with the House of Israel and the House of Judah. It will not be like the Covenant that I made with their fathers. But such is the Covenant I will make. I will put My teaching into their inmost being and inscribe it upon their hearts. No longer will they need to say to one another: know the Lord, for all of them shall know Me,' declares the Lord."

From where he stood, Jesus saw several people twisting around, turning their heads toward benches along the side where the women were sitting, and saying, "I think those are his sisters. Aren't his brothers James, Yossi, Simon, and Jude? I remember his father. A carpenter named Joseph, but he hasn't been here for a long time."

Having read God's rebuke of any who might ostracize their fellow Jews, Jesus would have returned to his seat, but he was approached by several worshippers who tried to touch his garment. Hoping to avoid a commotion, he quickly made his way outside, followed by the disciples and the several afflicted congregants, where just a short distance from the entrance, Pietists surrounded him.

To two of those pleading to be healed, one Pietist said, "He is possessed by Beelzebub," using the popular, derisive alteration of the deity's name, meaning "lord of the flies." Another then added, "It is only by the Prince of Demons, Beelzebub, that he casts out demons! No relief from physical malady is worth losing your soul!"

"And if I cast out demons by Beelzebub, by whom do your sons cast them out?" Jesus retorted. "And how can Satan cast out Satan? If he is against himself, how will his kingdom stand?"

Just then, beyond the edge of those who had gathered to hear the exchange, Yossi, Jude, and Mary were approaching. Intending to join the concluding service, they became distressed at what they saw.

As they reached him, hoping to stop whatever he was doing, Jesus gently placed his hands on a man who asked to be healed. His quiet blessing was barely heard over the angry insults of the Pietists, and one of them gleefully declared, "See—nothing has happened! Look, you are not healed. He has no power from God. Satan cannot heal you!"

Failing to restore the man's health, Jesus said, "No man is a prophet in his own home." It was an old saying and did not mask the fact that his effort depended on the faith of the recipient. Following the retreat of others awaiting his touch, a Pietist called *out, "Here are his mother and two of his brothers. Let them take him. He's their problem."*

Mary, enabled by Yossi and Jude to reach the midst of the crowd, tried to pull him away, but Jesus, seeing his family believed what they had heard—that he was mad—became incensed.

"These aren't my family," he said. "Who are my mother and brothers?" Gesturing toward ordinary members making their exit from the synagogue, he declared, "These are my mother and brothers," adding, "and these are my sisters," seeing they had just come out. "These who are here to do the will of God are my family!"

As Jesus led his band past the encircling Pietists and began to ascend the market street toward a less public place, a voice taunted his disciples. "You think he is a prophet? His is not ruach ha-kodesh, the holy spirit. It is ruach-Beelzebub—the spirit of Satan! That's his power. You should come with us!"

Several of the disciples stopped and turned toward the one who said it, and one of the Zebedees replied, "To you we are doubtful Hebrews. All you think about is our family tree, where we came from. You won't even let one of us touch your sleeve, as if we are defiling you. And you say we should come with you?"

"The Kingdom is coming," the Pietist responded. "But you still have time to cleanse the sins of your ancestors. Even if they were foreigners. You still have time to change."

Wiping his point on a soft cloth, Matthias pondered this last entry. In these years of Roman hegemony, the Pietists suspected any ignorant local with an odious Galilean accent of being descended from mixed marriages. Their ignorance of Torah had led to the stigma they were not even true Hebrews.

To make the heading, Matthias again selected a broad-tipped point. He reflected on the next passage, knowing his words would make record of Jesus' most cherished teaching. All Jews believed God had formed the creation from his own spirit, breathing life into Adam, longevity into sages, and had transformed Moses, turning his doubt to a vision of the covenanted land. Such was the nature of God's spirit that it might even purify those marred by ancestral sin. Isaiah's message from God—"truly Ephraim is a son to me"—gave scriptural testimony that Jesus' own followers were no exception— not a tax collector like Matthew, nor a self-aggrandizing poser like Simon, nor these simple fishermen who loved him. In the words of the sages of the Salt Sea sect, recipients of the holy spirit would all be B'nai Elohim, sons of God. Blessed by Torah insights, teachers such as Jesus, or uneducated disciples too, could be Adonai's firstborn—if they lived according to the commandments.

Matthias again introduced his entry with the broad point.

The holy spirit and sons of God

Jesus then said, "They don't need to prove they have a pure family tree. The holy spirit is changing them to sons of God."

"These?" an elder Pietist scoffed. "Look at what they know— nothing! And they come to one for help who uses Torah to twist their minds. If his is the holy spirit, Satan has his kingdom!"

So shaken were several of the disciples by this pronouncement, their confidence in Jesus appeared to falter, and one or two looked at their teacher in a different way—like netted fish under his scaler's knife.

Without hesitation, Jesus addressed them, his gaze fixed on the Pietist whose words were so arrogant.

"Blessed are you when men such as these revile you and persecute you and utter all kinds of evil against you because of me. It is no different from how they treated the prophets. But all sin will be forgiven the sons of men, including their insulting this son of man. But whoever insults the ruach ha-kodesh, God's holy spirit, will not be forgiven, either now or when the Kingdom begins."

Another Pietist then spoke, cajoling the disciples. "Sins of your family tree must be erased over time. Anybody who says different is lying to you—and has an evil purpose. Do you want to be like fools joining an army of Satan? Leave this so-called teacher and learn with us!"

"Hypocrites!" Jesus replied. "You have committed sins far beyond these students. You do anything to call attention to your piety, but you conceal your misdeeds, hoping God won't see them. I tell you, compared to the plank in your eye, theirs is only a splinter. So take out the plank in your eye before you judge them."

Jesus had walked several steps along the road, intending to lead his group away, when he saw a few of his accompanying acolytes whispering to each other about what they should do, though none turned to leave.

"Can a blind man lead a blind man?" Jesus asked, turning to face the Pietists. "You are like the blind leading the blind."

Ignoring him, one of them attempted to persuade the hesitant ones. "If you study with us, believe me, you'll learn a lot more than you're learning from him."

Then, a young man who had thought he might follow Jesus spoke up, saying he had to remain behind to help bury his father, that he could no longer delay since he was obliged to do so immediately after Rosh ha-shannah.

Watching him go toward the Pietists, Bartholomew wondered aloud whether his father was truly deceased.

"Let the dead bury the dead," Jesus answered sarcastically, but then regretting his harsh response, said, "Never mind. God comforts all who mourn."

Noting the triumphant look on the faces of his Pietist adversaries as the young man joined them, Jesus wondered whether their offer had also tempted his twelve disciples. So he said to them, "You are the salt of the earth. But if salt has lost its taste, how shall its saltiness be restored?" He was telling them that if they left, they should not return. Then he added, "Do any of you believe if they teach you and you learn what they know, you will know more than I do? When you are fully taught by them, you will know only what they know. But if you learn what I teach, then you will be sons of God."

Upon hearing him again say they would be sons of God, the Pietists began growling that he was guilty of helul—blasphemy— but a moment later, having failed to lure the rest away, they scurried off like wolves whose prey proved too heavy to drag back to their lair.

Seeing them go, Jesus said, "Anyone who studies with them is no longer good for anything except to be thrown out like tasteless salt and trodden under foot by men."

As he would eventually confide to me, his earlier instruction about not judging others had sunk beneath the storm tide of his own anger.

Only slowly regaining his composure, he realized Thaddeus was asking about the Pietists having a plank in their eye. "The eye is the lamp of the body," he explained. "If your eye is sound, then your whole body will be full of light. But if your eye is not sound, then your whole body will be full of darkness."

Though he never said it, in that darkness, they might no longer see him as their teacher.

Undaunted, he hoped to free them from their stigma as northern locals, so-called am ha-aretz. If they studied Torah and became sons of God, there would no longer be a shadow over their ancestral tree. As Joel prophesied, with the onset of the Kingdom, even the outcasts would receive the holy spirit and be prophets.

In the quiet that followed that contest for his own disciples, Jesus informed them there was a family wedding that he would attend. Cana, a picturesque village about a half day's walk, was in the direction of the Sea of Galilee.

The Cana wedding

As they set out, he could see their reluctance to join him. His family had been so hostile, believing he was acting like a madman, that they could not imagine being welcomed to the festivity. As they walked along, stopping to rest more than was necessary and shortening the time they would be at the wedding party, a group of men were hammering nails into the frame of a hut, preparing for the coming Feast of Booths.

"Everyone of you who listens to my teaching and acts accordingly will be like a wise man who built his house on a rock foundation," Jesus said, still feeling a need to reassure them. "And when the rain fell and the winds blew and beat upon that house, it did not fall because it had been built well."

The wind and rain were the gossip and accusations of the Pietists. The houses that did not fall were the souls of those who studied Torah with him.

133

As they again walked on toward Cana, Jesus told them, "And everyone who studies with me and then ignores what I say will be like a foolish person who built his house upon the sand. And the rain fell and the winds blew and beat against that house and it collapsed. And it had a big fall."

Descending from the low hills of Galilee, past the summer-browned fields and harvested vineyards, Jesus stopped only to purchase a large wineskin from a street vendor, and finally the group arrived at the wedding party.

When they reached the entranceway, his mother stepped forward and, seeing the intended gift in his hand, immediately berated him for coming late. "They ran out," she said, as if it was his fault.

"What does it matter to you or to me, woman?" he replied coldly. "It's not my wedding."

Somewhat unsettled by his mother's criticism, he would attempt to make amends.

Though water was added to wine at all weddings, Jesus could see from the light pink color in the pitchers that the guests were making do with a mixture far too diluted to have much flavor.

After he and several of his disciples finished rinsing their hands under the spigot of the water vessel set out for that purpose, he handed the wineskin to the servant and told the man to pour the wine from the skin into the same container.

His mother was standing there when he made the suggestion, and she observed the servant's reluctance. The large jar was intended to cleanse the hands of the guests, not to dispense wine. As he knew, many ordinary Galileans were purifying their homes and attaching an aura of holiness to the household water vessels, as if they were living in a temple. To him, sanctifying ordinary water for washing was just another arrogant claim to be holy like the priests.

With the party winding down and plainly hoping to avoid a commotion, Mary told the servant, "Do whatever he says."

Pleased that that there was now stronger wine available, many did step forward to help themselves. And one said, "Look what he has done now. He has turned the water to wine!" To the one who made the sarcastic comment, it seemed Jesus thought himself equal to the high priest who, on the Sukkot Feast of Booths, poured water and wine on the altar, praying the winter rain would be turned to the wine of prosperity.

One of the guests, upon helping himself to a glass of the rich mixture, said, "People usually serve the strongest wine first and water it down later, but now we have the strongest wine last!"

If he had expected the gathering to pay him such attention, he did not say. But even the bridegroom took notice of the line formed to refill their glasses. When he inquired of the steward what they were all doing, thinking it was an odd thing to see them drinking water used to wash their hands, the steward believed he was looking for a compliment. "Common people save the watered-down wine until everyone is drunk," he replied, "but you have saved the best until now!"

And it was just about then, as Jesus told me, that he thought he heard somebody say, "Good health to the shetuki."

"Shetuki is shetufi," a companion remarked more loudly.

Others who possibly heard it had turned to look at him. They may well have been startled to hear so blatant an insult.

If a woman whose husband accuses her of adultery becomes pregnant, popular opinion says a healthy baby is God's verdict that she is innocent. But if the baby turns out to be deformed or crazy, it means the husband is not the father. Though any individual who cannot name his own father is called shetuki—a silent one—those who show madness as evidence of their illegitimacy are shetufi— crazy ones.

But it made no sense. His father was Joseph. And Joseph had never accused his mother of adultery.

For the moment, it seemed the one voicing the remark was drunk. But it disturbed him that they would not only make him the target but also his mother.

When he looked in her direction, she was wiping her eyes, and he saw she was weeping. She too had heard it.

What they said about him had nothing to do with her. He would tell her this was only about him. As he went to her, she said weakly, "If you continue like this, no one will marry you!"

"It's not the right time for me to get married," he answered.

But even as he said it, he was deeply troubled by something in her manner that he had never seen. She was looking at him as if he were a stranger.

For an instant, a shadowy face in enfolding darkness seemed to be claiming him, speaking to him from somewhere, a foreigner who worshipped false gods calling him, "my son."

His concern about false accusations of suspected wives, the Pietist fashion these days, was turned into a defense of his own mother. Could she have done such a thing?

Standing and giving testimony before a tribunal of wedding guests, only God could render the verdict. If she turned out to have violated her betrothal to Joseph and conceived by some unknown man, everything Jesus was teaching and doing might be Satan's work. Now he understood the reason for her remark that nobody would marry him. A shetufi not only was somebody who showed signs of madness but was one born in sin to an unknown father. Marriage to such a person would be a curse on the offspring.

His disciples, having heard the emotional exchange—whether or not they understood—averted their faces. His brothers and sisters were saying good-bye to the other guests. His mother no longer cast her gaze in his direction but made her way to the other side of the room.

Alone, he saw one who looked at him as if to blame him. It was his brother Jude. Even in that instant he studied Jude's face, searching its contours for a similarity to his own. His brothers were Joseph's sons, offspring of his mother's aunt. Her death had made the marriage of his own mother to Joseph a possibility. If Joseph was not his own father, neither were these his brothers.

James the Zebedee was standing next to him, asking whether he would make the trip to Jerusalem for Atonement Day and the Sukkot Feast of Booths. The question was one of separation. Jesus saw the other disciples standing by the door, waiting for James. They were leaving.

"Go," Jesus told James. "I will not be coming to Jerusalem. Find my cousin John there. Perhaps he will help you understand the holiday and its prayers."

The way he saw it, just when he needed them, they were deserting him. He felt utterly betrayed. Did they not appreciate that without him, they had no hope of being accepted by their fellow Jews? More than that: they had little hope of entering God's Kingdom. Few teachers had the inclination or were endowed with the spiritual depth to open the gates to their kind!

Without him, who would offer them the ruach ha-kodesh, the holy spirit? Who would deem them worthy to learn the traditional meanings of Torah?

Outside, he saw his mother and with her, his brothers, if he could still call them that, waiting for him in their cart. His disciples were gone. Saying nothing, he climbed up, and they all set out for Kfar Nahum, where they would stay, I believe, at Jude's house before continuing the next morning to Jerusalem for the Day of Atonement.

That night, Jesus fell into a half sleep and had a dream or perhaps a vision, which he told me about as if relating an actual event.

He saw himself sitting with his disciples, teaching, when several Pietists appeared with a woman. She was being forcefully pulled by her arm and was standing before him against her will.

One of them said, "You say a man should not divorce his wife on grounds of suspicion, that we do so to be free from our wives, but what about one such as this? We have found her with another man, having intercourse. The law says we should stone her. What do you say?"

He tried not to look at her. Instead, he made marks with his finger in the dust of the ground.

One of the disciples said to the Pietists, "You see? He is giving you the answer. If you understand what he is writing, you will know."

"We know it is nonsense," the Pietist said. "You read it to us if it means something!"

When none could read it, a Pietist said, "Well, Master? This woman was caught in the very act of committing adultery. And Moses has ordered us in the Torah to condemn women like this to death by stoning. Are you afraid even to gaze upon her?"

As he looked up, Jesus could not make out the features of her face, and darkness surrounded her. From her bent frame, he sensed hers was the progeny of a broken Covenant spanning centuries, a crippled people waiting for their Creator.

Then he saw a face of many faces. It was no woman; it was his own brother Jude, and James, always showing that sadness, and the disciples. He saw their faces in hers.

The Pietists were waiting for his answer and as he turned toward them, they looked to be the guests at the wedding, and they were all in the Temple courtyards.

"Will you not condemn her?" one demanded.

Would they execute her and so themselves? he wondered. The Temple was now fortified against her by gates of exclusion, each nuance of the Torah made into bars of iron.

Then slowly, the darkness surrounding her lifted, and a parade of people behind her were all the same person. She was the prostitute, and she was the lame and blind and deaf. She was the leper, and she was the ritually impure. She was the one who did not share her food with God but collected taxes for the emperor, and she was the one who cheated and lied and stole.

"What will you say?" a Pietist asked.

In that moment, he knew she was Israel, the abandoned mother. In her eyes, he could see all those who were being exiled from God, waiting for the bridegroom of her youth, their Creator, to declare her innocence.

God's silence was the day's darkness. If God did not speak and forgive her, she would be forever lost in its lightless shroud. There would be no Kingdom.

When he looked about, to see what his accusers had decided, they were gone.

"Woman, where are they?" he asked. "Has no one condemned you?"

"No one, sir," she replied. And he understood her words to mean, "It is up to you."

Then he saw it was his mother, her expression sad, as it was on his thirteenth birthday when he asked why Joseph almost never came to visit them in Nazareth.

And just as he would have said, "I forgive you," he was startled by laughter. In the odd way of dreams, Jesus was awakened by the sound to discover it was his own.

"I was intending to forgive her, when I was the one who needed forgiveness," he told me. "What my mother had done was give me a father who I could feel within me, tempting me to be a god, as if I had the power to forgive sins against God.

"And still she stood there, waiting. But now, if I forgave her, I condemned myself by acting as one with divine authority to do so. So all I said was, 'I don't condemn you.' But she was gone, and I was awake."

It was in that state of mind that he determined to make the pilgrimage to Jerusalem and seek God's answer. He needed to know whether he was evil or good.

If you have ever been to Jerusalem during the festivals, you know how steep the climb is when you make your way up to God's house. The Temple mount was originally chosen by Solomon because it is defensible. Now we have Romans quartered everywhere and that has eroded even the memory of its purpose.

When he arrived at the foot of the mount, Jesus avoided meeting anybody he knew. He made his way upward, mixing in with the hundreds of pilgrims who slowly ascended the difficult slope.

Temptation on the Jerusalem Temple mount

About halfway, there is a place to rest. Those with infirmities and crippling handicaps often stop with their bedding near an outdoor bath named the Shepherds' Pool, built on a small plateau, where others, unafflicted, also may pause for a short while before pressing on.

I gathered from what he told me that as Atonement Day was soon to begin, transfixed gazes were on the calm and glassy pool, and none took special notice of him as he found a spot to rest.

Only when the surface changed, crenellated by what seemed the breeze from an angel's wing, did the sickly gathering surge forward, flopping down the stairs or sliding into the soothing cool water.

They were a familiar sight to him, waiting for God's presence to hover over the water as on the day of Creation, and form their lives anew, so they would be welcomed whole into the Kingdom.

Offspring of sin, these souls would be cleansed by the water's purifying touch. The satanic past, that father of torment, would be gone.

Was he one of them? His healing and teaching—were they signs of madness? Such was the doubt he felt as he beheld their misery.

The breezes that blew in that place were infrequent and short-lived, and only a minute would pass when the air was once again motionless. It was a strange sight. Those who were able to find a place for their mat near the edge were waiting, though the sun was blazing hot. Then the surface of the water seemed to ripple and come to life, and after managing to immerse their bodies, they finally dragged themselves out to test their bones for a miracle. God did not always answer their prayers, but all knew this was the year when the Kingdom could begin. And there were stories and rumors of cures and healings.

Forcing himself to continue on, Jesus ascended the full height of the Temple mount and stood at the outer edge of its great courtyard on the north side. It was a vantage point from which he could see far to the east, into Moab and Ammon, where the Nabateans had their kingdom.

But the image of the crippled and lame by the Shepherd's Pool remained with him.

"Could I be doing all these miracles of healing if Joseph isn't my father?" he wondered. "If some Roman soldier, or idol-worshipper, or a Hebrew who was himself married took my mother from Joseph . . ." No ridicule by Pietists matched the contempt he felt toward himself at that moment, having let his disciples think he was the chosen one and that they need only heed his teaching to be saved from their pasts, as if his was pure!

Taking a step closer to the edge, he lamented bitterly, "If I am so holy, it is impossible that I even die!"

He knew no angel would save him and that he would plummet to his death. Drawn forward by the dizzying height, the soil and sand gave way underfoot as he peered down, slipping, first slowly and then with nothing to stop him.

And this is what he said aloud, as I recall him telling me, word for word.

"I had always thought Joseph was my father. Now he is taken away. I had always thought that by the holy spirit You had made me one of Your sons. Now You are gone from me too."

But a voice, unexpected and tempting, said, "You can rule them all. There will be only a Torah of my spirit. I am your father."

As his feet were coming out from under him, he recognized the words were formed by the scraping noise of his sandals, become a voice of temptation, ugly and strange.

Then it was too late. He could no longer right himself.

Scoffing at his fate, he mocked himself bitterly, "If you are God's chosen one, don't be afraid. The rocks below will be as soft as loaves of bread."

About to plunge headlong down the precipice, Jesus knew he was utterly human. There would be just his broken body for them to find below.

At the point of falling, he saw the Siloam and Kidron brooks where they emerged from the Jordan, and even as small as he was, from that far, he could see John immersing a group of pilgrims on their way to the Atonement Day service.

"God, I do not want to die!" he cried out. "I ask forgiveness for my sin of acting as if I have your powers. Cast me not down this steep slope!"

Only then, he would tell me, a strong breeze pushed him back and gave him the support to again stand safely on firm ground.

Jesus' baptism by John

Immediately he found a descending path, and half stumbled, half ran down the Temple mount. Against the throng of pilgrims making their way up, he managed to keep on until he neared the narrow watercourse where John was talking to several men. From their tone and attitudes, they were apparently Levites from the Temple administration.

"I am not the messiah," he heard John say, answering a question.

"Then who are you?" one of them asked. "Do you think you are the prophet Elijah?"

"I am not," he answered.

"But why are you immersing people?" a third one persisted.

Seeing a family start making their way across the shallow, rock-studded water, John called to them, "Akov, akov!"—an answer, if the officials could understand Isaiah's prophesy, that was, "The crooked shall be made straight," referring to the sullied lineages of the northern pilgrims.

As he turned to wade toward them, he said to his interrogators, "Do not presume to say to yourself that we, unlike them, have Abraham for our father." And pointing to the rocks, he added, "For I tell you, God is able to raise up children of Abraham from these stones!"

It was just as the officials turned to go, remarking that they need not pay attention to this madman, that John noticed Jesus standing there.

He was not prepared for what he beheld. John could see that the denunciations of him as an emissary of darkness had found their mark. The one who had taught others to hold no grudges, cancel all debt, and even forgive enemies appeared too weary to step toward his open arms to embrace him.

As Jesus took several tentative strides, intending to be immersed by him, John said, "You should be the one immersing me."

"Just do what is right," Jesus replied.

Feeling John's hands on his shoulders and then on the top of his head, he slowly lowered himself under the water and, once fully beneath the surface, thanked God for saving him.

The first word he heard as he rose was John's greeting—"Dodi, my dear cousin"—accompanied by his affectionate embrace.

Recalling that moment, Jesus later told me it was as if God had spoken, for the word was echoed by passing pilgrims singing the Song of Songs as they climbed upward. Dodi Li, my beloved. My dove that is in the clefts of the rock in the covert of the cliff, let me see thy countenance, let me hear thy voice. Dodi, John's greeting, had glided toward him and seemed to rest on his shoulder, gently with his touch.

CHAPTER FOURTEEN

Matthias had fallen asleep without an afternoon meal and awakened when the shadows were already pointing south. Rising quickly from the bed, as if he had to be somewhere, though he did not, he put several round pittot bread loaves over the coals to warm them. Poking at the charred embers of wood, he saw there was not enough fire for soup and added small branches of dried cedar. As he took the flint fire-striker and began sparking the kindling, there was a loud knock at the door.

The visitors were the widow who always inquired of him and a man.

"Good afternoon," she said. "Are we interrupting?"

Indicating with a gesture they should make themselves comfortable on the pillowed bench, he replied, "I was just putting on some soup. Please have some."

"Thank you," she said. "You go ahead. This is my brother. I have told him about you."

"A pleasure to meet you," Matthias replied.

"Yehonatan," the man said, nodding politely.

"I hope you have been kind in what you told your brother about me," Matthias said. "And if you would like some," he again offered, it will be ready in a moment. There is ample."

"We ate at the normal hour," the woman replied. "But don't let us disturb you. My brother has a question for you, if it would be all right."

He searched his memory for her name, as he was unable to recall it. "I have no way of knowing why I should be able to help. But what is on your mind?"

"My sister says even Gamliel listens to your opinions."

"Gamliel listens to all opinions. That is how he became wise."

"My problem is this," her brother began. "Three years ago I had more than enough money for my own needs. My youngest brother, a tanner, is a cripple. That year, his health was especially poor, and he could not work, so he could not afford to pay for skins. He needed money to live, until he would feel stronger. I wanted to help him.

"The third brother of us three owned a house. He is hardworking, and he too wanted to help our afflicted brother, so he sold me his house and took only a small part of the money for himself. The rest he spent on paying a tanner to do what my other brother could not. His investment went well enough for the leather to eventually be sold to a sandlar. Now our afflicted brother has enough to eat and is prepared for the next season. And my brother who sold me his house is working hard, as usual . . ."

"But?" Matthias inquired. He put a ladle in the bronze pot, took a taste, and added a handful of coriander.

"But he wants his house back."

"You have finished paying for it, is that right?"

"Yes, and even if I was willing to return it to him, he doesn't have my money to pay me what I gave him for it."

"Money that went to your crippled brother."

The widow interrupted, "Matthias, Yehonatan has let Hezzie live in the house. And he gave him a very fair price."

146

"I'm sure," said Matthias.

"I told you," she said to her brother. "He understands these things."

"Yehudit, please let me tell him," her brother scolded mildly.

"Yehudit may have too high an opinion of me," Matthias responded, pleased to have seemed to know her name. "So why are you seeking my advice?" he asked, sitting down to eat. "You think what you think."

"Because Hezzie, my brother, has petitioned the Sanhedrin for a hearing. And I want to know what his chances are."

"Three years ago? As the seventh was just beginning?"

"Yes."

"He will have his house back," Matthias said. "You may not use your brother's inability to repay as a reason to keep his house. He asked for it back within a year of the transfer. The Torah is clear that within a year, an individual who sells his house may ask for it back. Even though you paid him for the house, his debt to you, the amount you gave him, is fully canceled by the law of the seventh year. If one day he is able to return the money, perhaps he will. But you may not demand it from him or damage his name by telling that he has committed a wrong. So tell me . . . how is your brother, the tanner, doing?"

"Fine. He is doing better," Yehonatan said, his flat tone hardly concealing his disappointment.

"You fulfilled a commandment to have helped him. It will come back to you."

"Thank you for your opinion," Yehonatan said, standing and turning to go.

"We should let you finish your meal in peace," Yehudit agreed. "Have a good new year." Matthias opened the door and saw them out, wishing them blessings for the coming season.

"I may have other blessings but not the house," the brother remarked. "That will not be mine."

"Haver, my friend," responded Matthias, "it never was."

After the door closed behind them, the silence that followed allowed his thoughts to attend a different issue.

He still had to put some things together for the trip before another hour passed.

CHAPTER FIFTEEN

*A*s they neared Jerusalem's Sanhedrin square, Matthias thanked James for the ride. "This will be fine, my friend. I will walk the rest of the way."

Gripping the reins tightly, James had a gloomy awareness that he would once again be forced to tolerate Simon's claim that his brother was speaking to him from heaven. Given their ignorance, Andrew, Thomas, and the Zebedees would prostrate themselves before his false god. Even Thaddeus might succumb, and there was no telling about Matthew and Philip.

Instead of immediately entering the Center, James made his way up the Temple mount, where he would seek Gamliel's advice.

Skirting the outer side of the southern wall, he peered down the ridges of rock and grass toward the Salt Sea, visible in the distance.

After turning the corner and reaching the eastern side, James found himself standing behind a curtain of long white tunics. As the sonorous voice drew him forward, several elders, stroking gray beards, made room for him to pass.

The sage was reciting Torah law. "On this day, atonement shall be made for you to cleanse you of all your sins. You shall be pure before the Lord. It is a law for all time."

After a brief pause, he offered his commentary. "And this evening at sundown we will begin our fast," he said. "But is it important to fast? What if the fast hides our sin behind false piety? Therefore, God told Isaiah, 'They ask Me why when we fasted, did You not see and bless us?' And Isaiah heard God's word: 'Is the day of fasting I desire meant for men to starve their bodies, bowing your head and wearing sackcloth and ashes? No. This is the fast I desire. Let the oppressed go free. Share your bread with the hungry. Take the poor into your home. When you see the naked, clothe him. And do not ignore your own family. Then shall your light burst through like the dawn. Then when you call, the Lord will answer. He will say, Here I am. And you shall be like a watered garden, a spring whose waters do not fail.'"

"Do those who worship a false god, have reason to hope?" James heard his own voice almost as though someone else were speaking.

"Come forward," Gamliel said, "So I may see you."

James was quickly given a corridor through the several of those gathered just ahead.

"James? Well, I thought I recognized your voice," Gamliel said.

"Shannah tovah," James said.

"A good year to you, my friend." Gamliel replied. "Tell me again what you want to understand."

"Some of those who studied with my brother are marred by ignorance, knowing little Torah, and I am afraid they are exalting his memory, making him a false god."

"You must teach them about Jonah," Gamliel said. "His story is about them."

"And what shall I say?"

"From what you are telling me, those so devoted to your brother when he was alive have given up on his teaching, changing Torah's message to exalt themselves. When that happens, they are like others who have lost faith in Adonai and made a false god who will listen to their prayers. Jonah did not want God to give the people of Nineveh a second chance when they, like your brother's circle, turned toward

150

idolatry. And what were those people like? They were ignorant. Worse still, they were living lives of greed and hate. But God commanded they be given hope—a second chance. On our Atonement Day, God has given us that same message to deliver: We are all His creation. This includes the ones who are ignorant of Torah, even doubtful Hebrews who worship false gods. They too can return. There is hope for all of us."

"But I am afraid—"

"James, return to the others. Tell your brother's disciples his teachings live on in the Torah, as does the spirit of all its teachers."

"Rav todot—many thanks. I will try," James said.

"I wish you peace," Gamliel replied.

As James nodded respectfully, he felt a tug on his sleeve.

"I'm glad to have found you," Bartholomew whispered, somewhat out of breath from the climb. "Simon is claiming he has seen Jesus. And he is about to present witnesses who say the same."

James preceded Bartholomew down the slope, their pace quickening. Finally, they reached the door and pushed it open. Inside, there was a general buzz as the disciples whispered excitedly to one another.

"You don't know what has happened, eh James?" Simon said, as if James never was part of the group. "Well, how could you? You have just arrived. But we're about to have a meeting. Tell the Marys to join us. Even you will be amazed."

After leading the way, as the others heeded his summons to gather on the upper floor, Simon took his customary place at the front of the room and addressed them.

"Brothers and sisters," he declared, "several of you have already heard me talking downstairs, but here are the details. I have the news we have all been waiting for! As most of you know, I went to the

Galilee several days ago to see members of my family and yes, to do some fishing! I expect that later we shall enjoy some of the catch, since there is plenty. I was with Thomas and the Zebedees, and there was a man on the shore yelling his advice to us in the boat about where to cast our net. We couldn't believe what happened. When we pulled it in, there were so many fish, we thought the net would tear. After rowing back, we saw the man was standing next to a charcoal fire, obviously pleased we had enough to share. Thomas? You tell the rest," Simon said.

"I had doubt it could be him," Thomas said. "But when Simon said it was Jesus, I asked the man if he was a ghost. And to prove he wasn't, he asked me to touch him. 'You can see I'm no ghost,' he told me. 'I have flesh and bones.'"

"By then," Simon interrupted, "we had put fish on the flames, and the next thing, he stood near to the fire and said . . . well, go ahead, Thomas; finish it."

"That's when he said, 'May I have something to eat?'"

Upon hearing this news, several exchanged words of glee, even grasping and hugging each other.

"And?" asked Simon loudly, intending everybody to pay close attention to what followed.

"And then," said Thomas, "he took a piece of the grilled fish and ate with us."

"Well?" Simon asked the gathering, "Isn't this what some of us needed? Of course there has been doubt. We mustn't blame ourselves for that. But let the Zebedees say what they saw. James and John, please come forward so we may hear."

"I confess until I beheld Jesus in the flesh, alive, as he was before his crucifixion," John the Zebedee said, "I too wondered whether his body had truly ascended to heaven. But I touched him, and he was real."

"I touched him too," James the Zebedee confirmed.

"Do any of you have anything to ask us?" Simon inquired.

"Did he say he was Jesus?" James bar Alpheus called out.

"No. But I know it was," John said.

"I am sure it was Jesus!" Thomas declared.

Just then, Mary, the widowed mother of James bar Alpheus, who was now the wife of Cleopas, came through the door, speaking rapidly. Having herself become a devotee of Jesus, owing to her son's encouragement, she had been helping with the preparations for the meal but departed suddenly after Simon's news.

"Cleopas is coming," she said. "He has something important to tell all of you."

Hardly had she finished her few words before her husband's footsteps were heard on the stairs. "I am sorry to disturb your meeting," he said as he entered. "Until now, I have been afraid to say what happened. I thought maybe I was crazy. But Mary has told me what happened to you, Simon. You will want to know—I had dinner with Jesus only days after he died."

Stunned by the news, there was gasping and open-mouthed expressions of amazement as he continued in excited tones, saying he had been walking on the road to Emmaus, just outside the Jerusalem city limit, when Jesus came up to him and walked at his side.

With all gazing, transfixed and fallen silent to hear every detail, only James bar Alpheus displayed obvious displeasure at his stepfather's appearance, loudly grinding his teeth and looking like a cow chewing its cud.

"I thought he was an ordinary man," he began again. "I didn't recognize him. And he talked about our sacred books, especially the prophets. The more he talked, the more I realized he was referring to himself, that he was about to usher in God's Kingdom. Then I went to eat, and he joined me. As we broke bread, I thought to myself, what the angels told my wife is true! This must be Jesus. Mary, my wife,"—he pointed at her—"told me that she had a vision of angels who revealed that Jesus was still alive. And that's how I realized it was Jesus!"

"Blessed be his name," Simon said. "And blessed be those who have seen him as well as those who have faith, even though they have not. Matthias will certainly want to record these holy events, don't you think, James?"

"I trust he will put them down as they are told to him," James replied. "And you are Cleopas," James said, turning in his direction. "Mary, you bring him so rarely. It is good to see you. But tell us, Cleopas, if he still showed the pain he had on the cross or if he was in good health, as we always knew him?"

"I didn't notice any pain. Maybe he seemed a little tired. But we walked a long way, and I was tired too. I can't say if he looked as he usually did because I was never fortunate enough to have met him. Not when he was alive."

"Well, thank you for sharing this good news," James said. "It is no minor matter to hear such things. And what testimony, Thomas! That you and several others were with him on the lakeshore. It is hard to imagine."

"Now we can believe he is with us and have no more question about it," Thomas responded, pleased his word seemed to matter.

"And I understand you immediately recognized him and while eating fish together must certainly have talked about everything that had happened," James persisted. "It was like old times."

"It was," Simon said, staring at James. Could Andrew have been right, he wondered. Jesus' brother was no ordinary adversary. His eyes were red with blood. And his hoarse voice sounded almost boyish and sing-song.

"And you, John?" James asked. "Was it like old times?"

Both Zebedees nodded but sensed the question was more an expression of disapproval that they would make up a story like this one.

"But Cleopas, may I ask you another question? Was his beard as it always was?"

"His . . . his . . . beard?" Cleopas stammered. "I don't know. I never saw him before that day."

"What kind of question is that?" Simon demanded.

Ignoring him, James prodded Cleopas, "But was it nearly as long as yours?"

"Yes. I think it was. And it was a much fuller beard. Like that of a prophet."

When the room was silent, James knew he had made his point. Jesus had only a very modest beard.

Taking his measure, Simon inquired, "But tell us, James, whether your efforts to raise funds were successful today. We will require a full treasury for spreading the news that Jesus is alive."

"I have brought words of inspiration, the true wealth of our group. I wish to have you hear my brother's voice."

"As we do," Simon said uneasily, still doubting Andrew could be right. But if James had a demon, they would need to expel him from their midst. Disguising his thoughts, Simon lauded, "And isn't that what we've been saying? He's communicating with us in messages only the worthy can hear." Feigning shared belief, he added, "If you have instruction from Jesus, we are all ears. But I'm sure you won't take too long."

Dismissing the rude request that he be brief, James followed Gamliel's advice, saying, "These are some of Jesus' lessons concerning the Day of Atonement. As you know, it is a day when we come before our God, Adonai, and ask forgiveness for our sins. But do not think that is how we achieve repentance. We must fulfill his commandments, caring for the poor and needy, the widow and the orphan, seeing to the well-being of the unfortunate, and correcting our wrongs."

"Well then, thank you, James," Simon interjected.

"Do you remember my brother's teaching?" James inquired of the disciples, ignoring the interruption. "Your tongue is one of the smallest organs in the body, but it may spark a fire that spreads. Remember how they spread rumors that Jesus twisted Torah law? But that wasn't true. Will you now believe what his enemies said about him? I hope not. He told you to obey the Torah and love your neighbor as yourself. Then the Torah will give you a rich life. You are servants of the Torah's laws, not its masters. But if you are servants of the Law, and God is the ruler and master of the Law, how will you be the master of other men? Do you think God will forgive you for playing ruler over others? There is only one Lawgiver, and He is the only judge and has the power to acquit or to sentence."

"Wonderful even to hear so faint an echo of your brother's voice," Simon said curtly, catching sight of Andrew, who was nodding to him as a sign the demon was speaking. "Of course," Simon added, "dispensing with its provisions, we disciples are moving into the Kingdom much as one steps on a stone crossing a brook. Those who take longer will be welcome when they finally see the eternal glory that awaits them. But really, I imagine we are all smelling the aroma of our meal. Shall we let them know we are ready?"

As if he had not heard him, James went on, "Some of you may think of selecting from the commandments this one or that one that suits your circumstances. But if you keep a law, such as giving charity, and break others, such as adultery, do you think you will be forgiven? No. You see, if a man keeps some commandments but violates others, it is as if he has disavowed the entire Torah. Is it for you to decide which of God's laws to keep and which not to keep? If you do this, you claim to be the judge of the Torah. Rather, behave as though you are to be judged by its laws. And take advice from those of us who knew Jesus best."

"Thank you," Simon said, exhibiting pronounced indifference, even while Andrew was now raising his eyebrows and jutting his chin in short, sharp thrusts toward James, beckoning his brother to appreciate the satanic threat in their midst. "Now that James has brought his talk to a close—" Simon adumbrated, only to be further interrupted.

"There is more."

"Not too much more, I hope," Simon insisted, pursing his lips.

"A final matter requires comment," James said, his voice gravelly and hoarse.

"I share the confusion about my brother's murder. If he was close to God and filled with the holy spirit, how did our Creator permit him to suffer and die so vile a death? If God did not forgive my brother and saw fit to punish him, is there any hope for us whose sins must be far greater than those of Jesus? One day, I hope God will reveal the reason he died as he did. Still, among us are those who pretend to have the answer. They say he did not die. His tomb was empty after the crucifixion, and his presence supposedly has reached some of us through the holy spirit or, even now, in person. But I say, if you want to bring my brother to life, do it by accepting the laws of Torah and bring hope to all people: Hebrews and gentiles and to Hebrews of an uncertain past, like some of us here today. If you have begun to believe Jesus is a god, remember God loves you, and you can repent having made him a false god. Remember how God punished Jonah because the prophet wanted Nineveh's idol worshippers to be destroyed. But God saved them, as he will all of us. On the Day of Atonement, you need only ask for a second chance and, as Jesus taught, give a second chance to others. Then your light will burst free, and you will be as a watered garden."

Refusing to even look in James' direction, because doing so might be taken for acknowledgment that what he said had merit, Simon said testily, "The light of his teaching will burst free as long as it is not kept under a bushel. That is why we are all depending on you to find resources to support our work." Then, to quickly blunt the point of James' last words, he added, "But one thing you should all understand about Jonah. Wasn't he in the belly of that giant fish for three days? He was. Jesus too was in the tomb three days. He was placed in the tomb on Friday, and our sisters, as well as Matthias and I, found it empty on Sunday. Just like Jonah, so too has Jesus risen and is a sign to this and future generations."

Having taken a seat, James again rose. "My brother prayed we be spared. He was not like Jonah, who wished the idolators of Nineveh to be destroyed."

Simon seemed pleased. "Our lord's brother is right!" he declared, addressing the others. "Jesus was far greater than Jonah!"

With these words, discussion of serious matters was concluded, and the mouthfuls of food being served provided an excellent excuse for the silence that had descended on the group.

Preparing for the fast, the fresh-killed partridges were not salted as usual, an omission intended to lessen thirst. They were served with delicious large legumes, slightly sweet but perfectly offset by a sparse amount of rue.

When James finished his portion ahead of the others, having refrained from overeating, as there was another meal to follow at his father's, he expressed his appreciation for the fine fare to Martha and Thaddeus, the cooks, and rose to leave.

"You may recall I stop in to see my father today," he explained.

Undeterred from expressing his suspicion, Andrew had reached Simon's side by the serving table and quietly urged him to notice James' suspicious-sounding elocution. "If I'm right," he whispered, "it's trying to possess the rest of us with its ideas. But just look at its eyes!"

"Keep still," Simon cautioned.

"Of course," Andrew answered, thinking he grasped the reason. The likely outcome, were he to expose James' demon, would be to advance its purpose. The other disciples might believe he and Simon were both mad to even hint such a thing. Then, the others could unite in support of James, saying Jesus was a false god, and they should all observe every Torah law—probably its very intention—thereby falling into Satan's trap. "But did you notice his eyes?" Andrew insisted. "A match for his voice, for sure! They're turned red with blood."

Curiosity as much as suspicion got the better of Simon, and he made his way across the room, just as James reached the door. "Be sure to wish your father a good fast," he said, concealing his purpose.

"I will," James responded, his words barely audible. His reddened eyes, just for a moment, made Simon's skin crawl.

"What's that?" Simon asked.

"Sorry. You probably noticed I can barely talk," James replied, rubbing his eyes deeply with his knuckles and added, "It's the damned thistles. When their flowers turn pink in this season, so do my eyes. And my voice goes too."

Studying James' face, feigning interest more typical of a physician, Simon finally declared loudly, intending Andrew to hear, "Thaddeus makes delicious soup. It's a sure cure for what's possessing you."

A few minutes later, intoning a final "amen" to their blessings over the food just finished, Simon looked at Andrew with a twisted smile. As so often, his younger brother had again played the fool in a misguided effort to support him against James. Impervious, Andrew smiled back, taking it for a sign of gratitude.

***

After the door closed behind James, Simon addressed the gathering. "But my dear friends," he intoned, "here is truly important news."

"About our lord?" Andrew trumpeted, not suppressing his admiration.

"Indeed. What I am about to convey is so earthshaking that I already have sent an epistle to Paul for his dissemination. I am happy to finally know why Jesus suffered as he did. Like you, my faith wavered—and I waited for him to tell me, and now he has. He has told me to recall his words the night of his arrest and then we shall have our answer. Did he not tell the Temple police, 'If I am the one you are looking for, let these others go'?"

"I remember those words," said Andrew.

"I do too," said Thomas.

"Who will ever forget them?" chimed in Matthew, joined by others.

"And on the morrow, will not the high priest send to its death a sacrificial goat carrying the sins of the people, a goat that will perish

160

so none of us need suffer for what we have done in our lives? Do you not see that Jesus was telling us he would die in our place and asked God that our suffering be his instead!"

"You think Jesus was like some goat?" Simon C'nani bellowed, making no effort to restrain his anger.

"No, of course not," Simon replied. "Jesus was kind and compassionate and was more like a gentle lamb, befitting his sacrifice during our Passover. Matthias, who was with us in the garden when they came for him, will record his words, 'Since I am the one you are looking for, let these others go!' Then, when Jesus was dragged before the high priest, didn't Caiaphas show even he understood, saying, 'It is best that one man die instead of all the people'? In the days of mourning that followed Jesus' crucifixion, Matthias told us that is what the high priest said."

"He said that," Thaddeus agreed. "According to Matthias, Caiaphas thought Jesus' execution would satisfy his enemies, saving the rest of us."

"And thanks to Jesus we are alive!" John the Zebedee's falsetto praise rang in their ears and caused several to turn toward him. "It's true!" he added. "He died to save us!"

As their murmurs subsided, Thomas rose to speak. "Peter," he said, "should we still ask God's forgiveness for our sins or, because he died for us, are we already forgiven?"

Matthew answered before Simon had a chance. "Jesus said to forgive others or you will not be forgiven. Therefore, you should take your oath before God that you will do that, and then God may forgive you!"

"How is it possible?" Thomas persisted. "To them, we aren't even pure Hebrews. And our souls are stained by sins we don't even know about. You think they want us standing alongside them praying?"

"It will be a long time before they think we are Jews like them," James bar Alpheus added.

"But it's not up to them," Philip said, meaning it was up to God.

"That's true!" Simon admonished, his harsh tone taking them by surprise. "We have been freed from the earthly bond and already are in the Kingdom, revealed to us through his messages from heaven."

"What are you suggesting, Peter?" Andrew asked.

"Just this: are we so desperate for the approval of these hypocrites that we should plead with them to accept us? Shall we fast and be mournful as if our lives are still stained by sinful origins? Or are we ready to accept our own royalty as Jesus' elect? I say, do not fast! Do not wear sad faces! Anoint your own heads and be earthly rulers, receiving Jesus' word and spreading it to all who are worthy!"

"Even John's followers fast," Simon C'nani called out.

"Are we John's followers? If you must fast because you feel Jesus' loss," Simon declared, "then let that be your reason. Do not fast as others do. They think if they are forgiven their sins, God will send his chosen one. But we know Jesus is the one God sent, and though gone from this realm, he is alive."

"Amen, amen," several proclaimed loudly.

"Brothers and sisters," Simon responded, raising a hand to request silence, "if you know the good news about Jesus being alive in heaven, teaching us, and appearing to some among us, why should you be sad, unless you don't believe it?"

Saying this, he cast a sharp glance at Bartholomew, as he suspected Bartholomew's moody silence indicated disapproval. "And why should we give the priests a role in our forgiveness? The priests are still led by Caiaphas, who handed over Jesus to be crucified. Do you want them to be your spokesmen to God? We should be our own priests! I say, if we must confess sin, then let it be to each other!"

"Jesus did not forgive sin," Philip asserted. "He only believed that God would."

"Is there a difference? How many men who walk this earth can speak for God?" Simon declared, turning to the others for approval. "This is why everybody must hear the word of God's true son, just as we are telling it!"

"Ye'hee ritzon l'phanav. May it be according to His will," Matthew answered, in the words of the traditional prayer, drawing the discussion to a close.

CHAPTER SIXTEEN

With the sun overhead, the trees formed short shadows along the fields of pale-brown scrub, lengthening only slightly by the time he reached his father's house.

Even before he had turned in from the road, Elizabeth was waving and calling to the others, "James is here!"

Bringing the cart to rest just behind another, he dismounted and embraced his aunt.

"Happy holiday," she said, hugging him tightly. "Don't look so surprised to see me. It's the new year, isn't it?"

"And to you! Everything smells delicious."

The air in front of the outdoor beehive-shaped clay oven shimmered with waves of heat, and an outdoor table had been set for the afternoon feast.

"Stewed meat and wonderful prunes! But I hope you're not too hungry. It will be a while."

"I can wait," James replied, having little appetite left to eat a second time. "Shalom, Jude!" James greeted his brother, as he emerged from the house. "Where is Abba?"

"Alive," came Joseph's familiar voice as he emerged from the house with James' sister.

"Come give me a hug!" she exclaimed.

"This is what's good!" he said, wrapping his arms around her and his other sister together, as she too kissed his cheek affectionately. "But where are the others?"

"Not Simon but Yossi will be here later, I hope," Joseph replied. "Are you ready?" He had been waiting so they might go together to the City of the Dead. "Shall we?" his father asked, walking over to the cart.

"Of course. Here, let me give you a hand."

Leaning heavily on James' forearm, Joseph climbed aboard. "But what about you, Elizabeth? Won't you join us?"

"Not this time. Somebody has to keep an eye on the oven. Maybe after the Feast of Booths."

Jude climbed the rear iron step, shut and hooked the back panel, and took a seat on the side bench. Seeing he was ready, James turned the horse's head toward the road and clicking his tongue, called, "Sah! Go!"

Before long they approached the gate of the necropolis.

Its tomb entrances were almost invisible. A casual passerby might not even notice the thistle-covered mounds with hewn-out doorways, each leading down carved stone steps.

Near the entrances, large terracotta pots filled with neft fuel were aflame.

As they approached theirs, other visitors emerged from one tomb, and James could see several had been crying. Joseph greeted a woman he recognized as a neighbor, and she nodded with a sad smile.

Coming finally to their own, Joseph reached into his shoulder purse and retrieved several clay lamps. Handing one to James, he then located a jar of oil, advising Jude, "Just light it from this."

The cork came open easily, and after Jude poured a small amount into the lamp, James kindled the wick from the nearby neft pot.

Careful not to slip, they descended slowly into the cool, dark chamber to a niche with a small, ornate limestone ossuary that contained the bones of the deceased. Inscribed on it was the name "Hannah." She was Mary's mother. Another ossuary, just to the side, was inscribed "Yoakim," Mary's father.

In uncharacteristic fashion, Joseph squeezed James' hand. "Take care of her, James. When I'm gone, please make sure she has what she needs."

"Who, Abba?" James asked, wondering how he might take care of somebody already dead.

"You know who I mean. Mary," Joseph replied, placing the lamp on the flat top of her parents' ossuary.

His father's concern for Jesus' mother—despite only rare references to her all these years . . .

Not taking notice of James' furrowed brow, Joseph then instructed Jude, "Light the next one so we can see where we are going."

Leading the way, Joseph located a somewhat larger bone container, one with the name "Shulamit" carved near the marble molding along its upper edge. Beautiful, finely sculpted rosettes decorated its sides.

This time Joseph asked James for three of the lamps from his purse. Little was said as he kindled one after the other, placing them atop the fine white-stone lid.

As he prayed aloud, extolling God, he was joined by James and Jude chanting the traditional words taken from Ezekiel and Daniel. "For all eternity I will be holy to you, and I will make myself known to all the nations, Adonai proclaimed."

Upon finishing the sanctification, Joseph took the jar of oil and told his sons to pray silently for their mother. He would go into the dark alcove just ahead and leave lamps for his parents, as well as Elizabeth's husband, Zechariah, whose ossuaries were there. Then, bending down to avoid hitting his head, he disappeared into the dark recess.

Meanwhile, after completing a private meditation, James waited for Jude to open his eyes.

"Jude?"

"Yes."

"Do you remember her?"

"Of course!"

"I was only three. I remember her holding me and singing while she bathed me," James said. "It's the only memory I have."

"She was like a queen."

"That's what Abba says."

"So. That's what she was like," Jude told him. "If you ate too quickly, she would tell you. And she worried we swam too far out in the sea."

James saw his brother was searching for his memories, trying to see her as she had been.

Sparing him a return to that day, when as a nine-year-old, his mother was forever gone, James said, "Here he is."

Joseph's flickering lamp illuminated the arched opening and upon making his way out, he brushed the white limestone powder off his tunic where it had rubbed against the wall and returned to their side.

James was stunned by the sight of tears pouring down his father's face. "Abba? Are you all right?" he asked.

"He's fine!" Jude snapped. "It's a grave, isn't it?"

"Come," Joseph said. "Let us return to the house."

The horse tugged the cart gently over the road's bumps and furrows, and Joseph groaned, causing James concern.

"Abba?"

His father's lips were moving silently, and he seemed to be talking to himself, but as the horse reached the entrance path, James saw the breeze had dried his tears and so held his peace.

Pleased that Yossi was there helping the four women, Joseph announced, "The boys and I will take a mikveh bath and be ready in a few minutes."

Afforded the privacy of the fence behind the house, he would enter first, stripping off his clothing and immersing himself in the cool water filled continuously by a nearby brook. When he emerged, Jude followed, and then Yossi. James had brought their satchel of white tunics from the back of the cart, and Elizabeth handed him Joseph's.

Once seated at the dining table, having thanked God for creating grain and wine, Joseph said to Jude, "Well, give me an answer to this riddle. Once we purify ourselves with atonement, how is it we may even suffer more demons than before?"

"I don't know," Jude answered. "Ask James. He'll have an answer."

"Not really," James said.

"None of you?" Joseph asked. "Yossi or my daughters? Elizabeth?" Receiving only quizzical glances, he continued, "You know how there are crazy people who come to the Temple. Their families bring them. It was at the end of the Atonement Day service, nearly twenty years ago, just after Tiberius became emperor . . . somebody was screaming and carrying on, just as crazy as before. So he asked me why God hadn't chased away his demon."

"Who, Abba?" Jude asked, chewing a large mouthful of meat.

"So I told him the soul is like a house," Joseph continued, refusing to be interrupted. "On the Day of Atonement, we sweep it clean. But then the house is empty . . ."

For a short while, the only sound was the scraping of plates, as the riddle awaited a solution.

"Other demons would find the house nice and clean and want to move in!" Joseph suddenly exclaimed, laughing loudly. "He actually said that. How he could make me laugh! Of course, I couldn't let him think praying caused demons to possess you. He'd never pray again! So I tried to defend God. But I didn't know then and I still don't know why God seems to punish some people. I still don't know . . ."

"Matthias hopes to see you soon," James said, trying to free his father from the apparent reverie that gripped him.

"He loved Torah, didn't he, James? Reciting the commandments at twelve. Give to the one who begs, and if he does not repay you, do not ask. If someone needs your tunic, give him not only your tunic but your coat too . . . and the rabbis said such wonderful things about him."

"Joseph!" Elizabeth hollered sharply, as one might awaken a sleeping person.

Snapping out of his dreamlike state, Joseph wiped his mouth on a cloth, insisting they should finish the meal so they would not be late.

When they were done, after James helped his sisters onto Joseph's cart where they found seats next to their father, he returned to his own, taking the reins to lead the way. Jude, who sat alongside, looked back every so often, but said nothing. When they'd been underway for a half hour and were making their slow ascent up the hilly approach to the city, James turned to his brother, probing his thoughts. "What's got you so quiet?"

"Nothing," he replied irritably.

"I think Elizabeth is worried about him," James observed.

"He's always like that after a cup of wine," Jude said. "It's nothing new."

After pulling his cart off the road as close to the Temple as permitted, James turned to see his father just rounding the bend.

Upon securing the horses near grassy patches, they made their way together amid throngs of worshippers, finally reaching the two southern stairways with large open gates above. The steps of one were much wider than the other and had been especially designed to enable pilgrims, carrying their Passover lambs, to exit without bumping into each other. Often used on the Day of Atonement by Pietists and the wealthy as an entrance to avoid contact with less-observant pilgrims, James recalled a time he was with Jesus. As they were about to ascend the steps together, Jesus said, "Let's enter through the narrow gate. The wide gate is the one rich people enter. It's easier for a camel to pass through the eye of a needle than it will be for a man who thinks only about riches to enter the Kingdom of God."

Finally, they were in the main courtyard facing the sanctuary, and several members of the Sanhedrin, making their way toward their reserved area, stopped to greet Joseph.

"We miss you," one said. "Maybe you should come back."

"Happy new year," Joseph replied. "It's good to see you, as always."

James smiled at them, unsure whether they had any idea that he was Joseph's son. Just then, he noticed one of the women he had seen earlier at the cemetery. She paused before making her way to the balustrade and watched the Sanhedrin members paying their respects to Joseph.

"Who is he?" the man with her asked. "He must be very important."

"He is the one we met earlier. He is the man from the cemetery," she replied. Then she added impatiently, "Ba'ali, husband, don't you recognize him?"

Making her way toward them, guiding her husband forward by his sleeve, she introduced herself. "We are your neighbors," she said to Joseph, completely unaware of James.

"Happy new year," he responded politely. "Yes, I think we have seen each other."

"I forget your name," she said.

"Joseph, and this is my son James."

"Have a healthy fast. May you all be inscribed for a good year," she said, nodding also to the several Sanhedrin members she had just interrupted.

"To you as well," Joseph answered.

After she took a few steps away, they all heard her say, "He is Joseph. You remember. We see him at Arimathea, the cemetery."

"He was at Ir ha-mayteem?" her husband asked, embarrassed the others had overheard her vulgar pronunciation of the necropolis' name.

"Of course," she said. "He is very important."

CHAPTER SEVENTEEN

*W*hen three stars appeared overhead and the crescent moon was fully visible, the gathering of worshippers waited in hushed anticipation. Levites had taken their places on the fifteen semicircular steps leading to the forward area of the sacred Priests' Court, and a singer chanted the words of the prophet Joel, which commenced the Day of Atonement.

"Turn back to me with fasting, weeping, and lamenting. Rend your hearts, turn back to the Lord your God, for He is gracious and compassionate, slow to anger, abounding in kindness, and renouncing punishment. See a time is coming when I will pour out My spirit on all flesh. Your sons and daughters shall prophesy. Your old men shall dream dreams, and your young men shall see visions. Blow a horn in Zion, gather the people, proclaim a fast. For on this day, atonement shall be made to cleanse all your sins. You shall be pure before the Lord."

Then two silver trumpets sounded, a prelude to the prophet's words of hope. A mood of contemplation imbued every heart as Joel's ancient message heralded the coming Kingdom and the anticipation of a renewed Covenant. God would keep His vow to provide for His bridal People. No longer would the ash of drought darken her fields.

As Levites sang, the assembly swayed gently to the words.

"The ground must mourn. For the new grain is ravaged, the new wine is dried up. Watercourses are dust. Farmers are dismayed and weep over wheat and barley. To you, Lord, I call."

Other Levites, to the far side of the stairs, responded, "A time is coming says God when I will sow the House of Judah and the House of Israel with the seed of b'nai Yisrael, the descendants of Jacob. Then you shall be like a garden watered by an eternal spring. I dwell in holiness with the contrite and lowly in spirit. I will not be angry forever. No, I who make spirits fall also create the breath of life. I will heal them. I will forgive them."

Looking about to see whether any of the disciples were there, James spotted Thaddeus and James bar Alpheus. Bartholomew was with them. Then he noticed Matthew too. Searching the crowd, however, he could not see Simon or the others.

Among the large number of worshippers, James noticed, were some deformed by age and illness. Almost certainly, there were also tax collectors who raised money for the Roman occupation. On this day, as his father had taught him, none might turn away those who entered the Temple to pray. But when his brother had taught that very same message concerning the coming Kingdom of God, he was killed.

Swaying slightly back and forth, James closed his eyes. *Why God?* he wondered. *The one whose voice was passionate, proclaiming his faith in You that all might have hope in Your forgiveness—how is it You surrendered him to their accusations, as if he did something wrong in Your eyes?*

Bowing to the ground and confessing his sins, James tried to forgive God.

***

The next morning, not long after sunrise, crowds made their way to the Temple and stood in family clusters, chatting among themselves and greeting fellow congregants.

Jude had gone off to relieve himself, leaving Joseph alone in his usual honorary place near the front. Noticing him, Matthias came down the steps reserved for Sanhedrin members and wished him a good fast. Just arriving, James was pleasantly surprised to see Matthias chatting with his father.

"Shalom, James," Matthias greeted him.

"So you are mixing with the plebeians!" James replied, hugging his friend.

"Who are you talking about?" his father asked, smiling. "Not me, I hope."

Interrupting their banter, the loud clang of the magepha, a noisemaker designed to silence the crowd, announced the next part of the service was beginning.

Excusing himself, Matthias quickly ascended the steps to the Priests' Court fronting the sanctuary and returned to the rows of Sanhedrin members standing across from the massive altar of sacrifice.

As the monumental Nicanor doorway of the Sanctuary opened, all were transfixed by the sight of the lit menorah, as well as the purple curtain concealing the most sacred chamber, the Holy of Holies. Then Caiaphas, robed in pure white linen, with a jeweled breastplate and turban, emerged from his own quarters and made his way forward.

While many worshippers looked downward to avoid the disagreeable sight, a bull was led to one side of the Priests' Court and dispatched. The animal's near-instant death, as required by Torah law, without even a squeal of pain, would have almost seemed a staged event, except that its blood was collected in a gold goblet and handed to Caiaphas. Loudly reciting a text from Leviticus, the high priest walked ceremoniously back and forth, sprinkling it around the lower part of the huge stone altar, invoking God's rule over life and death.

Then the moment arrived when he would do the same as Moses' brother, Aaron, and the high priests of Israel since the earliest days of the nation. Before him was the velvet curtain that separated the People from God's spiritual presence on earth. If he went behind it with an impure heart and so was caused to die, there was a chain attached to his ankle, enabling his corpse to be pulled out.

When his figure vanished behind the long folds, James, to his own surprise, found himself praying that he die within. "God, let them all know Jesus' death was a sin, that it was not your will that my brother die!"

Just as Caiaphas entered the Holy of Holies, Joseph startled James by touching his arm affectionately.

"Abba?"

"My son, it's not even something he feels the need to confess."

As Caiaphas made obeisance to Adonai, all heard only his faint voice uttering the sacred divine name, passed secretly from high priest to high priest, and all knelt on the courtyard floor, falling prostrate.

With the fragrant smoke of incense spreading to the surrounding courtyards, he sprinkled blood of the sacrifice all about the Holy of Holies. Repeating his lustrations upon the altar's horned corners seven times, for expiation of the sins of the Hebrew nation, Caiaphas then placed burning embers at its center and signaled the waiting priests to ascend the ramp with the carcass. After the sacrificed bull was consumed in leaping flames, and the fire of immolation burned down, again becoming a glow, two goats were brought before the high priest. Laying both hands on the head of the one selected for exile, Caiaphas prayed for the banishment of all evil.

After the scapegoat was led away, the other was consumed on the altar, its blood too tossed on the sacred walls of the courtyard. Then the congregation joined the Levites, singing hymns of praise, thanking God for their many blessings and asking their sins be atoned by kindness toward others. Promising God they would keep His commandments according to Torah, their afternoon prayers had been completed.

Drifting toward the Huldah Gate, some took a moment for quiet conversation before returning home. Most would again assemble in the Women's Court for the closing service, but Joseph explained to James he was weary from the repeated trip and intended to say the evening prayers privately. Soon back at the Center, James, upon entering, was coolly acknowledged by Andrew and welcomed with a greeting by Philip and John the Zebedee. Matthew too had just come in.

"Where is Simon?" James asked.

"With Thomas," John replied. "I think they should be finished soon."

"Oh? Are they doing something important?" James inquired.

"Yes. Well, I don't know what you would say. But he is listening to Thomas confess, just as he did with us."

"Confess? What did you do wrong?"

"For sins we committed. You know. That's what we're supposed to do on the Day of Atonement, isn't it?"

"Well then, why didn't you come to the Temple? What does Simon have to do with your sins?"

"He is forgiving them."

Just as the older Zebedee said this, Thaddeus and James bar Alpheus entered with Bartholomew.

"Shalom, James!" Simon called to him from the stairs.

Without affording him the chance to return the greeting, Simon abruptly issued an instruction to John the Zebedee. "Tell Mary she can come now."

Appearing in response to John's call, Mary Magdalene saluted the group and ascended the stairs to join Simon.

"Who is he to hear anybody confess anything?" James asked Andrew.

"He takes our confession to the heavenly court."

"Are you serious? Matthew, did you hear this?"

Matthew looked at James with an expression of mild disapproval.

"He is amazing!" Thomas said. "Really, James. You should confess to him too. Your brother is listening to everything we say."

"And you all believe this?" James asked.

"We went to the Temple. Us and Matthew," Bartholomew said. "That's where we did our confessing. James, you waved to us."

"What do you want with those who don't want you?" Andrew demanded, rebuking Bartholomew. "You want Jesus' murderers to pray for you? You think God is listening to them?"

John the Zebedee reached for some nuts in a bowl and ate one as a show of solidarity with Andrew. He chewed loudly so all would see he had not been fasting. Upon observing his defiance of Torah law, James withdrew to his pallet in the adjacent room to rest.

A short while later, Thaddeus also stretched out for a nap. Before closing his eyes, he turned to James and asked, "Do you think Jesus is watching us from heaven?" When James didn't answer, Thaddeus said, "I don't know if I am going to the Temple later."

"Why wouldn't you?" James asked.

"They don't want us there. Nothing has changed. It's their Temple, and we are outsiders."

"Lev," James said, using his familiar name, "do you remember what my brother said? Ask and it will be given to you. Seek and you shall find. Just as Torah teaches."

"Simon tells us Jesus gave him the keys to the Kingdom."

"Didn't my brother teach that to him who knocks, the door will be opened? Did he leave it up to Simon to decide who should enter and who should not?"

As Matthew came in and found his mattress, others followed, and Thaddeus said to James, "If I oversleep, wake me. I'll go with you."

On the wane, the setting sun cast shadows like iron bars across the land, reaching the Temple courtyards. Accompanied by James bar Alpheus, Bartholomew, Simon C'nani, and Thaddeus, James tried to explain the awesome moment. "Tephilat Ne'ilah—the concluding service—is the closing of the gates of heaven when justice is decided for each of us."

Swaying back and forth in rhythm to the Levites psalm of praise, the congregation prayed Adonai would return to the midst of the bridal People, choosing a descendant of King David to rule his Kingdom.

***

Two days had passed since the Day of Atonement and that morning, Matthias, his presence requested by Simon, arrived as several disciples were on their way to find willow branches for building their Sukkot hut.

"With so many pilgrims, you'll be lucky to find a tree that still has its limbs," Matthias said.

"By the Siloam spring there are always plenty. We know where to look," Philip confidently advised, departing with Bartholomew into the bright daylight.

After enjoying the sweet honey and warm bread put on the table by Martha, Thaddeus and Simon C'nani, the strongest in the group, accompanied Matthew to the woodmakers' market to purchase poplar boards. As the aproned vendor watched, Matthew studied each surface with care. If the wood appeared weathered or darkened by seasonal changes, it was rejected, and fresh supports were chosen.

Soon they were back and Thaddeus held one post upright as Matthew measured its height using a hemp cord. "Not lower than ten handbreadths," he said.

"Tell him why!" came pleasant advice from James as he rounded the side of the building, managing to drop a heavy bundle of myrtle and palm fronds in a heap.

"The sages say the presence of God will not descend lower than ten," Matthew responded agreeably. "If a sukkah booth is to receive the presence of God, its roof has to reach at least that high. But you've done well. It's closer to eighteen. At least we'll be able to stand inside."

Upon entering the rear courtyard, Matthias announced his approval. "Coming along, coming along," he observed.

"Good morning, Matthias," James replied. "Good to see you're wearing an old work tunic."

"I'm glad to help. But the tunic is not old."

"Only joking," James said, placing his hand on his arm and soliciting a private word. "I'm sure Simon told you his tale of Jesus on the beach."

"Indeed. Quite a remarkable event," Matthias agreed, a twinkle in his eye.

"It must have come as some surprise to that poor man," James joked. "Can you imagine he had just awakened in the early morning and was taking a swim to clean off. He spots a school of fish and yells to Simon and the Zebedees to throw the net. How many times has that happened? Don't the children feed the fish with bread?"

"I've done it myself," Matthias answered.

"And the next thing, they are on the beach near the fire the man has made, asking to touch him to see if he is real. When he tells them he is absolutely real and not a ghost, they become jubilant and start poking at him to see whether he is made of flesh and bone."

Noticing that his amusement was no longer shared by Matthias, James continued, "Seriously, can you imagine what went through the fellow's mind? He probably thought of running away but instead invited them to grill the fish on his fire. My brother never was one for missing a good piece of grilled fish." Sensing the others were trying to overhear, James raised his voice, asking, "But why don't you teach something about the festival?"

"Well, it celebrates the fall fruits, especially the harvest of grapes," Matthias replied, as if that was the subject of their conversation. "And we take turns sleeping and eating in the sukkah," he added, returning to the immediate vicinity of the others, "to recall the miracle of shelter when we crossed the desert from Egypt to Canaan."

"We know that," Thaddeus said.

"It is a wedding," Matthias responded. "Or did you know that too?"

"Wedding?" Simon boomed out, having just entered the rear courtyard. "Is somebody getting married?"

"Matthias was about to tell us," Thaddeus answered.

"Well?" Simon persisted. "Who then?"

"We are," Matthias said.

"You and Thaddeus?" Simon asked. "That's nice."

After a moment of polite laughter, Matthias continued, "We are building our symbolic home for the spirit of God to be with us as provider and protector, like a husband, at least poetically."

"Go on, Matthias," Simon prompted, as Bartholomew and Philip returned with armfuls of willow branches. "What else?"

Though reluctant to play the teacher, Matthias realized the group was now listening. "Passover is the time when our people left her original home. A beautiful young girl, she—or we, that is—met our Creator at Mount Horeb and swore our eternal devotion, receiving the marriage contract, the Ten Commandments. Betrothed to God, we would be tested to see if our hearts were innocent as virgins and whether we would remain faithful even in the wilderness.

"As the time approached to enter God's land, we did what we could to show we were worthy and pure. Such was the Day of Atonement. And now, like then, we rejoice by expressing our love for God, hoping the Covenantal bond will be consummated in a great Feast of Booths wedding day, whether it is this very year or one to come. That will be the beginning of God's Kingdom."

"And where does Jesus fit in?" Simon asked. "Is he to be omitted altogether?" Seeing he had their attention, Simon answered his own question. "Of course not. Without him, what shall we expect? No, I tell you he is the cornerstone of our future! He is the one to rule in the coming Kingdom. That is what we believe, isn't it? That is what the wedding to God means! So let us build the sukkah booth, and await Jesus' presence, and hope he visits those of us who love him—as I am sure he will!"

Tossing a few willow branches toward Philip, Simon asked Matthias to join him in the upper triclinium. Once alone and seated at the table, he said, "You know, Matthias, most of them are like children. I recall how Jesus was often aggravated by their lack of comprehension and corrected their poor grasp of his parables."

"Did I mislead them?" Matthias asked, concealing his surprise that Simon belittled their acumen, the very shortcoming Jesus had found in him.

"No. Certainly not. But you should explain how God loves Jesus as his own son. That's all I'm saying. That's what they need to hear."

"You're better at that than I."

"Together, then," Simon suggested. "That's how we should encourage their faith. What I am planning is to bring them more of Jesus' teaching—to express his ideas as they are now given to me from heaven. A parable will emphasize their obligation to understand the revealed truth. Of course, we'll keep it simple so they will get it. Understanding the parables—that was the measure Jesus used to judge us worthy of his coming kingdom."

"Am I familiar with the parable?"

Simon weighed the possibility of disclosing too much. As much as he wanted to fully trust Matthias, he would best not forget that James was the one who usually brought him from Ephraim to Jerusalem. "No. How could you be?" he finally continued. "It is one I have directly from Jesus. You haven't heard it yet."

"Then I look forward to it."

"Good, good," Simon said, reassured and less guarded.

"But there's something else. It's about what happened two years ago." Pausing to emphasize the importance of what was to follow, he continued, "You could have turned down our invitation to be the twelfth. Why wouldn't you? Me, a coward, telling others to have faith in Jesus when I failed him so. Asleep, when I should have kept my promise to sound the alarm. Then, following behind like a stray dog as he was taken inside Caiaphas' house."

"These are different times. And you have changed."

"Even denying I knew him! My faith in him was gone, destroyed by his arrest. This couldn't happen to God's chosen one."

"And now?" Matthias asked.

"Now I know my weakness was part of God's own plan. All those things he had been saying, you recall, about his arrest, and prophesying his own death—they were not worries like we have. They were his intention!"

Uncertain what Simon expected him to say, Matthias simply nodded, encouraging his confidence that he understood.

"Of course, your being Jesus' true friend while he was on this earth, nobody needs to tell you. But there it was, staring me in the face—the truth that I had felt, as it was voiced from heaven by his holy spirit, that I had been right all along! It couldn't happen to him, not as it seemed. Jesus, as you certainly know, Matthias, had not really died! Beneath everything he said—and continues to say through me—was a concealed, deeper truth, leading to his kingdom, if we would be worthy to grasp the hidden messages."

"You've taken on quite a responsibility," Matthias observed, hoping his face didn't betray doubt over Simon's emotional display of self-adulation.

"Yes. How else can I put it and still be truthful?" Simon said quietly, as if sharing a matter requiring great prudence. "Matthias, I must save Jesus. I was a coward once, a coward because I lost faith in him. I let him die to me as the chosen one. But now I must show him I am changed, just as you say. Now, I will not let his voice be gone or his spirit be taken from us. Hasn't he already appeared to some of us? Satan may send his demons to stop me, but Jesus is alive! And this time I will not fall asleep!"

Outside, passing the front entrance, a loud voice spared Matthias the need to reply. "Etrogim! Etrogim!" a vendor of the aromatic citron fruit was calling out.

"I'll buy them for us," Matthias said. "My contribution."

"That's very generous," Simon replied, as if shaken awake. "Better hurry before he moves on."

Exiting quickly, Matthias arrived just in time to make the purchase.

Folding back the cloth that protected the gnarly, bright-yellow skins from the hot sun, the vendor pointed to the largest ones near the front. "These are my best," he said, holding one to his nose, proudly indicating the sweet scent, which in several more days would become an intoxicating perfume. "One hundred prutot each."

"I need fifteen of the largest," Matthias said. "If you give me a good price."

"Fifteen?" The man began counting them out, wrapping them in flax.

"Well?" Matthias asked. "How much do you require? Or will we be putting them back?"

"Two denarii."

Handing him the small silver coins taken from his shoulder purse, Matthias said, "Have a good festival," and turned toward the doorway as the man called out, "Etrogim! Etrogim!" pushing his cart in front of him.

After dragging the heavy sack to a corner of the lower sitting room, Matthias returned to the courtyard, where he resisted telling James about Simon's belief that he was Jesus' personal representative on earth. Sensing he was being watched from an overhead window, he would wait. Meanwhile, others were engaged in the festival preparations.

"Let's help Mary," John the Zebedee said, descending the outside stairs with his brother following.

Mary was struggling to carry the water pitcher on her shoulder as she rounded the side of the building. "We will eat before the sun disappears behind the trees," she announced.

As the Zebedees took hold of the heavy vessel by its handles, Simon too made his way down. "By then we'll be hungry," he said. "That much I can promise. And I see the walls are almost done."

"And I have onions and leeks," Thomas added. "But has Andrew come back? He has the meat."

"He'll be here soon," Simon said. "But I see Martha has brought cheeses and sesame cakes. We will feast like royalty."

***

With the first cool breezes of early evening, those still napping after the meal awakened slowly and joined the others, gathering for a meeting convened while there was still sufficient light.

Simon waited patiently for the disciples and James to find places in the upper triclinium. He handed each a cup as they arrived and poured them new wine, a sweet dessert customary for welcoming the fall season. "Matthias bring the scroll to the table," he suggested, "and prepare your writing point and ink."

When all were comfortably reclining, several on settees and others on large pillows spread around the floor, Simon raised the cup he held in his hand. "What a new season is beginning!" he declared. "Let me again wish all of us a joyous Sukkot Festival of Booths. I think most of you were outside when Matthias said it was a time of anticipation, a time when we await our heavenly protector as a bride awaits her groom, that it will be a wedding between God and those deserving to enter His Kingdom. Matthias, have I been true to your words?"

"That is our tradition."

"And James, even you have no objection?"

"Not yet."

"And it is more than a dream. There is truth in it. Let us recall what happened when Moses was on Horeb. He became so radiant from his closeness to God that upon his descent to their encampment, the people feared the change they beheld. What did he bring them? Guidance from God. Revealed through the holy spirit, which illuminated his insights from that day forward. And I tell you, brothers, something much greater has happened. For Moses only reached the top of an earthly mountain. Jesus has reached the heavenly realm, and there are no higher peaks and none their equal on earth.

"So I say, of course we anticipate the wedding. It will witness the coming of the true chosen one, the groom who will manifest God on earth. But some of you may not yet have reached this understanding on your own, and you are thinking, 'How will I learn these things?' Brothers, I have a parable to help you, one I have received from Jesus."

Murmurs of surprise and amazement caused a slight disruption, and then Simon advised Matthias that he was about to begin.

"Are you ready?" he asked.

"I am," Matthias replied.

"The Kingdom of Heaven will be like this," Simon said. "There was to be a great wedding, but the groom still had not arrived. And it had grown dark outside. Ten bridesmaids took their oil lamps and went to meet him. Five of them were foolish and shortsighted, and five were wise."

"Slower, please," Matthias said.

With measured pauses to permit the transcription, Simon continued, "The foolish ones did not take enough oil, but the wise ones went with extra flasks. And all fell asleep waiting. Then, at midnight, there was a stirring sound, and waking, one called out, 'The groom is here!' Seeing their lamps were running out of oil, and there was none to be spared by the wise bridesmaids, the shortsighted ones went to buy oil in the market. But by the time they returned, the wedding was taking place and only those who had been prepared were allowed inside. So be ready for the groom to come, for you do not know either the day or the hour."

Almost immediately, Thomas asked, "But who are the shortsighted ones?"

"Not you, brother. This has nothing to do with how you only see your food by bringing it close to your face. This is about a vision of our future. The ones who don't believe Jesus is guiding some of us from heaven and giving us his words to speak here on earth," Simon answered. "They will not be admitted to the Kingdom."

"But you say there were five. Are you talking about any of us?" Bartholomew asked, his right eye gone off fully to the side.

"I have only Jesus' words as I gave them to you. But if you believe that what I have just told you comes from him, I am certain you will not permit the flame of your faith to go out."

"And if there are those among us who do not think Jesus has given you a message for us?" James asked.

"That is the darkness of doubt," Simon replied. "But of course there is hope the night will be turned to day. Isn't that what Zechariah, our beloved prophet, said? Night and day will be the same on the wedding day."

"For Zechariah's prophecy to come true, we must now believe you speak for Jesus?" Bartholomew asked.

"Of course not!" Simon responded. "Only when I tell you Jesus has asked me to tell you something. Otherwise, I am like you. One of his sheep."

"What do you say, Matthias?" James asked.

"Jesus' teaching was certainly not limited to the past," Matthias answered.

"What a worthy twelfth you are!" Simon declared. "Hopefully, we may all share your wisdom. But when you return the scroll to its closet, come down and join us."

James waited for the others to descend first, and he stopped before reaching the door to ask Matthias, "Have you noticed how the five of them are almost a separate group?"

"You mean the Zebedees, Simon's brother Andrew, Thomas, and Matthew?"

"Then I guess you did notice."

Fitting the scroll carefully inside the wall cabinet, Matthias added, "They always call him Peter. The others still call him Simon, though I haven't heard Philip address him by any name at all. Five wise bridesmaids, and five who were without oil to keep their faith lit until your brother's return."

As they reached the bottom stair, Andrew immediately appeared, carrying a sack of pomegranates.

"Let me help you with those," James said, grasping a corner.

"I have it," Andrew replied curtly, hoisting it over his shoulder.

On their way outside to adorn the walls of willows and myrtle with the fruit of the season, Matthias turned to James. "You'll be visiting your father again, won't you?"

"I will, during the festival," James answered, surprised by an inquiry that seemed disconnected to the moment.

"Soon. Visit him soon. He has something to tell you." Not delaying further, Matthias led the way into the courtyard, and they joined the others in festooning the sukkah booth.

***

As James arrived at his father's house, two men were just leaving.

"Couriers," Joseph said as the visitors' cart wheels turned noisily. "They bring me news from time to time. Truly, I think they expect to find me dying or dead."

"Too bad for them!" James joked. "They'll have to wait a long time."

"I hate to be a disappointment. And if I care to admit it, their stopping by picks me up. Did you hear about the tetrarch?"

"What's the news?"

"Let's sit out back and I will tell you what they have just told me."

James was pleased to see that the frame of the sukkah was in place. He said he had brought plenty of palm fronds. "And this!" he added with a big smile, extricating an enormous citron from his purse.

"Look at that!" Joseph said. "I think that's about as big as they come." He pressed the yellow fruit to his nose, closed his eyes, and inhaled. "The bride's perfume is sweet! An etrog like this must have—"

"Grown in the Garden of Eden," James said, guessing his father's thought.

"Must have cost more than you can afford."

"Didn't you know you have a rich son? So what news did they bring you?"

"Rome has a newly appointed legate. A man named Vitellius. He offered Artabanus, the Parthian king, a fake peace treaty while at the same time secretly arranging an attack against him by Rome's allies, Iberia and Albania."

"Tiberius must have approved it."

"From what they just told me, the Parthian king sent one of his own sons to meet with Vitellius on a bridge over the Euphrates. And guess who was there acting as mediator."

"Antipas."

"None other. He suggested the king's son should reside in Galilee as a demonstration that the Parthians intended to keep their word."

"And the Parthians accepted those terms? Didn't they see the whole peace treaty was a ploy?"

"No. And it turns out that after the peace agreement on the bridge, Antipas immediately dispatched messengers to the emperor, describing the negotiations and taking credit for their success. What a fool! But with such luck! Vitellius' own letters reached Tiberius sometime later and were read by the emperor as old news. The result was that he extended no commendation to his new legate, and now he and Antipas are enemies."

"But you say the peace treaty was a deception. Why would the emperor congratulate either of them?"

"Because thousands of Parthians are dead. Now Vitellius hates Antipas, which should keep Tiberius from making him king of Judea. That's all I care about. You'll hear about it," Joseph said, pressing the fruit to his nose again and inhaling deeply. When James was quiet, Joseph prodded, "It must bother you that they don't know anything."

"Who, Abba?"

"The rabbis!" Joseph laughed at his own joke. "Your friends. So now that he's gone, I suppose they're teaching Torah—that ignorant Simon and the others."

"Even if it's true, there's nothing I can do about it."

"I don't know how you spend time with them. You're not Jesus, and you don't have to make his mistake of trying to save them."

"I am not trying to save them, Abba. I am trying to save him."

"Are you being funny, James?"

"At first it seemed so innocent. Saying he is alive in heaven, believing he will return when the Day of God happens. But it has changed. Some of them believe he's talking to them from heaven."

"Telling them to go to hell, ha. It's because of them he was killed. So they say he wasn't killed after all. Let them say it."

"They say he came as the chosen one."

"What a way to be chosen. Idiots. I'm the one who taught him! I guess that makes me God!" Joseph's sudden outburst startled James. "When he was just a boy, we all would go to the synagogue. You must remember—"

"And then you left. We almost never saw you."

"The Temple masonry took my time. And I had the Sanhedrin meetings. We knew Herod was on his way out. Then Archeleus single-handedly started a conflict with the Pietists, and Roman legionnaires enforced order everywhere! How could I move my family into that cauldron? But what about those palm fronds? And did you bring me some myrtle?"

"Yes, I have everything in the cart."

"What would you have me say, James? Few cared when he was alive; why should they care now that he is dead? Wherever he is, Jesus is at peace, and all their antics to wake him are not disturbing him."

"People are listening to them."

"Get us some water from the cistern and then come sit down," Joseph said. He accepted the water skin and then waited as James dragged over a short bench. "Did I ever tell you that Mary looks like your mother?"

"You may have."

"Do you remember her? You were only a child when she died."

"I remember her singing to me."

After taking a long drink, Joseph reminisced, "Her sister died two years before that."

"Hannah."

"Yes. And Yoakim already had been gone for several years. So Mary attended the school for daughters of priests, under the guardian care of my sister-in-law, Elizabeth, as you know."

"And her husband, Zechariah."

"Of course she was so much younger than I that I hardly thought of her in that way. But then, being left with the six of you and having no wife, and she having no mother, it just seemed natural. We'd get betrothed, and when she was ready, we'd be married. Elizabeth was right. I was in love with her—maybe because she looked so much like your mother or because I felt so old and she was so filled with youthful joy. You know our tradition. A widowed uncle who is not a blood relative is eligible and even desirable. The family holdings would be passed along to a family member, not to some outsider's children."

"And you were wealthy."

"There will be enough for you and the others, but it was a small ceremony. I listened as she swore her vow to love only me, and I said our ancient words, 'haray at mikudeshet li,' you are holy to me, and James, in my life, I will never have a happier day. Elizabeth took the witnessed marriage contract and put it away. I came to the school every day and took her to Elizabeth's. I was with an angel on earth. All my sadness at the loss of your mother was lifted from me. When vacation came, she was off to the house in Nazareth, where your sisters and often your brothers were her companions."

"I was there."

"But too young to remember when she moved in."

"You sound like you're talking about a different person."

Not saying he was wrong, Joseph pointed toward the branches James had heaped near the sukkah. "Bring me a myrtle, willow, and palm frond," he instructed. "We can bind them with hemp over there."

Even after Joseph failed at several attempts to tie the cord around the stems, James still did not interfere. His father's large hands, once a proud sign of his profession, had been deformed by twisted, large knuckles, making the task painful. Watching as his father's abraded fingernails futilely sought to complete a knot, James looked down, saddened by that faded past.

"Here. I can't," Joseph finally admitted. "You do it."

Watching his son skillfully bind the three species in the ceremonial lulav, he concealed his mild regret at needing his help. But there was something else on Joseph's mind.

"She was different to me in those days," he told James, as if remembering a dream. "Anyway, I thought it best she remain in Nazareth until unfolding events became less threatening. Archeleus was summoned by Augustus to explain a ruthless attack on neighboring Samaritans. Clearly, the ethnarch was not going to be king of Judea, as he hoped. In fact, he was soon banished, and the Romans put in their own administrator of Jerusalem, Coponius. It's hard to believe three decades have passed since she and I were betrothed."

"The betrothal period is usually a year. How long did it last?"

"It didn't."

"I don't understand," James said. "Was there a wedding?"

"No. Things went in a different direction. Elizabeth was pregnant with John. Mary went to visit her in Ayn Kerem. When they talked about Elizabeth's miracle, because she was past the usual years for a woman to give birth, Mary told her about her own miracle. She was pregnant."

"Elizabeth must have been amazed! How sad that Mary's parents were not alive . . . but when did you find out you would be a father again? I can only guess how that made you feel."

"No need to guess. Before I arrived for my afternoon visit that day, Elizabeth explained to her niece what it meant to have conceived during our betrothal period. Mary would now be regarded as married to me, and the wedding ceremony would simply be a beautiful party. Our betrothal bond, with the vows and contract, were what mattered."

"What did you say when Mary told you the good news? It must have been overwhelming."

"I asked her who the father was."

"What? Why would you say that?"

"Why do you think?" Joseph asked. "It wasn't me. That's why."

"That's impossible."

"For days I didn't eat or sleep. I couldn't talk to her. I was angry, and I was heartbroken. I wanted to blame her, but I blamed myself more—just an older man who had dreamed a foolish dream."

"What did she say?"

"Nothing. She didn't have to. It was in her eyes. What could she say?"

"Did she tell you who?"

"No."

"What did you do?"

"There were options. I could have accused her of adultery."

"You would never have done that."

"Do you know what the law says?" Joseph asked. "A man who abandons his betrothed when she is already pregnant is to be publicly whipped. I had to consider the probability that if I didn't accuse her, it would seem I was abandoning her."

"But you didn't."

"How could I? Mary is family. My niece. My deceased wife's blood."

"So you made her a home with us in Nazareth."

"When the time for her to give birth was near, I brought her to the house in Beit Lehem. It was the same time as the census. I enrolled her as my wife to prevent suspicion. I could never let anybody suspect her. A woman with a son and no husband—they would have called her zonah, a whore. If they came to know me as his father, then she would be all right. That's what I thought."

"So Jesus isn't my brother."

"He was the grandson of your aunt Hannah. He was your cousin."

"And he never knew?"

"Fifteen years is a long time. The neighbors either had never met me or had forgotten my visits when Jesus began his healings. The crazier they thought he was, the more they believed it was because he had been born in sinful circumstances. The stupid Pietists were saying Mary was a whore or an adulteress, and Jesus was her punishment—possessed by a demon. Did he guess? Not for a long time. But by his last year, he understood. He told Matthias he knew."

James rose from his seat slowly, feeling heavy and tired. "I will lean branches against the frame," he said. "But, Abba, have you told me all this so you would not be blamed for leaving us?"

"Is that what you think?"

"Nobody should say you left your wife, because she wasn't your wife. Nobody should say you abandoned your son, because he wasn't your son. Isn't that what you are saying?"

"You weren't much older than Jesus, and you are my son. If I'm only making excuses, what about leaving you and your siblings? There was work to do on the Temple!"

It was something James had never understood. But if he could be honest, he never considered himself any different from his brothers, Yossi and Jude, or Simon whom he did not really know because he was much older and had moved away. His sisters, sometimes with Jude or Yossi, would visit their father in Beit Lehem, mostly during the festivals. There, they witnessed his Sanhedrin colleagues showing him respect. Always they heard about his prestigious supervision of the stonecutters and priests whom he helped train as masons. But not Jesus. After he was twelve, reaching the legal age of maturity, Joseph did not invite him to visit his home in Beit Lehem with his siblings.

These thoughts were raging in him like a storm as he spoke.

"You said it yourself," James heard himself complaining. "You couldn't be in the same house with Mary. The truth is you moved away permanently because after twelve years of visits, teaching Jesus, playing the father to him, you still couldn't face the fact he was not your son."

"As he grew older, I hated pretending," Joseph admitted. "He was devoted to me and followed me around, learning everything I taught him, even carpentry. His honesty made me feel like I was repaying his love with a lie."

"I'll help you with the branches for the roof," James said, "and then I have to go."

"James, I did my duty to the family. Your sisters raised you well, didn't they? You came on the holidays." When James climbed onto the cart seat after covering the sukkah and didn't reply, Joseph said, "She never loved me as a husband."

Pausing, before snapping the reins, James showed his father deference. "Is there anything else before I go?"

"And I told Matthias that he should befriend Jesus if he could, staying by his side to see he was all right."

***

Back at the Center, James informed Matthias that he had made the visit.

"Are you shocked?" Matthias asked when James recounted Mary's infidelity.

"Of course! And you didn't tell me?"

"This was something for your father to say."

"So you expected him to spew out these buried secrets of disgrace," James stated. "But why now? Why ever?"

"Don't you understand?"

"Don't play games with me, Matthias."

"I'm not. You wanted to make Jesus human rather than a god. Your father has handed you a way. It wasn't my idea. It was his."

"No! You can't expect me to tell them he was born in sin! How would I do that to his memory? It's one thing to make him human, another to make him a mamzer! And Mary is my close kin. How would I do that to her after all these years?"

"Don't tell them. Just tell Simon if he creates a false god, you will reveal the truth."

"He could say something. Word could spread. I would never forgive myself."

"That is one secret he will keep," Matthias said. "I am sure of that."

"And Jesus. Was he truly your friend, or were you just spying for my father?" James retorted sharply.

Sighing, Matthias responded, "At first. But later on, I had never felt as close to anybody, but I could not always protect him, especially from himself. You were at Cana for the wedding."

"Yes."

"Then you know that what he related to me is true. Mary was crying because people were calling him crazy, saying he had no known father. That's when he knew he wasn't Joseph's son, and if he had given his students the unintended impression he was superior to the Shabbat or could forgive sin, he wondered if he was speaking with Satan's voice."

"Go on," James insisted, aware of Matthias' seeming reluctance to elaborate further.

"As he reached the top of the Temple mount that Feast of Booths just two years ago, he attempted to take his life. He told me only the distant sight of John revived his courage. He would ask his cousin to cleanse him so that he might be pure before God."

"That's why he was immersed by John?"

"Now you have your human Jesus." Matthias said. "Perhaps you can bring Simon's acclamation of his heavenly realm down to earth."

At that moment, the Center door swung open, and Thaddeus stuck his head in. "Are we going for a stroll to see the other booths?" he asked.

"Let's go have a look," Matthias replied. "James? Come. It will do us all good to get some air."

CHAPTER EIGHTEEN

$\mathcal{T}$he fourteenth of Tishrei, a cloudless, warm day, began quietly. As Thomas dipped his pita into honey, he replied to James' inquiry that Simon was in the upper meeting room with Andrew and the Zebedees but requested that he not be disturbed. "I'm sure the others will be up as soon as the aroma of food reaches them," he added.

"Any idea what it's about?" James asked.

"No, but I'm sure they will be down soon. Otherwise, the food will be gone."

"And he didn't invite you to hear whatever they're talking about?"

"Andrew is going to fill me in."

"It's just four of them?" James persisted.

"I was hungry," Thomas said. "So I decided to eat instead of joining them."

"There's plenty!" Mary Magdalene announced, carrying in an additional platter covered with thin layers of white cheese.

After setting the platter down on a small serving table, Mary Magdalene gave a friendly nod to James and called out, "Martha!" and explained, "She's been binding the lulavs."

"I'm here," Martha said, holding an armful of the leafy bundles in front of her. "And remember, the wire wrapping is silver. So make sure you don't throw it away when the festival is over. It's good for next year."

"Where is everybody?" Philip asked, just entering, wiping the sleep out of his eyes with the back of a hand.

"Upstairs," Thomas answered. "Four are still sleeping in the other room."

Moments later, the upper triclinium door swung open. "Are we too late?" Andrew called out. "Is there anything left?"

Each took a terracotta plate, heaped it with the breakfast victuals, and found places near Simon, who lowered himself carefully to his especially large pillow.

"Good appetite," he said, appearing to show an agreeable holiday mood.

"If you have a few minutes, there are some things I would like to discuss," James said, watching Simon spoon the silky amber honey onto his cheese.

"Have you found us a big donation?" Simon replied, pulling his cloth napkin to his lap.

"No."

"But you will, I'm sure."

"It takes time."

"You must tell them what it's for," Simon said. "Bankers and landowners understand buildings and architecture of stone, but you must explain they are building a temple of the spirit. When Jesus returns as lord, the temple will be of the spirit!"

"I'm not sure that's an idea they will follow."

"Not in so many words. Of course not. But James, you must use your gift of speech. Tell his story—that he was human in this life, but the worthy always knew he was more, that he was the one sent from heaven to rule."

"Simon, there are some other issues."

"Of course there are! But one step at a time. You mustn't expect yourself to have all the answers. And I will help you."

Acknowledging Simon C'nani with a polite salutation, Simon paused, as he and James bar Alpheus, Thaddeus, and Bartholomew overcame sleep and entered, apparently awakened by Mary Magdalene's announcement of the morning's fare.

"We all will help you," Simon reiterated, seeming to speak almost indifferently, not directly to James but to the Zebedees and Philip, who were seated across from him. "Surely, your brother is helping us to help you. And that is reason to have confidence," he added. "But what is really important is this delicious breakfast. We owe thanks to Mary!"

"In which case, I should feel free to confide in you," James responded, his heart racing in anticipation.

"Absolutely. If there's some advice you need, just ask. I will support your efforts fully."

When Simon's plate was empty, James rose. "May we talk privately, perhaps outside?"

"Now?" Simon replied. "It can't wait?"

"I thought you were finished eating."

"Yes, well, if it's important, and you're sure it won't take long."

As they walked from the door to the entranceway gate, James asked Simon whether he had ever heard the story of Jesus' birth.

"Not really," Simon answered. "Is it something we need to talk about now?"

"Did you ever wonder about it?" James delved.

"No," Simon said with some agitation.

James continued unabated. "Mary became pregnant by an unknown father—at least unknown to anybody but her."

Simon looked at James suddenly with shock in his eyes. "What? That makes no sense. Joseph raised him until he was twelve. Jesus has told us as much. No man would do that if the boy wasn't his. Why would you make up such a thing, James? About your own brother, no less."

"Joseph loved Mary. She was young. She was his niece. And he didn't want to accuse her—or be accused himself of abandoning her."

Simon's shock turned to disgust. "Why are you telling me this lie?"

"When we were at the wedding at Cana, do you remember how upset Mary was? He had poured wine into the water. People were mocking him, saying he was turning the water to wine, imitating the high priest's ritual of mixing water and wine on the Sukkot Feast of Booths," James said softly.

"I guess you didn't understand, even then," Simon responded. "She was upset. Mary always became angry with him. She wanted him to be ordinary. That's why Jesus called us his family. His mother and brothers didn't appreciate who he was, and they still don't."

"She berated him," James said. "The way he was acting, she said, people would avoid him and that if he continued his antics, nobody would marry him. We all heard him snap at her, 'Woman, I'm not ready to get married.'"

"What's your point, James, except to spread ugly lies and gossip? I really haven't time."

"Joseph was no longer living in Nazareth. Neighbors hardly remembered him, and some even thought Jesus was possessed by a demon, acting crazy. You know the popular belief. A crazy child is the way God punishes a woman who commits adultery."

"And you want me to take this seriously—that it matters?"

"It mattered to Jesus. He was conceived while his mother was betrothed to Joseph—born from adultery. That is why he attempted to take his own life."

"James, I don't know what strange world of falsehoods are surrounding you with darkness or who may be feeding your fantasies, but they don't change anything. To suggest such a thing—first, that he was a bastard and then that he tried to kill himself—is more than absurd; it is a sin."

"After her confrontation at Cana, that's when he first doubted his teaching was inspired by God's spirit, thinking it could be from that unknown father, a voice of Satan. There was only one solution."

"Were your ravings true, we certainly would know he tried to end his life. But of course the evidence is your word."

"He was on the Temple mount, on its corner precipice, and below, in the distance, just then, he saw John immersing pilgrims. That's why he went to his cousin and asked him to immerse and cleanse him."

As Simon stared at James, much like he was beholding a venomous snake, Martha appeared at the doorway. "Everybody has selected a lulav bundle. Here, I have yours!" her voice rang out.

"Splendid!" Simon said, still not taking his eyes off James. "And you intend to share these insults to your brother's memory with the others?"

"His teaching was profound. I believe he was blessed by God to see the majestic heights of Torah wisdom. But if you would destroy him by making him a god, I will do whatever it takes to save him by making him human."

***

Several bronze pans were stacked near the washing cistern, and Martha was showing them to Simon C'nani. "These are your responsibility," she said drolly, sounding like he was being trusted with an important job.

"Where's the lime?" he asked, picking up a rag dried on a rail in a row with others.

"Right here," said Bartholomew, carrying a sack. "Watch your eyes. This stuff burns."

"And when you're done, just open the spigot halfway," Martha instructed. "You can sweep out the crusts and flour without all the water going with it."

Not long after he had brought the first pan to a perfect shine, an elderly couple across the courtyard caught their attention.

The woman was inspecting their festival booth. "You call this a sukkah?" she asked.

"What else should I call it?" her husband asked.

"It's a small closet. We're going to eat and sleep in here?" she derided.

"There's plenty of room. You'll be surprised," he answered.

"Like last year," she scoffed. "I was curled up in it like a dog, and you had your feet sticking out the door because only half of you could fit inside."

"I made it bigger."

"Elijah couldn't fit in this. And he's invisible."

As the sun glinted off the copper pan that Simon C'nani was holding, Thaddeus approached. "Obviously, you have a talent for cleaning pots and pans!" he said.

"I'm sure you could do as well," he replied.

"The bride's home must be pure and spotless," Matthew called out from inside the sukkah booth. "Well, what do you think?"

Peering in to see hanging clusters of deep purple grapes alternating with bright red pomegranates, Bartholomew murmured his approval. Inside the Center, James had retired to a corner of his vestibule, from which vantage point he furtively observed Simon, who had just excused himself and was climbing the stairs to the upper floor.

"No doubt he has your conversation on his mind." It was Matthias who had located James. "You must have said something."

"I see you are on your way," he replied, pressing a finger to his lips so Matthias would speak more discreetly.

"It's easier to go early instead of pushing through the crowd," Matthias said, nodding.

"We'll all be leaving shortly. I thought I'd take a short nap."

"It looks like you got to him," Matthias whispered.

"He didn't take it well."

"No surprise. But be on your guard. He is surely thinking about what he can do."

"That I know."

"Will your father come tomorrow?"

"I believe so."

"Please wish him a pleasant festival if we don't see each other." With that, Matthias was gone, and James dozed off.

***

Like a rooster, Thaddeus was crowing, "Let's go! Let's go!"

Squinting against the red sun blazing through the small window, James put his hand protectively up to his eyes. "Thaddeus?"

"James, we're all leaving. You've been asleep."

Standing up stiffly, he half stumbled into the sitting room just as the others were filing out. Thaddeus patiently waited for James by the door, handed him the last of the bundled sheaves along with an etrog citron, and they departed.

Late Tishrei's autumn twilight illuminated the golden stones of the Temple's courtyard walls as the gathering found places to witness the libation ceremony. A raised platform fronting the Priests' Court along the eastern end was reserved for the deputation of Israelite leaders, who slowly climbed the low side stairs and took their places.

In rows cordoned off for the seventy members of the Sanhedrin, the esteemed dignitaries were standing to watch the arriving worshippers.

As they reached the balustrade overlooking the courtyard, Martha and her sister, Mary, along with Mary Magdalene, could see Matthias and his colleagues. Just behind his austere group was a low wall separating the Sanhedrin section from the altar, still emitting wafts of smoke from the earlier sacrifice.

To the far side, open and magnificent, the towering Nicanor bronze doors framed the inner seven-branched gold menorah, its flames illuminating the purple velvet curtain concealing the Holy of Holies.

As James stood with Matthew and Thaddeus, James bar Alpheus made his way toward them.

"Philip and Simon C'nani are here," he said somewhat breathlessly.

"Have you seen the others?" James asked.

"No sign, but Philip says they are definitely coming. Simon has told them we should all keep a lookout for Jesus."

Just then, a deafening, clanging sound of the metal magepha caused silence to spread like a wave across the crowd.

Stepping forward, the presiding officer of the Sanhedrin turned to face the open doors of the Sanctuary, watching as a selected priest lit the incense.

When the aromatic smoke rose and spread from its own sacred altar, the priest exited the Sanctuary and waited as the officer in charge announced, "Haverim, members of the Sanhedrin, priests, Levites and Israelites—His Excellency the High Priest will now kindly take his place."

Upon completion of these words, Caiaphas, adorned with his ritual linen tunic and bejeweled breastplate, appeared in the Sanctuary doorway and stepped forward.

Intoning the Torah law, he recited, "On the fifteenth day of the seventh month, Tishrei, you shall keep the Feast of the Lord seven days. On the first day shall be a solemn rest, and the eighth day shall be a solemn rest, and you shall dwell, each of you, in a sukkah booth."

All eyes were now on a delegation of priests, Sanhedrin members, sages, and elders, including renowned Pharisees, experts in Torah law who had formed a line behind Caiaphas and were exiting the courtyard in ceremonial fashion.

From their position, the three women could see them wend their way down the steep southern incline to the Siloam watercourse, finally passing through the Water Gate, continuing outside the city wall into the Kidron Valley.

Gathered high above, along the southern edge of the Temple mount, various officials viewed the procession as it came to the water's edge. Among them was Matthias.

Nearby, a rabbi was quietly speaking to his circle, teaching, "The stream at their feet is glorified in the centuries-old vision of the prophet Zechariah. When God again resides in the midst of the People, it is to flow all the way to the Great Sea and make the land fertile from end to end."

Interrupting his narration, the clarion call of two silver trumpets sounded by priests announced that the top edge of the sun was gone below the horizon.

As Matthias and other officials waved to those gathered by the water below, three more blasts were sounded from the silver trumpets, and all hands were raised as a signal that the holy time had commenced.

Stepping forward to the very edge of the Siloam, Caiaphas held the golden flagon for all to see and then submersed it beneath the flowing water. When he again held it aloft, filled to overflowing, Matthias and the other dignitaries saluted the event with joyous singsong shouts of jubilation.

In unrestrained glee, the courtyard's pilgrims waved their palm-frond sheaves and held the aromatic etrog citrons above their heads, as the gift of fecundity was on its way to the bridal People's home, God's temple.

Once the procession was again within the courtyard, an especially gifted priest sounded the first blast of the shofar ram's horn, tikkiyah, announcing their return with the sacred water, followed by a sequence of short blasts, t'ruah, a call to be ready.

As Caiaphas reached the semicircular stairs leading to the Priests' Court, he stopped.

Full silence had descended on the gathering.

Pressing the shofar to his lips, the priest sounded a long blast, prolonged and seeming closer. The water of salvation, as Isaiah had called it, was near.

Having assumed their positions on the semicircular stairs, the Levite musicians then started their musical accompaniment to the cadenced ascent of the notables led by Caiaphas, each step having its own meaning taken from the psalms of David.

As the Levite choir sang, "In my distress I called to the Lord, and He answered me . . ." the harps, lyres, cymbals, and trumpets were a rhapsodic measure of their pace.

Taking the next step, balancing the gold flagon carefully before him, Caiaphas joined in singing, "My help comes from the Lord. He will not let your foot give way."

Several steps higher, the sound of cymbals was louder and the chorus more triumphant. "We are going to the house of the Lord," the full assembly of worshippers sang. "May those who love You, Lord, be at peace. To You enthroned in heaven, I turn my eyes."

As he came nearer the top stair, their lyrics resounded. "Our mouths shall be filled with laughter, our tongues with songs of joy. Restore our fortunes, Lord, like watercourses in the Negev Desert."

Even as the musical accompaniment resonated across the courtyard, Thaddeus sought James' reply to a question. "Is this the wedding ceremony? It is beautiful, but I don't understand how it is a wedding."

"Listen to the next words," James said.

"Sons are the provision of the Lord," the gathering sang. "The fruit of the womb His reward. Your wife shall be like a fruitful vine within your house, your sons like olive saplings around your table."

"But I'm sure he understood," came a voice just behind James. "Didn't you, Thaddeus? Later. We shall explain some of these things."

It was Simon, who, with the Zebedees, had been standing there unnoticed.

"You are here!" James said.

"Why wouldn't I be? I look forward to seeing the day our lord returns. Perhaps he is among us even as we speak. But James, you look puzzled."

Turning his back to Simon, James gestured for Thaddeus to pay attention to the ceremony. "I am more eager for the Lord than watchmen for the morning," voices rang out. "Oh Israel, wait for the Lord, for the Lord is steadfast in His love!"

Seeing Caiaphas had reached the fifteenth step, all joined in singing, "Lift your hands toward the Sanctuary and bless the Lord. May the Lord, maker of heaven and earth, bless you from Zion!"

Responding with raised lulav sheaves swaying against the fading light of early evening, their perfumed etrog citrons in hands held high, the worshippers fastened their attention on the high priest as he made his way up the altar's ramp.

At the top, he turned to his left, where a large spouted pitcher filled with wine had been placed. Displaying the gold flagon for all to see, he also raised the wine pitcher, grasping it in the other hand. Then, holding them at arm's length so he would not splash his own feet, he prayed, "Adonai, blessed are You who causes the water of salvation to nourish the people and the land, who brings bread forth from the earth, and turns water to wine."

As the congregation's amen echoed across the courtyard and carried beyond to the hills of the city, Caiaphas tilted the two containers gently forward, causing them to flow together onto the altar.

***

Not long after eating the morning meal in their own sukkah booth, James led the group in prayers for winter rain, instructing those who were unsure how to shake their lulav sheaves in the six ritual directions—waving them forward, to each side and back, and up and down, while grasping the citron. Several followed his example.

"Will you join us?" James asked Simon, who stood watching.

"Please finish," Simon said. "We must all meet. There is something important that has happened."

James sensed urgency in his voice, and the group quickly followed Simon inside and found seats.

"Brothers and sisters," Simon began. "Rejoice! I have had word from Jesus!"

"Tell us!" Andrew called out.

"We have wondered how Jesus, while alive on earth, was sent to us from heaven, have we not? I know I have. People have made up stories to explain the miracle of his presence among us. Some who were enemies spread malicious rumors. I am sure I do not have to repeat the stories that he was evil, even a messenger from Satan, trying to raise an army against God." As he said this, Simon pretended to spit on the floor. "And I make no secret that I have prayed to him to explain his mysterious appearance on earth. Yes, your hopes and mine are fulfilled. Last night, when I was alone in the upstairs chamber, he came to me in a vision, and this is the news I bring you."

"Don't delay! Tell us," John the Zebedee insisted loudly.

"Here it is, then, just as he told me. It was Elul, the sixth month, in the thirty-third year of Augustus' reign, eight years before Tiberius became emperor, when an angel was sent by God to Mary, then a virgin living in Nazareth."

"Of course we know Mary!" Bartholomew interrupted.

"She was here only a few days ago!" Simon C'nani bellowed.

"Please. Let me go on, brother. These are our master's words. And it was during the time she was betrothed to the one we know by name as Joseph, of the house of David. The angel told her, 'The holy spirit will come upon you, and you will become pregnant and bear a son, whose name will be Jesus. And God will put him on the throne of David to rule over the Hebrew people and the world.'"

"But Simon, I've never heard Mary say such things," Matthew objected.

"Listen to Jesus' words, so you will understand. And Joseph, to whom she was betrothed, being a just man and unwilling to accuse her of infidelity, though he knew nothing of the angel's message, decided to end the betrothal quietly and without scandal."

"Even though he could see from her belly that she was with child?" Thaddeus called out.

"How is any of this possible?" Thomas demanded. "Joseph lived with Mary under one roof in Nazareth for the first twelve years of Jesus' life. We have that from James. Isn't that true, James?"

"My father resided with us that long. And he even visited from time to time in the years that followed, though seldom. But Simon, you surely will tell us about this too."

"You're right, James. I will. Then the angel appeared to Joseph in a dream and said, 'Joseph, descendant of David, do not fear to take Mary as your wife. But wait until she has her son Jesus before you make your bed with her.'"

"I never heard Mary say anything like this!" James bar Alpheus rasped. "And Jesus told you this?"

"Friend," Simon replied, "did you ever hear Jesus speak of himself as the son of Joseph? Of course not. And now you know why—not from me but from Jesus, who appeared to me. And those of you who have ears to hear will understand. And you who are worthy will be honored when the kingdom is revealed to all!"

"Peter, I have a question that is unpleasant."

"Then ask it, Andrew. I will try to give an answer."

"It is concerning you, James. I hope you will not be insulted. Is he still to be considered Jesus' brother? After all, James, you are Joseph's son. But now we learn that Jesus was not your father's son; rather, he was God's son by the holy spirit."

"Please, Andrew. Don't cause James added pain," Simon replied. "I tell you all, James was as close to Jesus as any brother would be. To us, James, you will always have a special place."

"As will you, Simon. Of that I am certain," James said.

Ignoring his comment, Simon went on, "Later, when we assemble after dinner, we will speak further about these miraculous events."

As the gathering began to disperse, James approached Simon. "May I have a word in private?"

"Of course. Just let me tell them about this evening's meeting." Turning his back to James, Simon declared, "It is a day to celebrate the return of Jesus to our midst! Prepare any of your memories for Matthias. He will be here at sunset to listen to your stories. And after we eat, we shall all go to the wedding festivities!" Off to the side and out of earshot, Simon said to James, "Oh yes, I'm sorry. What was it you wanted to say?"

"What will they think when I inform them Mary was an adulteress? That after realizing he had an unknown father, Jesus was about to take his own life?"

"Who would say such things about his own brother? Oh, of course, he really wasn't your brother, was he? But you would only prove the truth of my words. They would rightly see your slander as motivated by malice toward me. They would say you are angry because I denied your kinship with our lord. Well, James, he, not I, has disowned your kinship, and you constantly reveal it is so in your every rejection of his will."

Only a slight smile betrayed the confidence Simon felt at his tactics. He had rolled his dice, certain James would do nothing to hurt Jesus' reputation.

***

The sun had passed the tops of the trees, spreading cool shadows over the sukkah's branched roof.

Finding James resting inside, Andrew touched his arm. "I don't want to disturb you, but Peter has asked you to notify him the moment Matthias arrives."

"Is Jesus talking to him again?" James asked.

"I was telling him some of my own recollections, and Peter felt they are very important. Matthias is to record them without delay."

"I'll let him know," James said.

"Peter says it is a priority," Andrew asserted and then left without awaiting James' reply.

Not long after the sun dipped below the horizon, Matthias was following a bend in the path, enjoying the ease of walking down the slope, when James darted in front of him.

"Shalom, my friend!" Matthias said, obviously surprised.

"I'm sorry if I startled you. It is important."

"I can tell from your worried look. What has he done now?"

"He has told them Jesus was born to God's holy spirit, that Mary was a virgin."

"Should we laugh or cry?" Matthias responded. "And Joseph?"

"Joseph waited until Jesus was born, as an angel instructed. Then he took Mary to bed as her husband!"

"And you could say nothing."

"No, Matthias. Not without bringing shame on him."

"Simon knows you don't want to shame Mary either. He is clever."

"Andrew intends to share his recollections about something. Simon wants you to transcribe them."

"Let's see what he is scheming."

"I will go ahead so they don't see us together," James replied, walking briskly toward the Center.

***

The faint smell of frying fish pies—hashed with flour and flattened in spattering oil—wafted upward from the smoldering fire of the outside oven.

James and Matthias had eaten their fill and were thanking Mary for another of her Magdalene specialties when the disciples filed out of the sukkah booth. They carried their plates to a table near the washing cistern and climbed the outside stairs to the second floor.

Upon entering the room, Matthias was intercepted by Andrew, who handed him the box of writing utensils. "I have opened the scroll on the table for you," Andrew said, indicating a chair.

"Make sure he has what he needs," Simon instructed. "Matthias, did you eat well?"

"Thank you. It was delicious. And everything is here."

"Good. But what about us? Are we all here?" Simon inquired as they found their places. "It appears so. Except for the Marys and Martha. One of you get them. This is a time for us all to be together. And what a blessed night of joy awaits us. In a short while, we shall all go to the Temple courtyard and watch the lighting of the great menorah."

"If you have any questions . . ." James said, addressing the group.

"Why do they light such a huge menorah in the first place?" Simon C'nani asked. "We have the sacred seven-branched menorah inside the Sanctuary. Why is there a second one?"

"To honor the prophet Zechariah's vision that on the day God's presence returns to our midst, night will be the same as day. It is fifty cubits high, or as the Romans would measure it, seventy-five feet. There are eight branches, for the eight days of the festival, and each bowl of oil will burn for eight days, until the holiday is over. It is so bright, no one needs to fear stumbling on his way home."

"Thank you, James," Simon said, his tone suggesting they would now hear something more important. "Seven glorious days of unrestrained joy, followed by an eighth that culminates in the return of God's son to earth. Keep that in mind, brothers, as you look about for the surprise guests, who we hope will be witnesses, Moses and Elijah the prophet."

"What about Jesus?" John the Zebedee asked.

"You still don't understand?" Simon asked impatiently. "How will you be ready for the day that is coming if you are blind to what is happening in front of your eyes? It is Jesus' wedding!"

Before the exchanged murmurs had subsided, Simon continued, "Which is why we must ask Matthias to make record of that wondrous occasion when Jesus revealed his plans to us. Once cloaked in secret meaning but now revealed in a message to Andrew, who will forget the wedding at Cana?"

Filled with trepidation at creating a falsehood, one that even plagued Jesus toward the end of his life, Matthias took extra time wiping the point.

"Matthias?"

"Yes, Simon."

"Earlier I recounted the miracle of Jesus' birth as he himself told it to me. Please leave a space for that, and we will add it later. But now, Andrew come forward and speak from the heart."

216

"There was a wedding in Cana in the Galilee," Andrew began. "Jesus' mother was there, and Jesus was there with us, his disciples. When they ran out of wine, since the wine for the wedding was all finished, Jesus' mother said to him, 'They have no wine.'"

"You're going too fast," Matthias said.

"Shall I repeat it?"

"Just another moment."

"Take your time," Simon said.

"Continue," Matthias replied.

"It was about the wine. Mary had just told him they had run out."

"Yes. I have that."

"So Jesus told her, 'Woman, why turn to me? My hour has not come yet!'"

Interrupting, Simon exclaimed, "Let those who have ears hear! He was speaking of the great wedding, the one we now anticipate!"

"But I was there too," Matthew blurted. "She told him he wouldn't find a wife if he made a spectacle of himself. That was what she said after he started mixing the wine he brought into their purification cisterns. And he replied, 'It's not my time to get married.'"

"Matthew," Simon said, "will you not see that he concealed the truth behind words which, like brambles, caused the unworthy listener to stumble? Andrew, what happened then?"

"His mother said to the servants, 'Do whatever he tells you.' And Jesus said to the servants they should fill each of the six purification vessels."

The scratching sound of the point reflected the heightened pace of Matthias' writing, and Simon said, "A little slower, Andrew. But he told the servants to fill the vessels to the brim with water, did he not?"

"Yes. That's what happened. So he told them to fill the containers to the brim."

"But I saw him pour wine into them," Bartholomew asserted.

Ignoring him, Andrew continued, "Then Jesus told the servants, 'Draw some out and take it to the steward. They did so, and when the steward tasted the water, it had turned into wine. Surprised, the steward told the bridegroom, 'People usually serve the pure wine first and then water it down, but you have saved the pure wine for last.'"

"He poured wine into the small amount of water still left in those jars—the servants knew that," Matthew persisted.

"They didn't say anything to the steward," Andrew replied. "It was a miracle!"

"So you see, brothers and sisters," Simon declared, "Jesus spoke of his coming wedding—a time when there would not only be prayers that water be turned to wine, which we saw last evening but when indeed the water would actually be turned to wine, as Jesus did. Yes, it is hard to believe! But ask yourselves why. Don't you see Jesus was testing our faith to separate those worthy of him from those not. But did you take all this down, Matthias?"

Wrapping the point in a patch of soft fabric, he nodded, saying he had made the record as Simon wished.

"And James, am I wrong to conclude that you are overjoyed by this great vision?"

"How can you be wrong, about this or anything else? What does it matter if the wine was poured into the water? Your version is confirmed by Jesus speaking to you from heaven, I believe you say. But what did he tell you, Simon, about the days after Cana when he decided to kill himself?"

A noisy stir bordering on genuine commotion echoed loudly as the disciples reacted to James' words with expressions of disbelief.

"Yes," Simon said. "It is true."

"Jesus was going to take his own life?" a Zebedee called out.

"How is that possible?" Thomas demanded.

"Satan tried to fool him," Simon said. "Don't sons always think one day they will be equal to their father or maybe even superior? Satan knew that Jesus was God's son, and he told Jesus that if he wanted to rule the earth, all he need do was acknowledge him and claim his crown. Of course, Jesus had traveled a long way on his pilgrimage to Jerusalem, and as tired as he was, he believed it was God speaking and that he was being given his inheritance. But when he stood at the edge of the precipice, obeying the false instruction to jump and, by surviving, prove his identity, just in time he recognized the tempter's voice and stood back. Brothers and sisters, in this episode we have a lesson. If you listen to Jesus, you need not fear Satan's temptation. But let us all express our appreciation to James for reminding us to include the temptation Jesus experienced on the Temple mount. Matthias?"

"Yes, Simon."

"Before we roll up the scroll, will you take a moment and record several more details?"

"Of Jesus on the Temple mount?"

"Yes. But let's let them go down first. No need to delay. I suggest the rest of you freshen up. It is nearly time for us to go."

As the others made their way downstairs, Simon turned to Matthias, ignoring James, who remained. "Maybe put in that Satan challenged him to jump off the edge, actually hoping he would die. Oh, and I think we can add that Jesus took forty days to reach the mountain, so his pilgrimage was part of God's own plan."

"Aren't you inventing things?" Matthias asked.

"Not at all! Don't rabbis explain our lives with stories? We must capture the truth that we are all tempted by Satan. Well, it is getting late, and you can include it in the future."

"I have heard enough nonsense," James said. "I am going to get ready."

***

Nearly bumping into a man who had stopped to catch his breath on the steep ascent to the Temple entrance, Mary Magdalene politely wished him a good year.

"To you too," he replied and then whispered to James, "Kittian," the code word for Roman spies.

Turning slowly, James observed an odd-looking man leaning against a tree by the path, wearing a linen head-covering draped down to his eyes. "How do you know?" James replied in a low voice.

"He's just watching people pass by."

"Have a good festival," James said, nodding appreciatively.

"He is following us," Mary whispered, after they had gone on a ways. "As soon as we went by, he started walking between the trees."

"Act normal," James answered. "We have nothing to hide."

At last, amid a crowd of congregants, James felt safe. As one known to seek funds for a group whose leader they had arrested and executed, his activity was likely to be monitored by the authorities.

"No sign of the suspicious fellow," he observed as they made their way through the entrance.

"One of the things I don't get," Mary, Martha's sister, said to James, "is why we must be up on the balcony while you men are all below."

"They are afraid of us," Martha said.

"Are we so dangerous?" her sister joked.

"Some say women invite temptation," James suggested. "And they believe men must separate themselves. Not too many years ago, the Pietists made a fuss over women pushing forward, pressing against them, apparently bringing out their evil inclination."

"You mean arousing their interests?" Martha asked, smiling.

"So sad. What fun it must have been!" Mary Magdalene joked as they reached the stairs to the overhead balustrade.

"They give us a pinch on the behind and blame us," Martha said. "But what's going on? The priests look like they're fighting over something."

Inside the courtyard, two towering menorot lampstands, each with four golden branches becoming eight by proximity and topped by large bowls, were gleaming brilliantly in the setting sun. Positioned to the side of the semicircular stairs, glorifying the sanctuary, they towered over the gathering worshippers.

"The young ones are competing to see who's fastest to the top. They make torches for lighting the bowls of oil. But their seniors make them vie for the cloth," James explained.

"Must be special material they use," Mary Magdalene observed.

"Actually, their mentors are traditionally less than generous to their young protégés. Hard to see from here, but it's their old underwear. Keeps the boys humble—at least that's the idea."

As Martha was about to ascend the balustrade stairs, she said what had apparently been on her mind. "James, your brother often made us smile."

"It's true," her sister agreed. "Shall I tell you? That last Passover when I was putting oil on his feet, after he had come to the Bethany house covered in dust, Simon and especially his brother Andrew became aggravated at the sight. I was just giving his toes a good cleaning, and they didn't want my wiping to become too affectionate. But Jesus set them straight. You don't want the lord's feet to be dirty, do you? He was so sick of Simon always calling him lord."

When James suddenly seemed saddened, Martha added, "You remind us of him. I can picture the two of you laughing together."

"Thanks," he said, realizing what they meant. To them, no matter what Simon claimed, he was still Jesus' brother.

Once they were on their way up, he turned to see who else he might recognize and immediately noticed a furtive figure appearing for a brief instant, moving in short steps quickly out of view. It was the man who had been following them.

Intently scanning the crowd to see where he had gone, James' concentration was broken by two boys with their tightly furled palm fronds held like swords, dueling with each other and interfering with his view. When finally restrained by their father, the spy was nowhere to be seen.

"You must not do that," their father was saying, grasping the bigger boy firmly by the arm. "You may hurt each other with the sharp points."

"He is a Roman," the boy quipped.

"I am not!" his little brother snapped.

"We are all Jews," the man said. "And if we use our lulavs as weapons, it is to put out the eye of Satan! So aim them toward the sky. And don't stick anybody with them!"

Spared further concern by the sound of cymbals announcing the competition of the four young priests, the bigger boy exclaimed, "Look, they have the oil!"

As James navigated the torrent of worshippers still assembling, he heard his name called, and he looked about to see Matthew and Thaddeus and James bar Alpheus.

"You made it!" Matthew said. "We couldn't find you."

"I'm here. But where are the others?"

"Several are closer to the front."

"And Simon?" James inquired.

"We haven't seen him," Thaddeus replied. "But we saw Matthias with other men, dressed like dignitaries."

"That's the Sanhedrin," James said.

"He says he will see you in a day or two."

As the Levite musicians, who were positioned on the semicircular stairs, began playing their flutes, further conversation ceased.

***

Through the frond leaves covering his eyes, Simon had observed Mary Magdalene, Martha, and her sister talking to James, but they had not spotted him. Secluded as he was among the clusters of worshippers, he would wait until Jesus revealed that the time was right for what he was planning. Demon or no demon, he would do whatever was necessary to stop James. About Matthias, he was less concerned. *No wonder the Lord loves him*—he thought. *Such innocence in a man of his stature!*

Weaving his way between the onlookers, Simon reached the area where the Zebedees were supposed to find him.

Transfixed, the assembly let out squeals of joy as the competing priests suddenly raced to the foot of tall ladders propped against the four lamp-stand branches that framed the northern side of the Nicanor doors. Then, burdened by heavy containers of oil—each holding the equivalent of 180 large eggs in volume—they began their race to the top.

Every rung was a perceptible challenge as they climbed upward, with the large vessels resting on their shoulders and only one hand free to assure they wouldn't slip or fall.

"It's not something I'd do!" a loud voice exclaimed in Simon's ear.

"You startled me!" he said, seeing it was John the Zebedee, with his brother at his side.

"I'm for the short one," his brother James declared. "Even I am taller than he is."

Gaining the pinnacle first, one with short legs and a broad back was leading.

"Zechariah's vision is coming to life before our eyes," Simon informed them. "It is the beginning of the wedding."

After pouring half the oil from their vessels into the bowls atop the branches, the reduced weight eased their descent, and the young priests returned rapidly to the ground and raced to the far side of the stairs, to the base of the menorah's other four branches. Again, they ascended and filled the bowls, this time with a tall, skinny priest in the lead.

Upon completion of the task, the four, now at the foot of the ladders, gripped the torches they had earlier wrapped with oil-soaked priestly undergarments, lighting them from handheld lamps.

Against the darkening sky, the smoky torch flames created tails of light as they were carried upward. Surprising them all, an underrated young priest had overtaken the others and was now acknowledged with waving lulav palm fronds, brandishing his torch proudly upon reaching the floor and extinguishing it in a nearby cistern.

The bowls atop the monumental menorah were ablaze with a fiery glow, transforming the front of the Temple and illuminating its majestic entrance as a gateway to God's habitation.

"And if I tell you," Simon asked, turning to face the brothers, "I wasn't the one who told you to join me here—but it was Jesus, would you be amazed?"

"I didn't do anything wrong," John said, shaking his head. "What did I do?"

"Only good. Both of you," Simon responded, placing his hand on John's shoulder. "You and James and I have been invited to see God give his son to mankind, consummating the wedding we have waited for."

"You're . . . you're saying . . . us?" James stammered, pointing at himself with his free hand.

"Soon you shall see. Meanwhile, enjoy these festivities, which are blessings meant to honor our lord, Jesus."

Imbued by the prophet's message of God's imminent Kingdom, Levites sang and played their instruments, their chorale concluding with three blasts of the shofar, signaling the start of the People's prayer for fecundity. Raising his hand to quell further discussion, Simon indicated the Zebedees should be patient and enjoy the music of the coronation.

Meanwhile, just across the courtyard, James was explaining the ceremony's dramatic climax to James bar Alpheus, who appeared uncertain about what he was witnessing.

"If you listen to the words," James said, "you will hear how the bridal People must first wash, preparing for her nuptial era, for a wedding between us and our Creator, which we hope will occur in our own lifetimes."

"In that day," the Levite chorus resumed singing, "a fountain shall be open to the House of David and the inhabitants of Jerusalem for purification and bathing. 'I Myself,' says God, 'will be a wall of fire around Jerusalem, and I will be a glory inside My House. I will dwell in your midst and in that day there shall be neither sunlight nor cold moonlight, but there shall be a continuous day—only I know when—and there shall be light in the evening.'"

In their reverie, many worshippers listened with closed eyes and envisioned their beloved king, described in images of the song. He would stand atop the Mount of Olives, incomprehensibly majestic, causing the mountain to open and pour forth water, uniting the eastern and western seas with eternal fecundity.

Undulating to the sonorous music, the bridal People held their perfume-sweet citrons high overhead, her palm-frond lulavs like skirts waving gaily, with myrtle leaves rustling in anticipation. On the balcony, James could see Mary Magdalene and Martha and her sister Mary, their pomegranate-red apparel matching the sky.

The melodic prayer having subsided, men formed circles and began dancing while jugglers on large platforms, accompanied by the Levites' harps, lyres, cymbals, and flutes, sent varied objects high into the air. Always eight in number to symbolize the days of the festival, flaming torches were hurled aloft, as well as fragile eggs, spinning knives, and seemingly impossible glasses of wine, which remained full and upright throughout.

Then, just as James caught the attention of the overhead women with a wave, a celebrant took his hand, pulling him into the frenzied circle, shouting "shalom" above the din, and linking arms in the dance.

James saw who it was, and a tremor of fear coursed through his body. "Why have you been following me?" he demanded.

"I am sorry if I worried you," he replied. "I am no spy."

"And I am no Kittian sympathizer," James said, seeing his features were Hebrew, and he could be hunting down Jews who collaborated with Romans.

"Nor am I a Sicarri rebel who would stab Kittians and their ilk. There is no dagger under my tunic to do harm to you or anybody else."

James broke free from the circling dancers, intending to move away. He had no reason to trust the words of so suspicious a stranger.

Undeterred, the man insisted, "You must visit me in Beit Zaida. We will talk there."

"Visit you? Is that what you said?"

"I'm sure you know Beit Zaida."

"Even so . . . why would I? I don't have the slightest idea who you are or why I should care."

"I have something to tell you about Simon. You should make the trip. Ask any neighbors for Nathanael's house. They will point it out."

Before James had a chance to reply, the man bowed his head politely and was gone.

With the ceremonies drawing to a close, everybody hugged and took playful bites from each other's etrogim, the citron juice running down their chins.

"We should be getting back," Matthew finally said, as the others wiped their faces and nodded in agreement.

All were worn out, and some of the men were even slumped against the walls, dozing with their heads resting on each other's shoulders. James, again joined by Matthew and James bar Alpheus, as well as Thaddeus, who kept up at a distance, made their way along paths illuminated by the huge flaming menorah. They finally reached the Center, where the last embers of conversation should have burned themselves out, giving way to a peaceful night, but something had happened.

Upon their arrival at the Center, James and his companions immediately met with questions. Nobody had seen Simon or the Zebedees or had any idea where they had gone.

"Are you sure they weren't with you?" Thomas repeated, obviously worried.

"I'm telling you I have no idea where they are," James responded. "Certainly we will see them later."

"Unless they were arrested," Andrew said.

"What reason would there be for that?" Matthew asked.

"Maybe you can tell us," Andrew replied, directing his remark to James.

"I have no idea. And why would I?" James retorted.

"If somebody wanted my brother arrested they might make up a reason good enough for the Romans. Or the Jews."

"You think I would do that?" James asked.

"He has made you angry. We all know that," Thomas said.

"I take you at your word, James. And I believe they will have a simple explanation, when they get back," Philip advised, attempting to mollify the sharp tones arising from their concern.

"Philip is right," Simon C'nani said. "Let's not blame each other for something that has not happened—though I wouldn't put it past the Romans."

"Thank you, Philip," James said. "We are already living with too many imaginary notions. But maybe we'll see them at the Temple in the morning."

***

Late into the night, they remained awake, nervous that there was still no sign of Simon. In the light of the oil lamps, James observed, the disciples' faces reflected anxiety and exhaustion.

"Where is Matthias?" Andrew prodded James, annoyed because his eyes were closed. "He should be here."

"Maybe he knows something," Thomas said.

"He would be here if there were bad news," James said, half asleep. "No doubt his colleagues insisted he join them."

"At least he could inquire," Andrew said. "Isn't that the reason we chose him as our twelfth? So he would have influence with the authorities? Or is he using his influence to follow your bidding, James? Maybe you'd like all of us to die on a cross."

"As I recall, Simon proposed he be your twelfth," James said, barely managing to keep his composure.

"Simon." Andrew mumbled his name as if talking about a stranger. "If you ask me about my brother Peter, I will know who you mean."

Just then, the front entrance swung open, startling them all, and as if summoned to calm their angry exchange, Simon entered, carrying a smoky oil lamp. Immediately behind him, also with lit lamps, were the Zebedees.

"Where have you been?" demanded Thomas. "We're waiting for you!"

"Are you all right?" Andrew inquired. "We thought you might have been arrested."

"I don't even know where to begin!" Simon declared. "It has been the night we were waiting for!"

"Tell us!" Thomas exclaimed.

"We had just left the Temple" John said. "And the path that leads down . . . well, it was not the same."

"Not the same?" Andrew asked. "What's that supposed to mean?"

"It was different. It was leading up a hill. And in the moonlight, when we turned around to find Peter . . . well, there he was."

"So he was there," Andrew said impatiently. "And?"

"No, not Peter. There he was!"

"He? If they don't mean you, then who was it?" James said impatiently.

"Who do you think?" Simon asked. "It was Jesus. But don't look at me like that, James. Rejoice in what you will now hear! And he led us to a high mountain."

"Of course he did," James said. "And then what?"

"I know what you all must think," James the Zebedee exploded angrily. "You can believe we are crazy if you want. I don't even know how we were on that mountain. It was like a dream."

"I believe you," Thomas said.

"And we were amazed by the sight we beheld. Jesus' face began to glow, and his garments became as white as light," Simon said.

"Whiter than any bleached tunic," John the Zebedee attested.

"No fuller on earth could bleach them that white," his brother confirmed.

"Then two figures emerged from the mist," Simon continued. "At first I had no idea who they might be, but they walked over to Jesus and were talking to him."

"What did they say? Did you hear them?" Thomas asked.

"No. But I knew what it was about," Simon said.

"Tell us, Peter. Tell us."

"Yes, Thomas. They were Moses and Elijah, and they were hailing him as the chosen one in the coming kingdom."

"But what did you do?" Andrew asked. "You just stood there?"

"You can imagine how frightened we were," Simon said. "So I suggested he let us make three sukkot festival huts for them—that was the only thing I could think of."

"Can you imagine?" John the Zebedee interjected. "The three of us."

"So he is alive," Bartholomew said. "If what you say is so."

"He will be among us. I told you. He is the groom on earth. The wedding is his wedding. And the only ones invited," he added, looking at James, "are those who know and believe he rose from the dead. So those who doubt Jesus is alive in heaven and refuse to believe he will be our ruler in the kingdom, perhaps your faith will be illuminated come the morning's light. Meanwhile, please sleep well, if you can."

As the group finally ceased chattering about the wondrous events and were stretching out on their pallets, Simon said, "There is one thing more. This too happened. While I was inquiring about building them the sukkot booths, a luminous cloud surrounded them, and a voice said, 'This is My beloved son, My chosen one. With him I am very pleased.' When we heard this, we bowed our heads."

"Yes, yes, that's what we heard," said James the Zebedee.

"And then Jesus touched us, and when we looked up, he said, 'Tell no one the vision you have had, unless they believe in me.' Isn't that what he said, Peter?"

"Tell no one what you have seen," Simon corrected. "And then he led us down the mountain."

"A miracle!" Thomas exclaimed.

"And a tiring one, I'm sure," James said. "For me too, who wasn't even invited. Just hearing about it is exhausting. So if you are done, Simon, I wish you all good night."

***

During the five days since meeting the man, James was unable to stop thinking about him. Could he really know some dark secret about Simon? "Unlikely," he muttered as he squinted at the sun's first light pouring in through the window. Drawing his shirt over his head, he stepped out the rear door, where singsong prayers resonated from nearby courtyards blending with crowing cocks in a cacophonic chorus.

In the dawn chill, dense fog hung several feet above the ground. A neighbor could be heard teaching his children to be vigilant so they might witness the presence of revered visitors from an earlier era. The Jerusalem morning mist in mid-Tishrei was like the cloud of God's presence, spawning claims by young worshippers to have recognized Moses or Elijah praying near their booths.

James bar Alpheus and Thaddeus were early risers and had been plucking the last grapes hanging from their sukkah ceiling.

Helping himself to a clustered sprig upon entering, James said, "I once saw Moses. Simon isn't the only one. Of course, I was a child, and my imagination was overactive."

"But did you see somebody who could have been Moses?" Thaddeus asked.

"It is easy to believe what you want to believe," James replied, observing James bar Alpheus had grown quiet in the days since his mother and Cleopas bragged about meeting the risen Jesus. "And in the mist, I guess my brother Yossi looked like a spirit or ghost. That was the only time anybody ever mistook him for Moses. I'm sure of that."

Martha brought a plate of cheese and honey with hot bread, interrupting their conversation. "All cleaned pots should be brought inside, since this is the day we take it down. And the small tables. We want to put away what we won't be using."

***

"Do you see them? The older ones can't even stand up straight."

"Who?" James asked, pulling back gently on the reins, as the downward slope of the hill steepened.

"The Pietists," Matthias said. "They dig their thumbs in the ground to show they can go no lower when they prostrate themselves, always trying to prove they are holier than anybody else."

Coincidentally illustrating his words, a man wearing extremely long fringes and an oversized phylactery on his forehead limped across the road, holding the base of his back.

As several others also hobbled in front of the cart, ignoring the inconvenience they caused, Matthias blared, "They kiss the earth to show their humility before God, and then they can't get up without becoming lame! No wonder they take so long crossing a road!"

They had reached the wide highway north when James said, "If you wanted to hear something truly laughable, you should have been there last night when Simon and the Zebedees returned. I don't know how they expect anybody to believe them. It was some story."

"You think he let me leave without writing it down?" Matthias asked.

"Where was I?"

"Watering the horse."

"Matthias, how has it come to this? You and I only want one thing—to preserve Jesus' teachings and make his compassion a model for others. But every day, he is more the artwork of Simon's imagination. I shouldn't have said anything about his birth or how he nearly took his own life. He makes it sound like I'm the one throwing him down the mountain."

"It's not your fault," Matthias said. "So what will you do?"

"There's a man named Nathanael . . ."

"I don't know him."

"After dropping you off, I will visit him in Beit Zaida. He wants to tell me something about Simon."

"Where did you find him?"

"He found me."

"Simon is from Beit Zaida."

"That occurred to me."

233

CHAPTER NINETEEN

"*W*hy are you looking at me like that? You think it's easy to recall these things?"

As the knot loosened and he unfurled the scroll, the dove that had alighted on Matthias' windowsill turned its head slightly to the side.

"You birds think you know everything, ever since the Greeks watched you for signs from Zeus. But it's the prospect of sadness and regret—that's what makes me weary as I continue its passages."

To record more of this story, making a man from a god, who some are praying is a god, I should be better equipped than with this conduit, a point too narrow and feeble for the memories which follow.

Not too long after that Day of Atonement when Jesus nearly took his own life, he, like others, camped on the hillside of Jerusalem, anticipating the Festival of Sukkot, about to begin. Whether he joined others in helping to construct a hut, the festival's traditional habitation, I am not certain. I do know he would have been more than capable of doing so, given Joseph's training at an early age. But it really did not prevent his finding a sukkah, since it is a commandment to invite fellow Hebrews to dwell in your own if they have none. I recall he eventually located several of his disciples, inviting them to see where he was staying, and not long after that, we joined together in the vicinity of the Temple, witnessing the water libation and celebrating the fall harvest together. We waved the lulav and marveled at the jugglers eerily lit by the flickering flames of the huge Temple entrance menorah. Jesus, I can attest, had made peace with himself following his immersion by John. Here we are then, just after that Sukkot Festival of Booths, two years ago, little more than six months before he died.

Things were about to change.

The trail along the Jordan's sparkling water, glittering in the sun but so shallow after the rainless summer, was safe when you went in a group. The Samaritans rarely attempted robbery unless they were sure of success.

Simon, who at that time still had only the name Simon, invited me to join the others as guests in his house in Beit Zaida, but I thanked him and explained I would only be going as far as my own home—this place where I now sit. If I have not said so, it is in the town of Ephraim, in the shadow of Mount Gilboa, only a day's walk north of Samaria. Typically, the Pietists refer to the entire region as Ephraim, as if the Samaritans don't exist.

Here, a word about the Samaritans is relevant. Because Jesus' students, and the community of native Galileans are often insulted as ignorant locals, I wish to state they are not from the same stock as the neighboring Samaritans. Samaritans trace themselves back to an imported population of foreigners, settled in the land by the Assyrians, who intended to dilute remnants of Hebrew nationalism following the northern conquest. Of course, that was centuries ago. Because many such idolators intermarried with our people, those families cared little about Jewish practice, and their indifference became a sign they were not genuine Hebrews but had Assyrian blood. That may have been long ago, but the stigma is still a Samaritan trait.

Plainly, it is a demeaning insult to imply the Galileans are foreigners because they happen to be unfamiliar with Torah. I have taken a moment to say all this because of what happened next.

We had made our way almost as far as Aenon when we heard the sounds of laughter and splashing and perhaps singing. As we came closer, I recall my own amazement at the sight. It was a large group of men and women and children too, bathing in the river, and at their center, the bare-chested figure of John, bearded and scrawny but quite apparently jubilant.

For a short while, we stood observing them unnoticed. Then John espied Jesus and us and began waving. As I recall, a few of his entourage waded across and greeted us. This was truly a joyous thing to share. Before very long, we too had our shirts off and were dunking the ones who were near enough to grab.

I believe others remained nearer to John and actually complained that Jesus' group was immersing people in greater number. But neither of the teachers were the least interested, and by the time we had journeyed on far enough to be dried by the sun, voices just behind us were making mocking insults.

The pack of Pietists could have been wolves, yapping to each other in indiscernible little barking sounds. But Jesus was not one to be anybody's prey and turned sharply about to confront them.

As we stopped, so did they. Jesus said nothing, waiting instead for their leader to speak. Pushing back the oversized leather phylactery box on his forehead, he scoffed, "They call you rabbi, do they not? But how can you teach the ignorant am ha-aretz when Abraham is not their forefather?"

Jesus directed his first words to his disciples, saying, "Beware of false prophets who appear before you, disguised like sheep but underneath are vicious wolves," And then in response to the one who addressed him with the question, he continued, *"You can tell they are not born from sinful ancestry by their deeds. Could I pick grapes from thorn bushes or figs from thistles? A sound tree produces good fruit, and a rotten tree, bad fruit. A wholesome tree cannot bear miserable fruit, nor can a decayed tree bear fruit that is good."*

His students, he believed, proved their Hebrew lineage by studying with him. As they learned to keep the Torah's commandments, they gave testimony to their descent from Abraham.

"And you don't care if they were born from some unknown paloni almoni, maybe an idol worshipper or foreigner?"

"I tell you," Jesus said, *"you will be able to recognize their family tree from their fruits."*

"And you will promise them the Kingdom as Hebrews, even if they are in doubt? So, you are sent by Beelzebub."

"They ask me, and I tell them the same as you tell your own sons. Ask and it will be given you. Seek and you will find. You, who have evil hearts, ask me to defend myself to you. But don't you do the same as I? When your children ask you for a piece of fish, do you give them a snake? Or if they want to eat an egg, do you give them a scorpion? Why, then, don't you see if they ask to learn Torah, God's spirit may rest upon them, and they may understand the answers. In this way, God makes us and them His sons."

"So you think the holy spirit has made you God's son? The spirit you talk about is from Satan, not from God," another in their group railed. *"What you are doing is from Satan! You have an unclean spirit!"*

He had heard it before, in Nazareth, when others of their ilk offered to purify his students in four generations, if they would follow them back to their lairs.

Repeating what he had said on that earlier occasion, Jesus replied, "You can insult me, as I am only a son of man. And you sons of men may be forgiven for doing that to me. But if you insult the ruach ha-kodesh, God's holy spirit, you will not be forgiven."

We continued on, and there was no sign of them after that encounter. For a while, we went in silence and soon would be reaching my turnoff, when Jesus had us all stop and listen to his words.

"Do not concern yourselves with the question about your ancestors," he instructed. "The tree you come from is known by whether or not you do the will of your heavenly Father. So do His will as best you can."

Bidding them all farewell, I assured them I would look for them in Jerusalem on the twenty-fifth of Kislev, at the Festival of Lights, though circumstance would bring us together sooner than I expected.

Once again, as I bend over this parchment, I must put to rest a question that requires understanding. It is this: had the discovery of his uncertain paternal lineage led him to believe that he was actually God's progeny, born from God as His true son?

The opposite is true. His unsettling revelation that Joseph was not his father had caused him to briefly doubt that his inspiration came from the holy spirit—and to worry he could have unwittingly been an agent of Satan.

No. He didn't discover Joseph was not his father and then decide God was.

"That mischief fully belongs to Simon," Matthias mused.

Point in hand, again beginning his transcription, Matthias hoped to set aside the misconceptions daily born of Simon's supernal reverence for his lost teacher.

Shared by sages blessed to receive the holy spirit, the title "son of God" is accorded those who feel God's breath of creation upon them and seek to follow His will. This is asserted in the writing of our sages of the Salt Sea and, as Jesus would soon have occasion to say, in our psalms. As a title, it does not diminish the family tree or replace it.

But I shall shortly recount the moment when I witnessed his reply to Pietists who accused him of thinking himself God's son. And you shall hear him tell what he meant by it in his own words.

Kislev was a time of wary vigilance by the Romans—and in the north by Antipas—who were aware the Festival of Lights awakened rebellious ambitions. John's diatribes against the adulterer tetrarch and his so-called wife, Herodias, were likely to be forcibly suppressed in that season celebrating Judah Maccabee. And that is what happened.

The sad news, if feared to the point of presentiment, was carried by a messenger who understood not the least how disheartening it was.

Having inflamed the popular imagination with images of sin, declaring Antipas stood between Israel and her promised redemption, John was arrested.

It was from the widow neighbor, whose gossip was offered along with soup or cakes, that I learned the latest rumors of John's circumstances. Here are the words of our exchange, as I remember them.

"That funny man. You must have seen him," she said. "The one who cleans up pilgrims before they reach the Temple on the festivals. You know, in the river."

"Yes."

"They say he was a prophet. Maybe Elijah. The way he dressed and talked."

"I recall his bathing pilgrims on their way to Jerusalem."

"What they're saying is that after the Sukkot holiday, he camped to the north where the water was deeper. That he was in the tetrarch's region. That's why he was arrested."

When she told me, I tried to show no emotion, but in truth, I was overwhelmed. He must have been arrested shortly after we all bathed together. I knew John only as one knows an acquaintance and not even that well, but surely his arrest must have come as bitter news to Jesus, if he heard. I wished I was with him at that time, not by myself in my house. But I had returned here when they all continued on to Simon and Andrew's in Beit Zaida.

"Almost certainly it should not have come as a surprise," Matthias announced loudly, talking to the dove on his windowsill. "Not after he called Herodias a whore—and encouraged popular support for Aretas' attack!"

Determined that his next entry not reflect the fatigue of its author, Matthias lay down to take a nap. The dove, showing her approval, made a gentle cooing sound and flew off with a soft whistle of her wings.

CHAPTER TWENTY

*B*eit Zaida, as James knew from his occasional visits, was hardly a village. A horse could trot its perimeter in less time than it took to roast an egg. But it had a life of its own. It was comfortable even in the shimmering heat, as it breathed air like a living soul and drew cool breezes from the northern hills. From where James sat, high on the cart seat, the shoreline of the Sea of Galilee appeared to have widened with the dry spell.

Past shadows of nearby cypress trees telling late afternoon, he could make out fishermen hauling their boats close to shore, securing their nets. Only several years earlier—though it seemed a decade— the Zebedees and Simon would likely have been in their company.

"We're farther away than ever!" a voice behind him advised. "If it keeps on like this, we'll be walking a Roman mile to bring our supplies back and forth."

Had he not heard him, James would have known he was there by the smell of the catch. "Still, it's a magnificent view. But do you need a hand?"

"Don't trouble yourself," he replied. "Unless you would convey this in your cart." James leaned over from his seat, taking hold of a large iron hook, whereupon the fellow also handed up a heavy bucket of sardines and climbed aboard, sitting at his side. "You're not from around here. At least I haven't seen you before," he observed.

"No. I'm visiting. Perhaps you know him. Nathanael."

"That's a good one. Tell him you helped me carry this hook and bucket. He's the one who made them."

"Nathanael?"

"Doesn't matter he's small. Having hammered hot iron half his life, he's stronger than both of us. But I thought you knew him."

"We only met recently. I was looking for him."

"Well, just two turns ahead, and you'll find his house."

Pointing to a gate down a street to their right, the man said, "Here, give me that. And thanks for taking me this far. So tell him Judah the fisherman sends his greetings."

"Yes, I will."

Just as James finished tethering the horse a few steps from the gate, Nathanael appeared through the opening in a fence that separated his house from the next one over. "I use that building for my forge. I make ironware. But welcome. I'm glad you have come."

"Thank you," James replied. "Beit Zaida is like a glittering jewel in the sun. I was last here several years ago, at least."

"More like a pebble," Nathanael said, inviting him into the triclinium. "But we are blessed to live here."

"Are any of the Zebedee family still residents?" James asked, accepting a glass of water that Nathanael poured from a pitcher.

"Their mother. She is old and goes on and on about things nobody understands. But who would want to? She is rude, and her language is fitting a Samaritan."

"I see James and John all the time. Oh yes, I bring you greetings from Judah the fisherman."

"Forgive me for laughing, but it's not too necessary. He and I often play dice."

"He pointed out your house. And from what you said, you also know Simon."

"His wife still lives here, and her mother is getting old—like the rest of us, I suppose. Simon no longer visits them, as far as I know."

"But I probably shouldn't stay too long," James said. "Is there an inn nearby?"

"This is your inn. Let me show you the other room, and make yourself comfortable. The facilities are in back."

"Thank you. Just until morning, then, if it's no bother. But I should see to feeding my horse. He is at the tying post."

"We have a boy who loves the horses. In a short while, I will have a word with him about yours. But now is the perfect time to visit the synagogue. And of course, you want to know why you are here."

As they strolled down the street together, Nathanael slowed occasionally to greet passersby. When one of them and then another ignored him, it seemed impolite but might have been normal for people who saw each other daily.

Moments later, they were entering the large stone gateway of the synagogue.

Ornamented with carved relief images of flowers and scrolls, the cool interior was darkened by its arched ceiling resting on decorative lime-coated capitals, painted and colorful, forming sections for the stone benches. On the eastern side, toward Jerusalem, the wooden Torah cabinet was ensconced in an elaborate border of marble and housed behind a curtain, which Nathanael drew back. "The scroll is inside. But only the presiding officer has the key."

"It is beautiful," James said, "and what a chair!"

The monumental stone seat, with its front panel engraved "nasi," seemed more like a throne for a king, worthy of any man who bore its title.

"The president's chair, as it says. Eliezar ben Yehezkel sits there. Your brother would have seen it. I remember him."

"Did you and he talk with one another?" James asked.

"I'd heard so much about him from Simon and the Zebedee brothers that I felt I knew him, but we didn't talk very much."

"What did he say to you?"

Nathanael did not answer immediately. He led the way to a rear stone bench and gestured to James to have a seat next to him. "I never would have imagined," Nathanael began quietly, "that I would be confessing to Jesus' brother, repenting sins."

"I don't understand. Surely you have nothing to confess regarding my brother—and not to me."

"James, I see what a good man you are. And my heart goes out to you. I hope it's not wrong for me to say, but there is such sadness in your eyes."

"Please tell me."

"I was a follower of John, your cousin. It begins with that. If I flatter myself, I was a leader among his flock. He obeyed all the Torah's commandments and taught us. We were not all from here, and I think our following may have numbered more than a hundred. On pilgrimages to Jerusalem, those of us who were in his circle found him and kept in his company." He coughed and wiped his lips with the back of his hand. "I've breathed those iron vapors too long."

"Hard work, I'm sure," James replied, pretending not to have noticed the unpleasant smell of his exhaled breath.

"He immersed us, and we, in turn, bathed others—a ritual mikveh bath to cleanse our inner beings," Nathanael continued and then turned away to cough again. "He taught us to believe the Kingdom of God was coming. There would be a king to save us from the Romans. God would bless the anointed one with powers no army could stop."

"From the House of David."

"Yes, just as the prophets envisioned. This was before I had even heard about Jesus. But then Simon and the Zebedees, who bought ironwares from me—did I tell you that?—started talking about him, saying he could perform miraculous healings. Simon's face turned red with excitement every time there was some new story. He had cured his own mother-in-law and was permitted to heal on the Shabbat, saying that he had divine authority to do so."

Interrupting Nathanael, a Pietist entered, passing just in front of them, and walked to the ark, pressing his bearded face against it. After moving his lips in a rapid, wordless prayer, he turned and exited without a nod or greeting.

"You know what I said?" Nathanael asked, paying the man no attention as he left. "I was sarcastic. 'Sent by God to Nazareth? You must be joking.' And then he came here, just where we are sitting, and attempted to heal a sick woman, causing a disturbance. Like most worshippers, I thought he was wrong to do it. It was something you didn't do on Shabbat. But Simon's words were in my thoughts. Maybe he had divine authority."

"And that's when you met him?"

"Not quite."

James could not resist a smile at Nathanael's obvious desire to let the story unfold as dramatically as possible.

"I'm getting there," Nathanael said. "Time passed. And as you know, John strongly denounced Antipas as an adulterer. Meanwhile, the tetrarch's longtime Arab wife had run home to her father, the Nabatean Camel, Aretas."

"That was nearly three years ago."

"And John was arrested for encouraging popular sedition."

"Though he was innocent," James said.

"Innocent? Of course not. You should have heard his speeches. I only wish he could have lived to see so many of Antipas' fine buildings blazing to ashes! When John was arrested, do you know what that did to us? We prayed something bad would befall Antipas and his mock queen. His disaster would be our miracle."

"As it recently was," James said. "Only a month ago I had occasion to visit Kfar Nahum and saw the huge cloud from his camels' hooves. Surprising that he delayed his revenge this long."

"There were small incursions even before John's arrest, but Antipas still lives in that palace," Nathanael said, gesturing to the south, as if it were just down the road. "But you must have met John."

"As small boys. We exchanged greetings when Jesus and I visited John's mother on the holidays. But later on, I only saw him from a distance during the pilgrimages."

"Maybe you don't grasp what John meant to us. Of course to many, he was a demented fool, thinking himself an Elijah, dressing the part and spouting broken messages of salvation. When he proclaimed the Kingdom was near, they dismissed him as a ranting lunatic. But his words and cleansing were our path to God. Of course, I am talking to one who knows bitter loss. Forgive me."

"It's all right."

"It was then, when we first heard John was dragged off to Macherus prison, that Jesus came here again. He was at Simon's with the Zebedees, in his yard, and there were others, followers of John, like me. And Jesus too had just learned of John's arrest. You might have thought he would have talked about him. Said how great he was. Maybe that he was like Elijah. But he said nothing."

"And that's when you met?" James asked, trying to be patient.

"I stood at a distance, observing him, wondering what Simon found special about this fellow. After the debacle at this synagogue a year earlier, I had formed my opinion and saw nothing to change it. Finally, he stood up, looked around, and took notice of me by the fig tree in the yard. I admit I was nervous as he walked toward me. 'You are the one who never lies,' he said to me. It was what John always said about me. 'Nathanael,' I responded.

"He knew who I was and without a word extended his hand and touched the side of my face. At that moment, James, I had an experience I shall always remember. I felt love flowing into me, into my very being from the warmth of his hand. I felt I was a good person."

"He gave many people comfort during his life," James acknowledged. "I know what you are saying is true, Nathanael."

"Without another word, he left the yard and walked off into the darkness. I believe he could not share his pain over John's arrest with any of us. And no sooner was he gone from sight than Simon began talking about him."

"But what are you getting at?"

"You will soon see!" Nathanael exclaimed. "I knew about ruach ha-kodesh, that the holy spirit was a blessing from God. The ones who lived in the Salt Sea caves were known to embrace God's spirit and could pass it to others with their touch and their words—so too our sages, like Hillel and Gamliel. But I had never experienced it. I was desperate to understand how God could have taken John away and was yearning for an answer. I was now drinking in whatever Simon said."

"Which was?" James persisted.

"Which was that John was a messenger to prepare us for the arrival on earth of Jesus, King of the Jews."

"King of the Jews? He called him that?"

"Repeatedly, to us who followed John. Maybe not to the disciples because Jesus might get wind of it. But that had become your brother's title whenever Simon spoke to any of our group. John was just a messenger. James, you see what a small place Beit Zaida is. My reputation for honesty was something I treasured. I made it a rule—if I say something, I know it is true. And I went around heralding Jesus as King of the Jews. To this day, people who used to greet me look the other way. You may have noticed."

"I'm trying to follow," James said.

"How can you not see? I am the liar. Nathanael the ironsmith, a man supposedly incapable of deceit, I crowned your brother king with every word I spoke, in every conversation."

James became deeply thoughtful. "Not that it led to the charge over the cross," he finally observed. "The Romans could have found him guilty of that on their own."

"With all of us acclaiming him our messiah, our king, their false accusation sounded true. And I'm the one who served Simon's purpose, spreading that calumny. Without my telling everybody the supposed good news—that Jesus was God's anointed one—your brother might still be alive."

"So you had me make this trip to hear your confession? What difference does it make? It's neither for me to condemn your foolishness nor to forgive it. And if, in my heart, I forgive you, doesn't Simon deserve the same?"

"We are different, Simon and I." Nathanael seemed to be carefully considering his next words, so James exercised restraint and patiently waited for him to speak. "Simon's Jesus is based on lies," he finally said. "He isn't sculpting him as a god from misguided reverence. Even when Jesus was on the cross, Simon mourned only himself, an ordinary, often slow-witted fisherman who had spent his younger years netted by a wife he couldn't stand and trapped by circumstance that vitiated any prospect of respect. So he continues to fashion him, to make the false god who will save him from being so utterly unremarkable—like a robber who knows what he is doing is wrong but can't help himself because he fears he will be too poor to survive. Indeed, we are different! I mistook Jesus for God's anointed king—but unlike Simon I never knew how Jesus saw himself—just a son of man like any other; an inspired teacher but no more divine than you or me."

For several moments, they said nothing. Then James spoke again. "I shouldn't have come. All this has gotten me nowhere. What do you expect, Nathanael? That I will testify that Simon has been lying to create his false god, and its clay legs will crumble? To half the disciples, everything he says is revealed to him by Jesus."

"Yes, I want your forgiveness. Not for my sin, which is only cleansed by God's authority and certainly not by any heavenly Jesus, but for having worshipped and crowned the god Simon created. But I didn't mean to. I am sorry."

When James noticed that some spittle at the corner of Nathanael's lips was speckled with blood, he was reluctant to converse further. He stood up, saying, "If there were proof Jesus saw himself as a son of man like us and not as King of the Jews—and that Simon knew it—only then would his idol be seen for what it is. But there is as much chance of that as the heavens and earth closing like a book."

Nathanael led the way toward the entrance but paused and turned to face James. "There is one whose trust you must gain," he said hoarsely. "Though he has told me little, what he knows would unmask Simon."

"Who is he?"

"Not yet. If you want his help, you must explicitly denounce Simon for forcing Jesus into the mold of God's savior. Use the word 'helul,' heresy, and he will speak with you."

"Is it one of the disciples? Most of them can't bear the idea my brother was only human."

"Unless you do as I suggest, Simon shall have his way." Nathanael studied James to be sure he fully grasped his instruction.

"And what am I going to hear? Even my own group hopes that Simon is right—that Jesus is ruling them from above."

Nathanael had reached the entranceway of the synagogue, which was illuminated by the last light of day. "So are you good at dice?" he asked, as if he hadn't heard the question.

"I have played," James replied.

"Then listen for the one who surprises you by calling him Simon. And ask him about playing dice with Nathanael the ironmaker."

"Then it is one of the disciples!" James exclaimed but was deterred from further inquiry as Nathanael abruptly changed the subject.

"James, you must be hungry," his host said pleasantly.

After eating fish broiled on a metal platter forged by Nathanael, James was too tired to further strategize Simon's censure. Only when dawn broke and he was about to depart did he again refer to the ironmaker's advice. "Well, I wish you well, Nathanael. We will see what comes of your plan before very long. Many thanks for your help and hospitality."

"You are always welcome, my friend. How hard it is to believe that was little more than two years ago! Go with success, James."

CHAPTER TWENTY-ONE

$\mathcal{I}$t was after supper, and James was biding his time, not wishing to discomfit the disciples lounging in the lower sitting room. Several were discussing their coming vacations in the Galilee, where they would visit their families during the Festival of Lights. Jerusalem was closely guarded by the Romans during the celebration of Judah Maccabee's revolt, and speeches about the martyrdom of Jesus would be monitored. Matthias was, as James knew, remaining at home. It was prudent to spend the period away to avoid clashes with the centurion guards.

"I hope to visit my own house too," Simon said, "but there is pressing business with Paul. It won't suffice to hear from messengers how his work is going."

"Has there been news, Peter?" Thomas inquired.

"Well, perhaps it is worth hearing what our friends may tell us," he said, turning to Barnabas and John Mark, who had recently arrived from the north. "Would either of you care to report on the efforts in Tyre and Damascus?"

Mark, as they called him, gestured toward Barnabas, saying, "Listen to my mentor. He's a better speaker than I."

Lifting himself from the couch with the careful movement of a man whose weight required special dexterity, Barnabas faced the disciples and James. "It is good to see you all again," he began. "Tyre is no Jerusalem. For that matter, neither is Damascus or Antioch."

"Shalom, shalom," a few called out, expressing their welcome.

"I have been away too long. And Mark, I hope you will permit me to say you feel the same way. Brothers, from what you have told me in the past day, I understand the written story of Jesus and his teaching has yet to be completed. In the north, we await that. Our synagogues have the Torah. But Jesus' commentary—his voice—is missing. Should any of us think we can replace his words with our own? Of course not. But how are we to share his guidance and truth with our Jewish brothers in Tyre and Damascus or Antioch? Whatever we may say—even if we proclaim he is our inspiration—makes little impression.

"Naturally, once we have a scroll to share, a written witness to Jesus' life," Barnabas concluded, "Jews in the north—and I am sure this holds true here as well—will reflect on the written word. All who read and study it will be his students, and among them will be teachers to spread the net of him, who never caught a fish but has called together a school of us."

"What about the rumors?" Simon C'nani called out.

"What rumors?" Barnabas asked.

"Some of us have heard there has been an argument between you and Paul."

"I think we all would benefit from a written testament," Barnabas responded. "It's a perfect example of what makes it so necessary— that Paul claims Jesus said things that I seriously dispute. No need to deny we have our differences."

"I think you should speak openly with us," Bartholomew said, his wandering eye moving slightly away from the other.

"I am not keeping secrets," Barnabas replied. "Paul has told members of the Antioch congregation that their continued need for Torah is a sign of weakness."

"He's gone farther than that." All heads turned toward Mark. "I don't wish to interrupt you, Barnabas. You are a peacemaker."

"Say what you wish, my friend," Barnabas replied agreeably.

"When I told Paul he was misleading our Jewish brothers, he reacted angrily, urging me to go my own way—and you pleaded with him on my behalf, Barnabas. Then you too decided he had taken a wrong turn and joined me. And here we are. So it is best we air the dispute. Those of you who recall Jesus—is there one among you who ever heard him say Torah is a curse, a work of Satan?"

The commotion caused by the question was its own answer. Jesus had never said such a thing, and nearly all the disciples were vexed that Paul had blasphemed in his name. Among them, only Andrew believed devotion to Torah made observant Jews servants of Satan. But Simon still refused to bend, standing his ground against the temptation to label Torah an entrapment.

Surveying the angry group, he finally began calling them to quiet down. "I have received an epistle from the Jewish leader in Antioch to whom he made the remark. You should know that there was an argument between Paul and their congregation. When he tried to speak about Jesus, they flaunted the Torah and chased him from the synagogue with it, as if it was a sword—and he was humiliated. So he told them the only ones who needed the Torah were slaves to the Law and that since Satan wanted them to be his slaves, the Law came from Satan."

As they again began a loud stir of protests, he quelled their voices, loudly announcing he would be leaving the next morning to meet with Paul. "Silas and Barsabbas, who are here with us today, will join me." Off to the side, the two men raised their hands in a gesture of greeting, so the group might know who they were. "They are good men, and I expect them to fill in for Barnabas and John Mark,"

Simon continued. "Of course, I intend to find out what's going on. For now, let us not exaggerate the matter, lest small truths become harmful rumors."

"Rumors tell a lot," James said.

"I shall learn more very soon," Simon replied.

"And I too have heard a rumor."

"Is it something you wish to share, James?"

"I have heard that while Jesus was still with us, you are the one who anointed him King of the Jews."

"What?"

"His coronation, as I have it, was your own idea and that he never knew you gave him that title."

"I won't defend myself against this, as if I had done something wrong. It's not an accusation; it's a compliment."

"As it was told me, you said he himself was the sign God's Kingdom had begun."

"It is true! I was blessed. I recognized him."

"Thank God you did," squawked John. His brother James quickly followed, saying, "Amen, Peter!" And his brother, Andrew, added his voice. "Amen."

"But his coronation did not remain a secret from others," James continued. "Others passed it along in whispers, so that he never heard the title and had no chance to refute it. Instead, it bubbled like poison, which, when it came out, cost him his life."

"So this is your newest ploy, James? I admit it is beyond any measure of contempt I might have imagined. But it is no more a clever strategy to achieve control than your other devices. To suggest that I am to blame for Jesus' death is not a poor, misshapen accusation; it is bearing false witness."

"Is it?" James countered, his tongue feeling like a coiled snake about to strike. "Then let me not be taken for one fooled by the false god you have created, an idol represented as Jesus, whom we loved. He was a son of man who did not deserve his hideous end but returned to dust, as do all sons of man."

After these words, there was complete silence in the room. Simon directed his gaze at each disciple in turn, as if he was taking a vote on whom they would believe.

"Well, then, brothers, it seems I must reveal an exchange of words between me and Jesus that until this moment I had thought should best remain private."

"Tell us, Peter!" John the Zebedee declared, his voice discordant and loud.

"We have a right to know!" Thomas whined.

"James, you were not with us. It was while we were on the way to Caesaria Philipi, not long after John's execution. Everybody had dropped back, and I was walking at Jesus' side, so that it was just the two of us. And he asked me, 'Who do you say I am?' And I thought he was asking what people in general said about him, so I replied that some thought he was Elijah, and others believed he could be a return of John, who had only just died. But he made it clear he wanted me to answer for myself. So I said, 'You are the messiah king—the son of the living God.' That's when he said, 'You are Peter, a foundation of stone for my house. And I am giving you the keys of the kingdom of heaven. And whatever you decide on earth shall be decided in heaven—and whatever you deem worthless on earth shall be deemed worthless in heaven.' Then he instructed me to whisper only to the faithful that he was the messiah king until the time was right."

"Of course no one else heard him," James interrupted.

"Brothers, forgive me for having kept this to myself, but until today, revealing my name as Peter, as he gave it to me, was sufficient. Now I am forced to disclose the good news. Jesus was and is the messiah, King of the Jews."

"So he told you himself!" Andrew exclaimed. "Peter, I am proud you are my brother!"

"All honor to you, Peter!" Thomas proclaimed, and several others hailed him with ululation.

James felt the eyes of Matthew and Simon C'nani on him, and he noticed Thaddeus looking down.

As if the silence were witness to his triumph over James, Simon exulted in the sound of his own voice as he looked about and asked, "If any of you wish to join your devotion to mine, to celebrate the rule of our king who was our teacher, that would be welcome. Or James, have you more to say?"

Again there was silence. They all waited for his rejoinder, sensing a profound disgrace, and refrained from making any remarks that might interrupt his reply.

James realized at least several expected him now to surrender his position as president, rather than compete with one personally selected by Jesus to announce he was messiah king.

When James said nothing, Simon spoke again. "Thank you all. Thank you for knowing in your hearts that I spoke of Jesus as King of the Jews because that is what he wanted me to do—to you, the ones who are to exercise authority in his kingdom, and to others, as the word spreads to the faithful, the worthy. I hope, given the awful condemnation you heard this evening, making me Jesus' murderer— how, after all, does a man murder the one who is saving him?—that I will have your complete confidence."

Simon counted the murmurs of approval, noting the minority had shrunk to only Bartholomew, James bar Alpheus, Simon C'nani, and Thaddeus, with Matthew nodding hesitantly. He began to express his thanks, when Philip, reserved as he was, quietly offered his own thoughts.

"I for one," Philip said, "am not prepared to lose James as our companion, friend, and president. Let our discipleship not be deprived of his wisdom and counsel. Though he has not defended himself against your description of events," he said somberly, addressing Simon, "he cannot. He was not there. And I trust his honest intention to serve his brother's memory with passion and faith."

"But let's leave that to James!" Simon blustered. "None of you were there next to me, not to hear the words Jesus spoke to me. And you all know I am telling you the truth! But Philip, you surprise me! You have always believed in what we are doing. Have you changed?"

"We are doing good work, inspiring others with Jesus' teaching. It is what he told us to do," Philip responded.

"Not to engage in helul—heresy!" James declared.

"Then tell me Philip," Simon demanded adamantly, "what is the need to disturb our progress by sowing seeds of doubt?"

"Simon," Philip replied as he turned sharply to face James, "it seems to me that not everything you say comes from Jesus—not even the things you say Jesus said. We must all search our hearts to know what Jesus would have said or done."

"I agree," Simon answered, his brow furrowed by doubt at Philip's use of his former name. "I suggest you all think about these issues and that we talk about them after the holiday."

Somberly and without further debate, the group retired to their bedding or departed for an evening stroll along the adjacent walkways. Outside the gate, Philip stood alone as James approached. "It's getting cool," Philip said, not turning to see who it was.

"Yes. Jerusalem will be cold soon enough," James replied.

"You must have been surprised."

"By what you said?"

"Yes."

James nodded. "I was. And it raised a question in my mind."

"Ask. If I can answer it, I will."

"Have you played dice with Nathanael the ironmaker?"

Philip said nothing for a moment and then looked up at the darkening sky. "Soon there will be so many stars," he mused. "James, the answer to your question is that we must visit your friend. He must record the truth before there is no one to tell it."

"Matthias?"

"Yes."

"But what would you have him write?"

"He did not see that I was there, nearby. I know what Jesus said to him."

"About his name—Peter? About being the messiah and king?"

"Yes."

"What did you hear? And if it is important, why have you said nothing about it?"

"Simon and I grew up together," Philip said. "I love him as a brother."

"Then you are also from Beit Zaida?"

"Yes. And I played dice with Nathanael not too long before you visited him. Did he take your money?"

"I fell asleep before he had the chance."

"You'll hear what I have to say. But I will be ready at sunup."

CHAPTER TWENTY-TWO

Sudden shadows played across his closed eyes and then glittering light. Groaning slightly, Matthias opened one eye.

"Two of you?" he asked, squinting at the pair of doves on the windowsill. "Am I so important? And how is it that you are so small yet can shield the entire sun, letting its light reach me by folding just one feather?"

After a morning pomegranate and warm bread with honey, he splashed cool water on his face and dried off with the towel. He talked to the one tilting its head and watching him. "How I once loved your delicious eggs. But it's hard to eat the young of those who are your only companions. Well, it seems I too am trying to shield the world from falsehoods with a feather. Yes, maybe I am trying to do the same," he pondered, reaching for the writing point.

Following the Sukkot festival, those two years ago, as I have written, the others went on to the north without me, and I returned home only to learn that John had been arrested.

If I wondered about Jesus' reaction to the news, as I was certain word had reached him, I did not need to wait long. He arrived at my door the next day, plainly in a frazzled state of mind.

Again and again, he asked me to use my influence. Listing every possible recourse, even suggesting Elizabeth urge Joseph to do something, his storm of words finally subsided. The truth was grim. No matter that Joseph was John's uncle, or that I was a member of the Sanhedrin, the tetrarch was not likely to even note our pleas.

Never did such morose conversation—and prolonged silences—measure time. In many different ways to say the same thing, we found countless recollections of John's wisdom and courage, and there was darkness and despair in our unspoken thoughts. We were paying homage as if his fate was sealed.

Several weeks went by, and slowly the torment of our outrage found that quiet place of recess for painful preoccupations that no logic can resolve.

Before continuing, Matthias used the broad point, writing:

A paralyzed man lowered through the roof

And then he resumed . . .

Jolted upright by a sudden noise—the pounding of a fist on my door—Jesus and I were alarmed at the voice outside, demanding we open it. I refused, only to hear the roof being breached by force, with a cascading cloud of clay and straw coating this floor.

I could only stare in amazement at the sight of several large men lowering themselves into my house, aiding their companions, who were passing down a pallet through the gaping hole they had formed. Stretched out upon it, to my astonishment, was the fully prone figure of a man. Only then, at my suggestion, did they open my door from the inside, permitting others who were noisily knocking to gain entrance.

Brilliantly lit by the sun, the scene was altogether as remarkable as it was disturbing. For the first time I noticed Jesus' disciples were there too, almost all of whom I had come to know, and I was able to greet by name, except for one—an unfamiliar face but who is memorable because Jesus, with the dust still settling, introduced him to me as Nathanael.

Stopping to wipe his brow, Matthias now realized why the name had sounded familiar when James said he would visit him in Beit Zaida.

Then the commotion ceased, and Jesus was standing, looking down at the poor soul who obviously had only the least ability to even move his limbs.

To anybody who may one day read this account, please permit me to insert a word explaining the perplexing development. In our Torah, suffering and diseases are not always considered sure signs of God's punishment, but some maladies are more suspicious than others. Lameness and blindness, as well as leprosy—and paralysis, which afflicted the one on the floor—are in this category. Miserable individuals suffering from diseases caused by sin would require forgiveness from God, and that would coincide with their cure, a reward promised the penitent, according to our sages and prophets, when God's Kingdom began, if not sooner.

Fully appreciating these verities, Jesus showed sympathy and joined the man, kneeling next to him. Touching his forehead and face, he said, "Your sins will be forgiven. You will walk again."

The man's smile—and I bear witness—was as bright as water sparkling in the sun. Truly, it brought me and the others who saw it nearly to tears.

Then they all were leaving, carrying him out through the door, thanking Jesus and bowing their heads to him in the way one honors a dignitary. Two of them assured me they would stop by before the festival to completely rebuild my roof, and I told them the sunshine pouring in was welcome for at least a few days more. "We'll be here before it rains again," one assured me.

As they made their way out, several disapproving Pietists, having been drawn to the commotion, stood watching at the front gate, and I overheard Simon tell one, "Jesus has forgiven the man, and he will walk again," which caused the other to reply that Jesus was blaspheming, that only God could forgive sin. And several others chimed in, "He thinks he is God."

As the pallet reached the street, Simon kept on about the miracle we had just witnessed, calling it proof he had forgiven sin. Only the one named Nathanael plainly disavowed his oratory, telling Simon C'nani, who was within earshot, "If Jesus forgave the man his sins, and those sins were the cause of his paralysis, why didn't he get up and walk?" Following this remark, as I best recall, he set off in his own direction and did not join them again.

But Jesus had never made any such claim. All he said was, "Your sins will be forgiven"—not "are forgiven."

As the last of them reached the street, Jesus admitted to me, "It's easier to say your sins will be forgiven than to get him to stand up and walk away, carrying his bedding." Such was his sad observation, perhaps a joke at his own expense, because he could do nothing about the fellow's suffering.

After that, Jesus joined his students, and I was alone for several days, until the time came for me to make the trip to the Temple for the Festival of Lights, as it is still called by elders like me. More recently, some have begun to refer to it as Hanukkah, or Feast of Dedication, hailing Judah Maccabee's victorious rededication of the Temple two centuries earlier.

Upon arriving at the outer courtyard of the Temple, I could not have expected what happened. Naturally, the Roman centurions were patrolling the paths and roadways, and I could see legionnaires on the upper balcony of the Antonia fortress, which housed many of their men, but they typically had refrained from entering the Temple's sacred precincts so as not to incite resentment and violence by flouting Jewish law. Inside the arched gate, I caught sight of Jesus walking briskly toward the Portico of Solomon, with his disciples half running to keep up. He passed within thirty feet of me, not even looking up.

Had I wondered why he was in such a rush, that question was answered by loud noises made by fist-size rocks hurtling through the air in his direction, crashing into the massive stone-block floor.

Chasing him and his students, a group of Pietists hesitated as they reached the columned facade of the portico, probably afraid they would risk its damage by the continued onslaught. Moving to the side, so their missiles could be thrown without striking the masonry, they shouted insults and accusations.

I admit I was terrified. That was the first time I had witnessed what anger does to make animals out of sons of men. Even their words were spit out past snarling teeth. "If you think you're the messiah," one hissed, "why don't you just say so? How much longer are you going to keep us in suspense?"

The man's arm suddenly was raised over his head, and the stone he held was in plain sight.

By moving backward, so that the projectile would possibly abrade the ornate reliefs decorating the wall, Jesus had deterred his intention.

"I have kept the Torah's laws!" Jesus declared. "Which one of them are you about to stone me for breaking?"

His challenge gained several moments as they consulted with each other. Seeing an opportunity, I made my way forward and without even time taken for a greeting, I urged him to withdraw to the courtyard of the Treasury building, with its guards and Temple police. There, my own official capacity, I believed, would have a salutary effect.

"We don't intend to stone you for doing good," one finally roared, "but for saying you are God's son!"

"Doesn't the psalm tell us," Jesus replied, "'You are sons of God?' So the sacred text uses the phrase, 'sons of God' of all those who receive insight from the holy spirit. Yet you say anyone who says I am a son of God is transgressing."

I was aware several still held stones to throw, and I wondered whether they were truly prepared to kill a man because they disagreed with him. How many arguments and interpretations have been the daily fare of our Sanhedrin as we scribes, Pharisees, sages, and Saducees shape a consensus. Interpreting our laws and scripture with different opinions is the mark of our most illuminated conclusions.

Even as these thoughts crossed my mind, another called out, "Our father is Abraham!"

Jesus answered, "If you were Abraham's descendants, you would do as Abraham did! As it is, you want to kill me. That is not what Abraham did."

"Are you trying to teach **us***?" another replied angrily, aware of the reference to Abraham having spared his son, Isaac.*

Prompted one by the other, anger turned to rage. Several stepped ominously closer, shouting, "He is possessed!"

I cannot recall the manner of defense, if any, which his disciples may have attempted. Perhaps they moved as close to him as they could without placing themselves in danger of being struck by the stones. Joanna, who I later learned was the wife of Chuza, a member of Antipas' palace staff, stood out as the only woman.

This I do recall. As a stone hit the floor near his feet, we made our blurred retreat to the wide expanse near the Treasury, where another of these desert mongrels came forward and was about to strike. Just then, a nearby policeman intervened, stepping directly between us. The Pietists quickly tossed away the incriminating stones, scattering the evidence of their intent to commit murder.

Then, as if the matter was none of the policeman's business, one declared, "He has a demon!"

When Jesus made no reply, another added, "Are we wrong to say you are possessed?"

But another called out to the policeman, "Why bother to listen to him?"

"They want to kill me," Jesus countered, as a few more Temple guards approached.

The other replied, "You are mad! Who wants to kill you?"

Here again, recognizing several were from Kfar Nahum, I tried to intercede, telling them, "He did one thing—healing a man in Kfar Nahum who was one of your own. He thought the man had a demon, screaming like he did."

Completing the thought, Jesus added, "I asked you then, and I repeat it now—if I hoped to chase away his demon, how could I be from Satan?"

Hearing this, others who stopped to listen had the impression the police were about to arrest him. One said, "He is a good man," to which his companion replied, "He is leading people astray."

Among the Pietists, several continued making defamatory remarks. I heard one say, "How should he teach anything? His mother is a prostitute. He has no idea who his father is. He is shetuki."

The other answered, "No wonder he acts like a madman. Some say he even thinks he can forgive sin!"

At this point, I addressed the police drawn to the commotion. "As a member of the Sanhedrin who helps craft our laws, I think I speak with knowledge. The law requires a hearing before an arrest, and he has not been summoned for a hearing."

Nodding authoritatively, several nearby Pharisees expressed their agreement, and one even mocked the Pietists, scoffing, "Are you afraid he will lead you astray?" which caused several to become so irate they could only make gurgling sounds.

Another onlooker, whom I did not then recognize, telling from appearance neither a Pietist nor Pharisee, also spoke up for Jesus' right to be protected. Today, as I write this, I know it was Nicodemus, Joseph's servant, and I am certain he was in the vicinity to keep an eye on him. But I shall have more to say about Nicodemus farther on.

Angered by our support for their adversary, a Pietist, apparently aware I was a scribe, then denounced me. "What? You believe in him too?" the fellow barked. "None of us do!" And pointing at the disciples, he raved, "They are rabble—am ha-aretz! They know nothing about Torah! They are cursed!" His scathing insult fell on deaf ears, and he then turned to the nearest police official. "You should arrest him," he snarled, "or have you been possessed by him too?"

Impatient to return the Treasury environs to a peaceful mood worthy of the festival, the police finally dispersed the Pietists, cautioning them not to cause a further disturbance.

One thing I will never forget was how one of them, just as he was being escorted away, turned toward me and said ominously,

"You must be am ha-aretz yourself—born from sin—to think a prophet could come from those local Galileans!"

We did not remain in Jerusalem for the eight days of the festival. The pall cast over us by the ugly confrontation and our fear it might be repeated had taken hold. Numbering fifteen, there were, in addition to his group of twelve, only Joanna, whom I have mentioned, and me. At the beginning of our return northward, we stayed with Mary and Martha for two days in Bethany and then continued on.

After helping himself to a drink of water, Matthias returned to his task. He took a deep breath and touched the broad point to the parchment, meticulously crafting the large, dark letters:

Don't think I wish to abolish Torah

then continued with a fine, new point . . .

In the way one keeps still when a friend seems deeply troubled by private thoughts, we walked wordlessly for almost half a day. Only when he spoke was the silence finally broken, and I, for one, sensed a profound moment.

We'd been resting or napping on a stretch of grass, and several of us sat up from sprawled positions when he spoke. "Don't think that I wish to abolish the Torah or the prophets," he said, looking directly at Simon. "I do not wish to abolish them but to see they are taught and kept."

At the time, it struck me that he often respected Simon's leadership, if not a soaring intellect, and this was no more than a display of that high regard. Today, I admit I wonder whether he didn't have a premonition that Simon might mislead the others by making Torah seem a vestige of some antiquated past.

Certain I was then, as I am now, that those who voiced criticism of Jesus had found their mark, more sure than any stones they hurled. He still was concerned that he could be leading his disciples astray, even after his immersion by John, causing them to believe he was replacing Torah with his own laws or that he was master of the Shabbat and could revise or eliminate all sacred scripture. His next words were as direct as he had ever uttered.

"For truly, I tell you, heaven and earth will pass away before a yud, or the smallest jotting, will pass away from Torah. Whoever, then, is lenient concerning its laws and teaches men so shall be called least in the Kingdom!"

His tone of reprimand was not lost on the disciples. If they thought the Kingdom of God was independent of Torah, their false impression had been corrected.

Grown quiet like scolded children, the disciples spoke only sporadically about small topics, as we continued on.

From what he said next, I am confident that he was facing a quandary about how to explain the advent of God's Kingdom. He stopped and turned to face us. Looking about, he took notice of various strangers on the fringe of our circle, men who appeared to be listening with intense curiosity. No doubt, John's arrest had filled him with foreboding.

"This is what the Kingdom of God is like," he began. "A man throws seed on the land. Night and day, while he is asleep and while he is awake, the seed is sprouting and growing. How? He does not know. Of its own accord, the land produces first the shoot, then the ear, then the full grain in the ear."

When they seemed disappointed that there would be no sudden Kingdom of God—that it was concurrent with learning Torah—he looked about and saw a large bush by the road. "A mustard seed at the time of sowing is the smallest of all the seeds on earth. Yet once it is sown, it grows into the biggest shrub of all and puts forth large branches, so that birds can make nests in its shade."

Still dissatisfied, Andrew interrupted, demanding, "But when will the Kingdom be revealed?"

Jesus was crestfallen. Their surmise that he had foreknowledge of God's intentions was evidence of his worst suspicions. "No one knows except God," he replied moodily.

Then he told another parable. "A sower went out to sow his seed, and as he went, some fell along a path. The birds ate them, and some fell on rocky soil where they had little moisture, and the sprouts withered. More seeds fell among thorns and were choked off. But the seeds that fell into good soil grew many-fold."

Plainly confused, Thaddeus inquired what the seeds were. And James bar Alpheus wanted to know whether the disciples themselves were in the story.

Jesus almost never snapped at them in annoyance, but his words were harsh. Seeing we were not alone, he said almost inaudibly, "I am speaking to you in parables so no one else will understand. Don't you get the parable? How will you understand other parables?"

As we made our way, aware we had moved beyond earshot of any who might hear, he told them what the parables meant, because they were unable to grasp their meaning.

"Those who listen to the words of Torah and accept them will grow like the mustard seed." Adjuring Andrew to refrain from interrupting with his typical, impatient questions, he elaborated, "The rich soil is your honest and good hearts and must bear fruit with effort. Those who let Torah words be choked off, or who don't

have ears to hear them or the heart for them to take root might as well give themselves to Satan."

More guarded than usual, he concealed his ideas from what he had begun to recognize was dangerous scrutiny. Using the parables, a form of expression likely to befuddle any who harbored ill will toward him, he would explain them privately to his students, when he wouldn't be overheard.

I also suspect that, perhaps for the first time, he doubted his disciples' acumen, thinking some of them were incapable of growing, no matter what seeds of Torah he might plant. And as frustration so often spawns irritation, his own was close to anger. Comparing them to leaven, an impurity that is necessary for baking, I thought was a near insult.

"The Kingdom of Heaven will happen the same way a woman mixes leaven with three measures of flour," he said. "The leaven is hidden, but then the bread rises."

From their unhappy faces, I felt several recognized the three measures of flour were the Priests, Levites, and traditional Hebrews, which, by implication, characterized his own students as impure yeast.

Here, I will tell you, whatever faded memory may plague my record of Jesus' parables, there was one I shall always hear as if he had just said it. It was not about the Kingdom of God but was, I think, his way of reassuring them that they would not always be an "impurity" in Jewish society. If they chose to be part of God's Covenanted community and dedicated themselves to finding their way back from disregard of Torah, a welcome awaited them.

Here is what he said: "There was a man who had two sons, and the younger one asked his father to give him whatever wealth would be his to inherit, which he did. Not many days later, he went with the possessions to a distant land and spent all he had on prostitutes and loose living. Poor and without food, he found a citizen of that land to pay him a small wage for feeding his swine. Having barely enough to purchase a day's food, he was so hungry that he ate from the pigs' pods. Starving, he thought about the home he had left and lamented that his father's servants had bread to spare, while he was wasting away. What he had done, by acting with such disregard for his father, squandering what his father had given him, meant he no longer deserved to be part of the family. And he told himself, 'I will go to my father and tell him I am not worthy to be your son. Just let me be one of your servants.' But when he arose and returned, and his father saw he had come back, he embraced and kissed him, even while his son was saying, 'I have sinned against you and heaven. I am no longer worthy of being called your son.'

"But his father told the servants, 'Bring the best robe and put it on him. And put a ring on his hand and shoes on his feet. And bring the fatted calf and kill it. Let us eat and rejoice, for my son was lost and is found. He was dead and is alive again!'

"Now as the older son came back from the field and, upon approaching the house, heard the singing and dancing, he asked the servants about it. When they told him his brother had returned and they were eating the fatted calf, he became angry and refused to join the celebration. Even when his father asked him to come in, he would not, saying, 'For him who left your house and spent your wealth on harlots, you kill the fatted calf. Though I have obeyed all your commandments, you never have had such festivity in my honor.'

"To this, his father replied, 'Son, you are always with me. And all that is mine is yours. Now it is fitting to rejoice and be glad, *for this brother of yours was lost and now is found, was dead and now is alive.'"*

Did they recognize themselves in the parable? It is hard to say. On one hand, Jesus described them as the son who had squandered the blessings of their Jewish family, leaving Torah behind, only to discover they were hungry for its nourishment. But they would not be permanently exiled to the uncovenanted distant land if they repented and embraced the commandments, just as the older son, the traditional Hebrews, had always done.

But before they had a chance to inquire, as they probably would have, circumstances required a change of demeanor.

Around a turn in the hilly road, just approaching the Samaritan boundary, a group of Pietists crossed our path, preventing us from passing.

"We have a question for you," a brazen, bearded fellow said sharply. "Will you answer it?"

As soon as he said it, the face was known to me. He had been with the others who, like pack dogs, challenged us near Aenon where we had encountered John on the way north, following the Sukkot Feast of Booths.

Permitting no time for Jesus to decline, he said, "We have heard that you teach there should be no divorce unless adultery is proved. Isn't that so?"

Taking his measure, Jesus told him, "You have made your wives into whores by divorcing them so you may be with a different woman. How many of you have accused them of spending time with another man, so they might be sent off without the marriage contract's promise of security? I tell you that to divorce your wife in order to be with another woman who has caught your eye is adultery. And your wife who is sent away under such *circumstances is not divorced, so that she too becomes guilty of adultery by finding a new man she calls her husband."*

"But what about this?" the Pietist challenged. "If a man dies and is childless, our laws say his widow is required to at least consider marriage to an eligible brother of his so she may bear a child within the family. And imagine that she does so, and he also dies so that she again marries another brother who sadly suffers the same fate, all three leaving her childless. When she herself passes on and is in heaven, which of the brothers will be her husband?"

Here I must remark what brilliant level of intelligence Jesus showed in the face of the concealed threat, one I only sensed was hidden beneath the scheme of words.

In measured cadence, he responded, "Neither she nor they will be married any longer. They will be free spirits, like angels."

Later, when we were by ourselves and I asked what their purpose was, Jesus told me they hoped for a different answer, that he would say the woman did not have any right, even in heaven, to claim she was married to one brother while another brother she had married was still alive. That answer, had he offered it, would have been taken to reject Herodias' wedlock with Antipas, because his brother Philip was still alive at the time of their so-called wedding and was adultery since he had never given her a divorce.

Not satisfied that John had been imprisoned, they were seeking to give Antipas a similar reason for arresting Jesus. But the disappointment they felt was soon turned into embarrassment when Jesus showed he recognized their leader and understood full well his intention.

"What did you go out to see when you were spying on John?" Jesus challenged them in return. "Will you say with certainty

whether his teaching was from man or from God? You claim to know a true prophet. But you come from people who murdered Zechariah in front of the sanctuary doors!"

Outraged, one retorted, "Had we been there and been alive in the days of our fathers, we would not have taken part with them in shedding the blood of any prophet."

Jesus replied, "In saying 'our fathers,' you bear witness against yourselves, admitting you are the sons of those who murdered prophets. Now you would prepare the tomb of another prophet. But I have a question for you, you who are whitewashed on the outside but full of dead men's bones. A man had two sons, and he said to the first, 'Son, go to work in the vineyard today.' And he answered, 'I will not.' But afterward he changed his mind and went. The father went to the second of the sons and said the same. And he answered, 'I am going,' but he did not go. Which of the two acted according to his father's wishes?"

"Of course it was the first son," one of the Pietists immediately answered. Another added, "He was the one who repented and did as his father asked."

"Well," Jesus told them, "it was harlots and tax collectors who came to John first. Though they had refused at the outset of their lives to prepare for God's Day and His Kingdom, they entered the vineyard. You have seen it with your own eyes that his was a way of righteousness and still you do not accept it. You shut the Kingdom of God, neither entering it yourself nor allowing others who would enter to do so. You did not let them in during the years of tithing, and now, during the seventh year, you would keep them out by taking away the key of knowledge." The sharp rebuke was followed by words that ring increasingly true, even as I write them. "You would strain out a gnat," he declared, "and let in a camel!"

I grasped the allusion: John was the gnat, little more than an irritant compared to Aretas, the king of Nabatea, called "the Camel."

These Pietists had supported John's arrest for inciting the population against the adulterous tetrarch, while celebrating his marriage to their mock Maccabee queen, and in so doing had done more than John to ensure the Camel's revenge—a battle Jesus foresaw but which he only waged a month ago, shortly after I commenced this scroll.

Refusing to be further delayed by their arrogance, Jesus led the way forward, and we went northward, passing the outskirts of Samaria, just on its eastern edge by the Jordan River. Despised as the Samaritans are by most Jews, John the Zebedee made derisive remarks about them, acting superior because he didn't want anyone to think he had a mixed Hebrew ancestry like theirs. And Jesus told this parable:

"A man was traveling the road we are on and was surrounded by robbers. They beat him and took all he had and left him lying by the side of the road, half dead. A Temple priest passed by, without stopping to help him, and so did a Levite. But a Samaritan traveling this road stopped and treated his wounds, cleansing them with balm, pouring wine on them, and using spare bandages he carried in his pack. Then he helped him on his cart and took him to a nearby inn. He even paid for his room. You have heard me teach the Torah's commandment to love your neighbor as yourself. So I ask, who treated him more like a neighbor—the priest, the Levite, or the Samaritan?"

When all answered in unison that it was the Samaritan, Jesus replied, "So do the same yourself, or else the Samaritan will be better than you."

We soon reached the vicinity of an inn, and the Zebedees were having an argument. The older brother, James, apparently had control over their funds, money from their deceased father. So John, the younger one, said to Jesus, "Rabbi, tell him to give me money, that it is a share of the inheritance."

"Who appointed me your judge?" Jesus berated him. "Am I the one to tell you how to divide your possessions?" When John seemed stunned, Jesus added, "The Torah commands us not to covet, not to think your life is only about possessions. There was a man whose land produced so much that he needed new barns for storage. When he built them and they too were full, he told himself that he had all he needed for the future, and could eat, drink, and be merry without giving his possessions further thought. Then as he lay down to sleep, fully at ease, he heard the voice of God. 'Tonight,' God told him, 'your soul must be with Me.' And all the man could do was bid farewell to his possessions. Here, my friend, is what you need to understand. Your soul must be rich toward God. You can't have both money and God as your master."

If he hoped to convey his point by this simple parable, the next question from Thomas ended that prospect.

"Good teacher," he asked, "what commandment must a man do to inherit eternal life?"

Though I was just getting to know them back then, I had already seen that the disciples' questions often reflected their own personalities. Thomas, in this instance, showed his typical reluctance to believe anything not consonant with what he already believed. He had simply decided Jesus' parable was about the path to eternal life. Of course, it was much more a parable for the Zebedees, since John, especially, was always dwelling on money and arguing over the inheritance, instead of valuing the spiritual path. It was certainly not about inheriting endless life, which seemed to be a general preoccupation. Not surprisingly, Thomas' request for clarification completely ignored what Jesus had said only a moment before.

"But, good teacher . . ." Thomas again began.

"Why do you call me good?" Jesus retorted angrily. "Only God is good! And if you want to inherit eternal life, follow the Torah's commandments. Start with the Ten Commandments. Then do this mitzvah—give to the poor."

Recalling the exchange, he would lament on a later occasion that he had taught them that same lesson on Rosh ha-shannah but found it necessary to constantly repeat himself.

That night we stayed at the inn, taking up two rooms, with a private vestibule provided for Joanna. I recall an odd occurrence that strikes me today as having significance. Almost asleep, Simon, who was stretched out on a pallet near my own and quite out of earshot of Jesus, was speaking with his brother. He said, "Andrew, you see how he conceals his identity except to those who are chosen? We who understand his words are showing him our merit. Recognizing who he is—that is the key to the Kingdom, and those who cannot fathom his teaching are not included. Yes, those who know he is the chosen one are themselves chosen. That is how it works!"

Because I wanted to spare Jesus further aggravation over a seemingly insignificant remark, I never mentioned Simon's advice to his brother. Truly, I would not have let it interrupt my sleep, as tired as I was, but I had been kept awake by the sound of James bar Alpheus grinding his stubby teeth the night long.

At sunup, I continued northward with them, thinking that if I left his side and went home, despite their company, he would be in bleak solitude. His disciples had become almost distant and awkward toward him, while he was estranged from them mostly by his preoccupation with John, which distress they did not recognize or share. Bartholomew's wandering right eye, which I had come to recognize as a measure of his unsettled feelings, was emblematic of the moment's detachment, not looking at all in the same direction as the other. Then the separateness I sensed became surprisingly real.

On the border of Kfar Nahum, our group was met by several men who identified themselves as officials of the neighboring villages. The first to speak said that as representative of Kfar Nahum, his duty was to inform Jesus he could not enter. Immediately, his companions announced they were delegated by the councils of Chorazin and Beit Zaida to warn him to keep out—and he should not transgress their village precincts or he would be arrested. Adding salt to the wound, one after the other made it a point to welcome his students, recognizing that they had family and homes in the area and should not feel responsible for their teacher being banished.

What legal basis there may have been for so extreme a decision, I cannot say. Nor did they produce the list of grievances that led to this step. But Jesus was not caught up in the details of their injustice toward him.

"Woe to you, Chorazin! Woe to you, Beit Zaida!" he exclaimed, and then turning to the one who had first addressed him, he said, "And you, Kfar Nahum, will you be thought as high as heaven? You will be brought down as low as hell!"

Jesus led the way toward a grassy embankment and then waited for us to sit around him to hear his words.

"When you go from here and when you enter one of these towns," he began, "tell the people you talk to they should have faith in God's Kingdom."

"But we will stay with you!" Simon C'nani declared.

Undeterred, Jesus continued, "Wherever you go, stay with worthy people. If you wish people 'shalom aleichem'—peace to you—and they don't return your greeting, leave the place. Don't accept money or food from them, but shake the dust off your sandals and move on. Don't even take their dust on your sandals with you. And don't move to non-Hebrew territory or enter any Samaritan town. Go to others who are lost sheep of the House of Israel. Tell them the Kingdom of God is theirs too."

Noticing that several curious Pietists had ventured closer to overhear, Jesus said, "I am sending you out as sheep in the midst of wolves." Then, in the manner that had become familiar, using a parable to protect his teaching from their slander, he said, "There were not enough laborers for the harvest. So a householder went looking for laborers and found some who he agreed to pay a denarius for a day in the vineyard. Later, he found others who he also hired, and then still later he found others and asked them why they were idle. When they said nobody wanted to hire them, he hired them too. Then when the end of the day came, the ones who were hired last were paid the same as those who had worked all day in the scorching sun. But when the first ones complained, saying they should receive more, the householder answered that all were equal and that they had all received the same share as agreed."

It seemed to me then, as it does now, they understood he was saying good-bye. Their equality with all members of the Jewish people mattered little to them just then and the subtleties of his *story even less. Their bewildered expressions mirrored only a crushing sense of loss as they watched Jesus turn his back and walk away with me toward Ephraim.*

Many weeks went by, and his mood alternated between morose and angry. More than once he mentioned leaving for Nazareth, but I urged him to remain in my home, at least until warmer weather.

During that time, I recall my attempts to improve his humor with witty remarks about the disciples. "The Zebedees must drive you mad," I said.

"Boanerges," he replied, smiling slightly at his choice of their Greek nickname.

"Sons of thunder," I translated, adding, "but without the lightning. And Thaddeus, who listens with a gaping mouth—I'm never sure if he's amazed at what you're saying, or about to yawn and fall asleep. I suppose it's lucky he doesn't have James bar Alpheus' teeth, or we'd all be keeping our eyes shut, not to mention Bartholomew's eye . . ." But I did not continue about him or the others, because Jesus suddenly rose and went outside. Now, upon reflection, I can honestly say he never insulted them or made jokes at their expense. Nor did I do it again.

Then one day, a messenger came. He said simply and without grasping the impact of his words, "I bring a message for Jesus of Nazareth from Simon bar Yona. He sends you word that your cousin John has been executed. He says to inform you they will be meeting at the lake tomorrow morning." Numbed by the words, I thanked the fellow and gave him several prutot.

After he was out the door, Jesus said, "Will you come with me? I must go to the lake."

Word spread over the Galilee that John was dead, drawing his followers together like the plaintive sound of a shepherd's flute.

In a stream of groups, their number turned into hundreds, as they gathered on the southeastern shore of the Kinneret, as we also call it. By the time we arrived, the large crowd milled about on the grassy banks, burnished green by the fresh breezes of spring.

As a tear rolled down his cheek, Matthias rose quickly, lest it fall on the parchment. Determined not to become immersed in pity, he wiped his face with a damp cloth and rendered the next heading.

Jesus' eulogy for John

Watching from a distance, unobserved, Jesus said to me, "They are like sheep without a shepherd." He went forward, leading the way, and was immediately noticed. As the crowd became aware of his approach, conversations and talk subsided. Simon and Andrew, along with other of his students, excitedly rushed to his side. Not even referring to John, they began chattering about their activities. One reported that they had been doing exorcisms, and they'd met somebody doing the same thing. "In your name!" he added, as if to prove his continuing devotion.

"At least the one who does that is not my enemy," Jesus said to me in a private aside as we made our way forward.

Finally, we had reached the lake's edge, and he turned around, surveying the large assembly that was plainly waiting for him to speak.

Besides John's followers and Jesus' former companions, he saw, as did I, a recognizable cluster of local town officials, though this area was outside their jurisdiction, alongside Pietists—possibly so-called Herodians, the members of Antipas' administration who consecrated his adulterous marriage. Antipas certainly appreciated that John's execution was likely to cause a stir and even unrest, and these spies might have been there on his instruction or might have taken it upon themselves to keep him informed.

As he studied their faces and considered what to say, the parables were done. The stories that concealed meaning behind a shield of symbolic allusion were now put away. His only armor was what God might see fit to provide. He began slowly, determined that his voice be heard. His words, weighted with grief, carried steadfast in funereal homage to the farthest listener among them.

"Since the time John began his purifications," he proclaimed, "violent people have ruled, attempting to keep the Kingdom of God for themselves only, taking it by storm. Because he didn't eat and drink, they said he was possessed. Because I do eat and I do drink, they say I am a drunkard and a glutton and criticize me for sharing meals with those who have sinned.

"Well, I tell you with the utmost seriousness, one greater than John has never been born. He has been like an Elijah, keeping the Torah and leading you to God's Kingdom." Casting his gaze directly on the ones who were there as spies for Antipas, he asked them, "Did you expect to see him wearing luxurious clothes? Well, you wouldn't have seen that. The one who wears such clothes is the one in the palace. But what did you expect to see? Did you expect him to be like you, a reed swaying in the breeze going whichever way it blows?"

Angered by his obvious castigation that they bent their morals to match political benefits, one called out, "By what authority are you addressing this gathering!"

"What authority did John have?" Jesus replied. "Was it from you or from God? Answer me that. For I tell you that whoever spoke the unfounded words of accusation against him, those accusers will answer to God."

A Pietist on the edge of the group, perhaps wanting to expose Jesus' suspected claim to be God's messiah, snarled, "Give us a sign!"

Jesus took measure of their mocking taunts, aware that such malice might lead to blows. He told Simon, "Go to your boat. Take the others and make a place for me and Matthias," which he did immediately.

"The Kingdom of God is not coming with signs," Jesus then answered. "You show off your piety, but you know more about the weather than about the Kingdom of God. When you see a cloud in the west you say, 'Rainfall is coming.' And when you feel the south wind blowing, you say, 'There will be scorching heat,' and it happens. But the Kingdom of God is not coming with signs. People won't say, 'Look it's here' or 'Look it's over there.' The Kingdom will be in the midst of you. But for this adulterous generation, there is a warning. A man may not simply divorce his wife, sending her away, nor may a woman divorce her husband!"

In apparent disregard of all danger, his denunciation rang out, its target certain. Herodias had invoked Roman law to divorce her husband, who happened to be Antipas' own half brother Philip. As my friend well knew, John had died for making public pronouncements of these same charges—that a woman divorcing her husband without his agreement violated Torah, no matter if it had been granted under Roman law.

Even as a shudder coursed through him, Matthias proceeded, recording the heading and fearful events that followed.

Jesus becomes a fugitive from Antipas
At that, he turned and waved to Simon, whose boat was about one hundred cubits from shore, and with a somewhat urgent push

of my shoulder, he indicated we make our way to it and leave the vicinity.

To the hundreds of John's followers, I believe Jesus entering the Sea of Galilee was mistaken for a ceremonial immersion to memorialize their fallen leader. They thronged down the slope, as if this was the moment they were waiting for, and into the water, crowding toward him. Those nearest us, as we reached waist deep, grasped his tunic, which was already half submerged, and led a chant, "King of the Jews! King of the Jews!"

To this he reacted with visible temper, forcing their hands off him and pushing back fiercely, desperate to free himself. To me it was clear that he would not be taken for one who thought himself King of the Jews, nor would anybody witnessing this harsh physical rebuff doubt his revulsion at their suggestion that he was. In an odd way, the moment as I recall it, should have acquitted him of that eventual charge for which they took his life. Nobody who witnessed his wading hard against the tide to get away from that adoring crowd could believe he coveted their adulation.

Here, I must introduce Joanna in more detail. A woman of honor who had enjoyed Jesus' friendship, she was not present during this memorial but remained with her husband, Chuza, in Antipas' palace, where they resided. Chuza was a member of the tetrarch's custodial staff and overheard many conversations about political matters. When the Pietist spies brought word to Antipas about Jesus' denunciation of his marriage, as indirect as it may have been, Chuza sent Joanna to find Jesus and warn him.

We had pulled up on the shore at Magdala and awaited Mary, to whose house Andrew was sent for food and provisions. When Joanna preceded her to the boat, having guessed we might stop there as we sometimes did, she was breathless and plainly frightened. Immediately she informed Jesus what Chuza had heard. As reported by Joanna, Antipas was quick to inquire whether the mob at the lake all believed Jesus was their king, having hailed him as their monarch. According to what her husband, Chuza, told her, the spies confirmed that almost all did, excepting a few they overheard rejoicing that Jesus was really John reborn, once again among the living.

According to her account, Antipas railed, "What? John, whom I executed, has come back to life? He has risen from the dead? Is that what they think?"

Not lost on Jesus was just how ominous the obvious sarcasm was—and how serious in its possible consequence. If he were just like John, one they believed inherited his mantle, then the same verdict would be decreed by the tetrarch.

This was when Jesus told us: "Beware the yeast of the Pietists!" meaning they changed everything so they could trump up the charge against him. Of course, the yeast was the twisted truth that would cause false charges to rise against him, just as it causes bread to rise. Thomas, who was quite thin and always hungry, then was overheard telling Judas Iscariot, one young like himself, "He is talking about bread because we don't have anything to eat." This caused Jesus to bristle. "Why are you talking about having no bread?" he berated them. "Have you no perception?"

And the Zebedees also thought he was talking about bread. As I recall, Judas Iscariot, to whom Jesus had entrusted the purse, started to hand a coin or two to John, who said he would find a vendor. But Jesus, forgoing further pedagogy, warned John not to go to the public market. To avoid scrutiny, we should be patient and wait for Mary, who would bring a few loaves.

285

Then Joanna had more to tell. According to what Chuza overheard, Antipas interrogated his council, demanding, "Who is this about whom I hear such things?" And it was as certain as the sun shone, in Joanna's opinion, that he would do to Jesus the same as he had done to John—if he could catch him. I recall her dreaded words, "Antipas wants to kill you."

After a short while, Mary Magdalene came with a basket of bread and some fish too, which we all ate ravenously as Jesus addressed us. "Herod Antipas is a fox," he said. "Joanna, go and tell that fox that I am leaving his region."

Then he turned to us and said, "Go your own way. Foxes have holes and the birds of the air have nests, but I have nowhere to lay my head."

Simon next replied, "We have left everything and followed you. None of us has anywhere to go back to. Master, who shall we go to?"

After several moments of hesitation, Jesus agreed we would all take refuge in Philip's tetrarchy. Owing to Antipas' adulterous theft of his brother's wife, we could be confident Philip had little interest in abetting Jesus' capture.

Rowing from Magdala to the northern shore, we were beset by those breaking waves typical of the shallow water close to the beach. To lighten the craft so it would not become submerged, Jesus jumped out with one or two others and waded alongside. Then, we made our way inland.

Caesaria Philipi is a sprawling village set in the rocky hills. Even today, it is famed for its myths about Pan, the Greek goat-god that earlier inhabitants believed to reside in its wooded cliffs. With white jasmine flowers cascading like a drawn curtain to either side of a gaping cavern from which water flows, it is a seeming gateway between the splendor of God's creation and the dark world below. As we followed a shady path to a suitable patch of mossy ground near rock-hewn prayer niches, exhaustion had us all quiet, and I soon fell fast asleep.

Matthias rolled up the scroll and secured it on a shelf, intending to continue after an interlude in the vegetable garden outside his door.

To his surprise, as he leaned on his doorpost, attempting to fasten his sandal, the left one had shrunk and didn't fit on his foot. "But there hasn't been any rain. How did this happen?" he asked aloud, looking at it closely. "It can't be." Forcibly squeezing his toes under the front-strap, he realized that it wasn't the sandal that was the problem but that his foot was swollen. "My feet are already too big," he said. "Anyway it's more business for the sandlar. So let it be his luck."

Moments later, he was investigating the shiny surface of a cucumber when a familiar voice greeted him.

"Are you too busy to invite us in?"

Looking up, Matthias was surprised to see James, and even more so that he was with Philip. "This is unexpected!" Matthias said. "Of course you are both welcome. Are you stopping by on your way north?"

"Your house is our destination," James said.

"How are you, Matthias?" Philip asked.

"Fine. Yes, this is a surprise. Well, let me pick this one, and do come in." Standing up, he said, "The horse is having a snack, and so shall we." Their horse had found a patch of grass and paid no attention as they took off their sandals and followed Matthias indoors.

"So what's the news?" Matthias asked his visitors as they sat on two small couches against the side wall.

"We've come about Simon," James said.

Matthias sliced the cucumber and put it in front of them on a small table. "I see," he replied, bringing a jar of salt. "Dip it in here. It's better with salt. But has something happened?"

"I found Nathanael," James said.

"I don't know him," Matthias said. "But I recall . . . well, it doesn't matter. So?"

"You wouldn't," Philip replied. "He joined us after John was arrested and kept in our company only until they broke through your roof. If you saw him now, you might remember his face."

"Well, then what reason should I have for hearing about him on this occasion?"

"Nathanael was the leader of John's following," James said. "He's the one who Simon persuaded to believe Jesus was King of the Jews."

Looking up at the repaired ceiling, Philip said, "Seems like a long time ago they made that hole in your roof."

"It was," Matthias observed. "Nearly three years."

"Yesterday, based on what Nathanael told me, I accused Simon of giving Jesus the title over the cross."

"And?" Matthias probed.

"And he said that he was proud of it! According to him, Jesus confided that he was King of the Jews and asked him to share the secret only with those who were worthy. Then he turned tables on me, berating me for making him out to be Jesus' murderer."

"So you see, I am right. Well, friends, if you've come to me for advice," Matthias said, "I have none. James, do you think anybody can disprove Simon's claim—that Jesus confided in him that he was the messiah, King of the Jews?"

"I have evidence," Philip said. "I regret that I waited this long."

"What can you say? And whatever it is, why have you come to me?" Matthias asked. "Aren't the others more worthy of hearing your testimony?"

"Too many of them have adopted Simon's views as their own," Philip replied. "But you have a voice they cannot dismiss. If he is not stopped, our recollections, and his imaginary communication with Jesus, which you have been taking down at the Center, are to be the new Torah."

Standing up, James said, "The disciples know, as do I, how my brother loved you. He stayed with you in times of difficulty. It is fitting that you hear what Philip has to say."

"Is it to be for the sake of your brother's memory? Or if stopping Simon is the purpose, how will I do that?"

"When you speak to them, it may change everything!" Philip exclaimed.

"And so, Philip, whatever it is that you intend me to say will expose Simon's heavenly Jesus as a fantasy. With that, the Center's work in keeping his memory alive will be done."

Turning his back to Matthias, James held his peace while Philip spoke. "Simon did more to assure his death than Judas."

"You see, Matthias?" James blurted. "That is why he has kept him alive in heaven—to hide the truth about his own role in the arrest!"

Matthias was silent for several moments in contemplation but finally observed, "No, James. His heavenly Jesus proves that it is a crime that never really happened. The murder of God's son is an impossibility, acquitting him of ever wondering about his own guilt. Only if he believes Jesus is dead can he have done something wrong. He has no need to hide the truth, except from himself. His buried guilt is not for labeling him king; it is for being Simon, the man, and nothing more. But Philip, why have you only now decided to turn against him? And what will you say that may change things?"

Philip shared a brief look of satisfaction with James that Matthias would hear his version of events. "Is that what you think?" he asked, acting as if he didn't notice Matthias taking a parchment sheaf from a nearby stack and placing it on the table. "You believe this is the first time I've tried to stop him?"

As he stirred the powdered dye into a cup of water, Matthias said, "I am waiting to hear what it is you may say."

"Well, you must recall how we pushed against the choppy water to get to the boat and how Jesus so plainly fought to fend off the groping paws of the herd that threatened him."

"At John's memorial, that day by the lake?"

"Yes. I hoped Simon would admit the truth—that Jesus wanted no part of the crowd's anointing him king—but he had dreamed up his own interpretation. 'Yes, wasn't it wondrous to see him do that, calming those waves to reach the boat?' That's how he is changing it and will ask you to put down as true!"

Seeing Matthias had not begun to write, he continued, "Oh, and I thought Simon would admit how undone Jesus was by the circumstances, as mortal as any miserable fugitive. I reminded him about Magdala, how we stopped there, half starving in Dalmanutha, along the lakeshore."

"Yes," Matthias replied, resting the point on the table and listening.

"Simon's answer? He described huge crowds surrounding the boat when we beached it there. He said Jesus fed them all from one basket of bread—of course, the basket Mary brought had a bunch of loaves—and we were about fifteen in number, but he conjured thousands."

"We were glad to have a piece of warm bread," Matthias said.

"The multitudes," Philip continued through a broken laugh. "Simon says the multitudes were fed from a miraculous act, turning a few loaves into sufficient nourishment for all."

"So you tried to stop his fables," Matthias replied. "And even knowing your effort was futile, you would attempt the same thing now."

"But Matthias," Philip said, "you remember Joanna brought a warning from Chuza. From then on, we were fugitives. We managed to row all the way to the northeast side of the lake, past Beit Zaida, to the shoreline just within Philip's tetrarchy. With the boat overloaded by our number, the gunwales were nearly at the waterline and Jesus, aware of the possibility of sinking in the larger waves near the shore, jumped in, encouraging others to follow suit. And the craft floated sufficiently high to reach ankle depth as we waded to the beachfront. Of course, Jesus walked on water! That's how Simon tells it! He is creating a Jesus who can free him from his own skin!"

"If there is evidence, my friend, tell me," Matthias advised. "Otherwise, Simon's tales are but fashionable exaggerations, a poetic style even our rabbis use to interpret Torah."

Philip's demeanor became more somber as he again began speaking, and Matthias, noticing the change, faced the table, preparing to write.

"Not too many hours of the next day had gone by," Philip began, "when Jesus announced we were going to Jerusalem for Passover. As unimaginable as it seems, most of us had forgotten the festival was less than a week away. After purchasing an ass, we loaded it with sacks stocked with supplies and began the three-day journey."

"I was there," Matthias said, tapping the point impatiently.

"Following the inland highway, we approached the border between Philip's tetrarchy and that of Antipas. Jesus and Simon were walking ahead, as was their custom, and we had permitted them space for what seemed a few private words."

"I remember," Matthias nodded.

291

"And that is when he spoke to Simon. I don't think either of them saw that I had gone forward to find a fig tree and stepped off the road to relieve myself behind it. But I was nearby and could overhear their words."

"Is this what you believe is of such importance?"

"You be the judge, both of you. Nobody has heard me speak of their conversation until now."

"May I use your name?" Matthias inquired, as he held down a corner of the page, preparing to transcribe what followed.

"Yes. I expect that will lend it credence, though what you may choose to do with it is your decision."

Requesting he speak slowly, Matthias again wet the broad-tipped point, making a heading:

According to Philip

then, he began his transcription.

Returning to the road, I was just behind them, unnoticed. Jesus seemed preoccupied, telling from his long spell of saying nothing. Then he asked Simon, 'Who does everybody say I am?'

"*Simon replied, 'Some are saying you are John and others, Elijah. Others say you are Jeremiah or one of the prophets.'*

"'*But who do you say I am?' he insisted, plainly impatient with the evasive answer.*

"'*You have the message of the Kingdom, and we believe you are the holy one of God, King of the Jews,' Simon answered. I think it was the first and only time he admitted to Jesus what he had been preaching to John's followers, like Nathanael.*

"'*You have to stop saying such things about me!' Jesus said. It was the harshest rebuke I had ever heard him utter. 'If you don't, they are going to arrest me, and I will be put to death!'*

"*Simon then began stuttering but managed to say, 'God forbid! Adon, this is never going to happen to you!'*

"*Jesus slowed his pace, and turned to him, 'Why are you always calling me Adon, as if I am your lord and master? I am telling you to stop calling me lord,' he said. 'No one who calls me their lord will enter the Kingdom of God! You say you and others are doing exorcisms in my name? If they have done such a thing, on the day the Kingdom is revealed, I will deny knowing them.' Then, delivering his words in sharp reprimand, he said, 'Simon, you may say that you have been at my side, that we have shared meals together, but if you say I am God's chosen one again, I am going to say I don't even know you, that I don't know who you are or where you come from. What you are saying about me is from Satan! So get away from me, you who are doing evil!'*

"*Shrinking back to join the others, I hoped not to be noticed. I realized the gravity of what had transpired, and I was stunned. Still, Jesus' final words of rebuke reached my ears even as I retreated, and I will never forget them. 'Walk behind me, Satan!' Jesus demanded as Simon froze in his tracks. 'I don't want you at my side! You are not at the side of a god but of a man!'*"

Saying he needed to rest his hand, Matthias set the point down, and James said to Philip, "Thank you. Thank you for helping to save my brother."

"I wish I could have," Philip replied.

"What more does a man have when he's gone than the way people remember him?" James asked. "Simon's idol is not and never did resemble my brother. His false pronouncements are to sculpt his personal savior, as Matthias says. That is what Jesus meant when he chastised Simon. But Matthias, what do you have to say?"

"Though I was unable to make out the conversation, Jesus sounded angry," Matthias answered. "It hardly seemed like he was praising Simon. His recent claim that just then Jesus told him he was King of the Jews and named him Peter, gatekeeper of the coming Kingdom, is astonishing. From what you say, it was the very thing Jesus denounced as satanic."

"It is the measure of Simon's arrogance," James responded.

"I don't know how, if Simon believes Jesus is guiding him from heaven, he isn't afraid of being punished," Matthias observed.

"He has deceived himself and proceeds to deceive others," James said. "The voice of Satan is the only voice he hears."

"I am tired," Matthias said. "And this is a burden that only makes me more so. Unless there is anything to add, I must rest."

"Will you use my testimony?" Philip asked. "Do you expect to confront Simon with what I have told you?"

"We'll see what may come of this," Matthias said.

"Philip, permit me a word with Matthias," James requested. "I'll be right out."

As the door closed, Matthias said nothing. Whatever was on James' mind, he was about to hear.

"So you have taken down Philip's account. If I'm supposed to take that piece of parchment and read it to the group—"

"No, James. I'm not expecting you to do that. For now, let it be a written record. But when Simon sees he does not have Philip's vote, things may change."

James had never asked Matthias, but he not only wondered about his restraint toward Simon; he resented it. Only occasionally had Matthias suggested ways to make Jesus seem irredeemably human, such as exposing his birth to an unknown father and his suicidal self-doubt. But he showed no willingness to make those pronouncements himself. Instead of taking an active role in eviscerating their false god, he was letting Simon build his fortress of beliefs until they were impenetrable.

"Vote?" James asked.

"Without Philip, six are in his camp. Besides Simon, there is Andrew, Thomas, the two Zebedees, and Matthew."

"And, Matthias, if you speak out, you're afraid they will take a vote to exclude you? I fail to understand . . . you have been faithful to Simon's every whim."

"It's not about me!" Matthias exhorted, unable to mask his frustration.

"Then who?"

"If Simon has six, and I am voted out, having no right to be counted in my own behalf, you will have only Philip, Simon C'nani, James bar Alpheus, Bartholomew, and Thaddeus."

"Five," James mused, as the implication dawned on him.

"Simon has wanted you gone from the beginning. If I provoke him and he and his five cronies oust me, he would then have sufficient support to remove you from the Center."

"So, Simon, it is up to me to disclose Philip's testimony. Is that what you're saying?"

"I'm old, James. I kept asking myself, who will be there to safeguard Jesus' memory as they erect their egregious falsehoods about him, making the Center a Temple to their new god? In the years to come, only you, joined by those disciples so attached to your fellowship."

"So let it be this way, Matthias. My voice is already fading from any influence over their new Torah. Do what you should for my brother. He will always be that to me, no matter what they say about him."

As James rejoined Philip, they waved from their cart and soon were out of sight, leaving Matthias to unfurl his scroll and insert the new parchment with Philip's account. Finished sewing the last hemp thread, he searched for its place on the shelf, wondering whether the sun had gone behind the trees or his eyes had gone dim.

Sitting down heavily on his bed, he lay back, deliberating whether to expose Simon. "After I do that," he mused under his breath, "who will care about what Jesus taught—or even that he ever lived?"

As he was dozing off, Matthias prayed, "Adonai, give me strength to keep them from making him a god."

CHAPTER TWENTY-THREE

*P*aul stepped across the small rocks at the entrance, relieved when the elder did not inquire after Barnabas or John Mark, thus sparing him the need to mention their disagreement over the sanctity of Torah. He had more on his mind than preserving an entangled legal web of Torah practice. He would seek the key to pagan hearts, enabling them to unlock and enter Jesus' kingdom.

If he could find a common bond between Jesus' ministry on earth and pagan beliefs, Paul was hopeful these misguided worshippers would accept Jesus as the Christ. Certainly, were they to be baptized, Peter would be mollified, and his continuing doubt about this evangelic mission might be turned to enthusiasm.

The elder sensed the purpose of his visit—or so it seemed. Taking his arm, leading him farther into their cave sanctuary, with his other hand holding the collar of his robe shut against the momentary dampness, he told Paul, "We think of this time of season, when light and darkness struggle for dominance, as a time to worship with heightened solemnity."

Passing small clusters of initiates seated near the wall sconces, the elder slowed his pace, almost stopping. "You may be shocked or even repulsed," he said, preparing Paul for what he would see. "It will be strange to you that our priests bathe in the blood of the dying bull and eat its raw flesh."

Stymied by the prospect of such a baneful sight, Paul held his peace as they continued on. Then he heard a familiar sound, the loud cry of a wounded beast and that same discordant drone which occurred on his prior visit. This time, odd utterances were more discernible with each step.

"Follow me," the elder said. "It will be all right."

They had reached a cavern entrance festooned with hundreds of blazing torches, their blinding light causing Paul to hesitate for fear of stumbling.

"You see how light and darkness can have the same effect," the elder said. "Both may stop us from knowing the way." Taking Paul's sleeve, he tugged him gently forward until the sound of the priests' chanting was fully resonant, and they were in view through the torch smoke, which furled upward to a ceiling too high to see.

Visible at thirty cubits above, forming a roof of latticed iron, was a grate upon which a pierced bovine had collapsed and from which showers of blood cascaded down on the priests below, drenching them, dripping down their faces turned upward, dyeing their tunics red, and causing their chanting to become a warble as the liquid splashed into their open mouths.

Though difficult to see, two priests ascended ladders and made their way along the abutment bordering the grate. There, they appeared to carve open the beast, slicing its exposed flesh. After a short while, they returned to their group and passed a plate stacked high with the uncooked meat, from which they took and ate until it was empty.

"You are perplexed. Am I right?" the elder asked.

But receiving no response, except Paul's grimace from apparent nausea, the elder led the way back to the fresh air outside.

"It is not what I imagined," Paul answered. "We have different ways."

"Are you certain of that?"

"We don't drink blood or eat flesh uncooked."

"That is only the appearance of things." He gestured for Paul to sit on a stone bench near the cave entrance under a large cypress. "Yes, it is how I first reacted as a young man. What an awful impression it makes at first sight. But will you permit me to share a deeper understanding?"

"I would appreciate that," Paul replied.

"Our path is not a simple one. We do not see the choice like others. For them, there is good and evil. For us, there is what looks like it is good but is a disguise worn by evil to fool us and entrap us.

"When we enter the cave, we are entering the tomb," the elder continued, emphasizing his point with a raised finger, "the place of death. The body we so often have served with nourishment and niceties, we declare the work of the evil entrapper, the creator who has corrupted its every fiber with his poison. As we see the bull die, we are dying—and as it dies, we feel the moment is one of choice. Will we be altogether at an end, or is there some cleansing of the poison possible, a way to see light within the darkness? In the illumination of torchlight, some will see a bull dying and its blood pouring from its body; others will see the cruelty as a holy deception. Only those who see the bull as the source of true salvation are able to reach the presence and even enter the being of the true god. But perhaps I have said more than enough or even disturbed you. I hope not."

"And the pain of the bull as it is pierced . . . and cries out? That's part of your ascent to the heavenly realm?" Asked in a conversational tone, Paul masked his doubt there could be any sensible answer.

"I see. You think we don't feel its pain? Of course we do! It is our pain—but even pain can be a deception." As the elder paused to press the water skin to his lips, he searched Paul's face, aware a deep uncertainty was casting its shadow over his thoughts. "My friend," he said finally, "the beast's suffering is an illusion to test us. If we see its blood as nothing more than its body's fluid, we remain entrapped. The blood contains the true life, free of the evil god's power," he intoned. "It bathes us as we ascend to the divine realm. Only the suffering of the animal stands between us and salvation for all eternity. Those who see past its misery know their own is but a machination of the evil creator god, ever entrapping us in pain."

"But eating it . . ." Paul managed, almost gagging at the recalled image and slight stench still lingering in his nostrils.

"When we devour its flesh," the elder replied, pleased to think his guest's furrowed brow was an expression of intense interest, "we are eating the true god's body, becoming one with the supernal, luminary knowledge—the mazda of eternal life that is his blazing glory. The priests who chant the secret language lead us to the highest realm. We are not eating its earthly flesh. Can you understand? The beast's essence has become the true god incarnate. Ingesting the flesh, we become one with his gnosis, the eternal, pure light which illuminates all meaning."

"And death?" Paul asked. "We all die."

"For those who follow the path, death too is but a deception. One must pass through the darkness to reach the light—as we just did. But can you see yourself as one of us?"

Resisting the temptation to laugh, inasmuch as he now realized the elder had the very same purpose as he—namely, to win him over to his religion—Paul made no reply.

"I know what you must be thinking," the elder said. "These poor people. They believe a dying beast is their salvation. But, Paul, like you, we too have a savior. You know the Greek word soter, the intermediary who takes the form of different deliverers."

"Yes. I have heard Dionysus given the name soter."

"And others call him Mitra. I believe you are proposing we call him Christ, whose name was Jesus."

"Yes."

"Of course, in your doxologia he doesn't kill a bull," the elder said, smiling. "But in our way, the priest feels himself directly filled with the spirit of the soter as he dispatches the bull."

"I recall telling you our savior was himself killed," Paul said sadly. "His blood was spilled by the ones who have no light and live under the curse of the law, as you say. And we bathe in water to cleanse our sins, not in blood."

Sensing his desire to depart, the elder stood to face him. "Paul, to be like us, you must enter the realm of his tomb," he said earnestly.

"If I presented him the way you say, telling you about him as you suggest," Paul asked, "would you accept his identity?"

Laughing with unrestrained amusement, the elder slapped Paul's shoulder. "So are we talking about you or me? Who's the one converting? No harm. But I have my own soter. And I follow truth. Still, if the one I have worshipped all these years turns out to be your Christ, revealed as you say, how would I say no? Perhaps if by being submerged in the water, your initiates were dying with him and then emerged reborn, as we do from the cave, I might be more convinced. Still, for your Jesus to be our Christ, I urge you to find the spirit that was in his blood so that he may lead you to knowledge of the true god. In this way you will comprehend his suffering and enter the realm of eternal life."

Having shared the amusement of their misconstrued attempt to proselytize one another, Paul and the elder proffered mutual wishes for a good week.

"I hope you will renew your acquaintance with Simon, who now is called Peter," Paul said, climbing aboard his cart. "I think word of my being chased from the Antioch synagogue will cause him to pay a visit."

"I remember when he joined us for dinner in my home. I look forward to greeting him again. Meanwhile, my peace to you."

***

Less than a fortnight had passed when Simon made the trip north and was welcomed to the home of a Jew named Luke, a member of the Antioch synagogue who had been baptized by Apollos, a devotee of Jesus. Paul was not invited.

Feted with dinner by a score of brothers from the Antioch congregation, Simon reclined against his settee's cushion. Having early on taken notice there was no trace of blood in the platter put before him, he had fully enjoyed the meal. The meat was from a sheep killed and drained according to the commandment.

Seated at the table to his side, Silas and Barsabbas, who had accompanied him from Jerusalem, were engaged in gossip about Agrippa, Antipas' brother-in-law. Owing to his bizarre lifestyle, Agrippa's future was always a favorite topic.

"He may well be the Roman choice to replace Antipas," Barsabbas asserted, as the other guests listened politely.

"Impossible!" Silas moaned, as if suffering Barsabbas' ignorance. "After all, he made a fool of Flaccus. He was in debt, as usual, and saw a way to line his purse with gold from Sidon's treasury. Supposedly, he took bribes to represent their interests against Damascus."

"He's biding his time. You're right about that. Nobody has heard of him for months," Barsabbas acknowledged, swallowing a mouthful of food.

Directing his inquiry to his host—the man named Luke at the far end of the table—Simon interrupted their banter. "But tell me about Paul."

"Paul is a good man," Luke responded.

"Of course he is," another guest added. "But he doesn't understand us."

"He thinks he is offering us salvation. We believe that comes only from God," one across from the other declared, his wine splashing over the side of his glass.

"Are you and your neighbors persuaded by him to accept Jesus?" Simon asked.

"You mean us Jews?" one replied. "Not really, at least not the way he sees him. It is far more the teaching of Apollos that has us convinced."

"And who is Apollos?" Simon asked.

"I am," a dark-skinned fellow with an odd accent said.

"Then it is good to have shared a meal with you and to inquire about your lessons concerning the one I knew so well. Please tell me, who is your source?"

"What I know about Jesus' life comes from Barnabas and John Mark. They have spent the past year with Paul and, as I'm sure you know, have returned to Jerusalem. I believe they studied his teaching while in your company before coming here. So you are my true source."

At this obvious cause for amusement, they all chuckled.

"Are you from this region?" Simon asked.

"Alexandria."

"Then you enjoy the best of all worlds. There you have your Egyptian gods and here, so close to Macedon, your Greek gods are good company."

"I am a Jew. And the others will tell you that the worship of Greek gods in our region has been altered to suit pagan ways. Isn't Paul often in Tyre and Sidon? You will find their cult centers there. I'm sure he has an opinion about them."

"But why do you all sound so down on Paul?" Simon asked. "Has he offended you?"

"We don't want him to make speeches in our synagogue," one answered. "Our families and friends do not all share a belief that Jesus was sent to us by God. Yet he insults them for it."

"As if he is a judge, he says we who obey Torah are like slaves," another put in.

"He talks about the commandments with contempt," one of the older guests explained. "They are no longer from God. Just two days ago, he was claiming they only apply to those who still need them. That's how he puts it."

"And you Apollos? What do you think?" Simon asked.

"I believe what Jesus himself said, from what I've heard. No letter of the Torah should be changed. It is sacred. But there are ways to illuminate its message."

"Such as?"

"It contains the light to see and discover our path. The metatron brings it to those who are ready with open hearts."

"Metatron?" Simon queried.

"The one who descends toward earth, looking like a mortal but who is God's presence in the form of a man. He brings with him the truth of Torah from above and imbues the recipient with its essence. He enables them to see the future. These are the prophets and the sages. I believe the metatron chose to speak with Jesus just as he did with Daniel. Perhaps he has spoken with you, Simon."

"Jesus speaks with me through the holy spirit," Simon replied. "He walked among us on this earth as God's anointed. Surely your metatron obeys him, if such a one exists."

Simon was unsure what this fellow named Apollos meant but had the resentful feeling he was treading on the Center's prerogative. Whatever his ideas were about, they emanated more from speculation of the mind than the heart. Words heaped on words, Simon thought. Or did Apollos think his intention to play an important role escaped his notice?

"I haven't said it very well," Apollos admitted. "The metatron is a form of God. As such, he is an emanation of the supreme ruler. His feminine aspect is wisdom—sophia, as the Greeks call it, which comes only to the chosen."

Despite Simon's soporific haze from imbibing two glasses of wine, he listened to Apollos' discourse with an uneasy presentiment.

"She is luminous with the light of Torah, which the Greeks call logos," Apollos continued. "Perhaps the logos is not too different from the holy spirit . . ."

Every word Apollos uttered weighed upon Simon, returning him to the time when he was confused by Jesus' parables, before he perceived their secret message.

"I hope that accords with your own belief," Apollos cajoled. But aware Simon was studying his face, he abruptly ceased promulgating his notion of Jesus' theophany.

After a brief awkward silence, Simon bellowed, "You have so many foreign ideas! But what do you say about Paul? Is he not one of the chosen? Do you all deny he saw Jesus on the road to Damascus?"

"When we were baptized by Apollos," another guest ventured, sidestepping the question, "Paul found out and accused us of ignorance. It is a fact he calls Torah a curse."

Attempting to clarify Paul's idea, Apollos said, "He tells us John's immersions were a baptism of repentance for those who follow Torah. But if we want to be saved through Jesus, we should be baptized again—by him instead of me. Then we will know right from wrong directly from the holy spirit. That's his view."

As the meal was done and conversation turned from antagonism toward Paul to expressing gratitude for the fine banquet, Luke wished the gathering a pleasant evening, suggesting in a polite manner that Simon and his companions had traveled a long way and needed their rest. His home was to be the night's lodging.

After Silas and Barsabbas excused themselves and retired to their room, Simon turned to the few remaining guests about to leave. "Paul certainly seems to lack good manners," he suggested. "You all deserve his apology."

Responding with a raised voice, one said, "He forgets it is Jesus who is supposed to save the world, not him."

"It doesn't sound like you've been fooled," Simon observed.

"Nobody in our group has confused him with Jesus," he assured Simon, taking his leave.

Wishing Apollos peace as he was about to adjourn with the others, Simon caused him to pause for a last word. Aware the group was embracing Apollos' role, Simon marshaled his wits, determined to assert his authority. If he could control this man's agenda, it would thwart his apparent ambition.

"I wonder whether you have any opinion about our spreading the news of Jesus to the community of Alexandria," Simon said.

"Actually, I have thought about it," Apollos replied, pleased by the request to show his erudition. "The main miracle of Egyptian religion is the adoring protection of their mother goddess Isis. She enfolds her child Horus with love, so that he may grow up and bring about the resurrection of the fallen god Osiris."

"Do you think that will help them to understand what happened to our lord?"

"All their temple draperies and mosaics show her holding the child. Of course, they would appreciate the love Jesus' mother showed for him at the cross. She was there, was she not? They would picture her holding him as a child, embracing his fallen figure lowered from the crucifix. How should any of us ignore that agony?"

"I expect you are right," Simon averred, not answering the question about Mary's vigil at the cross. "Then I entrust you with that particular responsibility—to amplify the message of our lord's life and death in ways familiar to Egyptians. My peace to you, Apollos."

With the door closing before Apollos had a chance to reply, Simon took satisfaction in what was likely the fellow's bemused doubt about any sanctioned role in baptizing future adherents.

Guiding Simon to the guest room with its especially thick pallet and bowl of water, Luke paused at the door. "I hope you don't mind my curiosity," he said. "I also was wondering whether his mother was at the cross when Jesus died."

"In spirit, we were all there," Simon replied.

"Yes, of course," Luke agreed. "But in the morning, I hope you will permit me to make several suggestions."

"Ideas about spreading the good news are always welcome," Simon responded.

Weary from Apollos' subtle attempt to gain stature, Simon sank into the fine mattress of ground straw and chicken feathers. He could picture Apollos' eyes, confident, twinkling, as if his merit was measured by the appreciation of those he had baptized. But no stratagem to supplant Simon as arbiter of Jesus' plan for the kingdom would succeed.

In the enveloping darkness, as he surrendered to sleep, a table's shadow played across the wall, elongated by moonlight coming through the small window. Almost seeming to move as rays of light broke through passing clouds, it slowly changed shape. Somebody was in the room.

Barely visible was the familiar form of a tall, thin man. Swiping his hand across the table top, he found Simon's purse. Inside, there were only ordinary things—a piece of rough cloth for his teeth, a bone comb, some lemon-scented balm in a Roman jar, and a few coins but nothing of value. From beneath the wool blanket, too frightened to move, Simon peered at the man's scrawny back and arms, all he could see. If only he had put a gold coin in the purse, something of real value to give him, then the thief might take it and depart.

Returning the purse to its place on the table, the thief shook his head. "I don't want gold," he said but still did not turn around.

"Then what?" Simon exhorted, astonished that the intruder willingly made his presence known by speaking aloud, even seeming to know his thoughts.

"You have pretended something is yours that does not belong to you," the thief said, turning around and taking a step toward the bed.

"It can't be!" Simon said, terrified. "You think I have something of yours?"

The closer he came, the more he bore a semblance to . . . but it was impossible! His skin was shriveled, and his eyes had no light of life.

Weak and unable to rise from the bed to defend himself, Simon demanded, "Do you know who I am?"

"Of course I do," the thief replied through flaking, dry lips. "You are Simon."

"No. I am . . ." But as he would have spoken the name "Peter," he could not say it. "I am . . ."

"You always were Simon," the the skeletal visage rasped, taking another ominous stride toward the bed. "What you pretend is yours, never was."

"But I have the key . . ."

Pulling back the blanket beneath which Simon cowered, the thief, his voice suddenly gentle, jostled his shoulder, asking, "Are you all right, Peter?"

"Luke?"

"I see the blanket has fallen off, and with the cool night air, it's no surprise you were disturbed by dreams. Hearing you call out, I thought you might be asking my assistance."

"Yes, yes. Well, thank you. But no need for concern. Rich food, so delicious, has become more the cause of fitful nights than when I was young."

"I understand. Well, then, have a good sleep."

Closing his eyes, the blanket drawn to his chin, Simon could not quell his distress that the thief bore a countenance so like Jesus. Of course, he was an imposter, perhaps Satan come to thwart his mission.

Slipping into sleep, he would arise at sunup to hear Luke's ideas.

***

"We are Jews. That's basic to what we are prepared to accept," Luke was saying. "But I trust the eggs and honey are to your liking?"

"Delicious!" Simon replied, swallowing a mouthful. "I am also a Jew. So is Paul."

"Yes, I understand that," Luke assured him, "but Paul's instruction is sometimes too severe in calling for an end to our traditions. You hear how the others complain about his defamation of Torah law."

"I have never heard him speak against Torah. Perhaps he was angry when you expelled him from your synagogue."

"We have talked, and I believe he understands my viewpoint. He must find ways to interpret Torah rather than reject it. I have offered my advice."

"He listened to what you had to say?" Simon asked.

"Yes. And he seemed especially pleased to do so after I suggested he baptize me with the holy spirit."

"But what did you propose?"

"Peter, as Jews, we must recognize Jesus was one of us before we can accept him. Didn't God tell King David his descendant would be the messiah? So we must know his family background. We don't know anything about his origins. Certainly, if he was one of us, he was circumcised. Shouldn't we hear about that sacred occasion? And his ceremony of adulthood when he first entered the congregation of our people? All of us do that at twelve years of age if we have studied Torah. Paul shares no information about that. Perhaps I should hold my peace."

"What do you think we should do?" Simon asked.

"If I were spreading the news about him in the manner of a testament, I would find as many connections to Torah as I could. For example, that he, like King David, was born in Bethlehem."

"Which is true," Simon said, wiping his lips with a napkin and helping himself to a piece of cake.

"So I have heard. And then many Jews would say, 'Yes. He is the one sent by God.'"

"Are you as skilled with a point in recording your ideas as you are in saying these things?" Simon asked.

"I could explain the truth about Jesus to suit our fellow Jews. Yes, I have the facility you require, not only in Hebrew and Aramaic but in Greek. And I am versed from childhood in the passages of Torah and prophets."

Watching as Luke put an egg on his own plate and offered him another portion, Simon inquired, "But how did Apollos gain such popularity if he has combined Greek beliefs with our own? Doesn't he make Jesus sound more Greek than Jewish?"

"I do not ally myself with Apollos," Luke told him. "He says the metatron spoke with Jesus. I am saying Jesus *is* the metatron. Jesus was not a prophet. Jesus was the human embodiment of God. Let him be one who seemed human, like any son of man. Those of us who understand will say to ourselves, that was only his appearance. To us who are worthy, he was divine, just as the figure speaking to Daniel."

"I suppose we could reveal he was an embodiment of God's own spirit, like Daniel's vision of one on a throne. It would go well with the story of his birth."

"Oh?"

"That Jesus was born of God's spirit and that is why he never called Joseph his father, except that he raised him until the age of twelve."

"And Mary?" Luke asked, taking a bite of the warm bread and then passing its basket to Simon.

"She never knew a man. Certainly not before Jesus was born. But I see you are doubtful."

"Roman emperors have occasionally claimed their origins are the gods. We don't want proselytes thinking Jesus is that kind. But there is always some passage in our scripture to illuminate the divine plan. I am sure there are others who know the sacred writings."

"Matthew. If he finds his way. And our scribe, Matthias," Simon said.

"Well, together we may hail the day for which we have prayed, the day when we witness God's return to our midst. Soon, we may see the throne with one like a son of man descend to earth, surrounded by angels. On that day of our lord, we will no longer need an earthly king, not even a messiah. What Jew doesn't understand this? It is in every heart."

"I agree that is something to consider," Simon said.

"And let's not forget Elijah. It is good to emphasize how John was acting like Elijah, ushering in the era of the messiah's rule."

"I prefer we not give John too important a role," Simon responded, leaning back and pressing a cup of warm wine to his lips.

"Even here we meet many who knew of him. If we say John's baptisms paved the way for Jesus, they may be more convinced."

"Will you come to Jerusalem? We need you to record our ideas."

"You say you have a scribe."

"Yes. But I doubt his complete faith in Jesus. If you join us, I will put the point in your hand myself."

"It's an honor to have your trust. But I didn't know Jesus."

"In a way, neither did we. Not all of us recognized him."

"Then what I have heard is true. He never revealed who he was."

"In a hundred ways, he did," Simon stipulated. "But his sovereignty was always concealed behind a screen of symbolic teaching."

"Yet you understood."

"Yes. I was the one who did. That's why he wanted me to be a leader in the kingdom."

"Such a hideous end. And you never felt doubt?"

"Of course I did. My faith in him was tested by his arrest. His crucifixion should have been an impossibility. But then I felt his voice within me."

"What did he tell you, Peter?"

"The temptation to call him a mortal son of man like any other was trapping me in Satan's web."

In a crowing voice mustering confidence, Simon intoned the pronouncement he had delivered the disciples. "Others who have not yet heard him, still say God would never have done so cruel a thing to his son. Even James, his kin in our earthly realm, has said it was not God's plan. To stop their talk, I had to break a vow of secrecy to Jesus. When he called me Peter, he told me he was the Christ, and I was to have the keys to his kingdom, deciding who might enter and who not. Those words assigning me his earthly domain were a fortress against Satan's deception. So now you know."

Standing to leave, Simon placed the cup on the table with their breakfast plates and bid his host farewell. "I'm off to Tyre," he said. "Paul and I are to meet there."

"It was an honor to have you visit my home," Luke said sincerely. "And when I come to Jerusalem, I will tell you how we may find our savior's suffering in Torah."

"Is that possible?"

"We will find a way, Peter."

***

Only two days later, in the company of Silas and Barsabbas, Simon was the guest of honor at a home near the Great Sea. Paul had arranged the invitation.

As they sat together on the veranda, looking out across the white-topped furling waves, the thick gray clouds from Macedon made their way toward shore.

"It will rain in a short while," Simon said. "And tomorrow, the rain will travel with me from Tyre to Jerusalem."

"Priscilla has tent fabric that will cover you as you go and should keep you dry," Paul advised.

"But you don't seem to care," Silas said to Paul, addressing a topic of the previous moment. Paul had remained unresponsive to his suggestion that Syria's Roman legate, Vitellius, had less contempt for Agrippa than for Antipas, whom he despised.

"Of course, as I understand it," Silas persisted, "Agrippa will be king of Judea long before Antipas."

"Antipas the king?" Barsabbas said incredulously. "Little chance of that. And not Agrippa either."

"It doesn't concern us!" Simon snapped, his sudden display of irritation taking them by surprise.

"What I've heard is—"

"Didn't you hear me?" Simon demanded. "Enough! The two of you should avoid giving opinions."

For several moments, none of them said anything, until Paul broke his silence. "Tiberius won't favor Agrippa with the Galilee or northern tetrarchy the way he has behaved, much less make him king. Even his wife and children have left him."

Observing from Paul's patronizing tone and slight scowl that he was impatient to speak with him privately, Simon instructed Silas and Barsabbas to help with the meal. "Brothers," he said pleasantly, "please find your way below to the triclinium and offer a hand to Priscilla and Aquilla who are doing all the cooking."

"Perhaps my assistant, Timothy, needs your aid setting the table," Paul added.

"Of course," said Silas, standing up.

"Absolutely," Barsabbas agreed. "Whatever we can do will be our pleasure."

As the two men disappeared through the door, Paul said, "So are these the two you intend to spy on me?"

"Nonsense!" Simon retorted. "I am replacing John Mark and Barnabas, who you sent packing. These are fine men, if not always astute and will assist you in your work. Spies? Are you doing something contrary to the Center's wishes? Otherwise, why would I need spies?"

"Word of the Antioch affair reached you. Of course, I scolded those people. And I suppose they told their relatives in Ephesus that I immersed a dozen who wished to be blessed by the holy spirit. Isn't that where you spent the night?"

"You told them the Torah makes them slaves."

"You don't understand."

"Then please explain to me why you would have told them that."

"The people here have different beliefs. There aren't only Jews."

"Paul, the pagans are your main responsibility. So why are you saying such things to the Jews?"

"Should we have a different Christ for every group? You wish to anoint the Jews with the crown of the chosen. You join them at their dinner, observing dietary laws that exclude all others. You are no different from the ones who worship in a cave, keeping only to their own kind. Yes, some pagans even worship in the dark recesses of a cave lit by torches. Will I tell them one thing and the Corinthians or Ephesians another? Is there a different Christ for the Jews?"

"Your manner will hardly bring all believers together. They're already divided. Some are saying things like, 'I am for Apollos,' or 'I am for Paul.' I'm sure others will be saying I am for Peter. How can this be anybody's fault but yours?"

"Jesus speaks to us with one voice. All I hope is to pass along what truths I gain from hearing him."

"You who never even knew him are about to tell truths he has confided only in you?"

"Shall I inform you what he has said to me?" Paul prodded. "Then you will see I know him. Not as he was, wearing the mask of a mortal, but as one I have met face-to-face, blinded by his countenance, even like Moses when he received the commandments."

Angered by such arrogance from a man who considered his Roman education a mark of superiority, especially over simple Galileans like himself, Simon restrained a stormy rebuke, speaking as if saddened by something Paul could never understand. "That mortal's mask you speak of—you are not tormented by my memories. And how could you be? I do not hold it against you that you were never blessed by his teaching or ministry. How is that any fault of yours that he chose us disciples and never gave you a thought as we made our way from place to place, with crowds following him. It is a sorry fact that you never saw him tend even those crippled by diseases of punishment—the blind and the lame—forgiving their sins, curing even a leper. No, you never saw him at the Passover supper that night."

"Of course it was a sad time, and you will never know how I envy your being with him like that. But why are you still tormented, you whose faith has glorified his kingdom?"

Recalling the terrifying night's visage of the thief and fearful it would return to accuse him of lying, Simon spoke as if it was lurking . . . listening.

"We all missed Judas Iscariot reacting when Jesus said one of us would betray him. 'Surely not I,' he replied. If I had known what was in Judas' heart or that Jesus would be crucified—"

"What could you have done? It was never up to you!" Paul blurted, unable to control his outburst. "Is that what you think? If so, how can he be alive in heaven? Is the air he breathes in his heavenly domain your breath?"

Irresistibly, the dream had stained his thoughts. "He came to Jerusalem in order to keep the Torah's law. That is what enabled them to arrest him. He died in order to celebrate Passover, not to escape or hide from it."

"It is still you!"

"What do you mean?"

"You are still Simon. Peter was only an ambition, nothing more. You are the Simon who denied knowing who Jesus was on the night he was interrogated by Caiaphas and the others—so ashamed, afraid of being charged with a crime too, now calling your weakness a model for others, that they may transcend doubt as you have. But it is painful to hear you, hardly displaying the strength of one imbued by Jesus' heavenly voice. You sound more like a squeaking sparrow flying off at the least disturbance of his nest. Shall I call you Peter for the last time?"

Pounded by a gust of wind, Simon gripped the rail tightly and then turned, his legs enfeebled by doubt. He sat heavily in a chair under the eaves of the veranda. "Paul, do you say he was no Jew?" he demanded, his stern voice a facade. "You never saw his phylacteries. You never touched his tzitsit fringes. And how many meals did you eat at his side? Not one. There was never a drop of animal blood in his plate. What we did not do, out of ignorance of Torah, he did. And he read Torah in the synagogue, the very Torah you say is enslaving the Jews. He said it will never pass away, not even its smallest letter!"

"So he was a good Jew. And he is dead. And he was not the Christ. So it is over. Finished. Is that what you want? More important—is that what he wants?"

"But the Jews who keep Torah and follow its laws like Jesus did—you say they are living in sin!"

"Who else needs laws except those who are always tempted to break the law? Jesus was a Jew so he could show the Jews how to leave Torah and Satan behind, which happens for those who justify his death as God's plan, exactly as you have told the others. He came as a Jew in order to die as a Jew and end the era of criminals."

"Be careful, my friend."

"So let those who wish to follow the laws of Torah do it. They will enter the kingdom in their own time. If they wish to keep the Jew's diet, let nobody threaten them with heavenly punishment. And let nobody be forced to sit next to one eating foods they call sinful. But for the pagans, the animals of the world are no longer defined by those old scriptures. If Christ doesn't say otherwise, let people eat what they want!"

Simon rose stiffly, weighted by weariness, and caught sight of himself in the glassy, wet veranda floor, where the first drops had already formed a small puddle. It was the face he remembered, of an ordinary man, half asleep with wine, one who barely heard that wailing voice until awakened by his hand shaking his shoulder, urging him to keep guard. His reddened eyes were a testament to what Matthias told them days later—how Jesus had wept, praying to live, bowing before God, pleading . . . Jesus, the ordinary man who had appeared to him as a thief.

For just that moment, seeing himself in the water's reflection, Simon imagined Jesus forgiving him. "It is all right, Simon. It is all right to be just the fisherman you are. Only take me down from your cross and tell them you have made me a god to save yourself from the face reflected in this puddle."

Ignoring the dampness of the breeze as he looked out at the foggy sea, Simon longed for Jesus to be alive so he would have a second chance to embrace him as his teacher, to lay down his life for him—to have stayed awake! His face wet with tears, he recalled how Jesus had railed at him, even calling him Satan, refusing to have him walk by his side.

Paul thought Simon's cheeks were glistening from the droplets of heavy mist preceding the storm and took his broken smile as a cue to continue. "But of course it is up to you," Paul said. "Do you believe he speaks to us from heaven, or is that whole cloth woven from the fabric of your imagination?"

"I am the one to decide whether his will is served or not, especially by those who claim to have a message from him."

"Then it is still you, Peter. Well, let him be God's son and his death not be death at all, much less death on your account. Spare yourself that shame that only mocks his divinity. And let me tell you about the sign he has given me. The baptism is meant to reenact Jesus' death and resurrection."

"What's that you're saying?"

"You are as bewildered upon hearing it as I was. But the lord has told it to me. Entering the water and becoming submerged is to be understood by us, the apostles of the true message, as dying. By returning to the innocence of our first conception, wet within the darkness of our mother's womb, we may begin again, freed from the entrapment of our sinful bodies."

"You believe Jesus has told you this?" Paul asked.

"In the way the lord speaks. Doesn't he give us experiences that reveal his design? The cave of the mysteries practiced by these cults was the word of his truth. I admit I have visited one of them. To them, the cave is a tomb, and they die to the entrapment of law upon entering it. Now I have heard, as one hears through the holy spirit, the water of baptism is Christ's tomb. As his tomb was to our lord, so it must be to us!"

"What Jews will believe such a thing?" Simon demanded.

"Baptized, the faithful are to be blessed with rebirth, following our savior into eternal life, even as he has beckoned."

"And what about the Jews, Paul? You think they will accept the immersion is Christ's tomb?"

"You worry too much about them. Let them do as they must."

"You are well suited to the pagans," Simon said finally, breaking several moments' silence.

"Even more, he has told me the wine of the Passover feast must be his blood. He is God's sacrifice to the faithful. Just as the wine has always joined us Jews to Torah, those who wish to be with Jesus must drink it to be joined with him."

"You have that from Jesus?" Simon asked.

"I have it from the holy spirit."

"That the wine is his blood?"

"Yes, and the matzah his flesh."

"Who will believe such a thing? Am I supposed to tell the Jews who won't eat animal blood that they should drink the blood of Jesus? What Jew will believe in a messiah they eat?" Simon's laughter was shrill and fully absent genuine mirth. "I don't know, my friend, what you have been drinking, but it has spawned so many deformed ideas."

"Let the Jews run from it. I assure you the rest of the faithful will not. The worthy ones will understand the laws have entrapped them, and they must enter the tomb and drink the blood of the one slain in order to escape Satan's talons."

Below, sounds of voices interrupted their conversation. "It is the guests," Paul said. "Best we not make our appearance drenched to the skin."

"Will we be having the meal with a large group?" Simon asked.

"Not too many. But the local pagans do want to meet you."

"And have you any advice about what I should say?"

"Of course they have questions. Some of them are curious; others may accept Jesus. Several practice the mysteries of the cave and rebirth. You will want to attend to any questions from the one dressed in a brown tunic with a gold-braided sash. He represents a large community."

Following Paul, who paused to wipe his bald head with his tunic sleeve, Simon glanced down, but the puddle had become turbulent in the strong breeze, and he was relieved not to see his reflection.

"And others," Paul advised as they went inside, "include a few who revere the god Melkarth, a god they believe rules the earth and sea—one who seasonally battles death. They say he is subdued during the heat of summer and floods of winter but returns to life with the new crops springing forth from the ground."

Just as he said this, a sound of loud laughter reached them from below.

"They are a good-natured group," Simon said. "But what could have amused them, I wonder?"

"Don't wonder," came a pleasant voice. It was Priscilla, coming to find them, who, with her husband, Aquilla, were providing the afternoon's hospitality.

"One joked about your secret plan to circumcise them all as the price of lunch. I assured them the food was free."

"I see. Yes, they are good-natured. No harm in that. So let's meet them."

A moment later, Aquilla, noticing Simon was coming down, introduced him to the gathering. "Please welcome Peter, leader of the Jerusalem Center."

Greeted by the nearest guest just as he reached the bottom stair, Simon made no reply as the fellow giddily exclaimed, "Peace to you! I hear we have a savior!"

The subject had been raised too casually, and Simon turned to others who welcomed him.

"Don't hesitate to fill your plate," Aquilla said, bringing him a glass of warm wine. "We have plenty. On the table along the wall."

"Thank you. And thanks to all of you for coming here to welcome me. I see Barsabbas and Silas are well provided for and hope you will offer them your good wishes as well."

Continuing to accept the friendly greetings, Simon observed the platters of cheese and bread, with olives and steaming eggs surrounded by colorful vegetables. There were no animal foods, and Priscilla, who handed him a plate, suggested there was nothing he could not eat.

"You have a beautiful home," Simon said. "The linen embroideries on the walls are magnificent."

"I must do more than sew the seams of tents. My loom frees me to contemplate our lord and his teaching."

Even before Simon had a chance to reply, the same fellow who spoke of the savior was at his side. "Paul says he died to take away our sin, and his spirit is the source of life, so if we accept him, we may live on even past death," he orated. "Are you able to attest this is true?"

"His death ends sin for all believers," Simon answered dismissively. "But this all looks so delicious."

Another guest, standing close enough to hear him, said, "We understand he was God's sacrifice. Isn't that confusing? We know about offering a sheep or goat to Melkarth, with prayers for forgiveness of our wrongdoing, but what point is there in God's offering his own son? That is your idea, isn't it?"

Stepping up to Simon's side, Paul said, "It is not Peter's idea, friends. It is God's idea."

"Which must make sense!" another guest said loudly. "Or has God kept his reason a secret?"

"It is not a secret!" Simon responded abruptly. "He did not die. His earthly body passed from this realm. But he will speak to you if you are worthy—and that will take away all your doubt."

As the group was caught in the current of his words, they began to drift toward Simon.

"Of course you have doubt," Paul said, addressing the same fellow and then the group. "But have you come here to learn about Jesus or to promote yourselves? Peter, please don't take offense at these fine people. Listen to this, friends. Doubt is at the heart of our faith. The death of our body tempts us to say there is no meaning beyond death. Who is really tempting us to doubt the life beyond? It is the same one who tempts us to act in wrong ways and then punishes us for it, as if his law is broken when we follow our inclinations."

One of those who had not pressed forward to be near Simon—the elder who introduced Paul to the rituals of the cave—nodded his approval when Paul implied the lawgiver was a voice of Satan.

"You Jews are the ones with the most laws," a weathered-looking man then said. "I guess Satan has a special place in his heart for you."

At this, they all laughed boisterously, and none heard Simon whisper to Paul, "They think it's funny."

"Friends," Paul said solemnly, "is this how you treat a guest?"

"It's all right," Simon said. "Perhaps you are right. Satan may have discovered what a childlike people we Jews are. Who better to fool than us! But it is the voice and spirit of Jesus after he died that gives us proof of eternal life. And didn't he have to die for that to happen? How else would we be certain? So God, who loved his son, was only able to convince us through his death. Therefore, we understand he sacrificed his son for us. Not as you would a lamb or goat, no. But he caused him to be taken away so that his life after death would be a sign. To let his son die so that we would live—that is the truest sacrifice."

"And you say he speaks to you?"

"If I tell the truth, some of you will call me a liar," Simon said. "Yes, I have seen Jesus after he died and even shared a meal with him."

"I hope he didn't eat anything your God forbids, like octopus, or goat stewed in the whey of milk." It was the weathered-looking man who again had them all laughing at his snide comment.

"Grilled fish," Simon replied, unintentionally fueling their amusement.

"And what has he told you lately?" another guest asked, his eyes glazed by the wine. "Are we to eat only grilled fish in heaven, or will there be oysters and crabs as well?"

Responding sternly, Paul said, "He spoke with me too. As I have told you and so many others, he appeared to me on the road to Damascus. But you are all so afraid of missing your favorite foods. Is that what you should worry about? There is no need for food in heaven. But here on earth, you may ask Jesus what to eat. If you are blessed to hear his voice, then he may answer you."

Simon could see from their doubtful expressions that they could not fathom why the laws of the Jews were sacred, if, as Paul said, they were entrapping them.

"Some laws of our Torah are for all time," Simon explained. "Paul has surely said that adultery is a sin. You know murder is a sin. And stealing. And plotting to have what belongs to your neighbor. Yes, Jesus has taught us not to treat our neighbor differently than we would be treated. His words are found in our Torah. But the laws for gentiles were not spoken by him while he was among us. Today, from on high, he is guiding us through the walkways of the kingdom in altogether fresh ways."

At the point of invoking a new heavenly edict, one to win them over, Simon took a deep breath, paused, and cast his gaze at Paul, much like a man about to descend a treacherous slope. "I asked him about food," Simon began. "He gave me a vision that was his answer. Will you hear it?"

"Tell us," one said.

"Yes. We'll know whether your vision is true," another said, as if giving a warning.

"It happened when I was in the port of Jaffa," Simon explained. "While I was praying, I saw a huge white sheet being lowered from heaven. It reached the ground close enough for me to see it was covered with all kinds of animals, including wild beasts and everything we avoid eating that walks or crawls or flies. Even insects and bugs. Then there was a voice. It was Jesus, telling me to kill and eat. Of course, I thought that was impossible. These dirty creatures had never crossed my lips. So I said, 'No, lord. I will not eat profane and forbidden foods that I have never eaten before.' And Jesus said, 'Peter, what God has declared you should eat, you may not call unclean.' And I knew that what God had now made clean, I had no right to call profane or dirty.'"

"Thank God!" the man with the weathered face declared. "I'd go to hell before giving up my squid ink with dove's eggs. My grandmother's recipe, Peter, and one you too may now savor."

From the complete silence that met his lighthearted remark, Simon could tell his vision had been well received.

"Then whatever you eat," Paul said, amplifying Simon's words, "you are no longer sinning. The creation of the spiritual man has begun. The original Adam needed laws to govern him because his body was always craving satisfaction. He sated his appetite by doing wrong things, and so the laws were necessary. But if you are willing to believe the voice of Jesus is speaking to you through his holy spirit, then you need only nourish your spirit with his guidance and be free from the possibility of sin. You may eat whatever you want, because it is not your body that matters! Saying there are sins against your body is to worship your body. If you worship earthly things such as flesh, you are rejecting the spirit that frees you."

"Then why are we dining on vegetables and eggs and cheese?" asked one of the guests, reticent until then.

"Because those who are still freeing themselves from the law require patience," Paul said. "Silas and Barsabbas, who you see among us, and your neighbor, Timothy, and others who love Jesus have not yet heard him or only in a whisper. It is not easy to change a life of habit, especially when you have been taught it is what God demands. So let us respect the ones who are joining us but more slowly than others."

"What you say rings true," another said.

As the assembled group voiced their approval, murmuring words of assent, Simon inquired, "You who have been immersed by Paul, do you realize how you know in your hearts my vision is true?" Then, not awaiting their answer, he gave his own. "You have been blessed by the holy spirit itself. You are hearing the same voice as I!"

"Many of those you see still have not been immersed by Paul," Aquilla said softly.

"Ah, but friends, like the seasonal rain just starting," Simon intoned, turning to Paul, "can anyone refuse these fine people life's water? Paul, in the coming days, please baptize those who wish to be, in the holy spirit, in the name of Jesus the Christ."

During the next moments, more food was brought out and almond cakes were praised by all the guests. With the meeting concluded, conversation soon turned to leaving, as drooping eyelids indicated the time for an afternoon nap.

"We should go before the rain turns to a deluge," one guest said, touching Simon's arm in a neighborly manner.

Others joined in bidding him a good trip to Jerusalem and were about to depart, when a tall, wide-shouldered young man said, "Tell me this: regarding your law of circumcision, is circumcision still required of all those who would be covenanted by God?"

Paul, standing nearby, knew that an uncertain answer would possibly deter many from accepting Jesus. "Shall I answer?" he asked Simon.

"That's all right," Simon assured him. "Here is what you should understand, my friend. Circumcision is a denial of the body and of its lust. God gave Abraham, our forefather, a way of showing he didn't need his body to have faith. But the real sign of faith is an inward one, made by circumcision of the heart, not the flesh. That is the way we become Jesus' followers. So you need not be circumcised in the flesh if you are circumcised in the heart."

"To which, I would add this," Paul said. "Those who are circumcised because it is the law are still under the law and until they bear witness to Jesus, they should be circumcised. This rule applies to Jews. But if that is not your law, since most of you are not Jews, there is no need for physical circumcision. And for all people, when they hear Jesus and are free, then circumcision will no longer be necessary for any of them."

"I for one am greatly relieved!" another guest responded. "If I was to be circumcised before entering heaven, not even Jesus could persuade me to go. Lucky for me, I wasn't born a Jew!"

"I have one more question," a voice from the far side of the room called out. "If that's all right." Priscilla was one of the few local women who had embraced Jesus as her savior, and they all were aware of her importance.

"Naturally, I especially welcome your question," Simon responded.

"If we have sinned," Priscilla asked, "how are we to be cleansed? Will Jesus forgive us from heaven? Surely, to be worthy of entering the kingdom, the stain of sin must be removed."

"Your faith begins your life over," Simon said, addressing the entire gathering to show the question deserved special attention. "If you sin during the time between now and going to heaven, find another who has been blessed by the holy spirit, confess your sins to him, and through him as your intermediary, ask Jesus for forgiveness. Your prayer will be answered if your heart is penitent. But be careful of doing harm that has no remedy, or you may place yourself in the arms of the devil, and there may be no way out."

For the first time, the man with the weathered face spoke earnestly. "Then you say, Peter, that whatever we do that strikes you as wrong, you are speaking for Jesus, so we must follow your rules or be kept out of the kingdom."

"Yes, but we want to bring you in, not keep you out," Simon replied. "Jesus gave this lesson: If your children ask for something to eat, will you give them a snake or scorpion? Here is what he is giving: life itself, forever."

As the guests made their way to the door, several expressed their gratitude for the fine meal—with loud compliments, so Priscilla would hear—and embraced Aquilla, who bid them not delay, or the rain would soak them.

Excepting Simon and Paul, as well as Barsabbas, Silas, Timothy, and their hosts, the only one remaining was the elder of the cave, who had not ventured either a question or thought. Now, he said, "Peter, may I speak with you and Paul alone?"

"Of course," Simon answered, acknowledging his request with obvious respect.

"You say Jesus brings knowledge to you directly from the true God, isn't that so?"

"Yes," Simon responded, "but why don't we have our conversation under the eaves of the veranda? It will be more private there."

Outside, with the breeze from the sea growing stronger, the elder's long brown tunic was difficult to hold down and was getting wet with the spray. "I mustn't be blown out to sea. My wife would never understand," he said with a smile. "So I should not let this take more than a few words."

"I will do my best to satisfy you," Simon said.

"For us, who believe we must die to this world before we can be born anew, the challenge is often faced in opaque darkness. We enter it nonetheless, all to find our way to the one true God. By joining ourselves to his knowledge, we believe we can have divine immortality. Much as Paul has said, we too believe the laws governing the earthly realm are an entrapment. Even the luminary orbs of the night sky, so entrancing with their splendor, are only the deceptive web of the archontes, permitting no escape. And that raises this question: why should an old man like me, and others who have lived as I have, believe that the lessons of Jesus as the Christ are not just another deception?"

"Let me answer you this way," Simon said. "You too believe in divine knowledge, as you say. Yet if you achieve that knowledge, how do you know? How do you know you are experiencing the voice of God and not just hearing the entrapper, or as we might call him, Satan? Permit me to answer. If he tells you to subordinate yourself to his old laws, then you would immediately guard against his influence. Isn't that so? But just as the fresh wind brings in a day of rain, and we feel it is beginning, Jesus' spirit refreshes our beings with its new beginning. First comes the rain and then the harvest."

The elder made no reply, but his expression did not conceal his doubt.

Paul said, "Peter, I think we must share the tradition that is the secret of the disciples and Jesus' closest apostles."

Not wishing to expose his inability to grasp Paul's suggestion, Simon said, "Of course. Paul is right. You may proceed, Paul."

"The wine we drink on our festival of freedom is now given to us as Jesus' blood," Paul said. "Our journey is no longer from slavery in Egypt to the holy land promised to our ancestor Abraham, but it is from the realm of the entrapping law and its slavery into the realm of the one true God. Jesus' own flesh is our bread, our nourishment, so that as his body ascends, we are part of him and ascend with him into the kingdom of eternity."

If Paul wondered whether Simon would support his words, the elder's quick reaction prevented any discord. "It is wonderful that we have your Jesus come to save us non-Hebrews," he said. "I believe there can be no doubt that he is the Christ, just because he has freed you from your own cherished laws. That is my proof. Even more, your drinking his blood and eating his body is what our sages have always taught. I will spread the word. Your lessons from Jesus will be accepted by many of us. I only wish I had walked at his side as you did, Peter."

"In accepting him and justifying his fate on the cross as a sign from God, you are walking at his side, brother," Simon responded, and the two men embraced.

After Pricilla helped the elder towel off his moist face, Simon and Paul joined her and Aquilla at the door to wish him peace, watching as several companions then escorted him to their covered cart.

"I think you both could use a nap," Pricilla observed, guiding them to separate quarters spacious enough for each to have his own pallet.

"Thank you for your gracious hospitality," Simon said pleasantly. "A short rest, then, and we will be on our way."

Once the door was closed, and they were alone, Paul spoke. "Did you see how well he responded?" he asked, stretching out.

"Yes," Simon said.

"And have you nothing to add?"

"I hope what you say comes from Jesus," Simon told him.

"Do you think you are the only one he talks to? And isn't the truth told by our success? But I think we both can use a measure of sleep. May the holy spirit be with you."

"And you, Paul." But Simon was afraid to close his eyes.

CHAPTER TWENTY-FOUR

*E*ven after soaking it for several days—in the morning and then in the evening before sleeping—the small cut on Matthias' foot from the sandal strap had not healed. The lime powder bleach provided only slight relief, replacing the itch with a sting.

"That was an eternity ago," Matthias said aloud, recalling how his mother would slice the skin off a cucumber and put its cool underside on his boyhood bruises. Reaching down from his bench to scratch it, he then retrieved a fresh writing point, stirred the dye, and began again.

As we crossed into the Decapolis, entering the eastern province of Antipas' tetrarchy, we were immediately among the long parade of pilgrims on their way to Jerusalem for that fateful Passover.

Given what I know as I transcribe these recollections, please understand how I believed any danger was receding as we went southward. With every step we took toward Jerusalem, there was less likelihood the tetrarch would hunt down Jesus. Or so I believed.

His personal castigation of the Pietists' adultery, even his denunciation of Antipas for a sinful, unlawful marriage, was no basis for an arrest, surely not in Jerusalem, where Pontius Pilate exercised complete authority. Unlike John, whose main crime, to call it that, was outspoken rejection of Antipas' rule, Jesus had done little to invite a charge of sedition. Mostly, we all knew

Pilate detested Antipas, so his inclination to aid in capturing Jesus hardly seemed plausible.

What is more, on the pilgrimage Jesus never said he feared Antipas' vengeful pursuit. Telling Joanna, as he had days earlier, to convey word to Antipas that he was leaving his tetrarchy, Jesus seemed to dismiss any thought that the threat would follow us to Jerusalem. To the contrary, from what I know now, he had keenly sensed the possible consequence of Simon's exaggerated reverence. As my last entry reflects, taken down in Philip's own words to describe Jesus' severe rebuke, he anticipated the continuing danger, a trepidation I now believe was the likely cause of his moody silence as we reached Perea.

No doubt Simon remained oblivious to the threat caused by his misguided coronation of Jesus as king. The very idea he had subjected Jesus to a possible charge of sedition in the manner of John, was incomprehensible. He spoke from the heart when he declared to Jesus that he could never be arrested or put to death. Simon had created an immortal Jesus—or at least one who would soon prove his divine powers by ruling the land. Little wonder Jesus predicted Simon would deny knowing him if he was arrested. Here, permit me to observe with due emphasis, though I shall revisit the moment in detail, that the Jesus put on trial was actually an impossibility to Simon. His lord—"Adon," as he called him—could never be subject to the cruel arrest that took place before his eyes. Having created a different, all-powerful Jesus, he was telling the truth when he denied knowing him.

Now, I should say that eventually a man's reduced eyesight is an unavoidable reality. Much like the words I put down, which are still clear as the letters flow from my point but by morning's end will be hard for me to see, so too was the contempt of Jesus' enemies increasingly far from our minds as we made our way beyond the tetrarch's reach.

Still, I recall being troubled by Jesus' moodiness as we continued on. Agitated and impatient, he cast furtive glances at the clusters of nearby pilgrims, appearing to estimate their purpose. When one of the Zebedees asked him about entering the Kingdom, instead of replying, he sauntered several strides to the far side of the road, attaching himself to a family group with children. Seeing he was only a few steps away from the rest of us, the Zebedees hardly hesitated to trail close behind him. "If you want to enter the Kingdom," he finally told them, "you must be innocent as one of these." Plainly, he took pleasure at the sight of the small children half dancing and skipping as they went. Then, sycophantically pressing still closer to Jesus, one of the brothers inadvertently caused a child at Jesus' side to trip and stumble.

He was furious. After helping the child to regain his footing, Jesus said, "You want to know who will be first to enter the Kingdom? If any of you would be first," he said sharply, "turn and become like these children. Otherwise, you will never enter the Kingdom! Whoever is innocent like this child will be first. And I'll tell you something else. If you cause one who is innocent to stumble, you would be better off drowning with a millstone around your neck!"

As they say, it is easier to see a ripple in calm water than a wave in a stormy sea, and the festive gaiety of our fellow travelers prevented the rest of us from any sense of impending doom. If Jesus was short-tempered just then, I thought the tiring trip had caused his impatience.

Continuing our pilgrimage, we crossed the river and made our encampment outside Jericho, on the side of the road. As I recall, our donkey brayed with satisfaction as we lightened its burden of our provisions for the night.

Under the Nisan stars, as the moon was nearly full, neighboring groups also cooked and sang, and our worries seemed far behind.

After waking to the sound of people moving about and breaking camp, we washed in the rivulet of a spring, refilled our water jars, and ate young dates from a nearby palm tree, with cheese, bread, and olives. I admit I take pleasure in my ability to remember such details, as they were days of indelible importance. That next morning, by the first watch, just as the last nighttime stars disappeared into the morning light, we were underway.

Upon reaching the outskirts of Bethany, now hot and perspiring from the overhead sun, we stopped to rest under trees by the road. Two then went ahead to inquire whether we might stay the night with Mary and Martha. Of course, we were welcome.

Not long after a great show of affection for Jesus, the sisters prepared dinner. While Martha began serving, Mary emerged from a side room with a small jar of nard and gently kneaded it into Jesus' feet.

Andrew watched the caressing movement of her fingers and became uncomfortable. "That must be very expensive," he said as she applied more.

"It is," Martha affirmed, carrying in a steaming tray. "And it's good she is being so generous with my nard. But Mary, perhaps you will assist me with the platters."

When Mary made no move to accommodate her sister, Andrew again complained. "The money for that ointment could be better spent on the poor," he said.

"Leave her alone," Jesus reprimanded. "I like what she is doing for me."

"Don't you care that she is leaving me to do all the serving?" Martha asked. *"Please tell her to help me."*

"You're worrying too much, Martha. You've chosen to do what you are doing, and it's exactly what we need. What Mary has chosen to do is a beautiful thing for me and exactly what I need."

Martha was not at all pleased with his attitude, and Jesus joked, "Well, I hope you will not punish her by taking away her good portion, just because she's chosen to take care of my sore feet."

I may well have been the only one who laughed. And I truly recall how Jesus shot a quick smile in my direction.

Later, when we were about to fall asleep, I overheard Andrew say to Simon that he was unsure what Jesus meant, that Mary should have her portion.

Simon replied, "Don't you understand? He is referring to his teaching as 'the good portion,' and because she bowed down before him to oil his feet, she will have her share in the Kingdom. It will not be taken away from her."

The next morning, after our last bite of bread, we sat around watching Mary and Martha clean the house of all remaining leaven. It was in that interval that Jesus spoke about our plans.

Distracted by the gnawing pain, Matthias soothed his toe with the peel of a small cucumber, eating the rest and quickly wiping its juice from his chin, afraid the parchment could get wet. With a broad point, he then emphasized the grim section he would next commence:

Jesus' final Passover

Several of us were to depart for Jerusalem, nearly two miles away. My responsibility was to take Simon with John the Zebedee and Judas and arrange the Passover meal. Upon finding a room large enough for our group, we would unload the donkey, and

Simon was then to ride it back to Bethany. According to plan, the three of us would purchase our lamb and after the sacrifice, John and Judas would help carry it back to the house selected.

"But where should we have the festival meal?" I recall Simon asking.

Jesus told him we should go into the city and find one of the men carrying a water jar to make the unleavened bread. When he entered the courtyard where he was going, we would follow him and speak with the householder.

Listening intently, Simon appeared awestruck, as if this was divine wisdom. His ignorance of the typical manner used by pilgrims to find Passover space caused Jesus to patiently advise, "Ask if he has a large guest room on the upper floor and if he says yes, tell him your teacher wishes to know if he and his students may use it for the Passover meal. He will show you one that is furnished and ready." With that, Jesus handed Judas a small sack of coins. "You are in charge of the money for the lamb," he said.

As we set off, Judas asked whether there wasn't an expense for the room we would use. I replied that nobody took rent for providing Passover quarters, but we would purchase our wine and matzah from our host and give him a gift of the lambskin, which made a warm covering.

Just to the side of the city wall gate, clusters of Roman legionnaires kept a casual eye on pilgrims streaming into the city. Because Passover was a festival of freedom, rebellious speeches or even violent outbursts of protesters defying their hateful occupation might occur.

Inside the city walls, Jerusalem's residents were all busily involved in preparations. Some sights were so common, they were almost part of the celebration. You would see mothers pushing

337

their boys through crowded streets toward a barber's stall. Others carried armfuls of clothing from tailors' shops, and still others stopped to greet each other with holiday wishes.

I do recall a man was waving a pair of sandals in the air, pleading with a shoemaker who was closing his shop doors. Forced to wait because our donkey's path was blocked, I heard him lament, "These are my only pair." The sandlar glanced at the man's bare feet and replied, "Just stay here." He took the sandals and disappeared into the dark interior, while the fellow stood aside, letting us pass.

As we made our way, frenetic throngs rushed to complete their chores. By the end of the second watch, when the sun was overhead, all shops were to close. Only those necessary for the people to be clean and well dressed might remain open until the end of the third watch.

After stopping at a stall to choose vegetables and bitter herbs for the table, we continued until we came to a nearly impassable knot of women waiting to enter a large building.

"It's a bathhouse," I explained. "This is their last chance to wash using bran or oatmeal to scrub off their dry skin. Leavened grain will soon be gone from every corner of Jerusalem."

Not much farther on, we began to hear a sound of rhythmic slapping that I recognized. We turned onto a wide intersecting street and walked in the direction of the sound until we reached the residential neighborhood. A huge cistern in an open square was the site of men filling their skins and jugs with water. Several pilgrims were on the far side, trying to find space for their groups. As a resident with a heavy jug came in my direction, I asked, "Do you have room for a group?"

"Maybe one of the others does," he replied. "Ours are taken."

Approaching several waiting to fill their vessels, I again inquired. All but one shook their heads. The one man shouldered his earthenware vessel with a grunt and replied, "Happy Passover. I think so. But you will have to ask."

As we followed a few steps behind him, the noise of slapping grew louder, and the sweet aroma of baking bread beckoned until he finally entered a gate to a courtyard, where a row of women, bedecked in flour-whitened aprons, were kneading dough. Without setting down his container, the man emptied it into a wide-mouthed jar on the table close to the women.

The one nearest us dipped her hands in the water and slapped the dough until it was thin and flat. Others immediately shoveled it from wooden platters into the large clay oven. Satisfied, the woman turned to me and said, "I think we still have space. My husband is inside. Ask him."

I thanked her and wished her a good festival. I then suggested that Simon go to see whether we would be welcome. As was customary, the tradition of offering strangers a place for the ritual supper included setting the table with dishes and glasses, as well as providing dining couches. Always, there were at least ten guests. Simon soon came from the house, pleased to say the owner had a room for us to use. According to plan, we would meet toward the end of the fourth watch, when Simon returned with Jesus and the others.

After watching only briefly as Simon unloaded our pallets and blankets for the night ahead, we turned toward the Temple mount. Much as the darkest day begins with a pleasant sky, there was nothing in the air to warn of the change to come.

We were almost up the long ramp that led to the patio just outside the Temple's courtyard wall when we heard the noise of money changers barking their competing rates.

I was uncertain whether Judas realized the coins would need be converted to pieces of silver. Seeing he was tentative, I steered him by the arm toward a nearby changer, a fraternal touch that today fills me with revulsion. "The coins of Rome or those minted by the Tyrians portraying emperors or local gods are prohibited as currency," I explained. "Give him two of the silver denarri or a Tyrian half-shekel, and he will put an equal weight of plain silver on his scale."

I am recording these details because so many have attributed to Judas a satanic greed. Here, I wish to note, I did not witness any pronounced interest in the funds he managed. Before I make record of the subsequent events, I should say something more about him. As you may well sense, I have often thought back to the time I am now describing. I still try to detect some clue, as if to smell his rotten interior like a dog sniffs the carcass of a dead beast. Admittedly, I cannot help a nagging sense of complicity or at least of failed prescience, which would have alerted me.

Judas Iscariot, whose place among the disciples I have taken, was young and unimportant. I venture to say his nondescript, pleasant manner made his deceit almost invisible. I don't recall any serious questions from him and certainly no contentious disagreements. My impression was that he accepted the other disciples were his senior, and he would do well to learn from them what was expected. Always courteous and helpful, he ingratiated himself by exhibiting self-censorship that was mistaken for modesty. Truly, it is a remarkable thing that he kept so duplicitous a nature secret, even from Jesus. I should observe this, which has occurred to me more than once: had Judas been a disguised Roman or perhaps a Pietist spy, we might have respected his terrible agenda as befits an enemy, but his was the apparent indifference to his own worth as a man and the creed he adopted that weakened any resolve to spare Jesus. Some have called him a traitor. But to be a traitor you must defy your own current allegiance. In my view, Judas Iscariot was never one of Jesus' devotees. His was the evil of falsehood, pretending affection where there was none. Most probably, I believe, his clinging to Jesus' circle was an attempt to accomplish that same self-importance he derived from telling the authorities where we went after the supper. To those who ascribe to him the dark heart of evil, I demur. He does not deserve the distinction of being special in that regard or any other.

If my impression is true, at that time he still had not been approached by the authorities. But it would not be too much longer before the warped prospect of personal aggrandizement showed its face.

Making our way up the stairs and through the Huldah Gate, we were swept along by the flood of pilgrims. Like a fine mosaic of many colorful stones, the congregation was an array of priests, Levites, and travelers along with residents who, like us, after rinsing their hands and feet from spigots of the copper basins, made their way to the inner courtyard to purchase lambs. We skirted teachers and their circles of students who had come from afar and reached an especially large gathering that was listening to Gamliel.

Judas and John paused with me to hear what the sage was saying.

"What is the central commandment of Torah concerning Passover?" he asked rhetorically. "In the second book, Shemot, we are commanded, 'The whole Assembly of the Congregation of Israel shall slaughter the sacrificial lambs.' Friends," he continued, "do you understand? Our individual sacrifices elevate

each of us to the stature of a kohane, a priest. Nobody is closer to our Creator than any other person, not even a high priest. On Passover, we learn we are all equal; we are all priests. Therefore, Torah teaches if you are unable to come to the Temple, then make your sacrifice in the yards of your houses, and each house will be like the Temple, a habitation purified for God's presence. Remove the leavened grain! Make sure not even an olive-size bit of it remains. Burn what you have not given non-Hebrew neighbors, and dump your Edomite vinegar and beers."

Matthias stopped transcribing just for a moment as he vividly pictured Gamliel, waving and calling out a festival greeting.

"Remember what was commanded of Aaron and his sons," the sage had continued. "You shall never offer leavened bread on our Creator's altar. Only the pure bread, free of any yeast from the air, may be offered. Yes, today we will offer the matzah, holding it high over our heads, as the priests do before tossing it on the flames. And we, like them, will eat the unleavened bread, joining ourselves to the People, all equal before God. For the Torah teaches, 'You shall be to me a nation of priests.'"

If any of those hearing his words made claim to spiritual superiority, the sound of several lambs bleating 'amen' reminded them and us of our earthly nature. I can recall Gamliel joking, "Clearly, they agree."

Is there life without laughter? Of course not, and I should emphasize that Jesus knew how to laugh. You must understand how deeply this Temple was a world he loved, even as my purpose takes me into the darkest of hours.

When John the Zebedee made the observation that the size of the crowd was too large for all to enter the courtyard, and the gate had been shut with many still outside, I explained the schedule.

On other festivals, the Temple gates are open at daybreak, but on Passover, the crowd needing lambs is too large to delay, and they are permitted entry at midnight. After each assembly of worshippers exits with their sacrifices, a second ceremony with new worshippers begins. This repetition is followed by another until all are done.

If I hoped my comments might increase their appreciation of the day, John's expression said otherwise. Appearing distressed, like a trapped animal about to turn and bolt for the exit, he seemed only slightly less discomfited than Judas, who wore the sickly expression of one who has eaten bad eggs. Against the backdrop of joy and devotion everywhere around us, their visible displeasure was almost embarrassing, which is why I probably see it so clearly in my mind.

I thought a change in tone might lessen their sense of detachment, so I shared a story that was about me. Owing to the size of the crowds, members of the Sanhedrin, such as I, were encouraged to arrive by midnight to resolve any disputes.

One such time when a complaint was brought and a hearing required, I conducted the informal proceeding. As it happened, while still dark, a torch-bearing Temple official called out to a Levite watchman, "Shalom Aleichem, peace to you!" but the fellow, who was curled on the floor fast asleep, did not reply. The official thought to teach the watchman not to doze again, so he lit the edge of the fellow's tunic with the torch and waited until the smoke was sufficient to awaken him. Predictably, the man immediately ran screaming to the nearest cistern to extinguish the patch of garment going up in flames.

"You're supposed to sacrifice a lamb, not the Levite watchman," was our unanimous opinion.

Unless I am imagining their reaction, Judas appeared not to have been listening at all, and John nodded his head with the utmost seriousness. It strikes me now, as it did then, that the failure to see humor in a situation is a sign of separateness and ignorance.

I tried again, thinking they might have restrained their laughter from a misguided wish to be polite. "Of course, everybody found our verdict to be funny," I said in a jocular tone. "But we did not fine the official, suggesting only that he choose another method of rousing one who overslept."

John kept nodding, while Judas was like a fish with staring eyes and a mouth frozen into a meaningless grin.

I admit I don't remember if I ever told Jesus that story.

"Damn needles in my toes," Matthias lamented, deciding the fresh air might help. Once out the door, the pain would go away. Blood had to flow. Across the way, Yehudit, his neighbor, had been hanging laundry from midday. On the clothesline there were fewer than ten items, and it seemed she was using the chore as an excuse to investigate his activities.

"How are you?" she called out.

"Fine. Hard work, eh?"

"It's better than staying inside all day," she replied.

"I know what you mean."

"Then why aren't you out more? Your garden is dry."

On the verge of being impolite, he refrained from saying, "So is your laundry," instead answering, "I will take care of it."

"May I give you advice?" she asked and then added without waiting, "You should go for walks. I see you are limping. It's because you are always at that table. I'm sorry; I shouldn't have looked. But when I do the laundry, I can't help it."

"I appreciate your concern," he said, turning to his door.

"I don't know why you sit there like that. All day, it seems."

"You are right," Matthias agreed, looking back politely. "Well, the weather is changing. It will take care of my vegetables. But shouldn't you take in the wash before it gets wet?"

Once in his house, he shifted the scroll to the far side of the table so he would be out of her view.

After catching his breath, he picked up the point and began again.

Here, a few words about my first encounter with Jesus seem appropriate. He and I had met in that same Temple courtyard just three years before the Passover of his death. It was the fourth year of the cycle, during the Second Tithe, and I did not tell him then that I was his father's acquaintance, only that I was a member of the Sanhedrin and was concerned about his welfare. Having journeyed to Jerusalem with James, about a year before inviting Simon and his brother Andrew, as well as Philip and the Zebedees, to study with him, Jesus' public exchanges on the Temple mount that derided the Pietists as hypocrites were already causing controversy. When I warned him not to give them reason to charge him as a public nuisance, I was doing it for my friend Joseph, at his request.

In truth, sentimental as I am, I thought it an opportunity to bring them together as father and son. Only later did I learn from Joseph—and eventually much the same from Jesus himself— that there was an issue of paternity. Because sons often rebel against their fathers, I simply believed Jesus was independent, never suspecting he was left, after age twelve, to his mother's care and then to his own devices. When he and I came to know each other, I realized he never referred to Joseph by name nor called him his father, so neither did I make mention of him. Only once, I believe, did he say his name. That was when John was arrested. "Can't Joseph do something?" he asked. Exactly why Joseph still cared about Jesus, not being his true father or ever playing that role after Jesus reached legal maturity was something I came to understand later and will record in its proper place, farther on.

Now, I shall return to that dread day.

As the Levite chorus commenced the second presentation of Hallel, their voices harmonized against the background of lyres and bleating lambs. Our place on line finally advanced to the stall where we procured our animal. Tugging it along by a cord, we ascended the stairs to the sacrificial court, moving slowly toward the waist-high rows of semicircular metal rings meant to keep the lambs' necks steady.

Twenty-four in all, socketed to the floor, they were divided into four rows of six, with a priest standing by each ring, holding a basin to catch the blood of the animal as it was killed. In such crowded circumstances, the priests were only certain of who was in front or behind them from the basins they were passed, which were either silver or gold and alternated from row to row to keep them separate.

Following my lead, John and Judas helped hold it still, while I placed its neck in one of the rings. Then, taking a perfectly sharpened knife from a priest in charge of the implements, I dispatched the lamb.

As the animal was slaughtered, and the basin filled with blood pouring from its neck, the priest passed it to the next fellow stationed along the row of rings until the one nearest the altar carried it forward and emptied it on the base.

According to Torah, no Hebrew was ever to drink blood or to offer it to God. As my father had taught me many years earlier, blood was the animal's life, and God did not consume life but created it. Neither would God accept the lifeblood of an animal as an offering, so that it was not to be burned on the altar.

Once all the lambs had been slaughtered and the blood found its way into the small drainage holes that led to the water channel of the Kidron Brook, the priests swilled and rinsed the area, whitening the altar base with lime-coated cloths to prevent it from becoming permanently stained.

Carrying our lamb to the housed shambles on the far side of the Priests Court, we navigated between large cedar posts with hooks to use for flaying the carcass, finally locating a marble table that had just become available.

As I cut away the fatty part as well as kidneys and lobe above the liver, John followed my instructions and brought us a copper bucket for their removal to the altar, where they would be burned as an offering.

Once we had completed the preparation and rinsed the remaining blood from the area, I took the pomegranate skewer from a nearby bundle provided for the purpose and thrust it through, from its mouth to its buttocks. Making use of what would be a convenient spit for roasting, John and Judas hoisted it to their shoulders and followed my lead toward the Huldah Gate.

In all, each of the twenty-four rings was to be the site of sacrifice of nearly two lambs per minute for nearly two and one-half hours, with each singing of the Hallel psalms taking nearly a full hour. By sunset, well over six thousand lambs would be sacrificed, each to be eaten by at least ten but usually fifteen or more people. The number of souls participating was thus more than one hundred thousand people, at least half of whom were travelers to Jerusalem, such as we were.

If you wonder what I was feeling as we descended the wide stairs, with the sound of the one-hundred-seventeenth psalm receding into the background, I will say I was happy. Having come to know Jesus, I anticipated a supper rich with rituals and teachings. My expectation was to share the historical drama of our freedom from Egyptian slavery and pray, as Jews had for several decades, that the miracle would soon be witnessed again.

God would betroth His People and save her from the occupiers. If memory serves me, I made it a point to tell John and Judas they should use the term Kittians, referring to our ancient enemy, if they wished to talk about Roman oppression.

Romans dressed as Hebrews, or even Hebrews acting as spies, were always a fearful possibility. Indeed, as I offered my advice, it is a haunting question whether Judas recognized his own countenance in my warning.

Just a few steps from the entrance to the house where we were to have our meal, a large clay open-topped oven was filled with wood, and tall, square stones were ready for the lamb's spit. Telling from the sun, we were well into the fourth watch and might expect the others to arrive in a short while. It was at this juncture that I suggested Judas take charge of roasting the lamb and that John and I would go to the city gate and wait for Jesus.

The sun was nearly down and light was fading from day when they came into view. After we exchanged greetings, Jesus said nothing and walked in the midst of our group at the side of the donkey, not toward the front, as was his custom. Thinking back, I believe he was purposefully blending in with us in order to avoid notice. As we again entered the courtyard, Judas was at the roasting site, busily straightening wooden staves that appeared to be only recently lit. He could have just advised the Roman police, not far down the road, about Jesus' arrival.

Very likely, that is when Jesus sensed Judas' intentions were turned against him. Though he told several others to continue roasting the lamb, because Judas appeared to lack skill at making a robust fire, I now think that Jesus was wary of letting Judas out of sight.

Having purchased a large, full wineskin from the owner of the house, we set our sandals by the door and climbed the stairs to the reserved room. After helping array the table with cups of salty water, bitter vegetables, grape vinegar, and Mary and Martha's sweet haroset, a spiced-date condiment, I put out a plate of three pieces of offering matzah, stacked one on the other. We were well into the fifth watch and the sun was setting as Jesus summoned us to gather round.

Wordlessly removing his long outer garment and then wrapping a large towel around his waist, he filled a water basin from a jug and, kneeling in front of me, began washing my feet.

This custom, having its origin in the difficulty of bending down to perform the chore on oneself, fulfilled the commandment to be clean before the Passover meal. When he was done, I dipped my hands in the basin and then used the towel, a corner of which reached the floor, to dampen and wipe Jesus' ankles and feet.

As I stood, I recall the expression on Simon's face. He was completely astounded.

Jesus responded to his look by kneeling in front of him, as he had done with me.

"Are you going to wash my feet, lord?" Simon asked, plainly dismayed.

Jesus took the towel and began cleaning Simon's toes.

"Never!" Simon said. "You shall never wash my feet, lord!"

"If I don't, you have nothing in common with me," Jesus replied as he continued swabbing his ankles. Trapped between his reverence for the messiah he had created and the revelation that Jesus' feet, like his own, had been covered with patches of hardened dust and clay, he watched as his teacher hoisted the towel's lower half to wipe away the encrusted dirt, declaring, "If so, lord, don't only wash my feet but my hands and my head as well!"

"You again say I am your master or lord? Then do what your lord does!" Jesus told him. "If you took a bath, you don't need the rest of you to be washed." The slight smile playing on his lips vanished as he turned to Judas and, speaking almost under his breath, added, "Though not all of you are clean."

Today, I may observe with certainty, even as the sun's descent beneath the horizon should have occasioned unbridled festivity and rejoicing, Jesus' outwardly calm demeanor did not disguise his growing premonition that his life was in danger.

Taking the plate of three matzot, he then led us downstairs and outside. He stood near the roasting fire and turned to the courtyard entrance gate, calling out loudly, "Ha lachma anya. This is the bread of the poor and the oppressed. Let all who are hungry come in and eat!"

After raising and waving the matzah over his head, he broke off and handed out small pieces for us to all hurl into the glowing embers as the ritual grain offering.

Upon sacrificing and roasting a lamb in the flames of our own altar and offering unleavened bread to Adonai, we had completed the ceremony, consecrating us as a nation of priests.

The lamb was carried in on a platter and put on a nearby stand. We found places at the table, with Jesus and I sharing the same couch, across from Simon. Exchanging looks of camaraderie, we raised our glasses, thanking God for life and the new season. Some sipped and others gulped the sweetness of the rich, red wine. After making the blessing over matzah, according to custom, all took a bite and dipped bright-green bitter herbs into the bowl of grape vinegar.

Even before I had swallowed mine, Jesus said, "One of you will betray me."

The room went completely silent, and I recall Simon motioning to me that I should ask who it was that he meant.

"Who?" was all I could manage. I was too stunned even to speak.

"One of you who has dipped with me in the dish," he replied. His voice was quiet, but we all heard him.

From their places around the table, the disciples protested, several saying, "You can't mean me," and others, "Surely, not I." And so it was they expressed their confidence that whoever Jesus may have meant, he was not talking about them. Oddly, as if far removed from any deceit, Judas, the last one to speak, as I recall, said quite innocently, "Is it I?" Hearing him, you might have thought he was guessing the answer to a riddle, almost in the spirit of an amusing game.

Jesus' reply struck a chord fully familiar to me as a scribe and expert in the law but which went over the heads of Judas and the others. "They are your words," he told Judas.

The usage was a standard legal formulation to challenge a witness. If a false accuser intentionally lied about a defendant's purported wrongdoing, his words of testimony were to be punished as severely as would the one on trial, were he guilty.

Jesus' reply to Judas was another way of saying, "You are a liar to deny what you have done, causing an innocent person to be taken to trial. As you would do to me, the same will be done to you."

But then, the moment passed, and my attention to it as a matter of concern quickly lapsed. If I had wondered at the strange accusation, my doubts gave way to the sundries of the feast.

What happened next, as unlikely as it seems, reveals much about that early evening. We ate, devouring chunks of lamb impaled on the small handheld wooden skewers, with matzah washed down by many cups of wine, not mixing water until we were almost done. Nuts sweetened with honey made a delicious dessert.

Here, I must return to Judas. Seeming to share the group's enthusiasm that they would again sleep under the full moon as in the prior year, he recalled how pleasant a place the grove was.

As we continued our meal and were reaching the end, Judas excused himself from the table. At the time, it did not warrant any special notice. He had been eating, though not finished with dessert, and could have had any number of reasons for stepping outside. Had I guessed, I might have said it was to relieve himself, or because he felt the need for fresh air. How I wish it were so! But Jesus was on to him. "Hurry up!" he told him. "You should go quickly!"

You might have thought, as I did, he was telling him to return promptly. But today, as I write this, I know he meant, "Hurry up so you aren't late. You wouldn't want them to think less of you."

Jesus' sarcasm forced Judas to see himself for what he was—and not think he was deceived.

Inebriated and full of lamb, none of us—and I include myself—hesitated when Jesus, only moments after Judas left, suggested we set out for the Garden of Gethsemane. There, in the olive grove, we would make our beds.

Only days later, when the unfolding horror replayed itself again and again, did it seem a telling sign that Jesus had said nothing about the story of Passover.

Even before Judas' departure, he had become preoccupied, never mentioning slavery or freedom, or the plagues that God brought upon Egypt in the time of Moses. Today, I am certain he was in a rush to vacate the premises, thinking Judas would bring the authorities to the house just as we were finishing the meal. Inasmuch as a cohort of soldiers entering the courtyard would risk serious disturbance, that proved not to be the authorities' adopted plan.

Finally done, we gathered our provisions and departed for the refuge of the wide, age-gnarled trunks of Gethsemane's trees, where God might answer his prayers and keep him safe. Ascending a modest distance on a low slope of the Mount of Olives, only our sandals grinding against the ground broke the silence.

When we reached the grove, Jesus told the disciples to stop and unroll their pallets. Simon and the Zebedees were to continue with us. Andrew—inquiring rather nervously, I thought—had asked Simon whether he should remain at his side but was encouraged to stay behind with the others.

After we proceeded another hundred cubits, he instructed the three to take up stations and keep guard. Simon would sound the alarm and immediately warn Jesus if he heard anybody coming.

Honored with such responsibility, as I recall, Simon assured Jesus that nobody would get past them and whoever tried would be stopped.

"You'll all run away," Jesus scoffed.

"I would lay down my life for you," Simon said.

"Lay down your life? You'll fall back and say you never knew me."

"Even if I must die, I will never do that," Simon insisted vehemently.

"Before the cock crows to announce morning has come, you'll likely deny you ever knew me. But stay here. And keep your eyes open."

Jesus and I had made our way between the trees, perhaps another hundred cubits, when we came to a small, open area, where he got down on his knees, turned in the direction of the Temple, and began to pray.

"Aveenu shebashamayim, our Father in heaven, yehi ritzon milfanecha, may it be according to your will, asay eemanu tzdakah vahesed, v'hosheeaynu—to show your mercy and save us."

And then, as if reminding God of the people escaping Egypt, he looked up and wailed loudly, "Ziman mikreh kodesh, zaycher litziyat mitzrayim, let the cup of freedom from Egypt and the holiness of that time be a cup of freedom from my pursuers. Avinu malkaynu, Father and King, adon haolam, Master of the universe, tikach mimeni kos ha-mavet, take away this cup of death."

Before too much time had passed, without saying a word to me or even looking in my direction, he raised his hand to indicate I should wait for him, and he strode off in the direction of Simon and the Zebedees.

Only moments later, he returned. "They fell asleep," he informed me.

"Too much wine and lamb," I answered.

"If he would go to prison or even die for me, how can he not even stay awake?" Not expecting an answer, Jesus again faced the Temple and lowered himself to his knees. "Alaynu lishabayach la-adon hakol," he prayed, reciting these traditional words, while touching his face to the earth. "Master of all things and Creator of the universe, my heart and soul are sorrowful to the point of death. As I fall koreem, bowing before You, I plead that You forgive those who are with me. They know not what they do. May You who answers prayer, shomayah tefillot, and for whom all things are possible, answer and save me."

Finally reclining wordlessly on our bedding, the silence almost seemed reassuring, as if nothing exceptional was going to occur. Time passed, and the farther the moon traversed the night sky, the more relieved I felt. Sleepy with the heavy meal and late hour, I opened my eyes just in time to see Jesus again going off toward Simon and the Zebedees, apparently intending once more to prod them from their torpor.

When he came back, he was plainly exasperated. "They can't even stay awake for an hour."

"The spirit is willing, but the flesh is weak," I said. The proverb might just as well have referred to my own dozing off.

"Their eyes were closed," Jesus said. "Simon couldn't even answer me when I woke him again. He and the Zebedees will almost certainly fall asleep a third time."

They never had the chance. Just then, the sound of harsh voices and a commotion startled us. There were lights of lanterns and torches coming in our direction.

The next moment, an official standing only several feet from Jesus demanded, *"Are you Jesus from Nazareth?"* Behind him were the disciples, surrounded by a mixed guard of Romans and Temple police.

Jesus did not reply immediately but looked in the direction of Judas, who came forward and said, *"Rabbi!"* kissing him on the cheek, the sign apparently preplanned with the arresting officers.

"You would betray me with a kiss?" Jesus asked him directly.

But Judas showed no inclination to defend or acknowledge his complicity and stood to the side.

"Are you Jesus, the one from Nazareth?" the arresting official repeated.

"Haven't you seen me teaching on the Temple mount?" Jesus replied. *"Ask them. They know me."* Pointing to several of the Temple police who had protected him from the Hanukkah mob, he added, *"They know I am no common robber or thief, for you to come here like this with swords and clubs."*

Instead of showing even a small sign of familiarity, much less compassion, one who had helped him on that earlier occasion affirmed coldly, *"He is the one."*

As they seized and bound Jesus, he put up no struggle, saying, *"Every day you saw me teaching in the Temple courtyards and you never arrested me."* Then, observing the others were in danger too, he insisted, *"If I'm the one you are looking for, let these others go!"*

Brave and selfless at a moment when Simon cowered in fear—and I, to my own disgrace, stood by speechless—his demand they be freed made an impression.

Though the disciples were shoved forward, as if they too were under arrest, the police permitted all to run off, which they did *without hesitation, just as Jesus expected they would. One, whose sleeping garment was momentarily in the grip of a guard, actually fled naked between the trees.*

Even Simon was gone from view, apparently having retreated into the darkness to wait and see what might occur.

At Jesus' side, before beginning our climb to Caiaphas' house for a hearing, I was only briefly interrogated by the captain of the Roman cohort.

Because I was known to them as a scribe and member of the Sanhedrin, the Temple police gave their advice to permit my escort, and the soldiers acquiesced with near indifference as we began our ascent of the steep Temple mount.

One question may occur to you, which, I must admit, tormented me then and still does. Why didn't I assert my authority in Jesus' behalf?

Forgive me for forgiving myself. If I sound as though I am standing before a tribunal, I keep pleading the case to God that I not be accountable for my failure to stop the unfolding horror. I admit I would do anything to have one more chance to intercede but now am left only with my skill as a scribe to attempt an explanation.

It's not an excuse, but for two decades I had been a man whose role in Judean affairs was to contemplate legalities, venturing carefully thought-out positions on proposed rules. Often, I would take down what others said, rebutting or endorsing ideas based on their merit. In that chamber of the Sanhedrin, members were more accustomed to hearing themselves speak than listening to the wisdom of others. And as that became habit, with each of us accepting the countless times no attention was paid to what they opined, this night's violent circumstance seemed utterly hopeless.

As I told others, in those sad weeks that followed, nothing would have given me a surfeit of pleasure greater than taking a sword to cut off the ear of one of those marauders, martinets who surely would have refused to hear any protest.

In my favor, you may recall how I asserted my official post during the near-arrest of Simon and Andrew by Levite guards and my exercise of authority with Temple police, during the Hanukkah melee. But I did so only because they were subordinates, required by law to weigh my advice. In Gethsemane, force of arms would have been the only rebuttal.

This scroll, you may now understand, has been a personal struggle, as if there is still hope for me to change what occurred that night. Wrestling with the demon of my silence, I am sickened by a sense that the arrest is still occurring, even as I put down the words describing it.

Surrounded by a contingent of armed soldiers—fearful Roman cohorts holding long spears—I was fully undone by their ruthless arrogance.

Bound as he was, Jesus kept slipping and falling, and they repeatedly hauled him back to his feet in a gruff and contemptuous fashion.

Opening the tall iron gate fronting Caiaphas' two-story house, one of the high priest's matron attendants waited until we were inside and slammed it shut behind the last of the entering Temple guards. She did not admit Simon who, until that moment, had been following, out of view. When I requested that he too be permitted to enter, one of the high priest's personal aides recognized me and advised that Simon be let into the courtyard, though not the house itself. There, by the oven for roasting the lamb, its charcoal embers still brightly glowing, Simon remained, warming himself alongside the custodians. High on the Temple mount, the Nisan night was cold.

Inside, the smell of lamb still hung in the air. Standing shoulder to shoulder, more than two dozen individuals gaped at the sight of Jesus being led into the large triclinium, making room as he was brought to the front. One of the few I recognized was Annas, Caiaphas' esteemed father-in-law, who had been high priest before him.

Because it was the festival's first day, only an informal arraignment was legal. Jesus could be asked questions, and if witnesses gave testimony to support a serious charge, he might be taken to Pilate for judgment and possible sentence.

As I surveyed the assembled group, I immediately noticed a large uniformed contingent who were neither Romans nor Temple police. They were Antipas' personal guards. Looking around to see whether the tetrarch himself was there, I thought it odd there was no sign of him. For some reason I could not immediately grasp, it seemed all the more ominous that he felt no need to be present.

Just then, as I moved closer to Caiaphas, I overheard the high priest asking one of the Temple police what had become of the others—Jesus' disciples. When told they had been permitted to flee, he replied, "It is better that one die for many, than many for one."

Never had I felt as heartsick as I did hearing those words. Jesus' fate was already decided.

To you who read this, one truth should be evident. Whether he heard Caiaphas say it or not, Jesus knew they had convened the hearing as a formality and not as a serious inquiry into his possible sedition. Antipas did not care whether Jesus called himself King of the Jews, except that it was grounds for arrest. He only wished to silence the insult to him and Herodias, to punish the one he believed would perpetuate the popular mockery of his adulterous nest.

Caiaphas spoke first. "You are Jesus of Nazareth?" he asked.

"I am," Jesus answered.

"Have you been teaching secretly about God?"

"I have spoken openly for everybody to hear. I have always taught in the synagogues and the Temple and wherever Jews meet. I have said nothing in secret. But why ask me? Ask them," he said, indicating the Temple police.

At these words, not wishing to be brought by him as a witness, the one nearest Jesus slapped him in the face, saying, "Is that any way to talk to the high priest?"

Jesus, somewhat shaken, tried to speak civilly. "If there is something wrong in what I said, point it out, but if there is no offense in it, why do you strike me?"

In response, voices from around the room called out testimony about his supposed wrongdoing.

"You say the Shabbat was made for you!" one declared.

"You say you are the son of God!" another proclaimed.

"You believe you can forgive sin!" a third witness blared.

"You act like the messiah!" a fourth rasped loudly.

"We heard them call you King of the Jews!"

But none said he had ever called himself King of the Jews. They knew he had not done so and to testify otherwise would have been to bear false witness.

"Have you no answer to make?" Caiaphas asked. "Tell us why these men are testifying against you."

Several of those standing near the front had long fringes characteristic of the northern Pietist community, and their identity was further revealed by large white patches of skin where oversized phylacteries worn on non-holy days kept the sun from tanning their foreheads. I had no doubt they were Herodians, those senior Pietists who were members of Antipas' council. At least some among them had been at the lakeshore spying on John's memorial.

As Caiaphas waited for Jesus to answer, I knew there was no reply that could acquit him. Even if he denied believing himself the messiah or King of the Jews, his words would be rejected as an attempt to conceal what was already assumed—that he did believe himself anointed by God. The lie—for surely they would label it that—would only further implicate him in perpetrating a fraud.

Aware the interrogation was a charade and that his guilt was already determined, Jesus refused to play the fool by answering and thereby legitimizing their calculated questions. He recognized the tribunal was a theatrical prelude to his indictment, and he abstained from making any defense of himself.

Impatient and in ill temper, Caiaphas angrily demanded he answer. "I adjure you by the living God—tell us!"

Still, Jesus refused to reply, aware they would not reconsider their verdict.

When the high priest again insisted, "Tell us if you are God's anointed," Jesus finally responded, "They are your words. It is you who has said it."

The standard legal formulation, "They are your words," used by a defendant to accuse a witness of lying, was indeed the same Jesus had spoken when Judas feigned innocence, even while complicit in his arrest.

Although the thrust of the words at our festival meal had escaped his disciples and made no impression on me, being half drunk, they were well known to the high priest. Caiaphas now stood accused by Jesus of bearing false witness, violating one of the Torah's most sacred commandments. The high priest knew in his heart that if Jesus made no claim to be King of the Jews, he would himself stand trial in heaven before God.

A deafening silence fell on the room. Frozen in time, I remember it exactly as it was. Caiaphas looked at Jesus as if seeing him for the first time, appreciating him as a worthy person, not a lunatic who had an inconsequential existence—one that nobody would miss. If you will believe me, given how we have all come to hate Caiaphas, I tell you he wanted to free Jesus. I saw it in his face.

But what could Jesus have said? I have asked myself that a thousand times. Even these past days, I imagine him shouting the words Philip has told me: "Anybody who says I am sent by God as King of the Jews is speaking with the voice of Satan!"

Matthias turned to cast his eyes on the flokati where Jesus used to sit, imagining him reclining and listening. "You were right, my friend," he mused under his breath, and feeling his fingers cramping as he again gripped the point, he observed silently, "The light of day will soon pass, and I have so much of his misery to record. It's almost too much for me."

Indeed, they would have called his denial a lie, and the lie would only further prove his deceit. So he did what he could, warning the high priest and the roomful of adversaries that they were themselves on trial for falsely accusing him.

Unnerved at the sight of Caiaphas' hesitation, one of the Herodian Pietists called out, "If you set him free, you are no friend of the emperor's. Anybody who makes himself a king is defying the emperor!"

Not the emperor, no. He wouldn't have cared about a religious fanatic. But Pilate had his own incentive for obliging Antipas. Though only recently the tetrarch sharply opposed Pilate's minting coins with idolatrous images for circulation in Jerusalem, a courtesy to his council of Herodian Pietists, the Roman procurator intended to forget their differences if he supported him before an impending tribunal, one to which he had been summoned by Tiberius. To wit, Pilate would accord Antipas the right to decide Jesus' fate in exchange for his favorable testimony regarding an unprovoked massacre of Samaritans. Fostered by shared interest, their new comity required only Caiaphas' acquiescence that Jesus be taken before Pilate for judgment.

If the high priest hoped to keep the peace between Jerusalem's Jews and the Roman authorities, he could not refuse. If he freed Jesus, no priest or Levite would escape the procurator's wrath. Pilate had crucified thousands, and his cruel revenge was as certain as the sun rises and sets.

Charged with proclaiming himself King of the Jews, Jesus was blindfolded according to the order of Caiaphas, who announced for all to hear, "Take him to the Praetorium, where the procurator is waiting."

If ever I felt helpless, it was as I watched Antipas' guards push him toward the door, his garment brushing against me as he went by. I would have said something to reassure him, but others were still calling out their accusations. "You are the son of God, are you not?" one again mocked.

Turning his head sightlessly toward the voice, he replied strongly, "They are your words."

Others taunted him with rumors that he intended to destroy the Temple. People were laughing. One guard, almost putting on a show for the onlookers, struck Jesus in the face and declared, "Prophesy! Who is it that struck you?"

Wetting the point and twisting its nib slowly to stir the dye well, Matthias pictured him being prodded to the door like an animal, with onlookers gloating over their proof that he was not anointed by God—as though he had ever thought he was.

We were a modest procession and had made our way along the narrow streets when I felt Simon tugging at my sleeve. His manner was almost like one embarrassed to be seen in unbecoming circumstances.

"Tell me what is going on!" he whispered nervously.

Inasmuch as I was walking well to the rear of the entourage of soldiers and guards, I could speak freely. "He's had a hearing, as you know, Simon. And now he's being taken before the procurator for judgment."

"But what is his crime?" Simon asked, almost whimpering.

"The charge is that he claims to be anointed by God as King of the Jews."

Though I was not looking at him when I said it, I can imagine he was thunderstruck. Simon knew Jesus had never suggested anything like that about himself. And he knew, as I have recently learned, that he, Simon, was the one proclaiming Jesus king, his words a contagion inculcating every willing audience.

Stopping his transcription with a glyph half finished, Matthias was suddenly aware of the astonishing consequence this moment had for Simon. Everything he believed about Jesus was rebuffed by the sight he now beheld, watching as his teacher was led to judgment. Recalling Jesus' warning to him that his reverence was from Satan,

Simon had, soon after the crucifixion, confabulated the only one who could acquit him of his own role in the gruesome outcome—and that was Jesus himself, as God's son. It would take a god to save Simon from what he had done—and even more, from being utterly mortal.

Crowing cocks announced daylight as we crossed the city and came to the quarters where the case would be presented.

As we arrived in the vicinity of the Antonia Gate, I had done my best to provide Simon with the details about the hearing when a centurion approached.

He was the duty officer to monitor those seeking entrance to the Roman headquarters. "Are you two with the accused?" he asked.

"I don't know him," Simon said. "I was just speaking to my acquaintance about the festival."

As he promptly walked away, I identified myself to the centurion and followed the others. Days were to pass before I would see Simon again, days that would feel like an eternity in Gehinnom—hell itself.

Matthias was finding it difficult to see his own transcription. "When the sun gets tired toward the end of the day, so do I," he thought, but began again.

The procurator's chair for hearing cases, a throne-like seat of judgment, was situated on a paved area known as Gabbatha. Of the witnesses, no Herodian Pietists and no Temple police had accompanied Antipas' guard. Neither was Caiaphas nor any other Temple official in attendance. Presumably, they had all gone off to worship at the Temple, as was required on the first day of Passover.

We had been there no longer than it takes a cloud's shadow to pass, when Pilate emerged, fully arrayed in his flowing toga, its opulent folds in one hand as he took his place on the seat of judgment.

Antipas' guards, now augmented by several Roman soldiers of the procurator's cohort, pulled off Jesus' blindfold and shoved him forward to stand before Pilate.

"Are you King of the Jews?" Pilate asked.

If I had doubted his complicity in what ensued, Pilate's quick summation of the accusation showed he was early on apprised of the charges.

Intending the procurator to know he saw through his sham performance, Jesus responded, "Do you ask me this of your own accord, or have others spoken to you about me?"

"Am I a Jew that I should know all about what the Jews are saying? It's your own people and the high priest who have handed you over to me. So tell me what you've done. Do you say you are a king?"

"They are your words," Jesus replied.

Seeming to take his measure, Pilate continued, "Where are you from?"

Not lost on Jesus was the profound consequence that he was from Nazareth, placing him in Antipas' tetrarchy and under his jurisdiction. So he said nothing.

"Do you refuse to talk to me? Surely you know I have the power to release you, and I have the power to crucify you," Pilate threatened.

"As God wills it," Jesus answered.

"Tell me where you are from."

Just then, stepping out from the recess of a nearby doorway, well within earshot, the purple-robed tetrarch made his appearance.

"He is a resident of Nazareth in my tetrarchy," Antipas said coldly, his voice flat and official.

"Then of course his fate is in your hands," Pilate said, showing no surprise that Antipas made so sudden an appearance. "But if he is a king, shouldn't we see how he looks in your robe?"

Pleased by the humor of such absurdity, Antipas placed his royal purple coat around Jesus' shoulders.

"So you are a king after all!" Pilate joked.

"You say that I am a king," Jesus said, but his attempt to again expose the false charge had a hollow ring against the arranged outcome of the moment.

Off to the side, members of Antipas' retinue had amused themselves with a thistle bush that they had pulled up and were twisting into a thorny wreath. Before the laughter at Jesus subsided, they had pressed it down on his head, forcing it to fit tightly, its thorns puncturing his skin. As small trickles of blood stained his face, a member of Antipas' guard made Jesus hold a reed and bowed before him in mockery, declaring, "Hail, King of the Jews!"

"Here is your king then," Pilate said.

"We have no king except the emperor," one said, his sentiment immediately voiced in near unison by Antipas' other guards.

"What do you want me to do with him?" Pilate asked.

"Crucify him! Crucify him!" they hissed.

"You want me to crucify your king?" Pilate said, laughing and sharing the joke with Antipas as he signaled that his own soldier should return his royal robe.

Then Pilate stepped down from the seat's marble pedestal and, almost as though the charade had gone on too long and become *tedious, made a short waving gesture, motioning with the back of his hand that they do what was planned without further delay.*

His purple robe over his arm, as the sixth hour sun shone too hot for its use, Antipas paused with apparent satisfaction to hear Pilate say, "Take him away. Take him away. Crucify him." Seeing his guard slapping Jesus in the face and spitting on him, the gratified tetrarch joined the procurator inside, where it would be pleasant and cool.

On the route leading northwest from the Praetorium to Golgotha, the procession, no longer accompanied by Antipas' retinue but solely Pilate's personal legionnaires, paused outside a carpentry shop kept open under Roman authority. Not more than a few minutes went by before a large wooden cross was hauled out into the street. There, the soldiers waited as one of the non-Hebrew workmen completed a crudely engraved sign, saying, "Jesus of Nazareth, King of the Jews." When they had attached it to the long beam of the cross, they raised the heavy cruciform timber and lowered its top onto Jesus' shoulders.

The Levite officials responsible for observance of burial customs always made shrouds available where the cross was constructed, and I went into the doorway and found the pile put there for the purpose of clothing the deceased.

Impatient for Jesus to move more quickly, the contingent's commander determined he lacked the physical strength to manage the ascent without assistance. Approaching a Cypriot bystander, a foreign worker not celebrating the festival, he demanded the man hoist and carry the dragging end.

What I recall is the deepening silence as we moved farther from the sacred precincts. Beyond the city gates, away from the Temple ceremony, the Levites' instrumental accompaniment of joyous blessings over the harvest grew more faint with our every step.

Trudging along, I was surprised by a hand on my shoulder and turned to see an old face. He was parched with the sun and had thinning white hair.

"You don't remember me," he said. "I am Nicodemus."

"Nicodemus?"

"Joseph's servant. I was there when they almost stoned him during Hanukkah."

"Nicodemus!" I exclaimed, so relieved to see a fellow who would share my distress.

As we continued on, he informed me that this year Joseph's sons and daughters had remained in Nazareth for the festival.

"So you were with Joseph last night?" I asked.

"I took Joseph to Elizabeth's, his sister-in-law, and we roasted a lamb brought by a neighbor. Then we went to his house, and I came here early as I usually do. Yes, I still help him on Passover."

As Nicodemus further elaborated, he had only just passed the gate of Antonia and noticed Pilate listening to a case, an altogether unusual occurrence on the first day of the feast. That's when a soldier replied to his inquiry, scoffing, "What? Don't you know that's your king?"

Hearing this, I inquired what knowledge Joseph might have of Jesus' circumstance.

"None. I will tell him. But how shall I describe it? I won't know how."

"It is all so routine to them," I observed, on the verge of tears.

Most bewildering, from what I could see, compared to Antipas' minions, there was no special cruelty in the Roman soldiers' *comportment toward Jesus. As Nicodemus and I traipsed up the steepening hill, they talked to each other almost casually.*

Then we were there. To one side of the flat area at the top, additional legionnaires were hoisting another crucifix. Inserted into its deep receiving pit, it was heavily weighted by a drooping figure, one whose intermittent cries sounded like a horn's blasts.

Jesus was next. Instructions were given by a commander to provide him the usual mix of strong wine and myrrh, a medicant used to relieve pain, but he refused the offer. Though it is only a guess, I believe he wanted the soldiers to hear his screams rather than be spared the barbarity of their work.

Shall I tell you about those screams? Per chance one who reads this will take satisfaction over his fate. That is my concern. No. Let none who bore him ill will take pleasure in so grim a record. Instead, let everybody know this: he was brave.

To prevent bodily fluids released upon death from soaking his apparel, the soldiers stripped him not only of his outer robe but the fine one-piece cotton undergarment he had worn for the festival. Completely naked, he was attached to the beams.

As nails were driven through his skin, through the bones of his feet and hands, I looked away, averting my gaze until the cross was raised to its upright position. When his eyes searched and found me, I saw he needed one who knew him as he was and not as conjured by the false witnesses and murderers, grotesquely twisted even beyond recognition he had of himself. I was his memory of who he had been as he stared down at me.

After his cross had been secured, another was raised to his other side with a different figure, a thief, I was told, found guilty of crimes against the Roman civil authority.

Telling from the sun, which was directly overhead, it was about the sixth hour, the end of the second Roman watch. As the soldiers played dice, I recall them finally deciding to let the winner have Jesus' undergarment. Desert wolves would have had more compassion.

To his credit, the other who had just been crucified made a last attempt at humor, saying he wished Jesus were King of the Jews so he might get them all down. If I tell you I believe Jesus smiled at that, you may be right that it was only a wish.

Nicodemus had found a place to sit and was witnessing what occurred from a distance. As I stood there, I recall thinking I had always felt the companionship of God, but just then, God too wasn't there. Amid soldiers who sprawled about, scattered like insects, Jesus and I were alone.

His eyes were closed much of the time, only occasionally squinting in my direction, where I stood vigil several cubits from the foot of the cross.

I believe it was after three hours, the ninth, near the end of the third watch when the soldiers were replaced by a new contingent, that Jesus spoke for the first time. He addressed me in a barely audible, rasping voice, saying, "Matthias, take care of my nakedness." As I nodded for him to know I would, the scraping sound of his words attracted the attention of a nearby soldier. Extending a long hyssop stick with a vinegar-soaked rag on it to moisten his dry lips and parched throat, he showed the only compassion I saw that day.

Moments later, Jesus looked up toward the heavens and in a loud lament, cried out to God, "Eli Eli, Lama sabachthani? Adonai, Adonai why have you destroyed me?"

My heart was rent in two by his question. For him to believe he was being punished by God was almost unbearable.

Seeing my face so full of tears, he spoke to me again. "Matthias, it is almost finished"—words to comfort me that his suffering would soon be done, so that I might no longer feel his pain.

The sun had already begun to set when he gasped, and the life went out of him. A Roman soldier, with the same regard he might have shown a slaughtered beast, took a long spear and jabbed it deeply into Jesus' side, causing his body to release its fluids. Then they took him down, and several carried him to a waiting handcart for removal to the public tomb.

Nicodemus was with me as we entered the dark cavern carved into the limestone wall, and he helped me lift Jesus from the cart, laying him on the linen shroud, which I spread on the ground. He and I said the traditional words of Ezekiel and wrapped the cloth around him. Enough remained to tear off a large piece, which I bundled under his head.

When we returned to the outside, daylight was fading. Because Torah law prohibits mourning on Shabbat, since the day's holiness is meant to sanctify life itself, I expected to come back the following day.

As we walked down the Golgotha slope, Nicodemus anticipated my question. "I will go to Joseph," he said.

"It is almost as if I have stepped back in time," Matthias thought, staring at the blurring letters just drying. With the light of day fading, as it had when Jesus expired, he rose to prepare supper.

Limping toward the stove, his better leg also feeling weak, he leaned on his table, looking down. "You too?" he asked, seeing it was swollen like the other.

Stirring the coals and bringing them to life, Matthias prayed for the strength to finish his scroll. On the coming Passover, he promised himself, he would expose the idol Simon created, and with the final entry complete, he would seal the record. His eyes heavy with sleep, Matthias felt a burden was soon to be lifted.

CHAPTER TWENTY-FIVE

The interior of the Center was cooling down as the early evening breeze blew gently through the western windows.

"Should we wait for Philip and Matthias?" Andrew asked Simon.

"When the lamb is done we will start," Simon answered.

"Looks like Matthew is getting along with Luke," Andrew observed, glancing at the two of them chatting in the far corner. "You, me, and the Zebedees. Thomas. Philip. Matthew. That's all we need."

"We'll see," Simon replied, keeping his voice low so Andrew would do the same.

"Shall I tell you about the parable?" Andrew asked. "I've almost finished it. I'll say he was a servant who did nothing to increase his master's wealth."

"That's good. Yes, they'll know who you mean. And Matthew has worked on his as well."

"But when will we take the vote? Perhaps it's better we don't wait for them."

"When the outcome is certain. If I think the time is right, I will call for a decision. And there is no need to rush. James has chosen to be with his father so he has already sown what he will reap tonight. But I think I hear their cart." After several moments, Matthias entered, leaning heavily with one arm slung through Philip's, a thick walking stick in the other.

"Shalom! Sorry to be late!"

"Shalom to you, Matthias," Simon responded. "But what happened? Philip said you and he would arrive this morning."

"My legs are full of old age. And they have a mind to say no whenever I ask them to walk."

"But we made it!" Philip exclaimed. "Matthias would not be persuaded to join his neighbor for the feast. He preferred our company, if you can imagine such a thing."

"It would have taken more than ordinary patience to listen to her jabber all night. This is the easier choice, I can tell you."

"We're all glad you could come," Andrew said. "And of course you will want to meet Luke."

"I've heard much about you," Luke said pleasantly, as he and Matthew came over to offer their greeting.

"Then I shall surely have a chance to correct their gossip," Matthias joked. "And where are the others?"

"Helping the Marys and Martha with the lamb," Simon said. "And I think Thaddeus is arranging the table. But you must be tired, Matthias. Let's sit together, and Andrew, bring some juice, please."

Accepting Simon's advice, Matthias stretched out on the straw couch, propping himself up on a large cushion, as Philip excused himself to go to the courtyard and join the others.

"Matthias, I'm sorry to see you like this," Simon said, gesturing to Luke that he draw up his own floor pillow while Matthew too found space to recline.

"It has been nearly three months," Matthias said. "I'm pleased to be here."

"As are we to see you again," Simon said.

"So what have they told you?" Matthias asked Luke, smiling broadly.

"That you were his friend, as much as one might be the friend of our savior."

"Oh?" Matthias responded. "You mean Jesus?"

"Well, who else would he mean, brother?" Simon asked. "But Luke, Matthias enjoys making comments that require elaboration. It is the art of the scribe, I suppose."

"Forgive me for doing that. Am I so obvious?"

"I have no hesitation to call Jesus our savior," Luke said.

"And what has inspired you to join the flock?" Matthias prodded.

"The same as you, I imagine. He is the one the prophets said would come."

"Luke is an expert in Torah," Matthew interjected. "Even more than we are. He has been immersed by Paul—and he knows Greek!"

"Very true," Simon added. "Luke, I know you are too modest to say so, but you have found Torah explanations for Jesus' death on the cross."

"Along with Paul, of course. I hope I am worthy of his trust," Luke said.

"Are you speaking of Paul or Jesus?" Matthias asked.

"Both," Luke replied. "Correctly understood, I believe Paul has been speaking Jesus' words. Do you think differently, Matthias?"

"Torah was the heart of Jesus' teaching."

"Isn't that what you say, Luke?" Matthew asked. "That if we hear Jesus' voice we may truly understand Torah."

Hesitant that his demur might sow discord or even worse, be mistaken for respect, Matthias seized the opportunity to change the subject as his stomach growled loudly. "The delicious aroma is making its way through the window like a messenger," he said, "and my stomach is giving an answer."

"We will begin the meal soon," Simon assured him. "But what do you say, Matthias? Isn't it a blessing from Jesus that he has sent us one who has such abilities? His insights are from the holy spirit. I've seen that myself."

"Please don't glorify me," Luke said. "Save that for the one who saves us."

"What should I say?" Matthias asked. "I say it is good he looks fit. Otherwise, I don't know how I will be hoisted up the stairs for supper."

"You have no need to worry. We will make it a shared effort," Luke assured him.

"Carrying me like a cross," Matthias said. "Are you sure you are up to it?"

Luke's slightly twisted smile failed to conceal his discomfort. "I'm not sure I would have put it that way," he managed, just as Bartholomew and Simon C'nani appeared at the door with their announcement. "If you're ready, Simon, so is the lamb."

Then, after their warm welcome to Matthias, Simon instructed, "Well, see to it that we don't keep the lamb waiting. And make sure Thaddeus has put out the water for us to wash each other's feet."

As Matthias stood up slowly, supported under one arm by Matthew, Luke said, "I must compliment you on your fine writing. Every word is so carefully transcribed."

Matthias averted his eyes, trying not to display a perceptible unease that the newcomer was invited to read their scroll. He replied with forced indifference, "Good to have your approval. But my walking stick is like an additional leg. Can you hand it to me?"

Picking up the cane required that Luke bend down before Matthias. Once again upright, he handed it to him, saying, "Well, I hope I can contribute as much to the new Torah as you have."

Hearing this, Simon interrupted. "No doubt you will. But Matthias will always be advised of our proceedings—and the record of Jesus' life."

"Aren't I expected to continue the work?" Matthias asked.

"Absolutely! But you will be relieved to know you have already completed your responsibilities and can take proper care of yourself."

"I had anticipated doing more, perhaps adding some of my own recollections."

"Luke will be an able hand, putting down what you remember. After all, brother Matthias, you are one of us, are you not?"

When Matthias made no reply, Luke said, "I feel privileged to record what you may wish to add, and I hope my interpretations enhance the treasured time you spent with our lord."

Just at the foot of the stairs, Philip reached his side, suggesting he would give Matthias the help required to ascend to the second floor.

"Thank you," Matthias said to Luke, "I have trained him to do it. But let the others go first."

Simon watched the disciples enter the upper triclinium and reminded them to swab each other's feet, as Jesus taught them, and then to find their places. Luke would be sitting next to him, an honored guest.

Patiently waiting as they reclined on the wide, cushioned chairs and benches, usually arrayed along the wall but which were now adjacent to the table, Simon surveyed the gathering with apparent satisfaction. Only Matthias was still to have his feet cleaned. Looking down at Philip kneeling before him on one knee, Matthias leaned on his shoulder, watching him gently wipe his swollen ankles. After a few moments, he gratefully suggested it was time to begin the meal.

"You're quite right!" Bartholomew announced, as he and Simon C'nani entered, carrying the lamb on its large wooden platter, followed by the two Marys and Martha.

"What a delicious aroma!" Thomas declared, as voices of approval chimed their agreement.

After they positioned the steaming meat on a side table and covered it with palm fronds to keep it hot, Simon, seeing all were seated, rose to speak.

"Before we begin our glorious ceremony," he said, "let me express the satisfaction I feel that Matthias is here with us. We have missed you, brother."

"As I have missed all of you," Matthias replied, nodding to each in turn.

"But what kind of ceremony is this Passover?" Simon asked rhetorically. "As we anticipate making blessings over wine and bread, let us feel the new time. And let us share with our neighbors the truth we have been given through the holy spirit."

With the stack of three pieces of matzah held aloft, Simon went to the triclinium door overlooking the courtyard and opened it. "Let all who are hungry for the bread of life come in and eat!" he called out. "This is the bread of our lord, Jesus of Nazareth, who has come to save us."

"Amen, amen!" many among the group resounded, though several, including Philip and Matthias, were silent.

Once again seated, Simon addressed them. "This is a time when we must all hear the words he spoke, coursing through our veins like his own blood. For us, Passover is his story, one that is conveyed by Torah, guiding us even now to follow his path. Luke?"

"If I speak," Luke said as he stood, "I admit I am humble before you who knew him on this earth. Still, I trust you will recognize my confidence, assured by his spirit that he will guide what I say. As we are about to begin our Passover with wine and matzah, I hope my insight will provide you with spiritual sustenance. What good fortune I have to know the subtleties of language! Searching our prophet Zechariah, I realized Jesus was expecting me to interpret words I had never before understood. 'The enemies of Israel will fall, and their blood will be drunk like wine. And it will be the blood of the Covenant.' I long wondered what Zechariah meant when he said the blood of our enemies could be the wine of the Covenant. Then I began listening to Paul, whom you know. Of course, Jesus became the enemy of Israel—and yes, they permitted his blood to be spilled—even to pour—from his wounds. So now we know why. It is his blood that is the wine of our covenant. Paul heard it directly from our Christ. 'This bread is my body which is for you. Eat it as a memorial of me. And this cup of wine is the new covenant in my blood. Drink it as a memorial for me.' Yes, to become one with him we drink the wine and eat the matzah. And so too will all Israel one day drink the blood of Jesus, whom they have made their enemy. And it shall be their new Covenant, unwittingly accomplished by Jesus' death! But Simon, I am sure you will help explain these deeper messages from Jesus."

Resuming his role as leader, Simon waited for Luke to take his seat and again spoke, this time while reclining.

"Hevre. Brothers—and sisters. Don't be surprised. What fools they were to think their malice toward our savior wasn't God's plan! Is there anything Jesus' heavenly Father has not planned? We are not the same as they. Think about this. For those Jews, this is the festival of anticipation. Long ago, leaving her home, the virgin bride, Israel, longed for her spouse. She sought him in the desert and was betrothed with commandments—and lived with the divine presence in the wilderness, finally reaching the land of fruitfulness and fecundity. Others may think the wedding vows will be spoken again, haray at mikudeshet li—to me you are a bridal people—but we know that the groom has already been with us. What they pray will occur again, we know already has. Don't most Jews tell the story of Moses' miraculous birth, chosen to free the people and finally lead their escape from Egyptian bondage? To them, the departure from Egypt with Moses was the beginning of that sacred journey. But for us, the true journey began when Jesus was born. Matthew?"

Matthew rose and began like one giving a speech. "Shalom, brothers. And thank you, Mary and Mary and Martha. Soon we will enjoy the delicious banquet. But I wish to share a parable that comes to me from our lord."

"Go ahead, brother," Simon urged.

"An angel told Joseph—the one thought to be Jesus' earthly father—to escape from Herod. 'Go into Egypt,' the angel said. 'Get up, take the child and his mother, and stay there. When King Herod is dead, then you may return.' And the three of them went down to Egypt until the angel again appeared and said, 'Herod is dead. Take the child and return to the land of Israel.' And they returned to Israel."

After pausing to see whether his words had made an impression, Matthew continued, "But what makes this a parable? That is what I myself wondered. Then through the holy spirit, my ears were opened. Jesus was the new Moses. He survived the murderous plan to have him killed, just as Moses did, and like Moses, he has come out of Egypt to save those who follow him across the region of death."

"Well, it is a short parable," Simon said as Matthew sat down. "Perhaps you will do it justice when you speak with Luke, and he helps fill in the details." Then nodding toward Matthew in affirmation, Simon exclaimed in a loud voice, startling them all, "Yes! What you say is indeed from the lord, Matthew. I bear witness. Still, in our hearts, because we are human, many of us fail to pass over the threshold of doubt. Yes, that is what we must do—'Pass-over.' For as surely as death passed over the houses of the Israelites in Egypt, we must again be reliant on God through Jesus to see death pass over.

Only now, we know the power of the creation is given us, just as it was through blood on their doorposts, finally to consume. For that is how we shall understand the blood of Jesus, shed for us as a sacrifice, taking with him all our sins, that we may become one with him."

Raising his cup, Simon saw that several hesitated. "Don't you want to remember Jesus?" he complained. "Isn't that what he asked through Paul and Luke? And that is what we are doing just now. Certainly we need to understand the mystery of his death. We want to justify it to those who desire a path to his spirit in heaven. But some among us still stumble over the crucifixion. Could such an end have been planned by Jesus' heavenly Father? None of us need feel less worthy for having asked this question. Only . . . be sure you do not answer it falsely. We drink this wine as his blood, so that death passes over us, just as it passed over him in the tomb. He has died to show us the way to life. Will you say no?"

In the silence so full of pending consequence, Matthias' voice filled the room. "Of course, King Herod was already dead ten years when Jesus was born. Otherwise, a nice story, Matthew. But help me up, my friend," he said to Philip at his side. He felt as if time itself paused to wait on him, but Matthias finally stood facing the disciples. "A few words, if I may," he said, looking at Simon.

"Of course, brother."

"I rise to share with you my love for Jesus."

"Then we are your servants!" Simon declared.

"He was my friend, as you all know. When he sought refuge from publicity, he came to my house. For many of those hours we spent alone, he told me about his love of Torah and talked of his People, Israel. If you hear him speaking to you from heaven, as some among you believe, you must know he never called his People an enemy. Never.

"So I rise now not to defend his murderers but to save Jesus. And from whom must I save him? Not the tetrarch who, with Pilate's acquiescence, executed him as he had John, but to save him from you who would do what they could not do. They could only crucify his body, but some at this table—worse than Iscariot himself—would crucify his memory."

"Your words are an insult to him more than to us!" Simon blurted angrily. "Do you intend to continue a sinful tirade? Surely your illness has reached your mind!"

"Let him speak," Luke said. "And then we shall explain what he has failed to grasp. Jesus' words were revealed only to the chosen."

"You weren't there," Matthias said to Luke. "Neither to hear his teaching nor on the last day of his life. But you would expect us to regard you as chosen—chosen by him. Shall you forget, Simon, that terrible Passover, the fifth day of the week, when he met us at Jerusalem's gate? What about the rest of you? Three years have passed, but well I recall how he kept looking around, worried he might—at any moment—be arrested. Doing his best to avoid notice.

"And who among us can forget his words that one of us would betray him? If his capture were God's will, would the fulfillment of a divine plan have been betrayal? Or will you say he planned the whole thing with Judas? Make your choice: if it's God's plan, call Judas a saint; otherwise call Jesus' death an atrocity!"

"Are you done?" Simon demanded.

"No. Not as long as one drop of this wine is called his blood!"

"Then finish your ranting so we may forgive you and move on," Simon answered.

"Forgive me?"

"Because you, Matthias, like his murderers, are only an instrument of God's will! Of course Jesus had to die to this life—so he would be raised from the tomb. Yes, all those who turned against him—and by your words you are now counted in their number—must be forgiven."

"Which is why Jesus said from the cross, 'Father forgive them; they know not what they do,'" Luke asserted testily.

"And who was there to hear him say such a thing?" Matthias retorted. "Were you there, Andrew? Or you, Zebedees, or Thomas? No. None of you. I was the only one of us who was there while he was on the cross. And he never said anything like that. You remind me of the Roman soldier using a vinegar rag to wet his parched throat so that scratching sounds were turned to words.

"But this wine you call blood is so cruelly invested with false meaning! Decide whether to drink it as his blood—or not. But before your hand brings the cup to your lips, hear this. You who were in the garden of Gethsemane know he instructed Simon and the Zebedees to stay awake and guard him. Is that the way of a man who intends to be arrested? So, Simon, you didn't care enough then to save him, and you don't care enough now. Instead, you do the thing he rebuked you for—still calling him lord. But your weakness hardly surprised him. When, outside his hearing at Caiaphas' house you denied knowing him, that was typical. And when you vanished, rather than follow him as he carried the cross, do you think he was surprised or that he looked around and wondered where Peter was? Your messiah was about to die. No wonder you couldn't watch. It wasn't the end of God's Kingdom—it was the end of yours!"

"Enough!" Andrew exclaimed. "Jesus is alive in heaven. Nothing Matthias says will bring his glory to an end! I say, let us drink this wine as the blood of one they chastised as their enemy and be one with him."

"If you do," Matthias replied, "picture him as I saw him and as I heard him. Hear his prayer in the garden beseeching God, wailing to aveenu malkaynu, our Father in heaven, not to let him be murdered. I suppose you will say that was the prayer of a man calmly planning to die! And then, on the cross, hear what I do every day and even in dreams: the words he spoke to God, not some fantasy created by this newcomer. 'Adonai, why have you destroyed me?'"

"Are you finally finished?" Simon asked, his voice hardened and cold.

"Finished? Again, you remind me of the Roman soldiers at the foot of the cross, impatient for Jesus to expire. What a remarkable question. You know, Simon, as I stood there, looking up at his mutilated body, he must have seen my pain at the sight of his, and he said, 'My suffering is almost done.' As his beating heart weakened, he made only one last request, that according to the tradition of our People, the Jews, he be wrapped in the customary shroud, that his nakedness be covered. Of course, that is what I did. When he died and was conveyed to the tomb, I took care of his body as he requested. And I said Ezekiel's words of mourning. And I wept."

"Poor you, Matthias," Simon responded. "If you understood, you would not have wept—unless they were tears of joy! But only some are blessed with knowing the revealed truth. Our deaths have happened and we, unlike you, Matthias, are now truly alive. We died to this world in the tomb of water that is the baptism and arose to the kingdom's light. Yes, the baptism is our way of entering Jesus' tomb and rising as he did to eternal life. Of course, you, Matthias, have bathed in the ritual mikveh bath—so ordinary a practice compared to ours. But there is no salvation from that water. So we true disciples know Jesus in our hearts and hear his instruction—the new Torah! We will join his heavenly realm through this matzah, which is his flesh, and this wine, which is his blood!"

"If memory could have a body, each of your words would drive a nail deeper into him," Matthias said. "What little difference his suffering makes to you. As if God would have ever permitted his anointed to know such agony."

"May I try to help Matthias better appreciate our savior's end?" Luke asked.

Simon surveyed the gathering and though several held their wine cups, Bartholomew and James bar Alpheus, as well as Simon C'nani and Thaddeus had yet to raise them. Philip had not even brought his hand to the cup.

"Please do, Luke," Simon said. "I have no words to restrain him."

"Nothing tests us more than the suffering of our lord before he went to heaven, even as Isaiah prophesied. Some of you may recall his vision. 'The one upon whom the arm of God was revealed is sacrificed for us like a sheep led to slaughter,' Isaiah said. 'He suffered the punishment that made us whole. By his wounds we were healed.' But you know this! You disciples who were with him felt his power to save you, even from death. Haven't you told me your experiences were lifesaving? Condemned by pasts shrouded in doubt, you have been raised from the dead and are reborn. It is plain to some and invisible to others. I have been told Jesus said, 'Let those who have ears to hear, hear.' He took your sins on himself and in so doing, he forgave you. His forgiveness is your salvation. Your knowledge of why he suffered—that his body died by appearance only, rose from the tomb, ascended to heaven, and guided you to bring his forgiveness to others—has shown you the way. I say, let us be one with him!"

Seeing only six were holding the wine cups, Matthias exclaimed loudly, "No! He never forgave anybody in the way you mean. Not from sin accountable to God alone. Always he taught what Torah commanded, 'Loose on earth what you pray our Creator will loose in heaven. Do not expect God to forgive you if you do not do the same to others.' So, like Jesus, we do what our rabbis teach. On the day we atone for our sins, we not only pray for forgiveness from God but forgive each other. But if God chooses to punish somebody with disease, or maladies of birth, or in ways we do not fathom, like Job, then no man may intervene. Jesus lamented that some among you were spreading the falsehood he had made such a claim. And when he feared his words and deeds had mistakenly encouraged you to revere him like a god, what did he do? He stood on the edge of a cliff, intending to end his life. His voice expounding wisdom of Torah— teachings he hoped would rescue you from your spiritual exile—had become, in your ears, a promise you would rule God's Kingdom. Ha! That deformed message, twisted by your evil inclinations, was one he knew only Satan could deliver. If it came from his mouth, spawned by his unknown paternity, he would end it rather than be Satan's servant. Instead, John purified him, and he upbraided your ignorance, brandishing a sword of truth that Torah must never be changed—not even its smallest letter. But he is no longer here to save you from your ignorance, and the false god demands a new Torah."

"Are you saying he never forgave me?" Matthew asked. "I had been a tax collector for the Romans. They know that parable, the one about me, telling that I was forgiven!"

"He gave you hope," Matthias replied. "He didn't tell you to pray to him, did he? And in the parable, who forgives the sinful tax collector? Is it Jesus? Matthew, here is the truth. Not far from me, in the garden that night, he prayed to God to forgive all of you for his death. Those among you whose false ideas coronated him king were unwittingly carpenters of his cross. Without you, Simon, Antipas would have had no charge to bring to Pilate. Yes, in the garden, that is when he prayed to God, saying, 'Father in heaven, forgive them. They know not what they do.' Such is the forgiveness men may extend to men."

Staring at Matthias as if beholding a scorpion, Matthew, already holding his cup, raised it higher and waited for Simon's sign they should drink.

"I am sure he prayed for us to be forgiven our trespass," Simon finally responded. "Not for abetting his arrest but for any unintended deprecations during his life. But you are right about this, Matthias; he never called Israel his enemy, though they made him one of theirs. I give you who hesitate this parable. The advent of the kingdom of heaven may be compared to the day the son of the king was to marry. There were eleven chosen special guests who arrived early—guests of the king himself. But many others, instead of accepting the king's invitation, went off to tend their usual business. So the king said to his servants, go to the streets and lanes of the city and bring the lame and the blind and the poor and the bereft to my son's banquet. Then, after the hall was full, just as the ceremony was to begin, the king saw one guest had no wedding attire. So he turned to him and said—just in the manner I am speaking to you, Matthias—'This one does not know my son will rule. He is not dressed for the occasion!' Where then, Matthias, is your garment of white, your knowledge of who Jesus is? How did you become one of us?"

Seeming to speak from a reverie, Matthew proclaimed, "It is true. Shall I tell the ending? The king recognized him as one like those who tried to kill his son, and he said to his attendants, 'Bind him hand and foot and cast him into the darkness. He may have been invited, but he was not chosen."

"You . . . you say I wished to kill Jesus?" Matthias stammered, his hand steadying himself by holding the table's edge. "You who were with him saw I was one he loved. And more than you know, I cared for him."

James the Zebedee, holding the glass, said, "Simon is right, Matthias. You are one of them. What you couldn't do to his spirit on the cross, you will try to do here. He came among us to redeem us from slavery worse than Egyptian bondage. We were the fallen, and he raised us, ignorant fisherman, who they label 'locals,' and he gave us hope. Not only won't they let us marry their daughters, but they won't even touch us without washing. But he knew their hearts were filled with greed and adultery. They are liars and hypocrites. Some of us needed forgiveness, and he forgave us. Others had no known Hebrew past, and he said our family tree would be told by our fruit, the good deeds we did. I ask you, shall we again suffer the exile that has been our misery?"

Swaying weakly where he stood, Matthias attempted to reply. "You know Jesus' contempt was for the Pietist hypocrites who pretend to be holier than anybody else. But he promised all of you what the Torah does—that the poor and humble will be inheritors of the earth, equals with all other Hebrews in God's Kingdom. It is you who would exile yourselves by calling your own People an enemy."

"They murdered him! And you say they were not his enemy?" Thomas declared, seething with anger. "He forgave them, but they still executed him and drained his blood! But they didn't know what we know—that it is the blood of the true covenant. So drink, brothers, and show the murderers they are servants in his kingdom!"

"How easy it is to forgive yourselves by blaming others," Matthias lamented. "Did any Jew testify at Caiaphas' hearing that he heard Jesus claim he was King of the Jews? None did. The charge, brought by Antipas, was based on what others said about him, hailing him as king. What others? Well, assuredly the Pietists never made that up!

No, brothers, it was the followers of John at his memorial gathering, grabbing his robe as he tried to escape, persuaded by Simon—and it was you!

"So do what you will," Matthias said, leaning against the table. "Imbibe. Don't let the Torah stop you. Don't let the prohibition against eating blood as old as Noah hinder your folly. Do your best to squander the wealth of knowledge he gave you. But those of you who loved him, I implore you, hold back! Especially, recall what you heard with your own ears. Who here will not remember that day he told us that every law of the Torah is sacred, and that one who changes even the smallest letter will be lowest in the Kingdom?"

"Again, you fail to see the lord's message!" Simon erupted heatedly. "When Jesus declared, 'Before heaven and earth have passed away,' he meant passed away with his death and resurrection! And of course, the one changing the laws must be lowest, by which he meant most humble. You are right, Matthias, to say he promised we poor and humble would inherit the kingdom. For us, the laws no longer apply! And you, Matthias, what a disappointment, lacking even a small measure of that humility."

"May I?" Bartholomew said, rising to speak.

"Anyone among us may say what they wish," Simon replied curtly.

Pausing for Matthias to take his seat, Bartholomew said, "It is really more a question than an opinion. Who here represents James? Should he be completely disregarded, just as our Passover ritual observance changes to an account of his brother's life? I do not speak for James but repeat only what we have all heard him say before. If a man keeps all the Torah's commandments except for one, he is guilty of breaking it all. James echoed his brother's instruction that we may not pick and choose. We may not change Torah to suit our desires, and I think we all agree Torah says do not drink blood."

As Bartholomew resumed his seat, the disciples were surprised Simon made no immediate reply but was suddenly staring in the direction of the salt broom leaning against the mosaic wall. Oddly, his glassy-eyed expression was that of somebody whose thoughts had turned to a different matter altogether, causing one or two to twist around to see what was holding his continuing gaze. Not discerning the object of his distraction, Bartholomew prompted, "Simon? I'm asking you about James."

"You think James would know it was Jesus if he came to him?" Simon scowled, his reverie disrupted. "He will come like a thief. To steal what is yours, if you let him."

"Who, Peter? Who will come like a thief?" Thomas asked, shifting uneasily in his seat.

All were paying rapt attention, awaiting his reply, as Simon seemed troubled and uncertain. When he reached down, appearing to rub the side of his leg, Andrew queried, "Are you all right, Peter?"

Not immediately answering his brother, Simon felt for the large iron key suspended under his garment.

"You think it's easy to guard Jesus' kingdom?" he demanded, tracing the key's outline with his fingers. But I won't let him steal it . . . that's why he comes in the night."

"Who do you mean?" Matthew asked, doing his best to sound matter-of-fact.

"Jesus. That's who," Simon asserted testily, not looking any of them in the eye.

"Jesus, a thief?" Simon C'nani thundered. "Have you been testing the wine to see if it's really blood? Maybe it has gone to your head."

"If you let him steal your immortality, he will take it. He will tell you it was never yours. But you must be ready for him. Only if you call him a common thief will he depart without it. He wears that garb as a disguise to test us. Chase him out, and keep your faith in Jesus as you know him, as the lord. Be ready, I tell you!"

"His brother James would never call him a thief," James bar Alpheus opined. "We can be sure of that."

"James again," Simon said between clenched teeth. "He has already twisted Jesus' glory as the son of God into . . . into a son without a known father—a bastard! So let him be punished by his own decree—that we acknowledge his paternity is different from Jesus' and that they are not and never were brothers. But hasn't he disavowed us as well? Except for Barnabas' funds, he's brought us nothing. But make no mistake; this isn't about money. Andrew? Did you not hear the word of Jesus about this very subject? Then rest your glasses as he tells you, and your hearts won't be deceived."

"Brothers," Andrew said, "I know we all wish to finish this argument, and some of us, at least, to join with Jesus through this wine as his blood. None of us," he added, acknowledging the Marys and Martha, "can wait much longer to eat the delicious feast, though I hope we will leave the bitter herbs to others. For us, there is sweetness in our knowledge that we are truly free through Jesus. But this is what I have heard from on high, coming to me as a parable, concerning James."

"A parable about James?" Philip ventured. "Is that supposed to come from Jesus?"

"There was a landowner who took a journey," Andrew began, not dignifying Philip's obvious doubt with a reply. "Just as Jesus left us with the knowledge of who he was—and is—the landowner entrusted several servants with his wealth. When he returned, two of the servants had increased the amount of his treasure, and they were rewarded, while one had acted differently, hiding it in the ground rather than investing it wisely. Do you understand? And the landowner said, 'To those who have, more will be given,' meaning knowledge of the lord's true identity as our savior. It is the knowledge of Jesus as the messiah and ruler that some of us have increased, while James has buried the wealth out of sight."

"Then add this," Matthew said, jumping to his feet. "To him who has not, even what he has will be taken away. And cast the worthless servant into the outer darkness!"

For a moment, the only sound was made by James bar Alpheus, drawing Matthew's attention, prompting him to add, angrily, "And they will grind their teeth in anguish, but it will be too late!"

"But Matthew," Philip inquired, measuring his words, "will you now believe all of Simon's fabrications are true?"

"He forgave me!" Matthew responded fiercely, his face red with emotion. "And those who reject him now will be rounded up like straw at harvest for burning!"

"Andrew is right," Simon said. "The new Torah is given us as the treasure of wealthy landowners. So let us drink this wine as a memorial of his blood spilled to save us, and eat matzah, becoming one with his flesh. And those who do not have our knowledge should be dismissed from this elect servitude to Jesus, our Christ."

"Just one more word," John the Zebedee said, rising to speak, glass in hand. "Matthias, it is true. You may have been invited, but you were not chosen—not by Jesus, as we have been chosen. Your invitation was to perform the scribe's job, to combine the new with the old, but you have failed."

"No one puts a piece of unshrunk cloth on an old garment," Matthias answered. "If he does, the patch tears away from the garment and a worse tear is made. And no one puts new wine into old wineskins. If he does, the wine will burst the skins, and the wine is lost and so are the skins. Your new Torah, as you call it, cannot be patched to the Torah. Again, I remind you of his warning: if you change even one letter, you will be the least in God's Kingdom. Such were the words of your teacher, whom you call a god. As for the scribe's labor, he must revere the scripture without appending it. Yes, Simon, I stand aside. Let another who chooses your company play the pipes for fools to dance. My legs are done keeping time to your tune."

"Then that's how it shall be. Again, we are eleven," Simon said. "And it is time to sip our savior's blood."

Surveying the others to see who raised their cups, Matthias gripped Philip's shoulder and rose to leave.

"Philip, are you leaving?" Simon asked as he too stood up.

"I will decide soon whether to continue here. But Simon, I am one of those Jesus chose. You cannot eject me as you have Matthias or vote me out, as you will James. And it is hardly an exaggeration that what you are doing to Matthias and James, you did to Jesus too. He warned you that if you continued to say he was sent by God, he could be arrested and put to death. You refused to accept his words. When he said repeatedly not to say he was the messiah, you twisted his meaning. It became your message that his identity was a secret revealed only to the worthy.

"Everything he did to help people—giving them hope, showing them God loved them, bringing the ignorant back to Jewish lives, even his healings—were made into distortions. Who here really believes he turned water into wine, or that he made that decrepit, wasted body of a paralyzed man get up and walk, empowered by your imaginary words, 'I forgive you'?

"And you, not Jesus, kept insisting his secret message was a key to eternal life and transcended our earthly realm. As Matthias says, you defied him and spread word he was King of the Jews, handing the charge of sedition to Antipas so he might extinguish the burning insult that his wife was an adulteress. You did it as surely as if you handed him his head on a platter. That was all Antipas needed. Under Roman law, Pilate could then order the crucifixion."

"Enough!" Simon exploded, "You are a traitor!"

"Am I? Simon, he never called you Peter. I heard him at that very moment, as I was the only one who walked unnoticed near you. He said, 'Get behind me, Satan. If you continue to call me savior, I will deny ever having known you.' Will you forget he also said, 'You are walking at the side of a man, not a god'? In truth, from the time of his crucifixion, you have forced these disciples to do your penance, keeping him alive so you won't see yourself as abetting his murder!"

"I would have given my life for him!"

"Die for him? That would mean he never ordained your eternal glory in his coming kingdom and was only a son of man. No, the imaginary Peter could never die, even though he has never lived! You cannot admit it because your escape from the world of Simon the fisherman would crash like a runaway chariot."

"So it is the two of you! Who else?" Simon demanded, his glistening eyes darting around the table.

"To you women, please forgive me for not enjoying the sumptuous banquet," Matthias said as he turned to go, "I do not detest you, Simon," he added. "I believe you loved Jesus."

"But why did you become one of us. Was it only to stop us?"

"We shared the loss and the grief. After he died, the terror in your heart at being abandoned . . . well, you couldn't bear it. So you made up a story that he didn't die. I thought if Jesus could save you, though he was gone, what a beautiful memorial it would be to his life. If you dwelt in the shelter of his teachings, you would be a living monument. As long as you were true to him, studying Torah, a source of God's holy spirit, he would be alive—at least in your hearts. I could think of no greater act of revenge on his murderers, and no more fitting act of friendship than to record his teachings and make them the cornerstone of a school—this Center."

"We are his chosen!" Thomas declared.

"He took you in as a shepherd takes in lost sheep," Matthias replied. "I wanted to show that same pity, though no longer. For what I see is an aberration of Torah and a rebuke of who he was. Simon, I have only recently learned of the exchange overheard by Philip. Now to join you in the final elimination of his memory, in order to acquit you of blame and exalt you as his anointed emissary is unthinkable. Didn't he once speak of the yeast of the Pietists, their distorting what he said to cast suspicion on him? Well, Simon, they are no match for the leaven in this place. You have done far more to cause his agony and undoing than they. I lament only this: that you were not worthy to preserve his message. He told you that you could be sons of God, prophets of a coming Kingdom. Inspired by the holy spirit, transferred through his words, he gave you what you needed to return from exile. His gifts were a blessing from God, but they did not make him God's messiah. You made him that. I came here and joined you, Simon, only to realize my burden was to save him from you. I hoped I would succeed so he might again be alive in your hearts."

Simon's words were measured like thrusts of a sword as he answered, "Yes, he called me Satan. You know why? Because part of me was lacking faith. I still wanted him to turn back rather than go to Jerusalem, where I feared he would be arrested and put to death. I was acting like you, Matthias. But then I heard his message.

On a deep, inner level, I knew it was impossible he would die—and I told him I knew it was impossible. Of course, he became angry. What I couldn't grasp was that his death as a son of man like us was necessary—to eliminate those who had no faith in his immortality. Sadly, Matthias, you and even Philip will not accept the miracle of his resurrection. For you, he is dead; for us, he is truly alive!"

"Well then, good luck to you all," Matthias said, as he and Philip squeezed past the seats of the others.

"If you know so much," Thomas demanded, a tremor in his voice, "before you run off, explain how his body went to heaven. All the miracles are proved by that one."

Pausing, Matthias replied, "One day he will speak to you again. Not from heaven but from the grave. Meanwhile, Luke, may your record of Jesus' life be worthy of him."

Against the background of the disciples' murmurs as they puzzled over his remark about the grave, Luke answered, "I accept that as your sincere wish. But it would have suited our endeavor to hear your recollection of his being lowered from the cross and taken to the tomb."

"Well, I'm sure you'll ask Jesus, and he will tell you all about it. Meanwhile, at least you should know one thing more about James," Matthias added somberly. "I see six of you are ready to drink, and you will be the ones to vote him out. But you should realize he was about to have success. Before Jesus' arrest, he had won the devotion of a wealthy member of the Sanhedrin. I believe James was doing his best."

"You say James solicited a wealthy Jew?" Simon asked incredulously. "Someone we know nothing about? And what has he done to show his devotion to Jesus? If he is generous, give us his name. Or have you so completely turned against us that you refuse to share it?"

"I believe, as Jesus did, that there is always hope for a man to repent—even you, Simon. I know little about him, other than what his servant told me when he helped me with the body."

"Helped you? And only now you reveal this?" Simon said in exasperation. "If he loved Jesus and may choose to sponsor our work, shouldn't we know his name? Well, who was he?"

"A secret follower. That's all I know," Matthias said as he and Philip reached the door to the stairs. "First, his servant came, and then he did. They folded aloe and balm into the shroud. I think he called his servant Nicodemus. His name? I only know how he introduced himself as a former member of the Sanhedrin. But I had no recollection of him."

"If you could recall, then I would put it down in the scroll," Luke suggested softly. "I'm sure Jesus would want his name to be honored."

"If I could only remember . . ." Matthias said. "Yes, I think it was an odd name. I recall his saying, 'I am Joseph of Arimathea.' Or something like that. I can't tell you more."

Descending the stairs slowly, Matthias heard Simon say, "I don't know where that town is. Well, we shall try and find it. And now let us drink!"

They were outside under the full moon, and as Matthias slowly climbed onto the seat, watching Philip make his way around to the driver's side, he said, "You must continue. They depend on you. Thaddeus, Bartholomew, James bar Alpheus, Simon C'nani. After you take me to join James and his family, go back."

The wheels began turning noisily, and as the cart lurched forward, Philip asked Matthias, "Who is Joseph of Arimathea? Was there truly such a person devoted to Jesus?"

"I will tell you another time," Matthias replied and pointed to the road toward Beit Lehem.

When the cart reached the entranceway, James appeared. "Welcome! Have you already eaten?" he asked.

"I'm not staying," Philip replied. "Just seeing to our friend's safe arrival."

"I'm famished," Matthias said, reaching behind him and retrieving a blanket roll of heavy wool, stored under the seat at the outset of their trip from Ephraim. Thinking it was a package of provisions, Philip had paid it no special attention.

"Are you sure, Philip?" James asked. "There's plenty."

"Thanks, but not this time. I need to return. Matthias will explain. Please tell your family I wished them a happy Passover. Perhaps I will see you at the Temple for offerings of the new barley."

As the cart disappeared behind the junipers along the entranceway path, James handed Matthias his walking stick and asked, "Can I help you with that?" He had noticed the heavy bundle in his other hand.

"If you don't mind," Matthias replied.

Securing it under his free arm, James said, "I sense bad news."

"Yes, well, we were expecting Simon to act," he remarked plaintively. "So you and I are both out. He has had his way."

Nodding as if he was not surprised, James inquired, "And Philip?"

"Philip was chosen by Jesus, so he's stuck with him. But let's not talk about it now," Matthias said quietly, slinging his arm through James' as they entered the dining area.

Delighted to see him, Elizabeth immediately rose from the table, showing her pleasure at Matthias' unexpected arrival, while the others joined in her words of welcome, "Baruch ha-ba. Happy Passover!"

Illuminated only by the multiwick clay lamps, a guest he did not immediately notice gleefully added, "You are almost as unexpected as I am!"

"Mary?" Matthias asked, squinting to see her better. "Mary!"

A moment later, she had helped him to a place at the table, arranging a large cushion, while the rest of the gathering looked on.

"You look surprised," Mary said.

"Yes," he managed, squeezing her hand affectionately.

"No more than I," she said. "But after all these years, how could I decline the invitation."

Joseph had maintained his seat, showing no special interest in their exchange, but he directed James to put Matthias' things away. "In my room," he instructed. "Then serve our friend."

When James was seated, Joseph offered Matthias an apology. "Forgive us for having started without you," he said sincerely.

"Abba?" James interrupted. "How could you have known he would join us?"

"Remember what I once told you?" his father replied. "There are things you don't know." But saying no more, Joseph lifted his wine cup, as did the others.

"Blessed are you, our Creator, who has created the fruit of the vine," he chanted. When they finished saying amen and drank heartily, Joseph inquired quietly, "Matthias, did you tell them?"

"Yes, I did. And I am certain their new scribe will record the name Joseph of Arimathea."

"What name? And what scribe?" Elizabeth asked, having listened more intently because they were whispering. "Are you two having a private conversation?"

"My neighbor calls me Joseph of Arimathea."

"And will you share this joke with the rest of us?" Elizabeth asked casually. "Joseph of . . ."

"Ari-ma-thea," Joseph said, obliging her as he usually did.

"Aren't we in the outskirts of Beit Lehem?" she prodded. "How are you from some other place? I can't even pronounce it."

"My neighbor calls Ir ha-mayteem 'Arimathea.' That's where our paths have crossed."

"City of the Dead?" Mary ventured. "That's the cemetery with my parents' tomb—and my aunt's. I should visit their grave."

"Me too," Elizabeth agreed. "It's been several years."

"Let's talk about other things," Joseph said, somewhat moodily.

"Tell us, James, what's new at the Center?" Elizabeth inquired, trying to be more cheerful.

"I'm out. Matthias has just come from there and can fill you in."

"So, Matthias, shall you fill us in?" Elizabeth persisted. "Leave it to me to find another happy subject."

"Don't be concerned," Matthias said. "And thank you all for inquiring about my health. Did anybody ask? I'm better than I look."

"We see you are in your prime," Joseph said, permitting himself a slight smile. "You and I should climb Mount Horeb."

"Anyway, there aren't too many things still to do or places left on my list to see," Matthias said. "You can always pack me up like old baggage to take to the Temple."

"What about the house, Mary?" Elizabeth asked. "I was asking you about it when Matthias arrived."

"The house is getting old, aunt."

"Along with the rest of us. But you are still only a child."

"Long ago. But you must pay a visit. Come north, and we will cook you a meal."

"James, I told your brothers not to join us this Passover," Joseph said. "Next year, if it is God's will. But not this time."

Mary suddenly appeared puzzled and cast a glance toward Joseph.

"From what we have seen in the fields, the barley harvest will be a rich one!" Matthias said. "I suppose that has them busy."

"Of course it does," Joseph said, holding up a platter of bitter lettuce and passing it around. As they each dipped a leaf in the blend of dates and nuts mixed with honey and spices, Joseph led their blessing, recalling their freedom from slavery.

"The haroset is my recipe," Elizabeth said, her attention directed toward Matthias, who still held the lettuce in his hand without having dipped it.

"Let me taste it!" he requested, too enthusiastically.

"Just near your wine glass," she said.

Somewhat embarrassed that his vision had chosen that moment to blur, as it had several times the past week in the poor light of late afternoon, Matthias accepted the small bowl, touching his hand to its edge, and then used the lettuce to scoop a mouthful.

"It's not very light in here," Mary said, "and the flickering makes it hard to see."

"What secret ingredients do I taste!" Matthias exclaimed. "You are a magician! Isn't she, James?"

When their feast came to an end, all joined in singing the hymns of Hallel, praising God. Though they at first seemed to James a naturally awkward group, given Mary and Joseph had not shared more than brief encounters during the eighteen years since he left her, everybody appeared content and drowsy from wine.

Following the final psalm praising God, Elizabeth asked Joseph why he insisted they spend the night. James could take her to her own house with Mary. But recognizing the stern expression on her brother-in-law's face, she and Mary quietly followed him to the room he had prepared. "This will do," Elizabeth said. "And look, Mary— even nice towels for the mikveh bath in the morning."

"Sleep well," Joseph said pleasantly, turning to find Matthias just down a hallway peering into a side chamber.

"This will be fine," Matthias said, the staff in one hand, his blanket-wrapped scroll in the other. Then, having noticed Joseph's bed was in the same room, he feigned surprise. "Who sleeps there?" he asked.

"I do," Joseph answered. "Who the devil do you think? Queen Esther?"

"I never mistook you for Queen Esther," Matthias jested, handing him the blanketed bundle.

"And James?"

"I'll see how he is faring and give him this. I hope you don't snore."

Finding a comfortable space on the floor to the side of the dining area, James spread a pallet provided by his father and was about to sprawl out when Joseph returned and spoke softly. "I imagine you are wondering why, after so many years, I requested Mary come to our Passover supper."

"It surprised me."

"You will understand tomorrow. When the sun rises, Matthias will finish this."

"What is that?" James inquired, watching as he untied the hemp band and opened the scroll on the table.

"It's about Jesus. It is Matthias' scroll. I will leave enough light for you to read it."

As his father went around the room extinguishing several flames of oil lamps along the far wall, James sat at the table, his disbelief

403

mingling with a sense of betrayal. How was it possible Matthias had written something so significant and not shared it with him?

"Abba, you have read it?"

"I couldn't show it to you until now," Matthias said, making his way to the dining area.

"You two were talking during the Sukkot festival. I remember wondering what you had to say that took so long."

"Memories. They are here," Matthias said. "And tomorrow will be the last of them."

"James," his father said, "he has been gone three years. In the morning we shall remember his last day, as it happened."

"But what do you have to do with it? How are you able—"

"Tomorrow. At sunrise. By then, I'm sure, you will have read it."

Bent over the parchment, he perused the details of Jesus' uncertain birth. Years were gone by, and he could almost hear his voice, powerful and precise. "V'ahavta et Adonai Elohecha, you shall love your God." James felt he was following his brother's footsteps, accompanying him . . . warning them to end their grudges, so they might be forgiven by God . . . admonishing them not to be like the Pietists who put on airs of holiness. "Don't give charity intending to be seen and honored," he could hear him say, "and don't stand all the time when you pray."

As he read on, unrolling the next section of the scroll, a lamp flickered, soon to go out.

Rebuking the self-righteous Pietists who pretended to be Pharisees, scoffing at their hypocrisy in the courtyard where his students hadn't washed their hands . . . the Pietists, like filthy pots and pans, cleaned only on the outside, a charade making their homes out to be sacred as the Temple, while divorcing their wives to be with other women. The passages taking him from one episode to the next darkened slightly when another of the lamps burned out.

Touching a leper had been unintended. The man grabbed at his fringes, and people said he had forgiven the sins that caused his disease. "Go to the priests, and don't say I healed you," he told the leper. But the man spread word that Jesus had power from God, and so did his disciples.

Unfurling the parchment to free a fresh section, James followed the path traveled by Matthias' fine lettering. Every time he healed in the synagogues on Shabbat, Pietists assailed him for transgressing the law, though there was no such prohibition in the Torah. So he asked them, if you care for a beast on Shabbat, is a person in misery any less worthy? But his disciples misunderstood, believing he was superior to the Shabbat and was anointing them his elect in the coming Kingdom.

Forcing himself to read more quickly, as another lamp became smoky and would soon flicker out, James came to Kfar Nahum.

The man who seemed to be possessed was a respected, observant Jew, ranting at Jesus for coming to destroy the congregation, as if he were sent by Satan. To have done an exorcism on him convinced the other congregants he was trying to shut him up. Jesus, responding to their accusation, said he believed the man had a demon. "Would Satan cast out Satan?" he asked. But they had begun to talk about him as a madman, some even suggesting he was the prophesied false teacher intending to create an army against God.

In Nazareth, on the new year of Rosh ha-shannah, his disciples seemed nervous when Pietists warned them not to listen to his teaching. Hoping to reassure them, he promised that the holy spirit would enable them to understand Torah and make them sons of God, just as the sages said.

The flickering lamp went out, and James looked about for oil but found none. If two more went dark, he would not be able to read.

Cana. There, the family wedding had become a scandal. Jesus poured wine into the hand-washing water and most guests were pleased to be drinking the stronger mixture. James remembered how Mary had become upset, exactly as Matthias wrote. Already, people were wondering who his father was. Shetuki is shetufi—the one who can't name his father goes mad. It was a rabbinic proverb. Acting like a crazy man, nobody would marry him. From the way she looked at him, he knew the truth, that her tears were for him. Joseph was not his true father.

Possibly born from the seed of an idol worshipper, he wondered how he ever thought himself worthy, mistaking, it seemed, the voice of the evil tempter for the holy spirit. Whatever teaching or healing led his followers to exalt him was from Satan. That he permitted them to twist his words to glorify him could be a sign he was possessed.

On the mountain ledge, the Temple at his back and the lands of Moab and the Ammonites beyond, he stepped toward the edge of the cliff and would have ended his life, were it not for John. Immersed by his cousin, he felt purified. When the time was right, he would tell the disciples in words, which were impossible to misconstrue, that they must never alter a word of Torah. If they did, they would be least in God's Kingdom.

Learning of John's arrest, Jesus retreated to Matthias' house. His cousin had been accused of sedition, inciting listeners against the tetrarch, even encouraging incursion by Aretas, the Camel. John had not curtailed his incendiary speeches denouncing Herodias as an adulteress, undivorced by Jewish law. How often Jesus had accused Pietist men of that sin! But not a woman. And not the tetrarch's wife.

His despair over John's imprisonment in Macherus was interrupted by the paralytic lowered through the roof.

James strained against the fading light, reading that Jesus never claimed he healed the paralyzed body of that poor soul, nor could he free him from God's punishment, if that was his malady's origin. Therefore, he said what any compassionate man would have: "Your sins will be forgiven." It was the credo of faith uttered by every Jew longing for the Day of God, when all would be granted a new beginning. When Pietists gossiped how he claimed to forgive the man, his disciples spread word that it was true. They may even have given rise to the rumor.

Keeping his place with his finger, James came to an unlikely wrinkle in the surface where a small fragment of parchment appeared to have been stitched in. The insertion told how, during that retreat, Simon preached Jesus was the one sent by God to save the worthy. Whispered words of coronation secretly hailed him King of the Jews. It was what he had learned when visiting Nathanael and had reported to Matthias.

In the month of Kislev, during Hanukkah at the Temple, he was nearly stoned to death for calling himself a son of God. All Hebrews can be sons of God, he proclaimed in his defense. That was the teaching of the sages and scripture, even found in the psalmist's verse—but the true son of God, as if he were born from the Creator or would alone reign over others? Never had he made so unthinkable a claim.

James drew one of the remaining lit lamps closer to the upper edge of the scroll, where the thundering proclamation almost shimmered with the light. "Do not think I am changing Torah. I am with you to teach you to keep the Torah's laws and fulfill them."

Fearful that he, like John, would be arrested, Jesus avoided any lessons that could be misconstrued as political rebuke. From then on, he would teach only in parables. Those intent on overhearing seditious talk, intending to inform the tetrarch, would be frustrated. Pietists vilifying him for distorting Torah would be stymied. Still, to his dismay, not only the Pietists but his own disciples were baffled by their complexity, forcing him to explain in private. Nonetheless, their inability to fathom his meaning had furthered the least desirable consequence. Simon explained beyond his earshot that the parables' difficult messages were designed to sift out the worthy from the unworthy because the time of the Kingdom was at hand. In saying this, he fully ignored Jesus' advice that Torah insight would grow gradually, like seeds planted in fertile soil. At a loss, they continued asking him when the Kingdom would begin, as if it were up to him. Angrily, he berated them, saying that God alone knew when.

Unbeknownst to Jesus, all the while, Simon was playing midwife to the secret messiah. Then came the expulsion by Kfar Nahum, Beit Zaida, and Chorazin. The stir over his activity had continued, despite his hope it would subside. Now, he was formally banished from their precincts and would need to find refuge elsewhere. Sending off the disciples, he encouraged them to spread a message of hope that all Hebrews, including them, would share in God's Kingdom. Meanwhile, he again accepted the quiet seclusion of Matthias' home.

When John was executed, Jesus emerged, and he went with Matthias to join John's followers at the lakeshore. There, he memorialized his cousin as one of the greatest people who had ever lived, echoing his fateful pronouncement: "No woman may divorce her husband." This affirmation of Jewish law, on that day, was understood for its intent. He had publicly rejected the tetrarch's adulterous marriage.

As he waded toward Simon's boat, the large gathering, wishing him to baptize them in the manner of John, followed him into the lake. Beset by them, Jesus' garment was nearly torn off as they grabbed hold of his arms and loudly hailed him, "King of the Jews." The Pietist "Herodians" present as spies, being members of the tetrarch's Tiberius council, brought Antipas the news: Jesus had been coronated king.

Holding the parchment flat to better discern the small letters, James almost expected Matthias to note Simon's tale that Jesus calmed the storm to more easily reach the boat. Instead, a brief allusion to the moment said only that he had been helped aboard.

Freshly stitched, the next episode described their flight to Caesaria Philipi. It was the detailed account of their short stay in Philip's tetrarchy, and Jesus' harsh rebuke of Simon for saying he was the messiah. They were the recorded words of Philip, told to Matthias, that Jesus said his reverence and adoration were from Satan. Declaring that Simon was walking at the side of a man, not a god, he told him he did not want Satan at his side. Unmistakably, Jesus told him, 'Walk behind me, Satan!' That was put down when he and Philip went to Matthias' house.

Though he had hoped to make the Passover pilgrimage unnoticed, Jesus was aware of the danger. Amid the throng, he hoped Antipas would neither seek his arrest nor find him. And as he sent others ahead to make arrangements, including Matthias, the chance sharply diminished that the tetrarch would accomplish his arrest in Jerusalem, a city whose administration was under the authority of Pilate, no friend.

When the smoking wick darkened the room with gray, tomb-like air, James extinguished its dying flame. In the remaining light, he could barely read the passages describing the final Passover supper and Jesus' arrest. Telling about his prayer in the garden of Gethsemane to be saved by God and his abandonment by the disciples, the final passages detailed the abuse during the hearing. To James, they were events painfully familiar from earlier conversations with Matthias. Still, one short section surprised him. It told that Antipas' Herodian lackeys, Pietists brought by him as witnesses, never testified Jesus claimed to be King of the Jews—the capital charge that led to his crucifixion. If his fate had depended only on their contempt and vilification, lacking, as it did, such actual testimony, their complaints would not have been sufficient to decree his execution. As Matthias noted, he had done his best to insert the truth about the Jewish witnesses' testimony in the disciples' so-called "new testament." As he had recorded it in their own testament, it read: "And the high priest sought false testimony against Jesus so they might put him to death. But their many other words against him, reviling him, did not include a charge that could justify his execution. And when Caiaphas asked Jesus whether he was 'King of the Jews,' he replied that such words were Caiaphas' own, meaning he had never thought such a thing about himself. Any who pretended to know otherwise and accused him of claiming to be King of the Jews would be bearing false witness." But his fate was decided in advance by the agreement between Antipas and Pilate. As Caiaphas admitted, were he to spare Jesus, appearing to overrule Pilate, his disciples would also die.

Then he reached the account of Jesus' appearance before Pilate and Antipas, bringing him to the verge of tears, at the end reverberating with his question to God—"Adonai, why have you destroyed me?"—and with his last words to Matthias—"Take care of my nakedness. It is almost over."

Just then the last lamp suddenly went out and the room was dark except for soft light of the full Nisan moon coming through the window. After tying the scroll with the hemp cord, he lay on his pallet and fell sound asleep.

As the scraping of the heavy table woke him, James propped himself on his e!bow and watched a tall, thin man slide several benches toward the wall. At first he could not see who it was, even squinting against the white sunlight pouring in through the window.

"Nicodemus?"

"Shalom, James. Your father says it's time to get up."

"The wine. I'm usually awake by now. But when did you come?"

"I still try to look in on your father from time to time. Especially on Passover."

"How long has it been since we've seen each other? Not since the crucifixion. Please let me do that with you."

As James gripped the other end of the table and helped push it against the wall, Joseph entered. "We may see you at the Temple, my friend," Joseph said to Nicodemus. "Thank you for your help, as always."

"It was good to see you again, James. Take care of your father."

"I don't need anybody to do that," Joseph said hoarsely.

"Have a good holiday," Nicodemus replied.

As the door closed, Joseph informed James that the women were relaxing in their room, waiting for Matthias to finish bathing. "Meanwhile, have some warm wine and matzah. I will see if he is able to climb out."

Moments later, told that Matthias was done, Mary and Elizabeth exited to take their morning bath.

Still holding the large flax towel, Joseph watched as Matthias used the backs of two benches to support himself while making his way to the table.

"James, please hand me the scroll," he said, sitting heavily.

After he unrolled it to the blank parchment page at the end, Matthias requested his dye and point. "And a small bowl of water for mixing," he instructed.

While his father located the wrapped powder in Matthias' bag, James asked what he would be writing.

"You will soon know," he replied.

"First, there is something we must agree upon," Joseph adjured, "but is this what you need?"

"It will be fine," Matthias replied, opening the small jar.

"Which is?" James inquired.

"That whatever you hear this morning and that Matthias records, it will be only for me and Matthias to tell. James, you may never speak of it."

"Why would I? That hardly sounds like a difficult request."

"It is not a request, my son. It is your oath before God, made to me your father. Will you swear before our Creator as your witness that you will honor me in this?"

"I have always honored you, Abba. I swear to keep this as an oath."

"Then listen."

Matthias dipped the point in the dark liquid and nodded his readiness to proceed.

"The end of this scroll is given as my personal record to Matthias, the only one among those who loved Jesus who was there when he died, which happened in the eighteenth year of Tiberius' reign as emperor of Rome, when Jesus was only twenty-seven years old. My words are the truth before God.

"I am Joseph from Beit Lehem, who raised Jesus in Nazareth as his son for his first twelve years. He was the son of Mary, the

daughter of the priestly family of Yoakim and Anna, whose sister I had first married."

Seeing that Matthias was waiting for him to continue, Joseph struggled to keep his composure. "Let's go on," he finally managed.

"My servant at that time, Nicodemus, came to my house to tell me Jesus had been crucified. Many questions swirled like a violent wind through my mind. What could be the possible charge? Who had brought charges? On Passover? Had there been a trial? Was the Sanhedrin called into session, with the Court of Twenty-Three rendering the capital verdict? Nothing made sense. 'Nicodemus, what for?' was all I could ask.

"Nicodemus answered me, 'For claiming he was King of the Jews. That is all I know. Matthias will tell you more.'

"'Matthias?' I asked. 'He was there with you, Nicodemus?'"

Matthias stopped writing for a moment and dipped his point. "And he told you how I had stood the entire time at the foot of the cross, giving him what comfort I could."

Indicating Matthias should resume the transcription, Joseph continued, *"Nicodemus told me how he and Matthias took Jesus' body to the public tomb and wrapped him in a shroud. With sundown, it was Shabbat, but I did not wait. Exercising the privilege accorded former Sanhedrin officials, I went to Caiaphas and presented myself as Jesus' father. He knew me well as a builder who had worked on the very Temple over which he presided. 'If he had not been tried and executed,' Caiaphas said, 'Antipas would have eventually rounded them up and killed them all.'*

"If he had meant to pay homage to Jesus for dying that others might live, his words were little consolation. Seeing there was no justification for the cruel murder, he sought to exempt himself from responsibility. Not in so many words, this is what I

understood: when Antipas promised he would testify before the emperor that the procurator's atrocities against the Samaritans were exaggerated, they made a pact. Jesus was Pilate's offering to Antipas in return for that testimony.

"The high priest was relieved when I suppressed my rage and requested the body. 'He is your family. Take him and bury him as is fitting. The Roman guards have orders from Pilate to release the remains when a family member requests private burial. I will inform them.' Those were his words.

"The body was in the public tomb, a rock-hewn cave, where it lay undisturbed for the Shabbat. After sundown, when it was dark, Nicodemus met me, and we took aloe and myrrh and a fresh shroud and went to the tomb. Off to the side, the large entrance boulder had been rolled away, and the guards were asleep. The others crucified that day were out of sight, either removed or farther in, where we did not see them. Matthias, who had been at Jesus' side for so long, had finally given in to exhaustion and found shelter in the Sanhedrin chamber and was asleep when this happened."

"That's where I was in those early hours," Matthias affirmed.

Taking a breath, Joseph continued with obvious difficulty. *"He looked so young, his face sweet and innocent. I took the bloody, stained shroud off him and began rubbing his body with aloe. I wanted to be gentle, as if he could feel my hands. I wanted him to be alive so I could tell him I loved him as much as a man ever loved a son. With the hardened blood on his skin finally off, Nicodemus helped me wrap him in the clean linen shroud, placing myrrh between its folds. Do you want to know if I said anything? Only these words: 'Oh Yeshi. Oh Yeshi.' And I prayed in my heart that somehow he could hear me."*

While wiping his eyes with his sleeve, Joseph saw that Mary was standing at the doorway of her bedchamber. Realizing she had overheard, Joseph stood up and faced her. As she came over, he started to tell her what was in his heart, but she held up her hand.

"I always knew you loved him," she said.

James, already stunned by what he had heard, was surprised when they embraced.

"Will you take us there?" Mary asked.

"That is why you are," he replied. "So finish like this, Matthias, with these words: *Others came and found the tomb empty, but of course, we had taken him. You who one day read this will know we believe his memory should be resurrected. Let him be to you as he was to himself and his God, a son as we are sons—a son of man, not the son of God but, imbued by Adonai's holy spirit, he bore a surprising semblance to our tzadikim, our sages. The clay god they created never lived and never died. The young man, Jesus of Nazareth, is in repose, buried like any other man. If you wish to show your devotion to his memory, then remember him as he was, never more than human and never less. Remember his own words, which he said to his students when Matthias was with him: 'Do not call me good. Only God is good.' Still, as one who loved him, I wish God had been good enough to save him. But I imagine Jesus would have told me, 'Don't lose faith. Adonai will redeem us all when His Kingdom is revealed.'*"

Matthias was squinting to better see the final letters he drew, when Joseph turned to James, who watched, mute and incredulous.

"I will answer your unasked question, James," his father said. "Because if you tell them, they will make pilgrimages to his tomb, as a shrine to their god, and even in death he will not escape. They will trample his memory until it is lost underfoot, disturbing his repose with a public display of the very reverence that killed him. For a time, they may say it is not even Jesus' tomb. Then they will say he only looked like a son of man but was a god become human. Such will be the testament to his life. For his sake, the sake of his innocence before God, that he tried to stop them from exalting him, that he never saw himself as a chosen emissary of the Creator, that he was not anointed king in his own heart but by his ignorant group—"

Mary touched Joseph's arm to interrupt his apparent loss of control.

"I have taken an oath," James said. "But what are you planning to do with this scroll?"

"Come; you will see," Joseph replied, as Matthias finished binding it with the hemp cord.

Just emerging from the bedchamber, Elizabeth tried not to seem left out and asked where they were going.

"You are coming with us," Joseph replied. "It would have meant something to him that you did."

"Him? Who does he mean?" she asked Mary quietly.

"Your son's best friend for most of his life," Joseph said. "We are going to Ir ha-mayteem. Jesus is there with your sister and my parents."

As the cart traveled the road rutted by the late-winter rain, Joseph apologized to Mary. "I was afraid you would seek to comfort Simon and the others, telling them how he had been provided a dignified burial. Your love for those who loved him might have turned you into their millstone. They would have used you to grind his remains to fit their mold."

"You might have trusted me," she said. "But I imagine you had your reasons not to."

"I didn't trust James either. And I am trusting you now, am I not?"

"You are."

"Mary," Matthias said, "just as those demonic Romans crucified his body, the disciples are even today crucifying his memory. And what for? So he will save them. They truly believe he died so they will live. And they even blame their fellow Jews for what happened to him, when none, not even Antipas' Herodian henchmen, testified he had called himself 'King of the Jews.' Only the disciples hailed him their king. If they hadn't . . . well, there was no other crime the bloodthirsty tetrarch could have brought against him."

"Simon and the others will never know about his tomb," Mary said, as the cart passed under the entrance arch.

Inside, the faint aroma of damp limestone, still wet with the morning's cool air, guided their small procession toward his wife's ossuary.

Once Elizabeth and Joseph had carefully placed small lit lamps on its top, they, along with Mary, stood back to say Ezekiel's words of mourning.

As his father turned and led the way, James bent low to pass through the entrance of a side chamber. It was the one containing the coffin ossuaries of Joseph's mother and father. Behind him, following carefully, Mary and Elizabeth entered with Matthias, who propped himself up with the wall as he went.

As Joseph lit several more lamps each from the other, using oil from a juglet in his satchel, he took time to say prayers for them and turned to a dark, recessed corner of the chamber. In the luminescent glow of the flame was a single ossuary coffin.

"It is as alone as he felt during his last day," Matthias said.

"We will all be buried here," Joseph responded. "He will have his family with him."

Unable to restrain herself, Mary suddenly cried out. "My son, my son," and lunging ahead, she draped herself over its stone lid.

Watching her body heave with sobbing, James started forward but was stopped by a gentle hand on his arm. "Let her mourn," Joseph said.

When she finally accepted Joseph's comforting arm around her shoulder, Mary stepped back but paused to caress the name carved into the side.

"Yeshua bar Yosef," it read.

"You call him your son," she said.

Turning to Elizabeth, Joseph answered Mary. "As Elizabeth's son John would say, 'God is able to raise descendants of Abraham from the rocks of the Jordan River.' Will I deny he gave me such a son?"

After James and Matthias had touched the ossuary and found solace in private prayers, they all joined in the traditional mourners' sanctification of God. Their words, increasingly loud, reverberated off the walls, until all again was silent. "I believe we were heard in heaven," Elizabeth said softly.

As the women stood back with Joseph, Matthias secreted the scroll behind Jesus' ossuary.

"May it come to light when God wills it, and may the world know what a wonderful man was here," he said aloud. "Let that be the day of his true resurrection."

Then they made their way out.

"So, Matthias, how shall we spell it?" Joseph inquired when they all were walking toward the cart.

"As my mother pronounced it. Matia," he replied, leaning on his walking stick.

Joseph was relieved that his friend needed no explanation of what he meant.

"Only please put it as close to his as you can. Or if you go first, tell James. I expect he will outlast us by many years."

"You appear to have quite a while to go," James said, having overheard. "But I will see to it."

CODA

"*Y*ou're sure James is coming?"

He watched her hands gently squeezing his swollen knee, as if she might reshape it. Sliding her fingers around to his calf, leaving white trails, she prompted, "Well?"

"Yes. He should arrive any time now."

"And he's bringing food? Because I have more than enough to share."

"The pies you baked for me are perfect. But what was that you were saying a moment ago—that Antipas petitioned Rome to make him king. Yes, I had certainly heard that."

"Am I hurting you?" she asked.

"It's fine."

"Of course, that was not in the stars," she said, dipping her fingers in the olive oil and again kneading his leg. "But I can understand how he hoped Rome would make him ruler of all Judea."

"He always had that dream."

"Of course he could never have guessed what would happen to Agrippa."

As if familiar with the subject, Matthias said, "You mean because of the money he owed."

"And the other matter. That's what Tiberius really arrested him for. It's hard to believe."

Reluctant as he was to depend on her for news, Matthias would seem a sorry soul to James, were he ignorant of events about which everybody was gossiping. "I've heard so many different accounts. Which one do you know?"

"After Agrippa's wife and children abandoned him—that was when the Syrian governor expelled him—he went to Rome and spent time cavorting with his childhood friend, Caligula. During a ride in his chariot, Agrippa spoke of Tiberius as an old has-been. In the version I know, he told Caligula that Tiberius would soon die, leaving him the government, and that he was far more worthy to be emperor. Of all things, the driver, named something like Eutychus, overheard the supposed compliment and later on saved his own skin on an unrelated charge of theft by revealing Agrippa's traitorous remarks. Is that what you have heard?"

"Yes, the same."

"Of course what happened next is the best part."

"How have they been telling it?"

"Just as you've heard, I'm sure. The one part that confuses me is why Tiberius did choose Caligula as his successor. They say his diviners told him to do so. Hard to believe, right?"

"Very."

"But you must have been happy when he was made emperor. All of Jerusalem was in the streets celebrating, or so I've been told. But you can guess who must have been dancing like a Samaritan."

"I'm not sure I know who you mean."

"Agrippa! To go from being confined like an animal in the prison of Emperor Tiberius to suddenly being the new emperor's close friend—well, I would have loved to see his face when they brought him the news."

"He must be relieved to be out."

When she started laughing, he had no idea why but knew he had made some sort of joke that depended on yet undisclosed details of the subsequent events.

"You are funny," she said, regaining her composure. "Yes, I'd say he's quite glad to be out. After all, how hard can it be to enjoy the comfort of that palace, now that Antipas and his house dog are gone? But let me do the other one."

As she propped Matthias up on his left side and applied a bounteous amount of oil, her application of pressure to the tender muscles that pained him so permitted a moment of private disappointment.

Never in the past decade had he been so unimportant. Even a particle of what she told him would have been worthy of a courier, conveying a sealed jar with the written record. Such was always provided members of the Sanhedrin. Now that he resigned, a courtesy would have been to keep him informed, as they always had. Bearing witness to those days of personal stature was a shelf lined with those message jars, vessels reduced to storage of herbs and spices.

"And are the people pleased with him?" he asked.

"Agrippa? My guess is he'll be made king before long. He already has power that Antipas never did. People say he was the one behind the exile of the tetrarch. I've heard Agrippa encouraged Herodias to remain here, except she was too proud and went with Antipas. Good riddance."

"So the streets of Jerusalem have been filled with people rejoicing."

"I'm sure the celebration of Agrippa's rule was almost equally about Pilate," she replied.

"Very likely," he said, sounding as if he knew what she was talking about.

"Elijah himself would never have expected him to be sent away like that. Caligula does whatever Agrippa asks. As the emperor's friend, he is like somebody sent by God. To think we have a ruler with the power to send away Pilate! And everybody is waiting to see the new high priest. Caiaphas' robes were filthy with Roman influence. But you know far more about these things than I."

Hearing James calling from outside, he took a cloth and quickly wiped his legs. "Please hand me the stick," he said. "I want to greet him on my feet."

Helping him stand, she suggested she go to the cart and carry any foods he had brought.

She entered with two large sacks, one in each hand, and put them near a water cistern at the side of the oven. A moment later, James came in.

"Let me put this down, so I may wish you happy Purim," he said, locating a spot on the floor for a large wineskin.

"So you look—"

"Like I'm still alive? Here's my angel. Yehudit, this is my friend James."

"Happy Purim," she said. "But I'm nobody's angel. So what have you brought?"

"Beans, peas. Already boiled. Olives. Cheese. Fresh bread, salted fish. And lots of wine."

"If you're still hungry after your feast, James, that's my house," she said, pointing through the window. "I have invited my brother and his wife. A few friends as well. There is always too much."

As she reached the door, Matthias again thanked her for the pies.

"You are already looking stronger just thinking about them," she said. "So enjoy!"

As the door closed, Matthias asked how Joseph was.

"He is in reasonable health."

"Mary and Elizabeth?"

"They're fine. Elizabeth doesn't go out very often. I promised to tell her and my father about you," James replied.

"Tell your father I'm packed for the ascent of Horeb," he said, lowering himself with a thud to the straw mattress.

"I will tell them you haven't changed."

"Hard to believe it's more than a year since we were ousted from the Center."

"Or since I've been here. After Tiberius died, I kept thinking I'd see you at the Temple. Then we learned you had stepped down from the Sanhedrin."

"Were you there this morning for the reading of Esther's scroll?"

"Yes. She saved the Jews again."

"Just as she does every Purim. They don't need me anymore than they need Mordechai. But Agrippa! Who would have guessed?"

"So you have heard all about it."

"Thanks to the couriers."

"And I'm sure you still offer your opinion," James said, knowing it wasn't true.

"Only by courier. But they know what I think. Nothing pleases me more than Antipas having been banished, except, perhaps, Pilate's recall by Rome."

"To Lyon in Gaul. And Pilate was probably also hated by Vitellius. He was about to attack Aretas, avenging the incursion against northern Judea, when Tiberius died. Vitellius was glad to turn back rather than do Antipas any favors. But Agrippa had been in prison five months by then."

"His luck to have been a childhood friend of the new emperor."

"But I think it's you who should be telling me the news, Matthias. And you've surely heard about Caiaphas. But why don't I start the cooking."

"I can't wait to see the new high priest."

"May I use this for the beans?" James asked, taking a clay pot from the shelf.

"Whatever you need."

"I'm no great cook," James said, filling one of the empty courier's vessels from a sack.

"Well, has Philip told you about their most recent embellishments of Jesus?"

"He has, and I am in touch with Bartholomew and Simon C'nani. James bar Alpheus, and Thaddeus have also met with me. Do you want to hear? It may be upsetting."

"I'll survive," Matthias said sardonically.

"According to Philip, Luke has fully accepted Simon's use of the holy spirit to guide their supposed history, as if it would ever come near him."

"You're talking about their tales—wading out to the boat and calming the storm, reaching shore was walking on water. Oh, and the bread feeding thousands."

"More. Everything Simon says makes its way into the scroll under Luke's hand."

"Let me guess. Jesus forgave the leper, and the paralytic man walked."

"And they've changed Jesus' memorial for John. Now they say he spoke of him as the greatest man born to a woman. It's meant to keep him human, compared to Jesus, who was supposedly born from God's spirit."

"We've done our best."

Searching out several branches from the nearby stack, James snapped one to a size that fit the oven but did not reply.

"Don't spare me the details," Matthias insisted.

"Whatever he declares is from the heavenly Jesus is now sacred history. The key to eternal life is believing whatever Simon says."

"A wedding guest without the garment of knowledge is thrown out," Matthias recalled. "He told that parable at the Passover meal and then threw me out. Matthew said the excluded ones will grind their teeth like James bar Alpheus."

As their shared laughter subsided, James was suddenly serious. "Simon claims he has authority over the others because his knowledge is not revealed by flesh and blood."

"But then why did Jesus call him Satan? Or aren't they bothering with that small detail?"

"For not accepting God's plan that Jesus would die—"

"Yes, I recall that's what he was claiming just before Philip and I left. But your brother was a fugitive and he acted like one!"

"Matthias, do you mean Jesus never personally told you his plan?" James asked sarcastically. "Hard to believe. And he confided nothing about the three-day journey to Jerusalem for that last Passover? Well, now you have it from Simon. It was a coded prophecy that after the crucifixion he would be in the tomb three days. My brother was completely aware of the grim future."

"And that's why he acted like a fugitive?" Matthias asked in disbelief.

"It wasn't fitting for the messiah to die outside of Jerusalem. So he didn't want to be captured too soon. Everything was planned by God."

"Simon no longer needs to deny what he has done," Matthias observed. "He has changed his role from unwitting complicity in

426

events leading to the crucifixion of his teacher, to the holy act of anointing him King of the Jews."

"Worse. Now he's made it that all who reject the idea that God planned my brother's death are possessed by Satan. Pietists aren't the only evil ones. Jews who don't believe he is their king are all the same. All are guilty because they don't call my brother the Christ. Belief in his resurrection has become an exorcism of the Jewish Satan. Oh, and to prove their point, they have invented a crowd of Jews pleading with Pilate to crucify him and let some murderer go free instead of him, in honor of Passover."

"There was no crowd calling for his crucifixion, only Antipas' men. But what murderer went free?"

"They've named him Barabbas, son of the father."

"We have no such name."

"Made up to mean 'son of Satan,' the one they say is the real god of the Jews. The masses wanted Satan's son to go free instead of God's son."

While the beans and peas were cooking, James turned to his friend, reciting a litany of distortions. "Baptism imitates Jesus' death and resurrection, and they say their ritual wine is his blood." Noticing Matthias' eyes were closed, James stopped talking, and taking in the sight of his poor state of health, again faced the stove.

"Those ideas were Paul's influence. Luke must have brought them when he moved to Jerusalem," Matthias uttered gruffly.

Trying not to show how startled he was by the growling comment from one who appeared to be asleep, James turned about, answering, "Yes, but not just Luke. Simon himself, after spending time with Paul, changed. He is ready to dispense with Torah laws that are unnatural to pagans. Now he goes as far as Paul. You may have met John Mark."

"It's a name I vaguely remember."

"He calls himself Mark. Originally, he was a protégé of Simon's. Then he was sent to join Paul—he and Barnabas."

"Yes, a younger man."

"When Paul preached that Torah was a book of laws only necessary for criminals, John Mark quit his side. But he is at the Center, helping record the disciples' accounts. Paul's ideas about wine as blood and matzah as flesh are now included."

"Enhancements to bring their messiah to the pagan market along with everything else they butcher."

As the fragrant smoke of herb-rubbed fish, cut and skewered for roasting, wafted from the oven out the adjacent window, Matthias indicated the storage chamber. "Behind you—that's where you'll find the plates."

"These are beautiful."

"The Roman glassmakers are skilled. Yes, and did you see the green pitcher? We'll use it for the wine."

"But where is the table?"

"That's it, leaning against the wall. Without legs, almost like me. So I can half sit up with it alongside this couch. You can sit on the flokati."

Pouring the wine, James said, "It hasn't been easy for Philip. Only because I plead with him to remain in their company has he agreed to it. But every time we meet, there is some other liberty they have taken with Jesus' life."

Matthias raised his glass and together, they recited the blessing. After each took a large swallow, Matthias selected a piece of warm bread from the basket and thanked God for bringing forth grain from the earth.

"Amen," James responded. "Tell me how you like it."

"I'm still alive," Matthias joked as he took a bite of fish from the skewer. "You were saying?"

"Luke has been linking Torah to Jesus, as if the prophets were providing clues to his life. Zechariah envisioned the messiah acting like King David. So Jesus now rides into Jerusalem on a foal with adoring crowds welcoming him. And just as Zechariah said there would be no more money changers in the Temple on God's Day, Jesus now turns over their tables and chases them away."

"He is supposed to have done these things?"

"It's their idea of his keeping a low profile."

"But he hid in the garden, praying not to be taken captive. They know that!"

"Luke has a way with words. Logic doesn't matter. You told how he asked you to take care of his nakedness. I'm almost afraid to tell you."

"They have changed that too?"

"Luke uses Greek to correct your misunderstanding."

"Jesus said what he said."

"Gumnos, of course, is the Greek word for nakedness. Luke claims he was speaking Greek and actually said Gune, a word that means woman. He has made it that Jesus told you to take care of his mother. He even says she was with you at the foot of the cross."

"And that is what they have written?"

"On a separate parchment not yet included. I suspect they will wait for a future apostle to insert whatever Luke has kept to the side. Turning water to wine is also recorded separately. At present, I believe they fear Mary may dispute falsehoods about her and create a problem among the disciples. For now, Simon is still deciding what else Jesus will say from the cross."

"And us?" Matthias asked.

"Us? Jews who reject Jesus the king will not be forgiven until he descends with angels to judge the world. Then all Jews will confess they were wrong and will be saved."

"We'll be waiting a long time, I suspect."

"Anyway, it appears he has gone from being a son of man to being one described by Daniel as having the semblance of a son of man, one day descending on a throne with angels all around."

"There is nothing more we could have done. As Jesus said to me from the cross, it is finished."

"That's not what he says anymore."

"What, then?"

"Luke has changed the Aramaic to Greek. They have him say, 'It is accomplished.'"

"As if his own murder was what he sought to accomplish."

"But Matthias, tell me this. You must believe they will find it. Otherwise, why would you leave the scroll with his ossuary?"

"There will be a day when those who care are able to follow the truth like footprints."

"Footprints that lead to the tomb?" James asked doubtfully.

"I'm sure we will have been gone a long time. So let's enjoy her pies, shall we? Heat them up."

Watching James use a charred wooden spatula to suspend two small pies over the glowing embers, Matthias said, "Wild berries. She confided her recipe is to mix some that are too ripe with younger berries."

Deeply inhaling the aroma, James said, "He loved pie like this."

After only several moments of their savoring the delicious dessert, James' wrinkled brow caught Matthias' eye. "So? You look confused."

"Why did you say he was from Arimathea?" James asked.

"Jo-seph of Ari-ma-thea," Matthias said, smiling broadly and sounding out the syllables.

"Yes, I recall my father saying it was really Ir ha-mayteem. The night we were voted out you and he joked about the mispronunciation."

"People passing his house on the way to visit their family tombs. They'd see him at the Temple, a member of the Sanhedrin. He was a notable. So, they remarked he was Joseph from the neighborhood of Ir ha-mayteem.

"It is to be the final footprint. His name will reveal its location—Arimathea—in the poor dialect they do not recognize. Surely they will include it, boasting the reverence of a wealthy Jew for their king. Yes, the one who follows the footprints to Ir ha-mayteem, City of the Dead, will find his remains and the scroll. But let me ask you something, James. Do they talk about me?"

"Simon wanted your name expunged altogether. But Philip, speaking for Simon C'nani, James bar Alpheus, Bartholomew, and Thaddeus insisted your friendship with Jesus be recorded. You are now the disciple Jesus loved."

"With no name."

"Not as they tell it. But you were with him at the Passover supper and then in Gethsemane during the arrest. Next, you were at the hearing before Caiaphas and at the crucifixion. You don't seem to have helped with a shroud."

"Good. Let them save that for Nicodemus and Joseph of Arimathea."

"For now, you are among those who came running to the empty tomb with Simon."

"A witness to his invented resurrection," Matthias lamented.

"I'm sorry," James consoled.

"No need."

431

James was almost finished wiping their dishes and rinsing them in the cistern outside the door. With the afternoon sun well into the beginning of the fourth watch, his visit was nearing an end.

"You should be on your way," Matthias said. "Best to reach Ayn Kerem while it's still light."

After propping the table against the wall, James sat on the flokati next to Matthias. "Before I go," he requested, "tell me one thing he taught that I should always remember."

"To love God, to forgive each other so God might forgive us, and to have compassion on the sick and tormented and those in need."

James' silence showed disappointment. He had hoped to hear words Jesus himself spoke.

"When I picture him here," Matthias said, aware of what James was feeling, "I sometimes talk to him as if he were alive. Depending on what I say, he looks at me with expressions of either aggravation or amusement, and if I touch on what happened to him, it's always the same—a look of kindness. I don't hear his voice anymore, but I imagine him sitting where you are. That was his favorite place."

Matthias had suddenly become teary-eyed, and his voice choked up as he continued.

"I will tell you this, James. I know he regretted that the seeds of Torah, as he called his teaching, had landed on rocky soil. His students could not grasp his message promising they might become sons of God if they studied Torah. As taught by our sages, the holy spirit, ruach ha-kodesh, may breathe life into us from Torah's sacred passages, even purifying lineages mired in sin. And then, we all may see a path to fulfilling God's will, much as a son honors his father. Such was his teaching."

"I remember some of that from your scroll."

"Instead, the disciples thought the holy spirit endowed Jesus with divine powers and believed he would make them subordinate gods in a pantheon to rule the coming Kingdom. Not all of them went that far, of course, but Simon's cadre turned Jesus into God's own son."

"As they are doing now, with complete abandon. Matthias, one more thing. Why didn't you tell me about the scroll?"

"In the beginning, I doubted my words would capture his. I didn't know. Maybe I would fail to inspire the disciples with my version of Jesus' life. And with Simon so contriving his Christ, I was afraid my record could become a matter of great controversy, confounding even the ones who cherished his memory as a son of man. He had vouchsafed God's love for them, the outcasts, and I couldn't let that be taken from them."

"And now?" James asked. "You have entombed his memory."

"That occurred to me. But then I remembered the words that he prayed in the Gethsemane grove: 'Forgive them. They know not what they do.' To let the scroll become common knowledge, condemning Simon and the disciples for exalting Jesus, the very ones he asked God to forgive . . . how could I? Only if the scroll was discovered in a distant future, would I honor his prayer."

"Of course you let Joseph read it."

"It was Joseph's story too, especially the final days. And he may be right—that everybody knowing the location of Jesus' tomb would only lead to devotees coming as pilgrims. But now the story is yours as well. You are his family. Bound by an oath, it is your solemn secret."

James could tell from his glassy stare that Matthias' spoken thoughts had led him to a deep, private reflection. About to ask whether he would be all right, James hesitated. The window's light had caught the features of his friend's face, and he knew he would not.

433

"Don't look so sad," Matthias said, emerging from his reverie.

"You have a good neighbor. She will keep an eye on you."

"You know who I have? I have your brother's words. They are 'sukkat shalom,' a shelter of peace."

Bidding his old friend farewell, James knew that was the last time they would see each other.

***

Several years had gone by since then. As James sat on a soft, grass-covered hill overlooking the Sea of Galilee, the calls of fishermen to raise their nets reminded him of his childhood with Jesus. How often they had heard the words now shouted, "Tarim! Tarim! Raise the net!" Glittering in the sun, the flopping fins and brightly colored flashing scales were their last haul for the day.

He had been right in what he predicted. A new apostle, one named John, had flights of fantasy higher than shorebirds could soar. He had taken events recorded by Luke on the separate parchment and mixed them with his own poetry about Jesus as God's son. Cana and turning water to wine was recorded as a miracle. Mary was at the foot of the cross with the disciple Jesus loved.

Everything on the separate parchment was now either in Luke's or John's version. But John had taken other liberties. Antipas and Pilate were only obeying the bloodthirsty demand of elders and high Jewish officials that Jesus be crucified—this, though none gave testimony or even accused him of claiming to be King of the Jews. Determined to find blame, John even changed the first day of Passover to the sixth of the week, so that Jesus' death appeared to coincide with the sacrifice of the Passover lambs, as if he were the Jews' sacrifice.

If these thoughts saddened him, James could not help smile at the disciples' inclusion of Joseph of Arimathea. "One day people will also know who you were," he said aloud, glancing at the sky as if he might catch sight of Matthias looking down. "Nestled in the clefts of your recollections, they will meet him as he was. Thank you, Matthias, for writing what was true about your friend."

Descending on clouds of thoughts from a place within James' heart, Jesus was still on the shores of the lake, teaching Torah, waiting for God. But the day had turned cool, and it was two days to Beit Lehem to see after his father's welfare.

CPSIA information can be obtained at www.ICGtesting.com
Printed in the USA
LVOW08s1443180215

427348LV00030B/1600/P